G000279861

GOLDEN CUB

Rosemarie Gilchrist

en Press

First published in Great Britain by Pen Press
All paper used in the printing of this book has been made from wood
grown in managed, sustainable forests.

ISBN13: 978-1-907499-72-2

Pen Press is an imprint of Indepenpress Publishing Ltd
25 Eastern Place
Brighton
BN2 1GJ

Printed and bound in the UK

A catalogue record of this book is available from
the British Library

Cover design by Jacqueline Abromeit

About the Author

ROSEMARIE GILCHRIST WAS born and brought up in Southern Africa. Her grandfather, the Cub's uncle, was on the Pioneer Column which opened up areas beyond the Limpopo River. Her father's family came originally from Dublin and Leitrim and on her maternal side she has roots in Africa which go back to the early colonial days.

The history of Ireland and Southern Africa are entwined in the family like a wild mountain creeper. Rosemarie has completed the circle by finding herself back in Ireland, in County Fermanagh where the Cub's family originated from and only a few miles from Leitrim and the shadows of Alfred and Emmie. Many of the characters in this book existed but some left no names and a few made their own way onto the pages for good or bad and helped to shape the destiny of those already there.

Both Africa and Ireland have changed dramatically since those days but history was made and cannot be altered and it is this history which sets the patterns of change and advancement and helps to mould the people who come afterwards.

Prologue

From Boy to Man

IT WAS A tale about him, the white boy, about his roots, his beginnings, his people. Josh never tired of hearing it. It had become a compulsive need. If he forgot one detail he feared he might lose himself for ever. It stirred emotions down in the depths of his soul.

Majinga, his tribal mother, had told the story again tonight as they sat by the communal fire. Again he had felt himself tingle with the mixed emotions of fear, horror and grief. Then something unfamiliar had crept in, a sudden fierce reaction. The desire for vengeance. He ran his finger over the small scar near his temple which he had received at his tribal initiation into manhood. It crossed his mind that perhaps at thirteen years of age he had left behind the child, emotionally as well as physically, and, under the cloak of manhood, vengeance had arrived.

He stirred the embers of the fire until the flames leapt up again. Majinga and those who had joined them to hear the tale, had crept off to unroll their sleeping mats and been swallowed in the shroud of darkness beyond the fire.

Josh was alone with himself, his thoughts and dreams. Looking into the shooting flames he was sure he could see the canvas-covered wagon against the tall cliff face, above it, the blackness of the cave. Three charred pieces of wood collapsed onto the bed of ashes. In his imagination he could see the three men watching the encampment. In the shadows, by the wagon, lay a white man and a woman, caught in the throes of terrible fever. Majinga sat between them, mopping their faces with a water-soaked cloth. The blackened pieces of wood appeared to him to move closer to the sick couple. In his mind Josh heard the tale once again:

"And *then*, little mother, what happened?" he heard himself asking.

"There were three of them, white men, hunters. At first we were pleased to see them, thinking they might be able to help. But they were not good men. They saw that your mother was dying and that your father also had the killing fever. They looked at what was in the wagon and at Kano, the herdsman's sleek oxen, the flock of goats and sheep, and greed entered their eyes."

"What did they do, little mother?"

"The tall one with the face of a hyena, the scar across his face, the ear without a lobe – he turned his gun on us. We could not understand all he said but we knew we were in danger. He waved his gun at us."

"And then?"

"And then, my child, I grabbed you up and ran into the thick bush of the krantz and Kano followed. We ran for a while and then we hid until the moon was high in the sky."

"I know, I know, and then you went back... And what did you find?"

"There was nothing there... nothing at all... Just two mounds of earth against the rock face of the krantz."

"You looked to see that it was my mother and father?"

"I began to tear at the earth of the mound in the moonlight. Kano helped me. Below the stones and earth was your father. His head had been clubbed in, perhaps with the butt of the man's gun. We knew the second mound would be your mother. We did not disturb her."

"No wagon, no animals...?"

"Nothing my child. No small memory for you. Just the scarred red dust, coals of the fire and flattened grass where the beautiful wagon had stood."

Again he was aware of that flare of hatred against an unknown enemy. He shivered. As a boy he could hide, now Josh was aware that he was trapped by his past. Dispossessed. His only release from this story would come from vengeance.

Something fluttered in the branches of the ancient Marula tree behind Josh, where the ancestors' spirits roosted with the mossies and starlings. The fire had died back to a cauldron of glowing ash.

Somewhere in the dark African bush a hyena howled at the first glimmer of the rising moon.

Chapter One

IRELAND – 1879

Emmie leapt down from the cart. She gave the donkey a brisk pat as she hitched him to the post outside the kitchen door of Belhavel House. Smoothing the apron which protected her coarse-woven navy skirt she went round to unload the flour bags. Balancing on the cart step, she reached for a bag while using her other hand to pat down the vibrant mop of wavy rich chestnut hair which framed her lightly freckled face. She was aware that people admired her hair and the way it accentuated her green eyes, personally she regarded it as a hazard. There was no escaping unseen from one's sins, or blending into the scenery. Apparently, too, it was to blame for her quick temper, or so her father said.

Carrying the first bag of flour she pushed open the kitchen door with her shoulder and went down two steps into the stone-flagged room with its large glowing range, glass-fronted cabinets and huge scrubbed kitchen table. Ada, the cook, was up to her elbows in flour, kneading a new loaf. Emmie smiled at her as she dumped the flour bag on the far end of the table.

"Good day to you, Cookie, and here's the flour for your next batch!"

"Ah, tanks me girl, an' me trying to keep all the pots a bubbling while that Mary-Kate takes her time wit the picking of them spuds."

"You busy with visitors then?"

"Only one this day, but we do have Master Alfred back... and a right row there's been about that!"

"Alfred back! I thought he was with the grand folks up at college in Dublin?"

"He was indeed but the college sent him home – seems his life of fun an' games has caught him out. Not enough work. Seems you need to do some book work to be a doctor!"

Emmie laughed.

"Never been too keen on work – or not unless it was with horses an' cattle or sheep. Can't see him bending over ladies an' ministering to their needs!"

Ada joined in the laugh:

"Sure, but he'd be in bed *with* them, not attending *to* them!"

Emmie giggled,

"He's fun is that lad, I'd always spend time with him, but he has as much sense as a grasshopper!"

Emmie went out into the sunshine of the cobbled yard and brought back the last two sacks.

"So, where is the disgraced one right now?" she asked as she put them down.

"Where he usually goes when trouble strikes!" Ada nodded her head upwards. "On the blessed roof!"

"Then I'll creep up and catch him at his sorrows," Emmie looked enquiringly at Ada. "Are the others busy elsewhere?"

"I think so; the parlour maid, Jes, she says they are in the Master's study. It seems there is some matter to be considered," she wiped her nose against her sleeve to avoid the flour, "the visitor, it's Mrs Barton, from Watersmeet, Miss Florence's mother-in-law."

"Miss Florence and Master Folliott, they disappeared in Africa, didn't they? I wonder, has there been some news?" Emmie looked questioningly at Ada.

Ada shrugged and tipped the dough out onto the table.

"I'll nip up the back stairs and see what Alfred has to say."

Emmie wiped her hands on a towel and went over to the door to the back stairs.

She was well aware that when the pressures of life became too much for Alfred he would remove himself to the flat roof of the house where he knew no one would venture to disturb him. There he could wrestle with his feelings of being misunderstood and ignored.

As she clambered up the steep stone stairs Emmie recalled the early years when her mother, the miller's wife, had come up to help at the big house overlooking the lake. She had accompanied her, hanging on to her skirts in the kitchen, and then being accepted to play with the youngest of the fourteen Lyons-Montgomery children who overflowed everywhere in the large house. She had found herself quickly accepted by the boys, a playmate always ready to join in every escapade and to prove she could do it better than them. As she had grown older it had been the school holidays which she had found herself looking forward to. The boys were back from boarding school and the girls could abandon their governess.

The unreliable, charming, Alfred Otho, known to the family as "Alfred O", had always been her favourite, followed by the two youngest, Beatrice and Kynaston.

She reached the top of the stairs and emerged onto the balustraded roof with its slate tiles and lead edgings. There were six chimney stacks on the roof and she soon saw Alfred. He was lying against one, with one jodhpurred leg across the other, apparently contemplating his elegant, shiny boots. She crept over, popped her head round the chimney stack, and whispered:

"Alfred, your sins getting to you then?"

Alfred jumped and then looked put out.

She had to admit to herself that although he might have been described as "of short and stocky build", he was undoubtedly also good to look at. He had a mat of dark brown curly hair, a clear skin with the slightest hint of a stubble shadow and intense blue eyes with well-marked laughter lines at the corners. His mouth was a mobile reflection of his moods. His manners and charm were already legendary in the locality.

"God, Emmie, you gave me a fright! What are you doing here anyway?"

"I'm hearing, down in the kitchen, that life is not running smoothly for you?"

"Damn right too, although I'd hoped the whole world wasn't aware!"

Emmie untied her apron and, folding it up, placed it on the floor next to Alfred and sat on it.

"So, you back from Trinity and only a few weeks into the term. What happened Al?"

"Bloody old row of black crows! I got hauled up for missing too many lectures and not turning in work. No damn sense of fun. Never wanted to do medicine anyway. Assumed I'd run the estate or get one of my own and do blood stock. Old man thought differently but didn't ask me, just signed me up for it – one son a lawyer, one in the army and one in business – just assumed I'd do as I was told."

Emmie knew better than to interrupt. She nodded encouragingly.

"Never did feel part of that crowd – no academic me. Rather be out racing or gambling, parties, or round at the Club. Can't stick sitting round with my nose in a book." He seemed to go back into himself and sat staring out between the balustrades at the silver-grey water which glittered invitingly at the bottom of the sloping garden.

"What did your parents have to say?" Emmie asked gently.

"Can you bloody believe it? The old man was waving this letter from the bank at me. Seems I managed to clear a year's allowance in one term and ran up a bit of a debt to boot."

"Can't he just pay it?" Emmie enquired puzzled. She had never thought in terms of Hugh Lyons-Montgomery having money problems. They were only for the likes her dad and the village folk.

"Won't bloody do it!" Alfred said curtly. He mimicked his father's voice: "Maturity is evidently not your strong point, my lad. You appear to be coming down with a first-class degree in wine, women and the rapid dispersal of cash."

Emmie absorbed this thoughtfully.

"So, what happens now, Al? Bloodstock?"

"Not bloody likely. Says he hasn't the capital outlay and the land isn't right."

"Surely your father can get you back into Trinity?" Emmie enquired in some surprise. She had heard that Hugh Lyons-Montgomery was a well-known Dublin lawyer and a member of the Westminster Parliament. She wasn't sure what all that meant but it sounded important.

"What for? It's not what I want to do, Emmie." For the first time he actually turned and looked at her.

"So, will you stay at home for a while?" she enquired hopefully.

"Don't know. Only got back today. I feel like a kid. Ma was there for the row and she didn't say a thing... At least I'm too old to be caned," he added, the slightest glimmer of a smile.

"Oh, Al! I'm so sorry you've run into trouble. Could you help your dad here for a while?"

Alfred went back to looking miserable. "He's never believed I could do it. Hugh, the eldest, was meant to take over. Then he went and joined the army and died in Rangoon – left us with nothing but a handsome painting of himself in his dashing scarlet uniform to adorn the hall. No doubt the old man will decide and tell me to do it whether I like it or not."

Alfred hauled himself to his feet and went to lean on the balustrade. She joined him. There was a strange solace in the empty heaven and, down below the skyline, the delicate etching of the bog-fringed, tweed-and-heather coloured mountains merging into the soft green of the surrounding hills. From there the eye trailed naturally down to the secure reality of their familiar lake, fringed with rhododendron bushes frothing with a haze of pink and purple blooms.

4

The sound of crunching gravel and the familiar rhythm of horses hooves, took their attention. They both moved round to the front of the house and Emmie leant over the parapet in time to see Tom Maguire from Manorhamilton sweep his jaunting car to a stop with a flourish in front of the steps up to the front door. By craning sideways Alfred reported the arrival of a tall woman with a black bonnet firmly clamped on her head with a few wisps of straying grey hair escaping round the edges.

"'Tis Mrs Barton," Emmie informed him.

"What's she want?"

"Seems there may be news about your sister and her husband in Africa."

Emmie noticed that he had gone silent.

"What's up with you, Al?"

He was slow to reply, watching his father greeting the lady, paying off Tom and bringing her into the house.

"I was thinking about Florence. She was such a lively person and she was also an artist. You know, Emmie, she was going to London to study art when she met Folliott in Dublin."

"So, you must go down, it may be good news."

Alfred didn't move.

"After ten years? No, it's not possible. I'll not rush down. Mrs Barton didn't like Florence. She was far too 'liberated' for her liking. She tried to persuade Folliott not to marry her, she even pretended to be dying for a while!"

"Why did they go to Africa?" Emmie asked. "I can just remember their wedding, it was like a fairy tale to a little girl."

"They wanted to escape his mother... And also there was no work for engineers in Ireland at that time." He stretched and stepped back from the balustrade. "We all missed Florence, she was such fun. At first the letters came regularly and we were thrilled when she had a baby boy, Josh. As I recall, they went up to the diamond fields at Kimberley and then set out for a gold mine in the north. That was when the silence descended. No further letters arrived. They seemed to have been swallowed up in the African bush."

Emmie nodded. The story, as it had circulated the village, was coming back to her.

"I'd best be going, Al, me dad'll be wondering what has become of the donkey an' cart." She touched Alfred on the arm, interrupting his reverie, picked up her apron, and set off for the stairs without a backward glance.

5

She wondered at the change in herself. At one time, hidden up on the roof, she'd have kissed him and tried to cheer him up without a second thought. Now she was aware of a gulf between them. His life had expanded and hers had stood still.

His world had moved into a sophisticated stage where she could no longer follow. Reluctantly she was forced to admit to herself that he was a gentleman and she was a village girl. As she made her way down the stairs she struggled with her resentment. She knew how to act like a lady, she was sure she could do it. But then – who would allow her to try? Alfred might like her but she knew he would never take her to Dublin.

Back at Killarga Emmie found herself rapidly drawn into the chores to help her mother, Colleen. She tried to tell her mother about the arrival of Mrs Barton and Alfred up at the big house, but her mother seemed distracted and was obviously only half listening to her.

"What's up with you, Ma?" she enquired after her mother had reached for the sugar instead of the salt for the second time.

Colleen O'Connell wiped her red hands firmly on the white apron which covered her "housework" dress. Her brown hair was looped back in a loose bun which framed an attractive face rapidly gathering lines from the passage of years and the physical hard work of rearing a family, helping her husband with his mill, and tending their land for the meagre crops which the rocky soil would allow.

Emmie noticed the apprehensive look which crossed her face as she glanced at her daughter.

Colleen sighed.

"I know yous always had dreams, my love, but now yous seventeen it's time to decide on the future. Your Pa and I, we've been talkin' an' we think it's time for you to get married an' to settle down."

"Ah, Ma, not that one again! You know I'm too hot-headed for most of the lads round here. I need to wait a year or two and find some chap from Manorhamilton or somewhere with a bit of life – Killarga is too quiet and dull."

Colleen lifted the lid from the stew and stirred the pot.

"There's many a good lad hereabouts but you're set against them. You've spent too much time hobnobbing with the gentry an' it's done you no good. You've a sharp tongue in that head of yours an' I blame myself for letting you spend too much time with the wrong sort."

"Give over, Ma, I'm not wanting to spend my days tied to a tiny cottage with a basketful of children an' a grumbling man to tend to."

"It's not such a bad life, girl. You're the lucky one with a Pa who runs his own mill; you've had shoes for Sundays and food and a cart. It's more than most round here."

"I know, I know, but there's other ways of living. I'd like to use the voice God gave me, to sing an' visit other towns and villages."

Colleen turned impatiently to look at her daughter.

"Indeed, you'd be like a tinker, on the move and hoping for a few pence. No, my girl, we're respectable people here. You'll do as we plan."

Emmie felt her temper rising. She had been trying to avoid this discussion for a long time. She told herself to keep calm but her hands were grasping the back of one of the old chairs and her knuckles were white. She found it difficult to stop herself from swinging round to shout at her mother to stop planning her life for her. At the same time she was well aware that all parents planned their children's lives – hadn't Alfred just said as much himself – so it happened in all families, even those brought up with carriages and cooks.

The room darkened as someone came in at the door. Emmie recognised the silhouette of her father. He was followed by his son, Sean and the young-est boy, Duggie.

"What's this?" Padraigh O'Connell said, sensing the atmosphere in the room. Sean and Duggie slid onto the bench at the table and were joined by the toddler, Finola.

Colleen looked up at him as she began to serve out the bowls of stew.

"It's her ladyship here, she's not one for our local boys."

"Have you told her then?"

"I have not, you tell her."

Emmie felt her dad's appraising look. She had a nervous moment won-dering what her mother was to have told her. She knew her big red-headed dad adored her. However, with matching tempers, they usually avoided open conflict by getting others to pass their messages. He regarded Emmie as the prettiest girl in the village, and also, as she could read and write, as the most intelligent. Now, however, she sensed there was no escape. Her mother was obviously not prepared to act as a buffer this time.

"Well, lass, we must see to your future and we've looked carefully at the lads round here and we've decided Rory Maguire is the best for you." He dragged his chair over to the table and picked up his spoon as though the matter was decided.

Emmie felt as though someone had thrown a bucket of cold water over her.

"What did you say? Who? You can't mean that great clod from the bakery, the one who thinks he's a gift from God above to all the girls hereabout?" Emmie asked in a voice choking with indignation.

"So," said Colleen, "He's not good enough for you is he not? He's a grand lad an' he'll take over the bakery from his dad one day, an' if you won't have him there's many as will."

Out of the corner of her eye Emmie could see Finola sucking her thumb and staring at her wide-eyed, while Sean and Duggie tried to make themselves as small as possible, sensing a row about to erupt.

She decided to try persuasion.

"Ma, you know you need me to help with the house, an' the cookin,' an' Da, you need me to write out the accounts for you..."

Her father lifted his spoon and jabbed at the air with it.

"Oh, we've talked to the Maguires an' they'll be happy for you to come down to the mill each day, an' ol' Maguire, he's happy to think you can help him with the writing at the bakery."

"Got it all organised, I see..." Emmie could feel her temper rising. "What am I? A sheep to sell to the highest bidder? Ah-ha, gentlemen, *this* one can write as well as breed!"

"Ah now, Emmie, hold on to your temper, gal. This lad's got more going for him than anyone else round here, an' what's more," he smiled persuasively at her, "he will eventually run the bakery, an' I'm hearing he thinks you're real beautiful an' he'll do his best by you."

"Ah no, Pa, you'd not do this to me, would you? He's only interested in fishin' an' countin' his money or goin' to the races in Leitrim. There's no joy in the miserable boy at all!"

Colleen could contain herself no longer.

"So, Rory McGuire's not good enough for ye! Sure you'll be thinking you're too grand for the likes of us too, ye spoilt whelp ye! Hobnobbing wit yer betters an' learning the ways of them!"

"No, Ma, it's not that, it's just I'm not wanting to marry yet," Emmie cried, feeling caught somewhere between fear and indignation.

"It's like I've always said," Padraigh interrupted, "it's this educating girls what's caused the problems. Along comes yer man from the Parliament and pays a teacher-lady. What good's that done the young'uns? Nuttin' but teachin' them to want what they ha'na got. What their da's canna afford."

Colleen interrupted:

"An' the wanting of men they canna have – an' dreamin' of towns – all dreams, my Emmie, not for us."

"So I'm never to dream! I can only have what you have, because I'm a girl I can't do anything, not even try to sing, an' I'm stuck for ever here, in this place," Emmie was shouting and banging her hands on the table, oblivious of the faces around her.

"Come now, lass," Padraigh's patience was running out, "It's not a bad place an' you've family all around to support you." He turned to Colleen, "You see what too much time at the big house has done to her, she's dreaming of fine clothes and balls and coaches to Dublin… Not content to sing at ceilaghs round here, she wants the life we canna give her."

Emmie rounded on him.

"I just want to *live*, not to be hidden away in the depths of Leitrim with nothing but babies and housework lying ahead of me…"

Finally, Padraigh lost his temper.

"Well now that's it, my girl. You'll do as *we* want for once. We've set a wedding date in September, an' we'll do the best we can by you, an' no more mixing with the Protestants by the big house. You hear?"

Emmie pushed back her chair and it toppled to the floor. She rushed out of the door, tears streaming down her face.

"I hate you all. Why can't you understand?" she sobbed as she went.

In the background she heard her mother advising her father to leave her alone.

"It's the shock," she was saying quietly, "Leave her be, Tom. Girls are emotional about marriage, it's the end of their freedom."

She felt as though the bottom had fallen out of her world. Suddenly there was nothing left. No dreams. No chance to sing somewhere like Dublin, to use that voice which everyone had always told her was so special. She'd sung at the big house and Mrs Lyons-Montgomery had played for her and taught her new songs.

Now she might as well forget that other world she'd been allowed into for a while, it would soon be only a memory as she struggled for a life with good, solid, boring Rory and the bakery.

She needed to be alone. Enveloped in her own collapsing world, her feet followed the familiar path through the uneven stone-walled fields and over the mearing ditches, across the hill and down to the silver water of Belhavel Lake.

To her annoyance, as she came down to the small beach, she found another figure on the edge of the water. Then she recognised the familiar square shape of Alfred and moved down to join him.

Alfred heard the light crunch of gravel and turned sharply.

"Oh, it's you, Emmie... I'm not in the mood for company."

Emmie ignored this abrupt greeting.

"I was hoping for peace myself, Al... It's marrying me off they're trying to do back home, and me not keen!"

Alfred looked interested. He sat down on a rock and patted the warm surface of the one next to him.

"Come on then, sit down here and tell me your sorrows."

Emmie sank her toes into the warm sand and smoothed her skirt as she accepted his invitation.

"Why you down here, Al?"

Alfred was quiet for a moment, staring out across the lake as though gathering his thoughts.

"I suppose it's two things, really. One is feeling hopeless about whatever my father will choose for me to do next – and now he is talking about me going back to medicine again. He just doesn't hear me when I tell him it's a hopeless cause," he sighed.

"Ant the other one?" Emmie prompted.

"It's Florence. It looks as though someone may have found her son, Josh, and that means she must definitely be dead. We've never really accepted that before."

Emmie nodded sympathetically.

"I suppose there was always hope she might suddenly be found somewhere in the depths of the jungles where she could not write to you," she sympathised.

"I suppose so. No one ever talked about it. My father wrote to the Governor of the Cape of Good Hope and to the newspapers there and in Port Natal and Kimberley. Letters came back but they always talked of the 'dangers of the interior' and told us that they might be farming in the far north or have succumbed to illness in some remote corner of the bush. No trace could be found."

"Ant it's Mrs Barton who brought the news?"

"Yes, she's had a letter from a preacher in Cape Town. Apparently it says he has heard of a white child, a young boy, who has been found living amongst the northern tribes. Seems he had this news from a soldier, one of Lord Chelmsford's men, who was saved by the child."

"Saved?" Emmie queried.

"Yes, but unfortunately, he gives no other details. Seems Harriet Barton had put an advertisement in the Cape Town paper asking for any news about the missing family, and this man saw it."

"So, what happens now, Al?"

"We've no proof it is Florence's Josh, and Father has to decide what to do. Mother wants the child home and so does Mrs Barton, the women are quite hysterical about it, but it's ten years since they disappeared and Father is worried it may not be the right child, the preacher might just be after the reward."

"What do you think, Al?"

Alfred shrugged. "I feel very sad about Florence and I think if he *is* ours he should come home, but right now I'm more worried about myself and how to persuade the old man that I'm not cut out to be a doctor."

"I see. So, it's going back to Dublin you may be?"

Alfred leant over and put an arm round her shoulders.

"I'm still here for a while... we can meet... what's this you say about your parents wanting to marry you off?" A smile spread across his face making his blue eyes sparkle, "By God, Emmie, he'll need to be a strong character to hold a girl like you – and he better be good at riding and fishing or he's lost!"

"Al, you're not much good. Don't laugh at me. It's serious. I'm not ready to marry some village lad. They're a dull lot," Emmie wailed.

"Sorry, Emmie, it's serious then, is it?" He took her hand and kissed it gently. "I didn't realise... who are they wanting you to wed then, lass?"

"It's Rory Maguire – you know..." she prompted him as he looked blank, "...the one whose dad runs the bakery in the village."

"Yes, yes, I remember him now. A big serious-faced lad who was up before the magistrate for telling people in the pub they should riot against their English landlords."

"Yes, that's him. But his dad did cane him ant he says little to anyone these days, but word has it he likes to gamble an' eye the girls."

"He's the eldest isn't he, so one day he'll run the bakery – that's not bad, Emmie, it would give you a position in the village?"

"But, Al," she began to sob on his shoulder in despair, "It's not what I want."

"What do you want then, Emmie?" he enquired kindly.

"I'm not sure, but I'm not wanting to marry. Honest, Al, I'm not."

Alfred gave her a kiss on the neck and moved her thick auburn hair so that it fell over one shoulder.

"I think I want to get away from this village, from the gossip and chatter and meet new people... you've always said I could sing, I'd like to try."

Alfred lifted her face up with one hand and wiped the tears off her cheek with a finger from his other hand. "You're a lovely flower and you deserve better. But, Emmie, you'd probably have to sing in music halls and bars." He tipped her face up and kissed her full on the lips. You have to be tough to do that."

"I know, Al, ant I don't care! Anything to stop the boredom of being locked away in County Leitrim." She put her arms round his neck and kissed him round his eyes and on his mouth. He felt warm and comforting with a delicious male aroma mixed with the scent of a freshly laundered shirt offset by the soft rush-laden perfume of the lough. She moved her body up against his. He responded and she felt her heart thumping in her ears. She gazed into his face and saw a look of excitement flit across his face.

She heard a sound and felt Alfred draw back. As she struggled to recover her emotions she heard the distinct creak of boat timbers and the rhythmic splashing of oars as the prow of a small rowing boat began to round the rocky point to one side of their beach. Alfred grabbed her hand and pulling her to her feet, he propelled her hurriedly into the rhododendron bushes which lined the edge of the small beach.

Once hidden by the dusty leaves he kissed her on the ear and murmured: "The stable boys have the afternoon off to attend the fair and fresh hay came in yesterday, let's make good use of it!"

Stumbling behind his crouching body she followed him between the woody stems and deep green leaves, a surge of excitement making her ache with anticipation and aware of the desire in his eyes as he had taken her hand to lead her forward. They kept to the leafy cover until the open ground came into sight between them and the stable block.

All was blissfully quiet in the soft spring afternoon and the back door into the stable block was standing ajar. Emmie straightened her bodice and walked as casually as her pent-up emotions would allow her, across to the door and into the cool darkness of the stables. Quietly, she tiptoed over the cobbled stone floor to the wooden stairs. No coachman or stable boys to be seen, just the warm pungent aroma of horses and the familiar stirring from their stalls. Upstairs she crept past the tack store and the coachman's rooms and reached the stepladder which led up to the hayloft above.

Gathering her cotton skirt up to her knees, she tied it in a bunch and began to climb the ladder with jerky excitement, the smell of fresh hay wafting down to greet her in heady waves of natural perfume. At the top of the ladder she looked down cautiously but there was still no one to be seen, so she grabbed the wooden supports and hauled herself, wriggling, bare legs waving frantically, up onto the floor above. The dust left a smear down her bodice which she dusted with the folds of her skirt. Then she looked round and smiled with uninhibited glee. The soft, sweet-scented hay was piled up to the roof in a glorious golden cascade. She selected a corner well cushioned with its scented mattress and burrowed down into its seductive depths, covering herself completely.

Alfred made the same journey in a state of heightened excitement which almost made it impossible for him to climb the ladder. He hauled himself into the loft and sprang to his feet, shedding his shirt and trousers with magician-like speed, peering round in eager readiness to throw himself onto Emmie where ever she might be waiting.

He twisted about like a stoat scenting its prey, peering into the pale gloom in growing frustration. No sound. No Emmie.

"Puss-puss-puss," he whispered softly. Then, more desperately, "Don't play, kitten, I can't wait!"

Suddenly the surface of the hay in the far corner bulged into a ball and a figure sprang up, arms outstretched, stark naked, hay raining down round her in a Catherine wheel shower. He could not resist a wild whoop of glee as he leapt over and, scooping her into his arms, sank down into the sweet-smelling straw, feeling the warm silkiness of her skin against the taut muscles of his chest. His hands ran down her body and she bent towards him, putting her hands on either side of his head and drawing his mouth towards hers with an excited urgency. He felt her hips yield towards him as her nipples pressed against his chest. With a shuddering gasp of excited delight he sank into her body and began to move to-and-fro as she dug her nails into his back and gasped in pleasurable surprise.

Emmie felt herself move in tune with him, her passion met and committed. Then she slipped slowly into a feeling of deep contentment, overshadowed by a sense of bewilderment at how quickly it had all happened. The build-up had been superb but the moment had passed too quickly.

She lay there, dreaming quietly, her hands running caressingly through his hair. It was then that she saw the wisps of hay on a higher plateau of the stack wafting down towards them. Watching their graceful descent, she became aware of a slight stirring in the pile up near the rafters. Could it be the stable cat, she pondered sleepily. She narrowed her eyes and her hands stopped stroking his hair as she concentrated her vision. She could have sworn she heard a sound, almost like a snigger. Then there was a violent sneeze and the hay jerked convulsively, sending more dust particles dancing into the shaft of sunlight from the granary door.

Her whole body jerked out of its delicious lethargy into a catatonic tautness. This sudden reaction and her nails digging into his back, brought Alfred's head up to look at her face. Emmie felt him roll hastily into the hay while searching up towards the top of the stack with his eyes. She moved quickly into a sitting position and began frantically searching for her clothes in the surrounding straw. Just then there was another muffled sneeze. She saw Alfred's face go scarlet. He shouted up towards the rafters:

"Come out, you peeping bastard! Show yourself, we know you're there!"

There was a silence, followed by a further sneeze and then, very slowly, the apprehensive face of Alfred's youngest sister, Beatrice, emerged through the strands of hay, her dark hair crowned in an incongruous golden wig of straw, her mouth twitching slightly as she struggled to control nervous giggles at the sight below. Simultaneously, the irrepressibly cheeky face of the youngest boy, Kynaston, and his great buddy, Duggie O'Connell, popped gingerly out from other corners of the stack.

Emmie looked at Alfred and they both stared in growing horror as the full implication dawned on them.

"Come on, you bloody bastards, where are the rest of your sneaking army?" shouted Alfred. "You travel in a bloody pack, bring them *all* out – *and* that mangy hound!"

There was a long pause and then a gray and black nose appeared over the top, close to the rafters. A pair of disconsolate brown eyes looked down at them through a wiry mane of hair. The appearance of Boru was the final blow to Alfred and he leapt up stark naked and began to claw at the tall stack in uncontrolled fury. The faces above watched in dead silence, eyes growing rounder.

Emmie found her dress and with some relief pulled it over her head. Immediately she felt more in control.

"Jasus, sure Al, will you shut up for the luv o' God ant get your drawers on! You'll destroy yourself entirely before you kill the little buggers."

She was relieved to see that through his rage her common-sense prevailed. He grabbed his clothes and began to pull them on furiously, inadvertently dragging both feet into one trouser leg.

"Get down out'ta there, you little turds ant let's have a look at ye," insisted Emmie to the faces.

Like lice from a fleece the three emerged and slithered down. The Irish Wolfhound whined and then manoeuvred himself sideways so that he slithered part of the way and jumped the remainder.

"Ant would you pull Ethel out of that too – you're never wit'out her along wit you, are you now?" demanded the scarlet-faced Emmie.

"Honest to God, Emmie, she's out there on the lake wit Lambert, fishin'," came the subdued reply from Duggie.

"Indeed to God ant my baby brother spying on his sister, sure the shame of it... Mary and Joseph is there no loyalty left at all?"

"Emmie, we weren't spying, we were only playing hide-and-seek," said Beatrice defiantly.

"Like hell you were," shouted the red-faced Alfred, now returned to decency. "Who was doing the seeking then?"

"I was," said a deep voice from the top of the ladder. The coachman, Emmie's Uncle Con, was staring pensively up at the gathering from the ladder, his head and shoulders showing above the floor.

"I was mending the harness out front and doin' my 'seeking' when Boru barked for me." His mouth pursed into a thin line. "Ant it's not them should be taking the pasting, it's you two – especially you, lass," he said, nodding his head towards Emmie and rising up another rung on the loft ladder.

"Your Ma must hear of this to make sure you don't develop a taste for it!" he continued, glaring meaningfully at her.

He brought his bulk up another rung so that he was almost on a level with Alfred.

"An' you, young sir," he whispered, "you should know better. Keep your lusts for Dublin City – there's plenty there to keep you satisfied. This lass is no cheap Pegeen from the bogs. Yer dad'll have to know – he can talk to you about respectability and honour."

Emmie felt the colour draining from her face. She looked at Alfred and saw that he had turned white, his indignation was subsiding rapidly.

Righteous glee had come to rest on the side of the children. They stared knowingly at Alfred and Emmie, and Beatrice began to giggle as she recalled the scene in the hay.

"Shut up, Beatrice," muttered Kynaston, well aware that his elder brother would eventually reach him in the privacy of the house.

Duggie's eyes were like saucers as he pondered the row at home.

"Jasus, Em! You'd best not come home," he stammered.

"Keep your mouth buttoned up," Alfred told him tersely, "No tattle-tale from you."

Duggie swallowed and bit his lip, putting the advice into action.

"Come now, yous," sighed Con, beginning to back down the ladder. Emmie saw her petticoat under the hay and hastily pulled it on. The two lads bundled Boru's back legs onto the first rung while Duggie and Kyn took his front section and they heaved and carried the long-suffering hound down the ladder in silence, apart from the occasional nervous whine.

To Emmie's consternation the air of gloom seemed to draw other people like a magnet. Ethel and Lambert wandered in with a small trout. Ethel shoved the fish out in front of her, about to recount the deed, when she suddenly became aware of the charged atmosphere and choked back her words. Lambert looked at them both and appeared to take two seconds to size up the situation, then glared accusingly at his brother.

Alfred looked as though he was about to protest to Con, perhaps in the hope of diverting the course of justice. Unfortunately, Hugh Lyons-Montgomery chose that fateful moment to visit his hunter. Like his elder son, one look at the crestfallen couple, the trail of hay, and Con's set expression and he had little need for detail. With a heavy sigh he saw his canter being frustrated. Hugh waved them all into the tack room and looked expectantly at Con.

Emmie could see that Con was seriously disconcerted. She guessed he had been going to deal with the situation himself. He would have given Alfred a fair lecture and threatened him with his father, but, she felt sure he would have said nothing to his employee at this stage. As for herself, well she knew that he'd have spared her nothing. It would be that belt for her however it went. How, she wondered, was he going to deal with the threats he had made in front of the younger children? She watched him shift uneasily from foot to foot.

"Con, you have something to tell me, I think?" queried his employer.

Seven pairs of eyes fixed on Con.

"Ach sure," he began slowly. "An' thems can all be off." He waved his arm to include the children and Boru from the hayloft, and Lambert and Ethel, who had slid in as curious onlookers.

Alfred's father nodded.

"The supporting cast may now leave," he drawled, opening the door.

Reluctantly they all filed out and the level of noise in the stables rose to a babble as they moved towards the courtyard. Silence descended on the tack room.

Con fingered the tweed of his jacket sleeve and cleared his throat. As a man of few words whose conversation was normally concerned with horses, he was wondering where to begin.

His employer took pity on him.

"Con, you and the small children must have found these two up in the hayloft… um… presumably cavorting for their pleasure? Am I to assume that, to judge from the expression on Beatrice's face and the bursting importance of Kynaston and Duggie, that they somehow managed to witness this event?"

"Yes, sir, that's just it – yous put it right fine!" said Con, with obvious relief at not having to find the words for himself.

A long silence followed. Emmie could see that, like her, Alfred was finding the silence and the steady tap of his father's riding crop on the tack room table, an unnerving experience. Hugh Lyons-Montgomery's normally amiable face was furrowed into lines of annoyance and his blue eyes had taken on a coldness which defied self-justifying comments from either of the accused.

Finally, the tapping stopped and his eyes settled on his son:

"What do you have to say, Alfred-Otho?" he said, ignoring the normal familiar family abbreviation of Alfred-O, making Alfred even more aware of the depth of his disapproval.

Alfred, Emmie realised as he spoke, was in a state of nervous confusion, and certainly his reply startled her as much as it did his father.

"Sir, I love Emmie, I want her to come and live with me in Dublin… we could marry and live on my allowance," Alfred stumbled out his ill-considered and hasty reply.

Emmie felt herself stop breathing for a moment as she absorbed what he had said and then she put a hand over her mouth as she appreciated the impact of the comment on those around her.

"Tis not possible!" interjected Con, before his employer could reply. "It wouldn't be right! *Ant* the girl is promised to another!"

Although his face was now ruddy red with annoyance, Hugh spoke coolly.

"Of course, Con, you are quite right. Ignore this nonsense. I have already discussed his damn arrogance with this young pup earlier in the day. What, I wonder, does the young lady have to say?" his eyes swivelled onto Emmie.

Emmie swallowed nervously under his steady gaze and grabbed in panic for anything she might say.

"Well, sir, to be sure, Alfred is a good friend and I'd not mind Dublin. But, sir, I'm not a bad girl..." at this point she was aware of Alfred's father raising his eyebrows in feigned surprise.

"My Ma and Pa, they'd not like it neither..." She tailed off into silence, nervously biting her lip and watching Hugh's face.

"Do you feel no shame for what you have just done?" asked Hugh, in genuine astonishment. "You, a single lass from a decent, God-fearing family, *and* promised to another?"

Emmie knew that her shame centred around embarrassment and chagrin rather than guilt. However, a shred of self-preservation warned her that this attitude would only cause a local scandal and her father, adore her though he did, would be forced to use his belt.

"Most truly sir, I have sinned terrible. Father Donohue will give me a penance... an' me dad will have much to say..." At this point she felt genuinely apprehensive and Hugh seemed to soften slightly.

Very aware of her uncle's presence she glanced nervously at Con out of the corner of her eye. He was staring at her sceptically, obviously not moved to sympathy of any sort by her fears of family retribution.

Hugh had turned his attention to his son.

"Alfred-Otho, I expect better of you! You understand our position in the County. You are *not* free to indulge your lust on your own property – *or* anywhere else for that matter." His voice had developed an ice-cold edge which made Alfred shift nervously.

Just as Hugh was drawing in breath to deliver his verdict there was swish of skirts outside the tack room door and his wife, Elizabeth, opened the door and said hurriedly: "Could I have an urgent word with you, Hugh?"

Normally so calm and unruffled, Elizabeth was looking distressed and flustered, with a high spot of colour on each cheek. Emmie wondered whether their sins were already common knowledge round the family. No doubt Beatrice would have wasted no time in spreading the news, she speculated.

Hugh looked over his shoulder. "Con, wait outside with the youngsters. I will be with you in a moment."

He drew the agitated Elizabeth on one side and closed the door on the others.

Presently Elizabeth reappeared, her head held high, and ignoring the trio in the passage she swept across the cobbled courtyard, shooing several inquisitive little maids back towards the kitchen.

Emmie and Alfred were escorted back into the room by Con, rather, she imagined, as a guard might return prisoners awaiting their death sentence.

Hugh eyed them both thoughtfully for several agonising minutes. He appeared to be making up his mind about how to deal with the situation. Then he reached a decision.

"What you deserve, young man," he said, addressing Alfred sternly, "is a damn good whipping in public. Instead, I intend giving you an assignment which will take you away from Ireland and your undesirable friends at Trinity for a year." He paused and Emmie glanced at Alfred from under her eyelashes. He was staring at his father in open-mouthed amazement, hastily stifled as his father continued.

"At the end of that time we will see what effect the responsibility has had on you. I will decide whether I withdraw all financial support or whether you have matured and earned my respect and a return to your medical studies." Hugh paused.

Emmie could imagine Alfred's emotions, out of Ireland for a whole year, no studying, no family lectures! What could it be that his father was planning for him? It was unlikely to include her. It began to dawn on her that it would mean facing the consequences of their fun in the hay all on her own. She put a hand out to steady herself on the table edge. Her world was crumbling once again. She could see herself disgraced and lonely, tied to the house for ever and destined to stay home looking after her parents for the rest of her life.

It was then that the first threads of an idea began to weave round in her head. She was forced back to reality as Alfred's father sighed and looked thoughtfully at her for a moment.

"As for you, my lass, I think your family will have a great deal to say to you. Con, you must take Miss Emmie home and say what you feel necessary. Unfortunately, I fear that the whole episode was turned into something of a public spectacle and news runs like wildfire round here. It may be that your punishment, young lady, will lie in broken marriage plans."

Emmie did her best to hide her delight at the thought. Hugh looked a little surprised by her lack of response.

"It will not be easy for your family," he remonstrated severely. She nodded and he turned his attention back to his son.

"And you, young man," Hugh continued, "will go out to Africa to find this child who might be your nephew and bring him back to Ireland."

Emmie caught sight of the mixed emotions, largely of delight, which flitted across Alfred's face. For a second she felt a pang of panic and then it came back – the idea born of desperation and rebellion. It was only a seed but it gave her a surge of excitement. She managed to drag her eyes down to the floor to hide her feelings. She looked at her bare toes and thought irrelevantly how undignified it was to be caught without her shoes, up at the big house.

Chapter Two

AFRICA – November 1878

CLIFFORD WILSON TIPPED his hide hat to the back of his head and wiped his arm across his forehead to clear the perspiration which was trickling down towards his eyes.

He was aware of a feeling of acute frustration. He had lived in Africa for six years and by now he should have accepted that things moved at an unhurried pace, regulated by dusk and dawn and the passage of the seasons. He struggled with his own concerns. There was no real reason that he could think of as to why he was being forced to wait for an answer about the boy. He had seen the chief, been well received, in fact. He'd amused himself by passing on Queen Victoria's greetings while wondering what that plump little dame would have said if she had known that a member of the erstwhile American colonies was using her name to his own ends in darkest Africa.

The dignified induna with his well-oiled body and his head circlet of clay and hair, had acted as translator between him and the chief. He had virtually acknowledged that there was indeed a white boy living with the tribe, but had not been forthcoming as to where he was. Clifford's gifts had been received without rancour and there had been no threats or further demands. He didn't really see what more he could do.

He folded his tall, lean torso down into a sitting position, stretching out his legs in their leather hunting trousers and battered veldskoen boots and adjusting the cream open-necked shirt into a more comfortable position under his leather hunter's waistcoat. There was nothing to do but sit in the deep shade of the old marula tree in the centre of the kraal, with his back against the vast trunk, and attempt to be patient. This was not something he found easy at twenty-nine years of age. He'd have felt better if he could have had his gun and his horse with him but politeness forbade him to come armed into a chief's kraal. He'd left them in the care of a young warrior beyond the entrance to the kraal, to the fascination of the local children who sat watching him in awe. The sun had baked his skin to a gentle, even, golden brown and bleached his hair to a blond curly mop. He'd cultivated a beard to save on razors and this was a darker shade than his hair, closer to his natural brown. Vivid clear blue eyes stared out at the world in an expression somewhere between challenge and expectation. He had long ago accepted responsibility for his own life and with this had come a healthy degree of confidence.

A slight breeze flickered across the area of hard-baked earth around the tree, bringing with it the woody smell of last night's fires and the sound of childish laughter. This reminded him of his own childhood. Not that there had been much to laugh at, once his parents had died. He'd only been nine when that tragedy occurred and he had found himself deposited without ceremony with his uncle in Minnesota, a frightened little boy, the youngest of nine children. They were a poor family and another mouth was not really welcome. He had struggled through to thirteen years, keeping his head down, doing as he was told, desperate for love.

It was then that the circus had passed through the town and he had run away, becoming an assistant to the stunt riders. It had been no surprise to him that no one had ever come in search of him. He'd loved the roving life and for the first time had felt accepted for himself and had found that hard work earned him not only a meal and cash but also the respect and appreciation of others. He'd managed to stay with the circus for three years and then his love of horses had led to a year with the Comanche on the plains of Oklahoma.

Soon after his seventeenth birthday he had fallen helplessly in love with a young Indian girl who was already promised to another. His reaction to a broken heart was a trip to Boston and the snap decision to join a trading vessel bound for southern Africa.

However, the sea and the narrow confines of a ship had rapidly lost their attraction. In Cape Town, with its enchanting backdrop of Table Mountain, he was delighted to feel his feet on dry land and wasted no time in abandoning the sea and joining Henry Hartley, a well-known hunter and trader. From the start Africa had fascinated him. He could still recall his initial excitement as he wandered through Cape Town market and found himself faced by the colourful meeting of East and West mixed with the earthy tones of Southern Africa. There were doe-eyed women in gossamer saris moving between the stalls piled high with fresh fruit and vegetables. Their men were often bearded and wore white robes and red inverted flower-pot hats. There were also European woman, much as he recalled them back home, as well as delicately coffee-coloured people, who chattered like an aviary of birds and seemed to do many of the manual tasks. Just occasionally, there was also a man or woman of a deep mahogany hue, whose black eyes darted round in almost as much confusion as his blue ones. He recalled the intoxication of colour, the lyrical babble of noise and, above all, the scent. It was a mixture of spices, roses and wild honey, drifting ahead of the salty sea breezes, wrapping round the people and settling in the folds of their clothes. He smiled at the memory of his wonderment. It had not taken much to convince him that trading merchandise had more to offer him than the life of a sailor on the turbulent seas.

His drowsy reminiscences were rudely interrupted by rapid chatter and the sound of running feet on the sun-baked earth, Jolted back into the present he quickly became aware of a cry which, like the wind round a crevasse, rose to a sorrowing moan soon taken up by other voices, steadily changing note to the dull growl of a threatening gale. Clifford leapt to his feet and began to thread his way towards the entrance where his horse and gun spelt safety. He was stopped by the induna who had translated for him.

"What has happened?" he enquired of the old man.

"Some of the newly blooded young men had gone on a leopard hunt and two of them have been killed. A party will go out to see what can be done."

Clifford saw a party of young men, holding assegais running by, their feet thudding into the powdered soil in well-drilled co-ordination, their eyes staring straight ahead. A myriad puffs of dust were slowly settling back. Clifford swung back to the old man and opened his mouth to ask whether he could accompany them. Before he could actually say anything the old man shook his head.

"There are enough people, that leopard will not wait. He will move away. One of the boys is hurt, perhaps you can help him?"

Clifford nodded.

"I need my saddlebag – it has medicines."

A young man led him back to his horse and he pulled the medical pack out of his saddlebag. It wasn't much but it dealt with the everyday bites, stings and scratches of the bushveld.

The boy, Napedi, a good-looking lad of about thirteen, was sitting on a mat by his hut while his mother crushed up a compound of plants. Fortunately, it was a flesh wound, deep but not fatal if it could be kept clean. Clifford washed the wound with fresh water and admired the boy's stoicism as he bit his bottom lip and stared determinedly up at the thatch-rimmed wall, no sound escaping him despite the pallor of his face and the winces of pain. His mother packed the wound with the herbal mixture. Clifford knew that the locals would be better at treating an open wound with their own preparations, but he bandaged it as a contribution. The boy seemed delighted with Clifford's handiwork and kept showing everyone his bandaged leg and pointing at Clifford in delight. It was difficult to make Napedi's mother understand that it would have to be removed when she changed the dressing, but the old induna who was still translating said they normally used a large forest leaf to bind wounds and she would know what to do, and yes, the long cloth of the visitor would be washed down by the river and dried in the sun before it was used again.

From the induna Clifford was able to discover that in the night a calf had been taken by a leopard and this had given rise to the hunt. Leopards normally kept to their own trails and areas but, perhaps because the land was beginning to feel the first tentacles of a drought creeping across it, the easy meat of a young calf had appealed to the leopard. Past experience had shown that a leopard who succeeded could well return to try again. In fact, one of the returning young hunters had told of a rocky lair with a shallow cave in the high krantz and the presence of cubs. However, the leopard had outmanoeuvred the young hunters, and, probably in protection of her cubs, had killed two of them.

Clifford was aware that this tribe followed the pattern of the great Zulu tribes dividing their young boys into groups of approximately the same age, who then formed what was known as an iNtanga; they then played and worked together and would eventually be initiated together. This group had been from the most recent initiation, their enthusiasm to display their prowess had caused them to move into action without waiting for the guidance of a more experienced hunter.

"What of the white boy?" Clifford enquired hopefully.

The old induna looked at him thoughtfully, then rose up from his crouching position and pointed towards the chief's hut.

"Tonight we are called for an indaba. The witchdoctor will decide his future."

Clifford was aware of a sinking feeling. He'd hoped to find the boy, negotiate his release from the tribe and move straight off with the child to spend the night at the de Groot mission station, several hours' ride from the kraal. A tribal chief's kraal was not a comfortable place. There were far too many warriors for his liking and now there was also this air of gloom and foreboding, the women keening their sorrow and their respect for the dead, in long drawn-out wails.

Now he knew that he might well be spending a night as a visitor in the kraal.

Was it all worth it, he pondered?

Rumours about this boy had come to his ears many months ago when he was shooting in the vicinity of these mountains. The gossip had brought to mind a brief letter which he had read some years past in the *Natal Observer*, which had been from a grandmother back in Dublin looking for a lost family in Africa. When next he had crossed the great Drakensberg range into Natal he had called in at the newspaper office in Port Natal and asked his old friend, the editor, John Robinson, to look up the back issues. Sure enough, the last news of the missing family had come as they headed north to the Duivels Kantoor in the Transvaal. The grandmother was offering a reward for news of her daughter, son-in-law and grandson – a substantial sum. Thoughtfully he had left the newspaper office, completed his business in the town and turned his horse back towards the distant mountains and plains of the Transvaal high veld.

Months later he was back in the valley of the silver mists, and had tracked down the tribe, hidden in their mountain eyrie. It had cost him a couple of good, if ancient, muzzleloaders to persuade the chief to part with the boy. He had the feeling that in fact the tribe were glad to move the boy on but were not averse to gaining something out of the deal. He sincerely hoped that this would prove to be the missing boy and that the grandmother would still be alive to pay the reward. He had never thought of himself as greedy but there was no doubt that the sum advertised would set him up in a decent small farm, fulfilling his dream of owning something valuable for the first time in his life.

It was evening before the chief called the indaba. The frustrated hunters were back. They had found the bodies but there had been no sign of the leopard. Their cave was empty apart from the remains of the calf, some bones and the leopard's own distinctive rancid smell. Moving along the rocky edge of the krantz in the heat of the day, the leopards had avoided leaving spoor and the hunters had soon lost what tracks there were.

A tragedy like this called for detailed enquiry. The chief hung his lion-tooth necklace round his neck and donned his ceremonial kaross. His wives rubbed him down with lion fat until his body gleamed like polished ebony. The indunas, the elder statesmen of the tribe, were assembled on either side of their chief, beneath the Tree of Great Wisdom. Gadunga, the witchdoctor, in full regalia of feathers, horns and paint, sat by his feet. The warriors lined the right and left of the quadrangle, the craftsmen and herders seated behind them. Across the far end of the hard-baked arena sat the women, with the chief's five wives in the forefront, resplendent in bangles, necklaces and headbands of beads. Behind them sat the children, divided by their ages into different iNtangas.

The sun was sinking like a ball of molten fire over the distant hills and the evening star was making its entrance onto the royal-blue cloak of the evening sky. Around the perimeter of the great square several fires were lit, and young boys held flaming torches round the chief and his indunas. Clifford was reminded briefly of his time with his American Red Indian friends, only a brief shadowy illusion against the creeping dusk, gone like quicksilver.

The chief rose and the cow-hide drums rolled out a tattoo. He began to talk, obviously recounting the incidents of the day. Clifford watched him raise his fist to the sky and cry out dramatically. A wail went up from all sides. The three boys who had returned alive were called to give an account. Clifford felt himself tense up and leant forward for a better view. One of the boys was undoubtedly white. So this was why he had not been able to ride out with him. He had been involved in the leopard hunt. Straining through the fading light, he could make out a thin, wiry frame and a mop of straight, fair hair which fell to the shoulders.

The lad was flanked by two boys of his own height; one of them walked with a stick and had Clifford's white bandage round his damaged leg. They took it in turns to recount their stories.

It was not difficult to follow the events, as round the perimeter people rose and acted out the hunters and the hunted. With the flames from the fire and the dodging shadows, the whole scene took on the dramatic quality of a ghostly mime, with the drums keeping up a slow, sombre heartbeat.

Gradually the final rays of the sun disappeared below the horizon and the sky turned from pink-tinged gentian blue to the star spangled navy velvet of the African night. The last boy finished his tale. Silence descended. Then the drums rolled and the chief rose to pronounce. The flaming torches threw a flickering light across his polished body and he held his audience riveted with thunderous declarations.

Clifford could only understand a part of what was said. He saw the witchdoctor rise from the ground like a horned demon from the under-world. Slowly and rhythmically he began to dance to and fro, intoning a chant which rose at intervals to the high-pitched squeal of a bush pig. The shadows flickered across his clay-daubed body and his eyes gleamed and glittered below the horned and feathered head-dress.

Clifford knocked out the ash from his pipe and pocketed it. He wished again that he was miles away, quietly sitting by a friendly hunter's campfire. What had made him think that this might be an easy prize? The audience were swaying and chanting and now the senior indunas were joining the witchdoctor and the drums were speeding up their rhythm. The three boys moved into the centre of the swaying, circling group and the chief's wives moved round them with a slow rhythmic, sorrowful chant. A saga was being performed, one which would enter the annals of the tribe for future occasions.

Suddenly a roll of drums pronounced a pause and the witchdoctor began to circle and gyrate. Faster and faster he spun, his fur tails and feathers whirling frenetically, howling a long drawn-out animal screech which sent shudders through Clifford's body and left him with every hair on his body standing up in superstitious terror.

Finally, the bizarre figure flung itself to the ground in a last wild gesture. The drums stopped instantly. A deadly silence descended for a half second. The figure on the ground, twitching spasmodically, slowly gathered itself and sprang to its full height shouting:

"The Golden Cub is to blame for our ill-fortune. The Ancestral Spirits have spoken – the one we took in as our own must be returned to the gods."

A great sigh went up from the audience and then a single, strangled sob. A woman broke through the ranks of the circle to fall at the feet of the white boy. The boy knelt and raised her up. As he did so one of the warriors left the ranks and moved purposefully towards the boy, his assegai raised at a killing angle. The woman screamed and pointed through the crowd to Clifford. The boy looked and hesitated. He turned again to the woman.

"Majinga, Mamapana," the boy said tenderly, the words floating like a whisper across the great square. His companion with the white bandage moved into the path of the warrior. At that moment the witchdoctor made a movement of his hand and a passage cleared through the ranks of the warriors, as if by magic, right to the spot where Clifford Wilson stood. The boy moved with dignity, turning once to lift his hand in salute to the woman, Majinga. The warrior followed him, his assegaai now at a less threatening angle and the chief held his peace.

Feeling the power of the occasion, Clifford wasted no time. He swung round and walked through the crowd towards the main entrance by the stockade of wood and thorn bush, praying that the lad would follow him without hesitation. He was well aware that one hesitant movement, one sideways glance, might break the spell and result in death for the child and possibly himself as an inconvenient witness.

Only as the horse, with the pair on its back, gathered speed, did the first sounds come from the great kraal. A female voice keened to the night a heartbreaking song which would stay with boy and man for the remainder of their lives. To Josh, Golden Cub, it meant the ultimate in sorrowing; to Clifford it brought back tingling goose-pimples and a prickle of superstition.

Chapter Three

AFRICA – December 1878 – January 1879

JOSH HAD HIS arms round the man's waist. His cheek was against the leather waistcoat and beneath him he was aware of the jolting thud of the large brown mare, her hooves steadily beating a retreat down well-worn mountain tracks. He clung on, every nerve jagged and raw, shock tremors convulsing his muscles, his eyes screwed tight shut to cut out mental pictures of the last hours. Gradually the bouncing discomfort settled into a swaying rhythm and through a haze of muscular pain he realised he had adjusted to the movement of the great beast's striding gallop. They were down on the flat country now, and around them the bushveld appeared to be bathed in a silver sheen of moonlight.

"Think forward, think forward – not back, not back," a voice within him repeated over and over again, to the regular beat of the hooves on the hard-baked soil. Slowly the pungent smell of the leather jacket, well-steeped in pipe smoke and the warmth of the body of the stranger, crept through to his semi-conscious mind. He relaxed his face muscles and became aware that he was alive and that the night was rushing by in a silver haze.

Who was this man of the pale skin? How had he come to be there at his hour of greatest need? Above all, where was he taking him and what might lie ahead? The gods of his ancestors must surely have come to his rescue. If it wasn't for the man's earthy smell he might well have thought he was only a spirit sent to carry him across the surface of the world to his next life. The smell of smoke from fires, cured leather and stale sweat… and something sweet, not a mixture one would credit to a God. No, this was a white man, a man like himself, a man who would have to blacken himself to be a real man. White men had strange ways, he had heard the wise men of the tribe talk… No, think forward, think forward…

The mission station was small. A collection of huts and one long mud house with a thatched roof which extended out like a neatly clipped fringe, forming a veranda down the front of the building. Nikolas de Groot leant forward in his chair and peered across the veld as the darkness disgorged the blur of a drooping horse picking its way between the scrub bushes, its head lowered, reins trailing loosely. It appeared to be carrying a man who swayed slightly in the saddle, his face masked by a broad-brimmed hat. There was something attached to his back, possibly a travelling pack.

Nik slowly unfolded all six foot four inches of himself out of the rimpi chair and leant against a veranda pole, the better to observe his visitor. He ran his fingers thoughtfully through his coarse gold beard disturbing the odd grey hair in the process, and wondered what the New Year of 1879 might be bringing to his doorstep.

Nik was a gentle giant, peaceable until roused and then dangerous to cross. His parents had not been happy to see their second son enter the church and they were totally mystified by his decision to become a missionary. A preacher they could understand, a man who read the Good Book to his flock and tried to tie together far-flung farming families in the unity of the Dutch Reformed Church. But to set out to convert the heathen, the very heathen who had killed his elder brother, this was quite beyond their understanding and they had turned all their hope and affection on their youngest boy, Karl. Nik understood their disappointment. All good boer boys learnt about hunting, cattle, husbandry of the land, how to read the weather and how to ride by the stars. Men learnt to read so that they could lead the family in prayers and bible reading and they learnt to write to be able to sign documents and understand what the document said. But to have the physique and strength of a farmer and then go into the Church, and still worse, to become a missionary, was regarded by many as an easy and cowardly option to the hard, tough life of the Transvaal boer.

Nik couldn't explain it himself. He only knew that he had always felt a sympathy and affinity with the black tribes. He had learnt their languages with ease. Writing and reading had always been a pleasure, not a chore. He had felt aware that he was different and hated it.

Thank the Lord for his wife, Renata. She had loved him for just the qualities the others found so strange. She had been educated in the Cape with her brothers and had horrified the Transvaal boers with her insistence on joining in "men's talk". They had been even more puzzled by her understanding of politics and religion.

In her he had found the ideal soul-mate – serious, committed and capable. Her lack of humour was something he regretted but she supported him in all he aimed to do. She knew her bible backwards and saw his conversion of the black peoples to Dutch Reformed Christianity as essential to save their souls. Renata never suffered from doubts, and had no time for them in others. Sometimes he found that her certainty irritated him.

The dawn was sketching a delicate finger of light along the horizon as the horse and rider reached the homestead and Nik went down the steps towards them.

"Welkom, meneer." He watched as the figure jerked from its drowsy posture and the brim of the leather hat tipped back as the man's tired face looked down at him.

"Goeie more Predikant de Groot," the man cleared his throat and licked his dust-coated lips. "Am I glad to see you!" he added with feeling.

Nik laughed. "Clifford Wilson crossing my path again. God bless you, man, a good start to the New Year!" Nik reached for the reins to guide the horse to the steps and then stopped.

"What have we here?" he enquired, noticing the bundle on Clifford's back moving. Then grinned. "Ag man, if it isn't a small boy! *Waarvandaan kom julle twee?"* he slipped back into his own language without thinking.

"It's a long story, Nik, but just for now our need is for a bed." Clifford swung himself stiffly out of the saddle and caught the sliding boy in his arms.

"But of course, man!" Nik led the way up the steps, "I forget myself, *kom jong,* we have a bed in Hettie's room. Put the lad down there. Koffie for you and then bed. Later you can tell all."

Nik watched as Clifford laid the sleeping boy on the buck-skin kaross which was strewn across the rimpi-strung bed. Then he led him round to the kitchen where a perpetually bubbling coffee pot sat in resplendent state on the old black range. He indicated that Clifford should sit as he poured out the coffee. He watched his visitor wrap his hands gratefully round the tin mug and drink deeply.

"God, man, am I tired and grateful to have reached you without an assegaai between my shoulder blades," Clifford said, peering over the rim of his mug at him.

Nik felt himself stiffen. He lived constantly on the alert for problems amongst the local tribes or uprisings against local farmers.

"Trouble man ? An uprising? A war impi? Perhaps you tell me something now?"

"No, I don't think you need to worry," Clifford reassured him. "Just bad 'mooti' and a lucky boy... They won't follow, they are glad to be rid of him." He put down his mug, smiling gratefully at Nik. "Can you cope with old Charity? She needs her fodder."

Nik nodded. Stooping automatically to avoid the door lintel, he moved off to see to the horse while Clifford returned to the bedroom, lay down next to Josh and fell instantly into a deep sleep.

It was the insecure feeling that he was floating on a springy cloud which finally dragged Josh out of sleep and back to reality. A confused haze of memories swam into his consciousness; slowly he opened one eye and then, in considerable amazement, both eyes. He found himself staring into another pair of deep blue eyes, down at the level of his head. The eyes were seriously curious and their owner was sitting on the floor with her head on one side and straight golden tendrils of hair gently brushing the surface of the floor as she considered this strange apparition which had arrived in her room overnight.

Hastily Josh pushed himself onto an elbow and the rimpi-bed swayed insecurely. He stared at it in disgust, then back at the girl. She moved upright, put her finger to her lips and indicated for him to follow her. He recognised the body next to him. It was the man, the one with the horse, the one who had saved him. Gingerly, he swung his legs off the contraption and followed the child with the hair like his own. She led him onto the veranda, down the steps and round the garden space to the base of a spreading acacia thorn tree.

The sun was extending its pale early rays over the distant hills and painting the sky with an eggshell-blue light splashed with pink. A delicate spiral of smoke rose from one of the huts and a clatter of buckets meant that someone else was greeting the dawn. A fat brindle pup waddled and wove its way across to them and a lean hunting dog strutted over to inspect the stranger. Josh felt disconnected. Nothing made sense, he had no gauge to judge by. It was a new world and anything could happen. The child looked about half his age. He sat down on the ground next to her and eyed her clothes with interest. She was covered from neck to toe in a long blue and white checked dress. Why, he wondered, would anyone want to cover themselves in this way? It must make moving uncomfortable and hot.

"Wat is jou naam?" she asked him and he looked at her blankly.

She tried again, this time in broken English.

"Wat iz your name?"

This rang distant bells. It stirred memories of a little boy in a wagon who had spoken this way with his parents.

"Josh," he said.

"J-o-s-h." She rolled it off her tongue thoughtfully. "The prophet, Joshua?"

Josh, bemused, just shook his head.

"My naam is Hettie," she said patiently. "Hettie de Groot. My Pa iz a Predikant. My Ma iz a teacher. Wat iz your Pa and waarom hef you no clothes?"

Josh stared helplessly at her. He wore his leather thong and his buckskin apron. What did she mean? He wished she would smile. Those solemn eyes stared at him with disconcerting directness. He shrugged, and just then a woman, like Hettie, clothed from neck to toe, came out of the end room of the house carrying a bucket. She saw the two figures beneath the tree and let out a horrified cry.

"Hettie, kom binne, kom gou-gou kind!"

Hettie jumped up and walked over to her with the fat pup loping behind trying to keep up. The woman was tall and fair, and painfully thin, with her hair drawn severely back into a tight bun, emphasising the pinched mouth, narrow nose and the deep-etched sorrow lines from nose to mouth. As Josh watched she bent down and spoke to Hettie, who looked regretfully over her shoulder at him, hesitated, then put her head down and followed her mother.

He watched the tall, thin woman march purposefully round the side of the house with the little girl reluctantly running to keep up with her.

Nik was bending over by the pump ladling water into a can, ready to fill the trough for the horses and donkey to quench their thirst before the heat of the day descended on them. He felt the indignation in the air almost before his wife, Renata, reached his side. He glanced round. Her normally pale cheeks were a bright, almost feverish pink, and she seemed to have grown several inches. Her grey eyes flashed with annoyance. She burst into staccato Afrikaans before she reached his side.

"And who is this half-naked white boy, dressed like a heathen kaffir, sitting in our backyard, corrupting our innocent daughter?"

Nik unfurled himself and gave her his full attention.

"It's the visitors, Rena," Nik explained patiently, "Clifford will tell us shortly… I gave them the guest bed in Hettie's room. The boy looked but a child. Hettie probably woke him up to talk to him."

He was tempted to add that he was probably not made any differently to the little herd boys who cared for the cattle and frequently played with

Hettie if they were in the vicinity of the mission station. However, he realised, looking at Renata's face, that she was too shocked and troubled to cope with this reasoning.

"It is not right for a white boy to be seen like this! It is indecent! No God-fearing Christian should demean himself in this way. The man must be mad to allow it. What will the mission boys think of a white boy dressed like an unchristian savage?"

Nik gently put down the can and, straightening up, looked down at his wife. This problem was obviously going to need his full attention after all.

"Woman," he boomed, "you will not be discourteous to guests, no matter who they are or how they dress. How often have I told you that there are *no* savages round here? Apart, that is, from some ignorant people of both colours who behave like hyenas. If the boy has no clothes, there is a reason... What is more, it is up to you to find him something to cover his nakedness which so offends your eyes." He saw Hettie staring up at him from behind her mother's skirt.

"More, dogtertjie," he said, to her, bending down and gathering her into his arms. "How is my little girl this day?" Hettie's face lit up into a beautiful smile and she threw her arms round his neck.

"Can he be my special friend, Pa?" she asked in her own language. "He is called after a prophet, his name is JOSHUA." She laughed. "I think he has not found Jericho yet!"

Nik joined in her laughter, a big loud booming laugh which brought Clifford out onto the veranda to see what was happening.

"See," Nik said to Renata, "you would take away the innocence of childhood in your concern for the unimportant – the child has barely noticed the lack of clothes."

Renata shrugged. "A child grows to a woman, Nik, a woman must know what is right and wrong and the responsibility is ours... you must also remember your position in the eyes of the heathen whom you seek to convert." She swung away up the steps.

"More, meneer," she greeted Clifford stiffly. "I will find something to cover your boy."

Clifford stammered out a greeting, looking at the indignant woman in some puzzlement. Then his face changed and Nik realised that he had suddenly remembered the boy.

"Pardon me, madam, I've an old pair of trousers in my saddlebag, they might cut down to something passable." He moved hastily off to where the bag was slung over the veranda rail. Now there was a twinkle of amusement in his eyes.

Renata appeared out of the house with a homespun cotton shirt, much mended, but clean and respectable.

Josh was still sitting under the tree. The big dog had his head on his ankle and Josh felt comforted by his presence. He had just seen some of the mission servants coming in about their business. To his amazement they were all dressed like the white people. To judge by their curious stares they were just as surprised by him and he was beginning to feel extremely self-conscious and awkward.

Just then Hettie appeared with Nik. Josh was aware of a huge suntanned white man with fair whiskers from his chin to his chest. Josh moved instinctively against the tree trunk but he noticed the dog bang its tail on the dusty earth in a greeting and then roll over with all four legs in the air waiting to have its stomach tickled.

Josh relaxed and looked at the man with interest. He was indeed large but the corners of his eyes crinkled into a friendly smile and his walk was slow and unthreatening. He stopped to tickle the dog but Hettie tugged him impatiently towards Josh.

"Hier is my Pa," she said proudly, displaying him like a prize specimen.

Josh inclined his head and kept his eyes on the vast man.

"Waarvandaan kom u?" asked Nik politely.

"Nee, Pa, nee, hy praat nie die taal nie... Probeer Engels," Hettie urged him impatiently to speak in English.

Josh felt the large man's eyes on his buckskin apron and then was aware of the eyes moving to the small initiation mark on his jaw just below his right ear. The scrutiny left him with no feeling of fear but a strong wish to meet with the big man's approval. To his tremendous relief, the whiskers parted in a smile and Nik, Hettie's father, addressed him in the Venda tongue, asking him where he was from. Josh told him of the kraal beneath the high krantz.

"So, that is your home, child, and you have sharpened your spears and move to fresh hunting grounds?"

"Yes, I did not wish this..." Josh's voice trailed away as he struggled against the turmoil of emotions inside himself. The man seemed to appreciate instinctively what he was trying to say.

"My child, you are at a mission station," he explained, going down into a squatting position to be nearer to Josh. "Now, I think, you must learn the ways of your own kind and then you will belong to both sides of our Africa." The tall man rose and Josh did the same. The man rested his hand on Josh's shoulder and steered him gently towards the house. Hettie danced alongside in happy glee.

Just then the thin woman appeared again. This time she was carrying a garment which she pushed into the man's hands.

"Get him covered," she ordered.

The man smiled down at him again and held out the garment.

Josh felt a strange mixture between annoyed resentment and relief, as he gingerly took the coarse-woven garment from the man.

At the same time the man seemed to think of something else. He bent down.

"You must want a pee, boy?" he said in the native tongue.

Josh nodded gratefully. The whole place was so strange that he felt as though he had been thrown into another world and the reality of everyday needs had taken second place. Now that it was mentioned he was desperate for that pee.

"Go now, Hettie," the tall man indicated gently, "Josh will soon be dressed and will come back to you." Hettie smiled, "Joshua the prophet, I will wait for you by the steps!" she ran off after her mother.

The man told Josh that his name was Nik. He led him past the rain butt to a small house with a door. "You need not call me Oom Nik," he said, "it is the polite form of address for someone older than yourself, but I would like you to just call me Nik." Josh nodded.

Josh found it hard to believe, but the man opened the door to the little house and indicated the hole in the floor with the seat over it. He explained to Josh that it was here he would pee and empty his bowels while he was staying in the house. Josh looked carefully at his face to make sure that he was not joking.

"But," he said, puzzled, "it smells bad, like an animal kraal that has not been cleaned... no, I think it smells worse than that!" The big man burst out laughing.

"I know! I know! But it is your first lesson in how the white man lives! When you are away from the house, in the bush, you may go where you like, but here you must use this place so that no one may see you."

"Why?"

The big man whom he was to call Nik, scratched his head. "I think perhaps it is thought to be cleaner!" he chuckled. "Anyway, in you go."

36

After this strange initiation they went round to a water pump near the trailing fronds of an old peppercorn tree. Josh watched Nik pump the arm of the contraption up and down and stared in amazement as brown water poured into the trough. He looked round for a river or a water hole but there was none. It was like magic, it just poured out of the mouth of the post. He bent down and looked up the pipe and caught some of the drips on his face and in his mouth.

"It comes from a spring beneath the earth; I have a pipe to bring it up. It is for animals, irrigation and washing. It is too bitter to drink," Nik explained.

Josh found himself propelled into the trough while water was squirted over him and he was handed a piece of slippery grease to rub on himself and then rub off. He was made to wash his hair with the same stuff and when the water had rinsed it all off he was handed a piece of cloth to dry the water off his body and hair. Back home in the kraal they washed regularly in the river and oiled their bodies, but the sun did the drying. Then he remembered with a jolt that he was no longer home, that what Nik had said was indeed true, he was learning the ways of the white tribe. The ones he could not yet call his own. There was a knot in his throat which he swallowed.

Feeling rather self-conscious in the shirt, but pleasantly surprised to find it comfortable, he followed Nik round to the front of the house. There he saw the other man, the one who had saved his life. He was sitting against the veranda pole at the top of the steps drinking from a cup. He lifted a hand in greeting.

"Well, there you are! And made a decent Christian, I see!" He came over and clapped a hand on Josh's shoulder and looked him over.

"A bit of a trim of that mop," he said, indicating Josh's shoulder length fair hair, "and we'll soon have you looking like one of us!" He squinted at the initiation mark and laughed. "Pity 'bout that. Your Irish grandma may have a thing or two to say about her grandson's tattoo. Not quite the respectable image, hey, lad?"

Josh stared solemnly at him trying to comprehend the language and to size up this man who had saved his life and turned his world upside down.

Hettie came out with a wooden bowl filled with porridge and a spoon for Josh and fetched one for herself. She made him sit down next to her on the step, and a black girl, who worked at the mission, brought them mugs and milk. Hettie picked up the spoon and began to spoon the porridge to her mouth. Josh watched in astonishment, then tried the same thing. It was certainly less of a problem than using one's fingers but it was very difficult not to be messy, especially as the food seemed very wet and hot. It tasted alright.

Clifford joined Nik and Renata in the cool dark living room of the mission house and they ate round a lovingly polished old yellow-wood table surrounded by the remnants of a more genteel society. A darkwood sideboard stood against one wall opposite an old Dutch cupboard and an ornate wall clock lent a feeling of solid stability to the mud-brick homestead. He told them the story of his discovery of Josh and their dramatic escape from the kraal. He avoided mentioning the reward. He looked over at their shadowed faces, feeling annoyed with himself for a sudden strong desire to have their approval. Normally he did as he wished, he had given up seeking approval when he was eleven years old. Life had taught him that survival was his own affair.

As she leant towards him across the table, Renata's troubled gaze caught his attention and brought him out of his reverie.

"But whose child is he, Meneer? Somewhere he must have relatives? Indeed how can it be that no one has come in search of him? Poor, poor child!"

Impulsively she turned towards Nik.

"Nikolas, let us take this child. We can teach him the ways of the white people and bring him up like our own. He could be God's gift to us to re-place our little Jannetjie, lost with the fever but two years ago, please, please Nikolas…" she implored.

Clifford was aware that he was somehow losing control. After his efforts to retrieve young Josh he was not about to hand him to someone else. He interrupted before Nik could reply.

"Thank you, ma'am, but this child has relatives in Europe to whom I must return him."

"Why?" Renata asked accusingly. "Why have they not searched for him, why is it you, a stranger, who has found him?"

"They thought him dead with his parents," Cliff replied.

"They could not have cared or they would have sent someone to look!" she shot back at him angrily, spots of colour reappearing on her cheeks. "He will have a better life with us, here. He will be brought up as our son and we would be proud of him!"

Hastily Nik interceded:

"Renatjie, Renatjie, los kind, los." He gave Cliff a searching look. "So, you know his roots and you will see that he is safely returned?"

Cliff nodded sheepishly.

"His parents were from Ireland. His grandmother wishes to have him back."

"You have a heavy responsibility, my friend. You must be sure that this child has adapted to our European ways and language before you put him on that ship or you will be consigning him to misery back in Europe," Nik spoke slowly and Cliff was aware of his close scrutiny.

Cliff felt himself coming out of the shifting sands.

"I suppose you're right. I'll see what I can do but I don't know much about children."

He was immediately aware of his mistake.

"Then leave him here a while, my friend. Renata and Hettie will soon teach him much and then you can return and take him on to his people. I can help him to read and write. He will be better prepared for the world beyond Africa."

The proposition held Cliff's attention for a moment but then survival and reality returned with force as he recalled the reward which would mean a farm or trading store of his own.

"Thank you, but the family know that I have gone to collect him and they will be making arrangements for his return. I cannot delay that long."

It could well be the truth, he thought to himself. There might be a letter awaiting them in Natal from the grandmother. He shifted uneasily in his chair, aware that they were both watching him closely. To ease the tension of the moment he rose and walked to the door to look out at the two children on the veranda step.

Hettie had her hand on Josh's arm. She was looking up at him and laughing. The sun seemed to bounce off her golden hair, the blue eyes were trusting and filled with admiration. Josh stared down at her in wonderment, an answering smile lighting his thin, serious face. He took a twig from her on which a green stick insect was balancing itself precariously on a shiny leaf.

Cliff had the uncomfortable feeling that this boy reminded him of someone. He couldn't quite pin down who it was. There was a vulnerability about the youngster when he was in close contact with the little girl. He had lost that wary, defensive outer shell with which he had approached his surroundings an hour ago. If this was indeed the Irish boy beneath the surface, Cliff reasoned, was he tough enough to cope with what lay ahead? His mind flashed back to the scene in the kraal. He recalled the way the boy had stood, erect and proud, despite the sentence hanging over him. Yes, this youngster had qualities of strength which emerged in times of crisis. These might well be tested in the weeks ahead.

He was suddenly conscious of the subdued talk at the table behind him. Renata and Nik were still discussing the boy's future. He heard his name mentioned and then he heard Renata protesting slightly louder:

"But Nik, what experience has *he* of small children?"

He couldn't catch Nik's reply but the question made him uneasy. He had never thought about coping with the boy when he planned the trip. It had all seemed so simple. He'd bribe the chief to part with him and then put him on a horse and they would ride back to Natal together. There he'd collect the reward, put the child on a ship and head off to buy his land. How could he have been so naïve, he wondered. Well, he'd hit the first problem as soon as he reached the kraal. Now he was facing the reality of another person in his life. A person with needs. It wasn't quite like collecting a puppy. Nik was pointing out that he, Clifford, had responsibilities. Christ! He'd never have got into this if he'd appreciated that he was expected to *teach* the child. Him... teach English, and reading, writing and arithmetic... teach the child about manners, about coping with other people, not to mention dressing and eating and washing! He could feel a wave of unfamiliar panic creeping up on him. Then it came to him... of course, now he knew who the child reminded him of... it was himself at the same age. He too had been left orphaned and unwanted. He shrugged the disquiet away. If he could cope, then so could this lad.

Although Clifford would have liked to leave quickly, he knew that his horse needed more time to recover. Hettie took Josh under her wing and gently introduced him to her world and from time to time he would reappear next to Clifford.

"Why does he keep coming round to look at me?" Cliff asked Nik. "You understand children, what makes them do this?"

Nik sighed.

"You have been thrown too quickly into fatherhood! Don't worry, you are his link with his other world. He is afraid you might go just as suddenly as they did! He is reassuring himself. Be patient my friend."

Renata cut Josh's hair and once the trousers were altered Cliff was reassured that he looked like any other boer farmer's son. In the late afternoon, while Hettie sat on the wooden fence swinging her bare feet, and watching the men talking, Cliff and Nik taught Josh how to use a gun and set up a target for him to use. He was an enthusiastic pupil.

Over the next few days Cliff noticed that the boy was slowly and hesitantly attempting more English words; each time he did this he looked startled, as though he had taken himself by surprise with the unfamiliar words. Nik too, he noticed, was watching Josh closely as he tentatively tried the new words, and then, finding that they fitted, began to use them with more confidence. He was still finding it difficult to cope with Cliff's American drawl and would frequently look round for clues.

Cliff felt ill at ease. He was aware of an air of disapproval from Renata and of silent criticism from Nik. Most worrying of all, he felt the hero worship from Josh. It emphasised the responsibility, and heightened his guilt. Having walked the path of the loner for so long he was not prepared for this sudden step into social responsibility. He wasn't sure how to cope and found himself far too often reacting brusquely and then felt guilty as the child looked puzzled or hurt and he would try to turn the situation into humour. Mostly the jokes fell flat. He realised that the boy's emotions and his comprehension of language were still insecure.

After three days Cliff announced that they must be on their way towards Natal, and Hettie promptly burst into tears and clung to Josh's arm. Renata shot him a look of disapproval.

"I will prepare you some food for the journey," she said with reluctance.

Nik went away and came back with a razor-sharp knife and a sheath for the boy to wear on his belt.

"Josh, this was mine when I was a boy. I have kept it sharp and dry and if you do the same it will repay you many times over. Come back one day, child, and tell me how you have used it."

Josh was nearly speechless with excitement at owning such a precious item.

Clutching the knife, he looked up at Nik, his face reflecting cautious disbelief.

Lapsing into his native tongue, he said: "This is just for me? For me *only*?"

"Just for you, son," Nik said, smiling fondly at him.

Without warning the boy bent down and kissed Nik's shoes.

"I will guard it with my life, man of the noble beard."

Nik lifted him back onto his feet with one hand and leaning towards the boy he said gently, in BaVenda, "In this world, Josh, you take my hand, there is no need to bend low to me, I am not a chief."

The boy nodded slowly.

The night before had echoed with the distant beat of drums and now, just as they were getting ready to leave, a tribesman arrived to talk to Nik. Nik listened to him and then turned to Cliff.

"Ambanjana says there is news of the gathering of great armies below the Drakensberg Mountains. It seems that Chief Cetchwayo has called in his war impis and a large European army is gathering in the valleys towards the sea. Cliff, this is what I feared. You and the boy must find another route. For some time now certain elements have been seeking to start a confrontation."

Cliff shrugged, "Perhaps this is just another skirmish?"

"No, man, listen to me. Theo Shepstone and Paul Kruger want to extend the Transvaal into Zulu territory. Agh, this land hunger is a terrible disease. It seems we cannot be content with all this." He waved his hand in an arc towards the horizon.

"We must become another warring tribe, grabbing new pastures, risking our families and wiping people off the earth as though we had never heard that commandment, 'thou shalt not kill'. We make ourselves as bad as the tribes we condemn."

Cliff looked down at him from the saddle and wondered at him. He had moved round amongst the Boers for some years now and he had never met a man like this. A man who seemed to see Africa as a single arena filled with men, not civilised Christians and wild savages, just men. Men with all their human frailties and their desperate need for strong leadership. Men who would kill and be killed and still pray, assuming that God was on their side. The most dangerous animal in Africa is man, and now he is turning on himself, he thought. He bent down and helped to haul the boy up behind him.

"It is sad, Nik, but we men love war. We love the excitement. We twist the truth to suit our needs. You cannot change us, Nik. Neither your Boers, nor the Zulus nor the English."

Nik nodded sadly as he hitched up the saddlebags.

"We'll do our best… and you, my friend, you must not risk this child… Take him to the Cape, the way down to Natal will no longer be safe. He is a vulnerable child who needs time to adjust to our ways. Remember, beneath that white skin you have an African child."

Cliff lifted his hat to the little trio and turned Charity towards the paths which would take them across the mountains and veld towards Lydenburg.

Josh waved back to Hettie, white and silent, as though he did not trust himself to speak. Hettie was sobbing into her mother's apron.

After a brisk start Clifford let Charity slow down. They had a long way to travel and time was of no importance. Josh was uncomfortable behind him on Charity's back. Cliff could feel him moving restlessly. It was when they stopped for a short break in the shifting shade beneath a flat-topped acacia tree, that Josh volunteered to run beside the horse.

"You'll slow us down if you do that," Clifford stated flatly, in what he felt was a voice which would brook no argument. The boy said nothing. He just stared out across the veld as though he had not fully heard. When they set off again the boy climbed up, but as soon as the horse was making a steady pace he appeared to lose his grip and fell off Charity's back. The fall was gracefully executed so that he landed on his feet and before Cliff could rein in he was already running by its side.

Feeling rather put out by this silent resistance, Clifford speeded up the horse's pace but Josh simply lengthened his stride and moved into a slow even lope which kept him beside the horse without any effort. Clifford was used to being obeyed. He felt irked by the boy's obvious lack of concern. He rode his horse in brooding silence, struggling with his emotions.

Josh was happy. Africa was spread out before him in its brown and gold splendour. This man, Cliff, who could ride and shoot and grow a beard, was riding by his side. The horse was relieved of the extra burden and the muscles of his own legs were unwinding and enjoying their freedom after the restrictions of the last few days. Running was as natural to Josh as to most tribal boys. With no form of transport they developed their athletic abilities at an early age, running vast distances to pass messages or to hunt the elusive game. His was a sense of incredible freedom, a feeling that he had joined the wind and was at one with the sights and smells of his homeland.

Clifford glanced down at him, aware of a pang of envy at the ease with which he strode evenly forward and at his total lack of concern as he covered mile after mile. His face was tilted slightly upwards and his chest heaved in and out evenly, every muscle co-ordinated in steady movement. It was his expression of pure pleasure which finally won Clifford over and restored his spirits. The boy had so obviously not meant to challenge him. It dawned on Clifford that he was doing what he was good at. He couldn't ride but he certainly could run. The envy changed to admiration and for the first time he felt glad of the boy's company. He smiled at him and slowed Charity to a gentle trot. Josh smiled back and seemed to acknowledge the softening in Cliff's attitude. Cliff allowed his mind to wander back to his own childhood. He recalled with a pang the carefully hidden moments of acute loneliness. The feeling that he belonged nowhere and to no one. He glanced sideways at the young figure with a flash of sympathy which he hastily smothered. He had survived by shutting away his emotions and he found himself doing the same again, but this time there was a small chink in his armour.

Clifford knew the hunters' paths and they climbed back out of the low hill and grassland country into the narrow valleys and dense forests of the Mamatzeeri mountains and Chief Magoeba's country. Progress was slow and Clifford frequently led Charity while Josh walked in the rear.

"Such big trees, my head nearly falls off my neck trying to look up to the top of them!" he remarked in his native tongue to Cliff.

"Why do you not shoot some of the wild pig who crash across our path? You have that thing called a gun, which makes you white men all so power-ful." He realised what he had said and quickly added, "Perhaps one day I too will have one?"

"Of course you will, lad," Cliff called back over his shoulder. "Wait until we reach the open country and I will let you practise with it."

They camped in clearings or on grassy ridges, their lonely fire a mere flicker of light in the inky darkness of the African night. Clifford showed Josh the wonder of matches and blankets, luxuries which had seldom made their way to the kraal. He was fascinated by the small lantern which Cliff lit at night.

"The sun has given you a piece of light which you keep in that strange gourd," he declared. "But this one travels with us – does it keep us safe?"

"No such luck," Clifford laughed. "It allows us to see just round us in the dark but a fire is the thing which keeps us safe from lions."

At first they battled by with a mixture of the Venda tongue, a smattering of other dialects which Cliff had picked up, and some stilted English. He was aware as he listened to the child that slowly Josh's English was increas-ing. He seemed to know almost instinctively how to shape some simple sen-tences. Often he could understand although he could not find the English to reply. To his surprise Clifford found himself trying to help him, uncovering an unfamiliar degree of patience in himself.

Occasionally they would see signs of the thatched rooftops of a group of huts in the distance and sometimes they could hear the distant sing-song of women's voices. For the most part they had this world to themselves.

Sometimes the track became almost a small road then quite suddenly it would deteriorate and they would plunge back into the winding tangle of the creeper-covered trees. After two days they began to emerge onto the grassy slopes. These led gradually down through rocky hillocks where fleshy-leafed aloes appeared to grow from rock crevices. Here and there the aloes produced a flame-coloured red-hot-poker proudly protruding over the gold and brown of the dusty low veld escarpment. The mountains grew more spectacular and waterfalls fell like silver strips of ribbon way above them. Now the tracks grew into broader well-worn ribbons of road which disappeared off in different directions and Josh began to meet more white men. Always there was time for a chat and the exchange of local news and Cliff struggled to explain what farmers and prospectors did. Hunters Josh could understand, but the others were a new concept for him to absorb. At one stage they stopped to help a transport rider who needed assistance to move his wagon out of a deep rut. He in turn took them to the edge of the escarpment where the land fell away into a vast canyon of lush bushveld topped by rock crags with strange flat tops.

"Look," Josh said to Cliff, lapsing into the Venda tongue in his excitement, "a giant God has lifted his head and shaken the roots of the world. The earth has come tumbling away leaving only these massive stepping stones across the valleys."

Cliff turned to look at him. He caught a fleeting expression of forlorn loneliness flitting across the child's face. Then Josh shook himself as though he was trying to throw off some niggling thought. Cliff caught the look and with unusual insight, put out a hand and rested it on Josh's shoulder.

"This is the Africa your parents left Europe to be a part of," he remarked kindly. "It gets into a man's blood, kid, it's what gives men wanderlust and makes it difficult for them to accept towns and law and order." He could see that Josh was grateful for the hand but the language was still beyond him.

"Is it your Africa, too?" Josh enquired innocently.

"Yes, boy, I came from across an ocean, like your parents, but I took my chances when they came. The man who helped me was a trader called Henry Hartley."

"A 'trader'?" Josh queried.

"We travelled by wagon and supplied people with lead and cartridges, guns, shoes, clothes and household goods."

Josh looked surprised, "You gave them these?"

"No, we exchanged them, sometimes for hides and food, but often for money." Cliff put his hand in his pocket and showed Josh some small metal coins, "People earn these for work and then they exchange them for goods."

Josh fingered the coins and tentatively licked one. Cliff laughed.

"They are not for eating, only for exchanging!"

Josh shrugged, "I would rather change for something I could eat!"

"How did you find me?"

"When I left Henry I decided to try hunting, I would bring back skins, ivory, ostrich feathers. Sometimes I went with two tribesmen and my horse and dog, sometimes with other hunters and a wagon. Up in the Zoutpansberg I heard a rumour about a white boy and then down in Natal I read a letter in the newspaper from your relatives asking whether anyone had heard anything of you. I decided to go and look for you."

Josh sat looking at him. With no concept of distances or newspapers or relatives, he was feeling helpless, but he swallowed and nodded, looking into the distance beyond Cliff's head.

Cliff got up, brushing a hand across Josh's head, "Give yourself time, boy, you'll slowly begin to understand. Now let's move on."

For two more days they moved down through the lush green, lonely world, where the bullfrogs sang all night and few people seemed to stay for long because of the fever. Eventually the track became busier. They passed through the thriving mining village of Pilgrim's Rest.

To Josh the world suddenly became a wonderland of new sights. They were moving down the broad valley towards Lydenburg. The small farms were visible around them. Local Pedi tribesmen were moving cattle along the road towards their kraals in the surrounding hills. Twice they passed farmers with cart loads of produce and Josh could not believe that so much food could be moved by one man. Several transport wagons passed by in a cloud of dust, their weary oxen pulling heavily loaded wagons full of mining machinery. His introduction to his first windmill filled him with amazement and admiration:

"The water comes out of that pipe into the dam! But where is the river?"

"It's a spring in the earth," Cliff explained patiently. "That windmill," he pointed up to the blue heavens and the grinding whirr of the ever-circling blades of the metal windmill, "is being turned by the wind and that pulls water out of the spring beneath the earth."

Josh shook his head in amazement. "I wish Majinga could see this!" Cliff was eager to move on.

Eventually the town came into sight, a sprawling village of white-painted houses bounded by straight roads edged by water furrows. Josh rode seated behind Cliff. He found himself holding tight to the waist in front of him and staring in incredulous amazement at the dusty main street with its row of wooden and corrugated iron shops, houses and a hotel. It felt to him as though there were people everywhere. There was so much dust thrown up by horses' hooves and the wheels of coaches, wagons and carts, that he felt himself quite stifled by it. There was so much colour.

Everyone was in clothes like his own, often far grander. He watched two small boys chase one another across the road... then he saw the woman. She appeared such a strange shape. She must indeed have a large bottom, he pondered. The wonderful blue dress had a deep sheen and endless flounces and frills outlining a tiny waist with a large flounce of material behind bunched out with a bow at the rear. Poor woman, he thought, such a big bottom could not be an advantage unless she had many children to carry on her back. She must look strange naked, washing by the river.

Yet the young girls in their light cotton dresses looked normal. In fact, they reminded him of Hettie with their long hair and fair skins. Only Hettie was prettier to look at.

"What's that?" He pointed in front of Cliff. "That woman has a bush on a stick over her head!"

Cliff chuckled. "That's an umbrella to protect her from the sun."

Josh tried out the word: "Um-brel-la."

"Actually," Cliff corrected himself, "It's a sunshade. It does the same thing only an umbrella keeps off the rain!"

This piece of information completely silenced Josh for a while. How was he to cope if even Cliff got the wrong words? He was quickly distracted, noticing that many of the women wore things like ox-wagon hoods over their heads, tied beneath their chins.

The men were mainly dressed like Cliff, but some of them wore shoes rather than boots and had quaint bows beneath their chins and many were without hats. In the first shop they stopped at, the man had a large white cloth across his front. Cliff explained that it was to keep his clothes clean.

Many people seemed to be friends of Cliff's. They waved or stopped to talk and looked as curiously at Josh as he looked at them. As they approached the hotel there was a sudden sound, somewhere between a squeal and a wild howl, and a mobile dust ball whirled down the street towards them.

Josh's grip on Cliff tightened. How, he wondered, would Charity cope with this attack by a mad dog? To his amazed relief Charity simply stopped and put down her head. The dog skidded to a halt in front of them. She nuzzled him gently. The dog leapt round and round the horse in an ecstasy of delight, Cliff loosened himself from Josh and slid down to crouch next to the hysterically delighted animal. Josh clung onto the empty saddle and stared in amazement as Cliff was nearly knocked to the ground by this unreserved demonstration of love.

"Zenda, Zenda," he heard Cliff repeat in amusement. "Steady, boy, I'm glad to see you too."

He helped Josh down and the dog slowed its mad twirling and viewed Josh with reserved interest.

"This is my dog Zenda," he explained to Josh. "I left him behind with Jack in case the dogs in your kraal were unfriendly. Your chief might have decided to feed him to his mangy pooches in return for you! He is very intelligent and he'll guard us with his life."

Zenda sniffed at Josh and then sat down to regard him with a straight, inquisitive stare. Cautiously Josh put out his hand and touched the brindled black and gold head. The dog made no friendly overture, but continued to stare at him and then walked slowly round sniffing at him. He joined them as they walked towards the hotel, pressing against Cliff's leg possessively as he led Charity round to the stables at the rear of the building.

Cliff saw that Josh was disconcerted and reassured him.

"He always takes a while to accept another person. It's best to ignore him. He'll come round. He'll watch you until he has made up his mind about you and then he will be a friend for life."

"Ah, an' this must be the young lad we've been hearing aboot!" Josh looked up at the hotel proprietor as Cliff introduced him. He was a cheerful red-faced man with a small sandy moustache and straight, thinning hair to match. His light brown eyes were alert and inquisitive, but kindly.

"I'm glad you got it right, Cliff. Growin' up in a wild kraal is no place for a wee lad. He needs guidance and there'll be uncles and aunties aplenty to take him in. An' mighty grateful they'll be to you, young Cliff!" he patted Cliff on the back and Josh was aware of a large red hand on his shoulder.

"An' you're a bonny lad, a mite thin and scrawny mind, but a bit o' teachin' an' you'll be a credit to yer family. Come lad, there'll be food in yon kitchen. Let's get ye both some grub and hear the story."

They stayed four days in Lydenburg. Josh was captivated by all he saw. He went round in a happy daze, staring in wonderment at the sights and sounds of a small town. The clothes and colours left him dazzled. The shops were like hives full of honey. They were full of unexpected miracles and delicious, often edible, surprises. He was finding out about this stuff called money. It certainly looked worthless, but it changed hands easily and people appeared to value it. He felt as though his head might well burst from constantly trying to absorb new information.

Jack was a kind man. His wife had died two Christmas's back and he liked the look of this tall thin boy with the smooth mop of straight, blond hair and the clear blue eyes full of wonderment.

"Aw, now," he said to Cliff, "I do wonder whether my young nephews in Scotland are like this... and how, I wonder would they have coped dumped into a native kraal many miles from civilisation, for several years?"

Josh looked at Cliff. He found Jack's accent a problem. Yet Cliff seemed to understand it. Cliff grinned at him and shrugged.

"He's plucky... And he's fit!"

Jack noticed the boy watching Cliff.

"Ay, lad," he commented to Cliff, "It's your approval he seeks; he sees now that you are pleased, and that's all he wants! Sure now he can earn a few pence helping in the stable!"

Jack soon noticed that Josh had struck up a friendship with a small chestnut mare that nuzzled his cheek and came up to him with a whinny whenever he entered the stable yard.

"I'm thinking," he commented to Cliff, "that lad of yours, he may have a way with horses – see how that wee mare will do anything for him!"

Cliff turned to look.

"You're right, and thank you for letting him earn, he's fascinated with money and what it can buy!"

Jack and Cliff talked trading, transport driving, and the merits of oxen and horses. They watched with amusement Josh's reaction to water gushing from a tap.

"But where is the river or the spring?" he asked them in amazement, peering through the window into the yard. He was shown the rainwater tank and also the borehole. After an initial display of disgust they even managed to persuade Josh that the stinking lavatory out in the hotel garden was indeed a necessity in a town.

"Ay," said Jack in some amusement, "he's no idea why we make such a fuss aboot bathin' an' dressin' in private!"

They eventually persuaded him to make use of the lavatory. He went in under protest, holding his nose and threatening to be sick, and shot out again as fast as his bowels would allow. To him, this mass soil deposit was the most revolting habit of these white townspeople.

"Like rock-rabbits," he moaned to Cliff, "but at least theirs don't smell! It's worse than penned oxen, theirs can be dried and used again!"

Cliff grinned sympathetically and bought him a twist of the amber sugar candy.

"Rot your teeth as well," he commented. "They say sugar does them no good neither."

This sweetness was one of the delights of the town for Josh. Honey had always been a scarce luxury and everyone in the tribe had listened for the sound of bees or for the little honeybird who would lead them to the nearest swarm in return for some of the comb. To exchange this solid sweet delight for bits of metal seemed so ridiculously easy.

The bar was crowded at night as men came in to look at the boy who had grown up in a kraal and to try to talk to him. Josh, struggling to understand so many different accents, was unaware that he was doubling Jack's normal clientele. Often the questions were stupid and after awhile he would wander out to rid himself of the pungent, bitter smell of the beer fumes. He wondered at their ignorance on perfectly ordinary tribal matters. Occasionally someone would come in who could speak BaVenda, but he found this made him long for the security of the tribe and his heart ached for his friends and for Majinga. He would drift quickly away and hide for a while with the little blue roan mare in the stables. She gave him a feeling of solid reassurance as he threw his arms round her neck and pressed his face against her coat. Slowly, he would slide down to her feet and fall asleep.

Cliff went outside to look for Josh and found him asleep in the stable. As he was about to pick him up Jack came in behind him.

"Mon, the boy's quite happy there. You canna change him too fast, rooms and doors make him nervous and beds lift him off the ground he is used to."

Cliff nodded and left him on the hay.

"Sure, white men are still strangers to him, but he's learning."

He dropped a horse blanket over the sleeping form.

The two men leant on the stable door and smoked their pipes in companionable silence while the noise level in the bar rose steadily.

"We should be off tomorrow. What's the war news?" Cliff enquired.

"We'd all like to know!" replied Jack. "Word is largely by the drums an' ye ken how garbled those can be! The last coach up from Kimberley said Lord Chelmsford had commandeered every damn horse and wagon in Natal and a great many from beyond."

Cliff took a puff of his pipe and exhaled into the navy blue night air.

"I hear that old Cetchwayo has got total control. The Zulus are bloody brave fighters."

"That's so, an' does Chelmsford realise it's not a rabble army? It's a wild, cruel and highly organised battle force... he'll be tryin' to fight a conventional war with straggling lines of communication... I fear the old Sassenach may be in for a shock!"

"I'm pinning my hopes on Chelmsford," Cliff watched his smoke drifting up against the sombre night sky where storm clouds were building up. "He has the horses, the weapons, and the weight and training of the British Army... not that I care much for them!"

"Ay, an' they do say that Fynney, and some of the missionaries, was explaining the strength of the Zulu army and some of the missionaries were trying to put him in the picture, but this man, Chelmsford, he thinks he knows better, snotty old general!"

"Shame in some ways, but I wouldn't think the Zulus could outwit guns and canon, would you?"

"Cliff, I hope you're right." Jack looked sideways at him. "I suppose you *are* going across the Drakensberg?"

Cliff nodded. "No alternative. The family will send the money to Natal. I need it."

"I hope the reward is worth it, lad." Jack grinned at him. "You've a responsibility there – he's nearly been under the wheels of two carts already and the mail coach driver brought him in by the scruff of his neck yesterday. Damn nearly upturned the whole coach trying to see if he could catch the lead bridles before they came to a stop. Gave the horses and driver a hell of a fright. Listen! Get him a job as a drummer boy with Chelmsford – they'll take him back!"

"What, and risk losing my reward because he gets killed? No, no, Jack, I'll see him safely onto a ship and then use the money to settle myself in Natal. Maybe a small farm."

Jack wasn't convinced. "Ah, mon! You'll noo settle, you'll be up an' off at the first whisper of excitement anywhere on the continent! Need a good woman, you do!"

The next morning they were getting ready to move on when Jack came down to the stables.

"The kid needs a horse. You canna make him run to Natal, mon." Jack nudged Cliff. "Come on, ye mean ol' money bag, look how he loves that wee mare."

While Cliff glanced over at Josh, Jack went up to the boy.

"Listen, lad, I'm giv'n ya that mare, her owner died wi' the fever an' left me his horse to pay for the care."

Cliff was about to utter a protest and Jack waved him down.

"No, mon, you can owe me a favour, you both! She's good fetlocks and she's a stayer. What's more, she's taken to you an' you'll work as a pair. Her name's Cobbo. A good horse an' a good dog is all a man needs, an' a steady hand with a gun an' maybe a few friends. Remember that, lad, an' you'll be fine."

"For me? Cobbo?" Josh pointed at himself and stared in disbelief at Jack.

Jack nodded and rumpled his hair.

"Yes, lad, all yours. You learnt quickly. Remember your Uncle Jack, lad, an' perhaps we'll meet again if the good God wills it."

Impulsively Josh threw his arms round Jack and hugged him. Cliff watched with a gleam of sardonic amusement.

"Thank God I won't have to put up with you running alongside and slowing us down!" he commented. "Thanks, Jack," he added. "Do the same for you sometime!"

Jack grunted. He turned away awkwardly, obviously overcome by the hug and the show of genuine delight from the boy.

"Plucky kid!" he muttered, almost to himself. "Jennie would have liked him... she'd have approved."

He took down the saddle and bridle and busied himself helping Josh, who was so excited his fingers couldn't thread the leathers properly.

Cliff and Josh turned and waved to him. Jack watched the man and the boy riding away and, leaping joyously alongside them, the brindle dog.

Chapter Four

AFRICA, mid-January to early February 1879

IT WAS THE fifth day on the track to Port Natal. Josh was aware that Cliff was watching him closely as he put the pony through its paces. He knew he was doing well and he felt a glow of pride. He was at one with the animal and it responded in a quick, alert fashion to the slightest movement of his knees, heels or reins. He heard a guffaw of laughter and swung his head round defensively to look over his shoulder at Cliff. Then he relaxed as he saw the easy smile on the man's face.

"Boy, you're riding as though you've been in the saddle since birth!"

"She understands me!" he responded happily. "She's my friend... like you," he paused uncertainly as Cliff rode up next to him. "You are my friend, aren't you?" he could feel himself yearning for the answer.

He was aware of a slight tension in the muscles round Cliff's mouth He had come to realise that this was a sign of impatience in this strange man who was now the only contact between his past and his present.

"Of course I am, you call me Cliff, don't you?"

Josh nodded, slightly puzzled.

"What else should I call you?"

"In this country young people use the term 'uncle' for older men, they say 'Oom Cliff'. I feel that we ride together and must watch after one another, I am not your uncle, I'm your friend. Do you understand?"

Josh felt as though he had suddenly grown an inch and he sat up very straight in the saddle.

"I am proud to be your friend," he replied. "I will do for you the things one must do for a friend." He drew on the reins and the pony stopped obediently. "I would also like to say that Jackalet loves her new name and it is right that she should be called after the man who gave her to me." The pony twitched her ears in response to the name.

Cliff nodded.

"You make a good team, Charity and I are proud to ride with you, and Zenda has accepted you," he pointed down at the brindle dog loping beside his horse.

For the first time Josh felt as though he belonged. It was a tentative feeling, tinged with caution, but it was there. He was at last aware that this strange, silent, white man actually liked him. He was offering him a form of acceptance. Cliff had acknowledged Josh's growing competence with the gun, his riding, and his emerging command of English. He could feel his ability in this direction growing day by day. Each day he was aware of listening, watching and soaking in his surroundings, as they rode across the vast canvas of Africa. The graceful herds of blesbok and springbok moved off in soft dust clouds as they approached. Everywhere birds flashed their brilliant plumage and watched the travellers with sharp-eyed interest.

They were at the beginning of a long haul over the towering peaks he had watched growing gradually closer during the past two days. Cliff called them "the Drakensberg", said in a tone of deep respect. It was the end of another day and they set about making leisurely camp in the slanting shade of a cluster of boulders with a fine view over the surrounding countryside. As the sun sank, the African night was rapidly unrolling its bale of inky-blue darkness across the tepid sky. The crickets were in brilliant, orchestral form, backed melodiously by a spring which, despite the lack of rain, still managed to gurgle and froth from beneath one of the boulders. It kept a patch of rushes and surrounding shrubbery a rich dark green in sharp contrast to the rest of the sun-baked mountainside.

Josh moved round the green patch collecting herbs and edible plants for the meal they were about to enjoy together with the spit-roasting guinea fowl which Cliff had shot earlier in the day.

"How do you know which ones can be eaten?" Cliff asked as he watched him from the camp fire.

"I learnt from Majinga," Josh replied, without looking up, "It's the job of the older children to watch for the plant food and bring it back… and also to search for the plants which heal."

Later, their appetites satisfied, they lay back under the stars, the flickering flames of the fire glowing warmly on the surrounding boulders. They talked about horses. Josh marvelled at the man. He seemed to the boy to hold the world in the palm of his hand. He had seen so much and he could draw pictures in words and carry the listener with him in his infinite wisdom, to undreamed of worlds across rolling oceans. Cliff told him of the horses the American Indians rode and the circus horses of his youth. Josh felt his head becoming heavier. Gradually the friendly scene, with Jackalet and Charity

54

tethered on the edge of the firelight and Zenda asleep at Cliff's feet, blended together in a feeling of contentment as he fell asleep.

Cliff was entertained by his new roll as a brother figure. It was a novel experience to be responsible for another human being and to bask in the boy's open admiration. For the first time in his life someone was interested in him personally and he was enjoying the novelty. He had almost forgotten the wild enthusiasm and spontaneous delight of boyhood and found himself recapturing some of the magic through Josh.

Down on the bushveld plains they had raced and whooped and yelled, startling every living beast and bird for miles around. But who cared? Total freedom was a heady wine. The odd heavy-winged assvogel (vulture), was swooping high in the limitless blue of the sky, viewing their antics with a mild tolerance and keeping well clear.

Twice they stayed at farms and enjoyed the hospitality of the home-steads. Once they had camped near the Crocodile River and another night had found them sharing their campfire with a transport driver and his mule team. He was making his way north with mining machinery.

Cliff found himself very relieved to be able to talk to someone who had just negotiated the spiny back of the great Drakensberg range.

"What's the war news?" he questioned the sinewy stubble-bearded man sitting on the wagon seat.

"They're on the move all right," the transport driver commented. "There'll not be many more wagons through the passes. It'll be too danger-ous unless the British can post protection at both ends of each pass."

"What about Chelmsford's army? I thought they were moving into ac-tion?" Cliff asked, disturbed by the news and aware that for a boy and a man to stumble into a marauding war impi from Cetchwayo's kraal would be an instant death sentence for both of them.

"Ag, that Lord Chelmsford," the driver growled, "he better start listening to the Boers' advice. Can't move all those men and guns, tents and food... hundreds of wagons he's commandeered... It's too slow." He shrugged ex-pressively, "Imagine trying to take that lot through the hills and mountains!"

"Surely they realise that?"

"Naw, you know the high-and-mighty, always know best! The Zulu he travels light and he runs, silent, like the wind."

Cliff nodded. "They could be all round him and his precious baggage long before he even noticed!"

"If I was you…" the driver leant confidentially towards Cliff, "I'd move real slow like. Once you're up over the summit you want to watch out. Camp well off the track and don't light a big fire. Just a small one after dark, enough to keep the leopards away. Sleep with your horses ready saddled and their reins round your arms. And, man, that dog – he better sleep with one eye open! Not a barker, I hope?"

"No, he is a proper hunter, knows what to do."

"Good, you want to pass as silently as possible once over the crest of the mountains… They could be in any gully, up any kloof, blend with the shadows they do… Good luck, mate. For myself, I'll not be back this route for a while."

They turned in, rolling themselves in their sleeping blankets within range of the glow from the flickering flames. Slithering down the mountain with a wagon of machinery had been a tiring and dangerous job. The transport driver was snoring steadily in five minutes. Cliff looked over at Josh. He had rolled the old felt hat which Cliff had given him, into a pillow and lay curled up facing the fire, breathing evenly. Cliff lay wide awake for some time, staring up at the mountain and pondering which route through the towering crags might be safest.

It felt to Cliff as though he had only just fallen asleep when he was jerked into wakefulness by Zenda. The dog was silently and urgently licking his face. He tensed and listened. Only the mules could be heard but they seemed restless and uneasy and against the pale navy line of the horizon he could see his horse's ears clearly outlined and pricked forward, listening. Silently he slid out of his rug, automatically reaching for his gun. He began to follow a cautiously creeping Zenda who was edging towards the uneasy cluster of wagon mules. They stopped together in the deep shadow of the nearest boulder. Zenda had his nose up and was smelling the soft breeze and all down his back a spine of hairs was rising in disturbed consternation. Cliff felt the dog tense and strained his eyes into the blackness.

Josh did not know what sixth sense woke him but he was aware instantly of danger, although he could see nothing. It was almost as though the air had stopped moving. He looked quickly at his companions. The transport driver was a leaden lump in the dull glow but there was no sign of Cliff. For Cliff and Zenda to have gone must mean that they were already aware of the danger… or were they in need of his help? Silently he sat up and began to quarter the night, quietly identifying each shape. Then he saw them. They were the darker shapes against the dense blackness of the boulder. Just as he was reaching for his gun there was a sudden crash in the bushes beyond the mules and with a roar a lion sprang at the nearest animal. The mule let out a terrified neigh, as the lion, its mane silvered by the faint dawn light, hurtled towards him and then slid to the ground in a crumpled heap at the mule's side as Cliff's gun let out a crack which echoed round the mountain like a million subsiding explosions.

All the hobbled mules moved rapidly to one side, whinnying and neighing in terror. The transport driver was on his feet, gun in hand, staring wildly round trying to collect his bearing, straight out of his deep sleep. Charity reared onto her hind legs in fright and Jackalet tried to pull herself loose from the tree she was hitched to. Josh leapt over to calm her. Zenda was circling the lion cautiously. Cliff seemed to have decided that, having alerted the surrounding mountainside to their presence, he might as well make doubly certain of his target. He fired again and the body convulsed and then lay silent. Zenda sniffed closer, decided the job had been well completed and trotted back to Cliff, tail up in a form of salutation for a job well done.

"By jingo!" exclaimed the transport driver, staring in admiration at the great bulk of the lion. "You got a right one there, lad!"

Out of the gloom from under the transport wagon, emerged his three native trek boys, their eyes shining in their strained faces. They were still struggling to wake and recover from fright at the same time.

"Ag baas, is big mountain king, very good mooti," commented one, staring at the body.

"Get on, you lazy buggers, get those mules under control before they break loose," blustered the driver.

It took some time to calm down the mules and the horses but eventually everyone settled to sleep fitfully until dawn. In the bright light of day it was only the great tawny body of the lion which convinced them that it had not all been a bad dream. Zenda was rewarded with tit-bits of meat from all the breakfast plates.

"Ag man, you have a good dog here, with him you'll be safe," commented the transport driver admiringly.

The lion pelt went to Cliff but Charity reared and bucked at the pungent smell of the pelt and Cliff had reluctantly to give it to the transport driver to sell on the Reef.

From then on it was a long, slow haul up steep and precipitous paths and the purple-ridged mountains hid range upon range of smaller mountains.

Gradually they eased up the escarpment towards the jagged summit of the Drakensberg to the mountain passes which would allow them access to Natal, and, eventually, the descent towards the sea. The scenery was rugged and spectacular. Two men and a horse paled into insignificance against the size and vast splendour of nature's backdrop.

"How," Josh asked Cliff, "can people be fighting over land and grazing when the whole world seems to lie at our feet, empty and free?"

Cliff groaned and rolled his eyes towards the sky.

"Well may you ask, lad. You heard that last farmer. He felt that with so few people and cattle around, his herd had the right to graze where they wandered. On the other hand, the Zulus are also cattle breeders and they see no reason to back off pastureland which had been theirs by right of capture from lesser tribes, since the days of their great founder chief, Dingaan."

"But surely there is enough for everyone?" Josh puzzled.

"Apparently not. You know how much a large herd will eat! It must be constantly moved."

Josh was reminded of the herd which he had helped to protect. Although he had not seen fighting at his kraal he had heard the older indunas talking about the successes and defeats of their youth. It was only their position in their remote corner of the Zoutpansberg range, which had protected them from marauding tribes, ever on the lookout for new flocks and herds and new land. He was aware from the talk of the tribal elders, that Zulu expansion had acted like a great plague of locusts, overrunning, exterminating and absorbing all within reach. He knew that few tribes had survived this "mfecane" unscathed. Many tribes, he had been told, were entirely wiped out. The indunas had talked of this period with awe and fear. Some had been small children at the time, others passed on the tales from their parents. Then came the white men, land hungry and carrying guns. At first they had appeared to be no threat but then it became clear that they carried their power in their guns. Guns made better and more effective weapons than spears and knobkerries.

To Josh it looked like yet more craggy mountains to be crossed, but on the 19th of January Cliff declared that they were over the summit and beginning the gradual descent.

Josh delighted in each day as it came and revelled in the mountain grandeur and the friendly companionship of horse and man. He hardly noticed that Cliff's replies were shorter and he rode more cautiously. No longer the easy relaxed figure of the resigned long-distance rider, but rather the alert tension of a hunter. He was combing every kloof and crevasse with his eyes for signs of movement, traces of smoke or disturbed birds. At night the rule was silence and they huddled close together, with Zenda alert to every sound in the undergrowth and the horse and pony sleeping equipped for a quick departure. They ate in the dark and kept their fire low to avoid the tell-tale smoke by daylight or flames in the night.

"It's not the most direct route," Cliff explained, "but it should be safer than the usual traders road, perhaps less likely to be marked out as a good spot for an ambush," he puffed on his pipe, staring up at the rock face above them.

Slowly, often leading the horse and pony by their reins, Zenda leaping ahead, they descended to the rolling hills of Zululand. The country was tinder dry, water in short supply. At night the presence of lions made sure they all slept lightly and they would rise early and catch up on sleep in the silent heat of the middle day instead.

"That hill with the large rock face," Cliff pointed across a valley, "that's alongside the traders route, we'll head that way now, it's easier to cross the river from there."

Josh glanced across at him.

"Do you think the war could be over?"

"I'd like to think so," Cliff replied, "but I can't believe we've been that lucky. We've seen no signs, not even drumbeats."

They both sat astride their horses looking down through the shimmering heat haze at the rolling hills below them.

Unknown to the little party, a few valleys away Lord Chelmsford, Commander of the British Forces in Natal, was about to have his world topple in upon him. His well-organised army would be routed in the plain of Isandhlwana below the Nqutu Range and above the Malakata and Inhlazatye Hills. He would lose five companies of the lst/24th, one company of the 2nd/24th, 100 Natal Mounted Police and Volunteers and 600 Natal natives. Not to mention all the bandsmen, orderlies, grooms, drummer boys and the surgeon, wagons, supplies, ammunition, horses and cattle. It would prove a devastating way to start a campaign. A terrible blow to the morale of the remaining regiments. Worse still, he would have to face the fact that a series of human errors were to blame and he was personally, at least in part, responsible for some of the miscalculations. He had underestimated the manoeuvrability, strength and cunning of his foe.

While he dispersed his forces to reconnoitre the area, the main impi of 20,000 men were squatting silently in a deep ravine of the Nquthu range, which led down to the Isandhlwana plateau only four miles from the camp.

The Zulu leaders were waiting for the auspicious rise of the new moon on the 23rd before making their attack. However, when a scouting party suddenly sighted them on the morning of the 22nd, they were forced to move and attack earlier than planned, on the day of the "dead moon", when, behind the cloudbank, the sun was going into an eclipse.

As the great ebony army rose and moved into swift action, down on the plain, between the Nguthu range and Malakata Hills, nine men were escorting a rocket battery pulled by mules. A mile behind them were their accompanying force of infantry from the Natal Native Corps. They had all fallen well behind their commander, Colonel Durnford, who was riding ahead with Lt. Henderson and fifty of Sikalis mounted men and Newnham-Davis with the famed Edendale Contingent. They were all making steady headway towards the Nquthu Mountains where they were under the impression that they would be heading off a small contingent of Zulus.

Suddenly, the men with the rocket battery sighted a messenger slipping, sliding and plunging on his horse down the steep ravine. In a helter-skelter whirl of stones and dust he reached the plateau and raced across to the little group. He barely gave himself time to splutter out a warning about "Zulu hordes", to Brevet Major Francis Russell, before he wheeled his sweating horse round and disappeared in the direction of the camp.

Russell, peering ahead at his Colonel's force, realised that he had no chance of reaching them and ordered that the mules pulling the battery should be wheeled round. He had barely issued his orders when a movement on the ravine rim, down which their messenger had ridden, riveted the whole group in a split second of total horror. All along the ridge, as far as Private Trainer and the others could see, wave upon wave of black figures appeared, hesitated and then lapped over the edge and began the wild scramble down towards the little band.

Realising the helplessness of his situation, isolated as they had become a mile ahead of one escort and a mile behind the other, Russell ordered the mules brought round yet again so that his tubes could be erected in the path of the oncoming enemy. Private Grant grabbed the lead reins and did his best, but the noise and dust of the advancing impi was too much for the mules and, before he could stop them, two broke away and jumped onto nearby boulders, refusing to budge. Private Trainer and Russell and some of the other men, finally erected one tube and lit off a rocket, but it fizzled out and before they could organise another the front lines of the enemy hit them with full force. There was no skirmish, so vast was the oncoming wave of Zulus that they merely overran the rocket battery, stabbing and trampling the men and mules as they swept by.

It seemed to Private Trainer that they came on for ever. His body was tossed and trampled and thrown to one side and the earth went on thumping to the steady onslaught of wave upon wave of warriors, their eyes set firmly on the distant camp.

At that point he must have lost consciousness because when the fog lifted from his brain and his eyes opened again, the noise had faded and only the dust was still trying to settle in a red veil over the scene of carnage. Gingerly he peered through his coated lashes and then, as the full horror returned, he began to check on his limbs. One shoulder felt stiff and useless and the arm throbbed in sympathy. An assegaai had glanced off his left leg leaving a deep cut but otherwise all appeared to be intact. Every joint screamed in bruised pain from being kicked and trampled by the passing hordes, but they showed signs of reluctant movement.

The plain lay in an eerie half light, a chill wind swept across him and was gone. Behind the clouds the sun began to emerge from the shelter of the black disc of the moon as the eclipse faded.

Someone else had made it too. He could hear hoarse puking, spewing and coughing coming from behind a nearby boulder. In the distance there was steady firing from the camp and a sound like an angry hive of bees. Around him all was silent apart from the man behind the boulder.

The dust was still settling in a ginger haze and already the faint buzz of flies was accompanying the steady drip hitting the pebble-crusted soil by his side. Looking up he realised that the body of one of the mules was lying across the boulder, blood still oozing from its many wounds. Peering round to make sure no Zulus had stayed behind to administer the "coup de grace" to survivors, he forced his protesting limbs into action and moved round the boulder.

Scarlet jackets were sprawled in twisted disarray around the battered remains of the rocket battery, a few black bodies among them. Propped against the boulder, dazed and uncomprehending, he saw to his relief, his mate, Private Grant. Kneeling by his side and considerably hampered by only having the use of one arm, Trainer struggled with his teeth to get his water canteen open and force some of the liquid down his dazed friend's throat.

"What the hell are we doing here?" Grant finally spluttered in a hoarse, puzzled whisper.

"Ah, you're alive, ye old bastard! Thank God for that, I was sure those savages had finished off the lot of ye an' left me to tell the tale!"

Grant flinched as he tried to move. He had a gash down one side of his face but the blood and dust had already formed a protective cake to stem the bleeding. He peered at the bodies all round him, then up at the rigid legs of the dead mules. Turning sideways he was sick again and clutched convulsively at his side.

Trainer glanced at him in concern and slid his good arm under Grant's jacket.

"Don' you start thinkin' you can leave me to face this load o' devils alone. No, no, laddie! You've not been stabbed, nor shot – it's something bruised or broken… ribs, maybe? See if you can stand. Come on, man," he reached out a hand, "we can't sit here to be finished off an' I don't see how the camp can hold out against those hordes."

Holding Trainer's good arm, Grant hauled himself gingerly to his feet then creased up with pain.

Just then, over on the far side of the rocket battery, they heard a groan. Leaving Grant propped against the rock, Trainer hobbled over and found Private Johnston trying to move himself out from under the body of Brevet Major Russell. His life had undoubtedly been saved when Russell fell on him, protecting him from the stabbing assegais of the descending warriors. He had an open gash down one leg but nothing was broken and he and Trainer soon fashioned a bandage out of his shirt tails and covered the wound.

Together they returned to Grant who was still dazed. Between them the two men used a tightly wound shirt, removed from one of the dead men, to twist round Grant's midriff and this seemed to support him and ease the pain. They checked over their six comrades but they were all dead.

"Listen, would you, to those volleys, poor devils, what a shock!" Trainer commented.

"Can't see nuffin' for that bloody dust." Grant peered into the haze. "Reckon we'd better move somewhere else, an' mighty quick too, don' you Johnston?"

"But where'd you go from here? We're bloody miles from anywhere!" Johnston peered round and turned, questioningly to Trainer.

Trainer scratched his head with his good hand and peered up at the hill behind them.

"We go up there," he pointed into the Nqutu range, "an' then move that'a way," he indicated along the rocky hills, "an' we must come out near that other camp, you know, Rorke's Drift." He looked hopefully at the other two.

Grant nodded. "Down by the Buffalo River what we crossed the other day?"

Trainer nodded, "Seems like it, 'fraid I can't think of much else."

Johnston looked dubiously at them both. "Reckon you can make it?"

"I'd rather try than be a sitting duck for them Zulus coming back," Grant muttered.

"Always a chance we might bump into reinforcements an' get help 'fore our wounds get worse..." Johnston tried to be optimistic.

"Look," said Trainer, "Grant, you get some water canteens from the others what's not goin' to need them no more. Let's get rid of these ruddy red jackets what can be seen to kingdom come, grab a Martini-Henry each, an' boys, check you got plenty ammo, you never know when we might need it."

Equipped as best they could be, they set off, creeping round the conical hill and across the plain towards the pitted, stony slopes of the mountain over which the Zulus had emerged.

Trainer's arm was in a rough sling, but it ached as he struggled over the uneven ground. Grant was still suffering from the blow to his head which seemed to be affecting his vision and Johnston was limping and trying to stop the blood trickling down his leg from his soaked bandage.

Trainer viewed the others wryly.

"We're a right sorry sight, lads, but least we're alive!"

Like ants they struggled up the stony side of the hill and then onto the ridge from which they could view the plain below.

"Don't look good, lads," said Trainer, wiping the sweat from his eyes and peering across at the distant blur of their besieged camp. "Looks like a plague of ants and no sign of them being pushed back."

"My God in heaven, look at that!" shouted Johnston, pointing over to the right. "They're bloody well pouring down like black molten tar, out of these mountains, straight onto the back of the camp. I hope those laddies are awake! I bloody hope so, or they're finished."

They all stared down in mesmerised horror.

"They're coming down on them from every direction and soon they'll be surrounded..." Grant peered dazedly down the slopes and wiped his arm across his eyes to see more clearly.

Trainer was the first to come to his senses.

"We gotta get round these bloody rocky hills and down beyond to Rorke's Drift… Warn them and get some help, an' for sure these white shirts may be tattered and filthy but they'll show up like pox on a pig. Like as not some savage'll see us and then we'll be done for. Come, lads…" He began again to scramble and slide over the dry rocky slopes away from the ridge and out of view of the valley below.

They moved further into the range, travelling towards the east in the direction of the camp at Rorke's Drift. It was a long slow march, each man very aware of his wounds and the scorching heat of the noon-day sun. They crossed the rocky beds of a couple of streams, hoping desperately for some sign of water to wash their wounds. The dying trees and bushes on the banks told their own parched story.

Grant slipped down a rocky bank and lay still. Johnston dragged him into the shade of a thorn tree.

"He's passed out."

He hastily poured a little of Grant's water onto a strip torn from his shirt and laid it on the boy's forehead. "What now?" he queried, looking up at Trainer's strained face.

Trainer sat in silence for a few minutes, struggling to get some relief for his aching shoulder.

"By my reckoning we should be moving towards the end of this lot o' mountains, then it'll be down through that swampy bit where our wagons got stuck…" he paused and said, almost to himself, "I'd like to know whether Chelmsford an' 'is column got back to the camp on time. I really would."

"If not," Johnston interrupted, "if not, the lads will be in a right mess," and then, as a second thought, "bloody wish I was there!"

Grant was coming round.

"Give him some of his water, Johnston. An' maybe you better use some of yours on your leg. The flies are a right pest!" Trainer swatted at them as he spoke and then winced as a sharp pain shot through his damaged shoulder.

Putting Grant between them they moved off trying to steady him as they went.

Perspiration was running down Grant's face and mingling with the blood from the gash and the red dust of the veld. He was swaying as he moved and only just conscious. Suddenly, they were out on a ridge with a view across the low lying plateau of the Banshee and Buffalo River with the mission station at Rorke's Drift hidden by the distant bulk of the Oskarberg. It was then that Johnston let out another anguished shout.

"Look, bloody look, the bastards! They've got a whole bloody army heading for Rorke's Drift as well – and they're way ahead of us. They'll bloody massacre them."

Winding across the valley like a sinister black snake but at a steady even running trot, were three impis of the Zulu army, approximately four thousand men in all.

"It's Rorke's Drift they're after, an' there's no cover, an' probably only a hundred or so men there at present... pray for them lads." Trainer summed up the situation.

Grant was sitting on the ground propped against a rock, staring almost uncomprehendingly across the plain. His blue eyes had a vacant glazed expression, a preoccupation with his own pain, which protected him from the full shock the other two were experiencing.

Johnston slid down next to him, his head drooping in grim despair while both hands still held his gun with the stock on the ground, pointing up to the cloud-bespattered sky.

"We're jiggered, man, we're caught on two sides, an' we'll never make it now... Where else is there to go?"

Nothing made Trainer madder than people giving up.

"What the hell! We'll come out of this alive if I have to drag you both by ye bloody boot laces," he shouted at Johnston. "Don't bloody let the bastards get to you – our lads'll be fighting them down by that godforsaken sphinx-shaped hill at Isandhlwana. We'll get through come hell or high water..." He nudged Johnston with his foot. "Come on, Johnston, get on your damn hooves and we'll move north along that ridge and try to get down beyond Rorke's Drift, cross the Buffalo an' go round to the camp at Helpmekaar, avoiding that black centipede if we can."

Johnston looked at him as if he had taken leave of his senses.

"That's fucking fifty miles, how the hell do you think we'll get that far in this state? I'm ruddy done in as it is, an' this lad's hardly conscious. Come night the cold falls like an icy blanket and we'll be bloody stiffs for the lions by morning!"

"Don' give me your problems, just get on your ruddy feet and an' let's get moving. Maybe we'll come on one of old Chelmsford's detachments... look, for sure sitting here ain't getting' us nowhere, we may as well keep movin' as die of bloody despair by this rock!"

Cursing steadily, Johnston staggered to his feet and began to haul Grant upright. They hitched him between them again and stumbled off along a northerly ridge of the range.

So engrossed were they in making their way over the uneven rock-strewn mountainside, skirting bushes and hauling themselves in and out of dongas (erosion crevasses in the mountain slopes) that none of them noticed the small party of Zulus. They were part of the inDluyengwe regiment, late for their call-up and hurrying to join their compatriots on their way to Rorke's Drift.

There were four of them and they had just come over the rise and were picking their way down the slope at a steady running trot when suddenly the one in front caught sight of the white soldiers below them. They stood as if carved out of the dark rock of the mountainside, totally still, blending with the early afternoon shadows, and watching the slow progress of the three below. From their vantage point they could see that the men were on an old game trail which led up a slope to an area covered in large boulders. Silently they began to fan out towards the same area, creeping from bush to rock, using the patches of shadow as camouflage.

A soft breeze was blowing at an angle up the face of the berg and it carried the scent of strangers to Zenda's sensitive nostrils where he was lying in the shade, while the small party took a mid-afternoon rest. Immediately the dog stiffened and rose with a slow, lithe, slinking movement, the ridge on his back bristling. The dark ears came forward over the soft tan fur of his face, twitching to catch a confirmatory sound. His stealthy movement caught Josh's eye as he lay back in the deep shade of a gnarled bush. Silently, he prodded Cliff in the back and pointed to Zenda.

Cliff had seized the chance of this rest in the shade to take his gun apart and was carefully cleaning the barrel with an oily cloth. He recognised the dog's disquiet and began hastily to re-assemble the gun. It was every hunter's nightmare to be caught in this position.

Zenda had sidled to the edge of the small plateau and was trying to peer cautiously over the edge, nose twitching, back stiff with suspicion.

Josh rolled onto his stomach and crawled across the dry brown grass to join him. The trained eyes of the hunting dog were the first to pick out the shadowy movement of the three indunas on the slope below. Zenda's tail stiffened to form a straight line with his back and a growl of warning, so low it was almost like a stomach rumble, escaped him. Josh gently parted the brown grass at the edge of the plateau and peered down in the direction the dog was "pointing". He had almost forgotten about the existence of human beings and was prepared to see a predatory animal of some kind. Cliff knew better. That slink, that deep controlled growl, Zenda reserved for the most dangerous of killers – man.

The horses were aware of a drama. They too had caught the scent of man on the breeze. They stood quietly, ears pricked forward, eyes alert, also watching the dog and the boy.

Then Josh's eyes adjusted to the mixture of shade and light on the mountainside below and he too saw the flitting shadows of the four warriors amongst the boulders on the slopes below. Leopard-skin bands round their heads, swinging monkey tail kilts and chest pieces of white monkey skin, each carrying the short stabbing spear, the 'iklwa', and a cow-hide shield. He had heard of these Zulu warriors from the tribal leaders in his kraal and he was thrilled to see them himself at last. He wanted to jump up and shout a welcome and run down to look more closely at their splendour. Something about the way they were moving stopped him. They were not in the proud running-trot of the warrior party. They were moving stealthily, keeping to the deepest shadows. The lore of the hunt was well bred into Josh and he lay waiting for the animal to appear.

He glanced at Cliff, who was slipping the last piece of his gun into place and beginning to move towards him. Masked by the grass, they lay and watched the scene below. Suddenly, Josh felt Cliff stiffen and simultaneously he became aware of the crunch of boots on pebbly soil and the sound of muffled voices. The sounds were distant but clear. Josh was bewildered. If there was game close by who would be making such a noise? Then it struck him that only white men would make so much noise and only white men would wear boots. Could they be farmers? No, they would be riding. Prospectors? Traders? Brigands? Would Cliff fire a warning shot? He glanced at him. No, he looked strained but perhaps he didn't want to attract attention.

Suddenly, the silent observers saw three white men in battered blue trousers, tattered white shirts and pith helmets. No wonder their advance had been so slow, Josh thought. The man in the middle was being supported by his comrades and appeared almost unconscious. The brown-haired, red-faced man on his right seemed to have two guns over his other shoulder, he was limping badly and he was arguing with the red-headed man on the left.

It was obvious that the red-headed man was in considerable pain and was only just coping with the man in the middle.

Then, with a feeling of shock, almost like a body-blow, Josh realised that the warriors were stalking these men. White men, like Cliff. He had never stalked men, apart from at play. One of the white men could not protect himself, which made it four against two. He glanced sideways at Cliff. He appeared to be watching but showing no signs of action. Something, Josh felt, had to be done. If the white men had looked alert and capable he might have been prepared to watch and to hope that the warriors would defeat them. However, under the circumstances it would be like killing the innocent lizards who did nothing but catch flies on the hut walls. Lying in the grass just ahead of him was a flat, jagged-edged stone. He closed his hand over it. It was cool to the touch and it was just the right weight to wing its way down to the group below and still have the force to do some harm.

Cliff saw him just too late. Just as the stone left his practised hand and flew down the hill to thud against the skull of the warrior, who had already raised his assegai to attack the three men. The blow was so unexpected that the warrior was unable to stop himself from letting out a howl of pain and surprise.

Immediately, the three men, still dragging their companion, moved rapidly behind the rocks on the far side of the track. Josh was helpless to do anything further, with Cliff lying across him and breathing fury down his neck.

There was considerable confusion amongst the warriors, the rock appeared to have arrived from nowhere to knock out their companion. By now the two soldiers had gathered their wits and, propping their friend against a giant boulder, they were loading their Martini-Henry's as fast as they could and preparing to fight back.

Josh felt sick. It wasn't just the weight on his back either. He was torn by indecision. His first instinct had been to aid the warriors. Then the unfair situation had hit him, one man already wounded, and he had acted spontaneously.

Through the grass stems Josh could just catch sight of the scene below. To his consternation he saw that one of the warriors had a gun and he fired a shot at the large boulder, narrowly missing a soldier's head as he peered round to get his bearings on the Zulus. Splinters of rock whirled wildly through the air. Leaving their unconscious friend, the three remaining warriors rushed forward in an effort to encircle the rock while they had the advantage. Just as the warriors broke cover, so two of the white men dived down the hill to a boulder lower down. Both men began to shoot and one of the warriors fell with a thud. The remaining two appeared to withdraw to consider their next move. Fortunately, it seemed that neither of them had noticed the badly wounded soldier left propped in a crevasse between two rocks.

Josh was aware of Cliff moving off him but keeping his hand over his mouth. He felt Cliff's warm breath in his ear.

"One squeak out of you, my lad, and I'll brain you with a rock like you did to that chap. That'll keep you quiet for a while too."

The hand was removed slowly from his mouth and he glanced sideways at Cliff, aware of a frosty glare which left him feeling confused and despondent. He peered back at the scene below him. No further warriors had appeared at the sound of the shots. It seemed that this band of four were travelling on their own.

Cliff seemed to have reached the same conclusion. From their vantage point on the hillside above, the two of them could see the warriors part and begin to move round, using the rocks and scrubby bushes for cover. They were obviously intending to move in on the men from the sides or rear and take them by surprise. Cliff muttered, almost below his breath, "Better help I suppose, keep on the right side of the British Army... couldn't do any harm." He rolled towards Josh.

"Don't you damn well move or I'll skin you!" he whispered fiercely into Josh's ear. Then he moved slowly backwards and disappeared into the undergrowth on the hillside. Josh lay tense and unhappy, Zenda by his side.

Trainer was battling to cope with one arm almost useless. Johnston helped him load but how long would they be together, he pondered to himself. Trainer braced his gun along a groove in the rock. This damned country! He resented coming to an end so far from home, with every chance of becoming carrion for the vultures. He was looking up the hill, watching for any sign of the next attack, when suddenly his eye was caught by a slight movement higher up the hill, where a small cliff face ended in a grassy promontory. It was the flash of sun on metal or glass. Could he be hallucinating? No, there it went again. Another savage with a gun? If so, why was he not backing his friends? Trainer dragged his eyes away to examine his foreground. They'd better come soon, he'd give them all he had... and then... no chance of a reload, the arm was almost useless... it might well be a blessing to escape the pain. The pain seemed to dominate everything, it damped down his will to live. He, Trainer, who normally no man could put down. He was crawling, captured by pain, and now probably by these bloody savages. If the worst happened he'd let them have him, walk out in front of the one with a gun… he didn't fancy that spear, no thank you. An Englishman should die by the gun. It was a death a soldier could understand, his parents would mourn, but they'd be proud… if ever they knew.

He felt Johnston move, next to him, and he heard him whisper, "What the hell are the blighters up to? I could get the one with the spear, mate, you go for the other one while I reload."

Trainer grunted.

"Anyway," Johnston continued, "what the hell are they doing with guns, we weren't told to expect that. Trust the demented old idiots in the army to be misinformed, an' how about the ruddy red uniforms which make us sitting ducks. Treat us like cannon fodder they do."

"You'll be spear fodder if you don't shut up and keep quiet," Trainer growled back.

It took all of Cliff's skill as a hunter to move silently over the gravely terrain. He knew he must get into closer range if his gun was to be effective. In fact he had only just reached the first of the big boulders when he heard the shot, followed in short succession by two more. He hastily moved upright and looked down the slope. Just ahead of him and sprinting for the cover of a rock, was one of the warriors. He raised his gun to fire and felt a blow to his back which spun him off balance and sent his gun clattering across the shale and rock. The other warrior must have seen him and moved back to give his companion support. Survival instinct made Cliff realise that he was about to be hit again by the man's knobkerrie and he rolled rapidly sideways. Simultaneously, there was a thud and a gasp behind him as his assailant was hit by a whirlwind of tawny fur. The blow knocked the wind out of him long enough for Cliff to recover and leap at him, grabbing the knobkerrie where it had fallen from the man's startled grasp. Lifting it high above his head he brought it down with all the brute force he could muster, to smash his opponent's skull. Zenda was standing over the warrior, snarling ferociously.

The whole incident had taken a few split seconds but the other warrior heard the noise and turned to see what had happened. It only needed that split second for a dazed and semi-conscious Grant to come round sufficiently in his crevasse in the rocks, to lift his gun, which Johnston had left loaded by his side, and take wavering but lucky aim at the last warrior, killing him instantly.

Trainer couldn't believe it. Salvation had sprung from nowhere. Just as he was about to give up, aware that he could not re-load fast enough with one arm to make another effective shot. He had seen the man stand up, the knobkerrie whirl, then both men had disappeared and Grant had suddenly come round enough to use his gun. Trainer glanced round for Johnston. He too was just emerging from round the rock, looking stunned but relieved.

The white man was coming down the hillside towards them with a large brown dog by his side. His face looked gray in the shade cast by the heavy-brimmed buck-skin hat which was set back enough to show some locks of tousled brown hair. He was rubbing his back with one hand and limping slightly.

Trainer was still looking in amazement at the man who seemed to have materialised from nowhere to save them, when, behind him, he noticed a boy scrambling down the rocky scree. He was a thin, wiry, blond boy in battered trousers with an old shirt hanging down over his belt. He was holding a gun in one hand and using the other hand to balance himself. He noticed the man in the hat turn and look at the boy, a flicker of annoyance crossed his face, then he shrugged and continued to walk towards Trainer.

"Ah, now," said Johnston, speaking to himself in his amazement, "I'm sure I've never seen such a welcome sight in all my living days... a man, his dog and a boy, walking calmly out of the wild bush to save us... there must be a God up there after all."

The boy disappeared from sight where the hard red earth dipped down at the bottom of the first hill. Trainer walked towards the man, holding out his hand in a gesture of grateful relief. Suddenly, there was a resounding cry of *"Usuthu"* and they were all aware of a warrior standing a-top the great boulder above Grant and aiming his assegaai straight at Johnston.

Everyone had forgotten the warrior whom Josh had knocked out with his stone.

The world seemed to go into slow motion. Johnston reached for his breach-loader, but afterwards he commented:

"It was like I was in a bad dream, the gun seemed a dead-weight in my hands, I could hardly lift it. There was a great bang, an' then I seen that warrior in all his skins, fall, twisting as he went, the assegaai spinning off into the distance. The noise seemed to bring me back to this world and I seen the boy standing on the hillside, the gun still at his shoulder. Then I seen him sit down very suddenly, his head on his arms and his shoulders shaking."

It was Johnston who reacted first. He began to run up the hill towards the boy as if his life depended on it. It was an uneven jogging run because of his wounded leg. The rocky soil fell away from his boots and a little cloud of red dust trailed behind him. Reaching Josh he threw his arms round him and hugged him in a great bear-hug.

"Lad, you're one hell of a shot, one hell of a fine lad – I'd be down there with a metal shaft through my chest right now if you hadn't moved. Come on, lad, I'll never forget this." Gently, he loosened the gun from the boy's hold and laid it on the ground. Josh clung to him as if he was a rock in a swirling river and shook silently. Johnston held him tight, slowly soothing his shock, talking gently. Presently they sat side by side, Johnston kept an arm round the boy's shoulders as his body gradually stopped shaking.

"Good lad! I've one like you at home. What the hell am I doing so far from home? I must be bloody mad! What's your name, lad?"

"Josh," came out in a quiet murmur as he responded to the man's genuine warmth and understanding.

"I killed him," he whispered, his eyes going glassy as he pictured the scene once again, "He was so proud, so magnificent, I should never have done it. He was a brave warrior, who was I to kill such a man?"

Johnston looked at him incredulously.

"Lad, he was going to kill me… Don't you understand… he was blood mad? You saved my life. He'd have killed you if he'd seen you first."

"I'd rather that."

"War's a nasty business, you kill or be killed. Right now you've fallen into a war and you have to be on the side of your people, the white people… that Zulu, he was a soldier for *his* people."

"But they're my people too! At least… we were a small tribe but we would have followed them if necessary," the boy pointed to the small tribal scars below his right ear.

The man stared, then ran a finger over the mark and whistled.

"Well, I'll be damned… where are your parents?"

Josh shrugged. "I don't know. I think they were murdered by some white men. I was raised by the tribe until Cliff fetched me away." He nodded his head towards Cliff, who was struggling to make a new sling for Trainer's arm.

Johnston was a family man, forced by debt to join the army. He missed his wife and children. The idea of being part of a black tribe was totally foreign to him.

"Look, lad, your tribes all war against one another. Sooner or later you would have been fighting other tribes and killing other warriors. You've just been forced to start early. Be proud that you behaved like a fine soldier, your tribe would have felt the same way when you killed for them."

Josh looked directly at him for the first time. It was a grateful glance and it brought Josh another steep step out of childhood. Johnston ruffled his hair and pulled him up.

"Come, lad, there's a very sick man down there who was also very brave. Let us see if we can do anything for him." Johnston moved off down the hill. Josh picked up his gun and followed him. His head was up, he would live with the nightmare but this man had understood.

They camped on the ridge overnight. Cliff and Josh taking it in turns to watch over Grant. Together they did the best they could for them with the medicines Cliff carried and Josh's knowledge of herbal cures. Johnston's leg was puffy and Trainer was in and out of sleep between bouts of pain.

They lit a small fire behind rocks and hoped that its glow would not be seen by any other Zulu war parties. They needed the warmth to ward off the cold night air of the mountains, their bedding blankets were needed for Grant and Trainer.

Everyone was glad to see the dawn sky and find themselves still alive.

Johnston woke feeling less feverish and refreshed by the sleep. The herbal pack which Josh had made and put on his wound had reduced the swelling and the inflammation. Trainer seemed worse and Grant, whose head wound had also been cleaned and packed, was better but still weak and befuddled.

In the night they had seen the red glow in the sky which outlined the Oskarberg and meant that Rorke's Drift was burning. They knew that they must cross the veld well beyond that area and make a wide track round to Helpmekaar, where the army had a supply base and medical unit. It was bound to be slow with Charity and Jackalet carrying Trainer and Grant, and Josh and Cliff helping Johnston.

"A restless night," Cliff commented to Josh, shaking himself as if to throw off a malaise.

Chapter Five

AFRICA – Late January to April, 1879

IT WAS A slow and cautious cavalcade which set off down the mountain. They were working their way carefully towards a narrow gully which should keep them out of sight of any stray Zulus who might be on their way to Rorke's Drift. An ominous pall of black smoke hung in the sky above the Oskarberg.

"I'd give a lot to know how they got on down there," said Johnston, nodding towards the smoke. "It don't look good, not when they was so outnumbered, been a long time but they must'a put up a good fight. That mission was small, and," he said, nodding at the smoke, "it were thatched."

Silence fell for a while as everyone concentrated on picking their way between rocks and scrubby bushes.

Johnston, Josh and Clifford were walking and Grant and Trainer were on the horses. Grant was semi-conscious but seemed to suffer moments of clarity between bouts of talkative rambling when he thought he was back in England. Clifford and Josh had done their best with the support round his ribs but obviously the swaying movement of the horse was causing him considerable pain and from time to time he moaned and they stopped to help him re-adjust his position or to give him a break.

Trainer's left shoulder and arm were firmly bandaged to his side with strips of his shirt, but having found someone else to steer the little group, he seemed to have lost his drive and will to live. Josh, walking by his side, realised that Trainer's leg, where the assegai had sliced it, was giving him considerable pain. He drew Jackalet to one side and insisted on rolling up the dirty trouser leg with its bloodstained tear. He called to Cliff to stop and the others gathered round. The wound was not deep but the dust and grime of the previous day's walk had infected it and the skin was puffed up, with a nasty purple edging.

"It's not just the pain of that shoulder, this wound is poisonous," he explained to Cliff, who stood up and felt Trainer's face. "He is hot, too hot."

"Bloody hell! It's given the man a fever, look how bright his eyes are? We'll have to treat that leg right now." Cliff looked round for a suitable spot to lay Trainer down and to light a small fire to heat up some of their precious water to clean the wound.

Johnston struggled to hold Trainer down while they lanced the wound, drained off the puss and cleaned it as best they could with their limited resources. Josh searched amongst the surrounding rocks and bushes for suitable herbs to boil in the water and pack over the wound.

Trainer began to suffer the icy fever shakes despite the heat of the midday sun burning down on them. They wrapped him in a blanket and waited for the phase to pass. Cliff was watching the sun nervously, not keen to keep the three men away from medical care for another night.

"Moving as slowly as this, circling wide to avoid any Zulu regiments, I reckon we've another four hours before we reach Helpmekaar. Won't make it before dark," he commented to Josh.

Cliff did not want to admit it to anyone, but he was fighting off occasional waves of nausea and hot flushes, himself. From time to time he found himself bending almost double with tummy cramps and the others had to wait for him briefly while he relieved himself. He was so seldom ill that it startled him and he was reacting by pushing himself harder, convinced that the symptoms would fade with time.

"Just something I ate, I expect, didn't cook it well enough..." he made light of the problem when Josh questioned him. To Cliff illness was a weakness. It was not one he could afford to indulge in.

He looked at the boy loading up the saddlebags, his serious blue eyes assessing the position and weight of each bag. He still felt aggrieved over the incident of the stone the previous day, and Josh's disobedience in arriving on the scene when told to stay behind. Reluctantly, he had to admit to himself that the lad had more than compensated with the vital shot which had killed the last warrior. Also, his native knowledge of medicinal plants and their healing properties was proving invaluable and he seemed alert and thoughtful, far beyond his years. In fact, Cliff conceded to himself, he was rapidly forgetting the boy's youth and treating him like a man. Especially now that they had these three soldiers to look after and steer back to Helpmekaar. He was grateful not to have come upon the situation on his own. Then there was this jealousy thing raising its head somewhat to his surprise. He hadn't expected it of himself, yet he had to acknowledge to a jealous pang that the soldier, Johnston, appeared to be able to bring out a side of Josh he couldn't reach.

He noticed that Johnston watched and encouraged the boy whenever he could. He appeared to be fascinated by Josh's knowledge of the plants of the veld and their medicinal properties. Despite the heat Johnston placed himself close to the little fire and watched as Josh prepared the herbal pack. While they were crouching in the shade of the rocks waiting for Trainer's fever to subside, he encouraged Cliff and Josh to tell him the story of the escape from the kraal. He listened in genuine amazement.

"By jingo! Well, I'll be damned!" he kept saying. He would put his arm round the boy's shoulders and hug him as though he was his own son. This rough and ready soldier had a warmth about him that gave unstintingly to the lad and brought out a corresponding warmth in Josh. For the first time Cliff heard him laugh and talk unhesitatingly. His language seemed to flow more freely, he was not struggling to find the words.

Still puzzling over the easy relationship between the two, Cliff fell asleep. He woke with a start to find Josh and Grant lifting Trainer back onto Jackalet's saddle. He glanced at the sun and realised he had been asleep for about an hour.

Grant swung into Charity's saddle.

"Why the hell didn't you wake me?" Cliff demanded in embarrassment.

"He's only just come round," Josh said, as he swung himself up behind Trainer, ready to hold him in the saddle. He glanced closely at Cliff, "You alright?"

Cliff pulled himself up. He noticed Johnston wince, and pointed at Grant. "Get him off that horse. Johnston, that leg of yours won't go far in this heat and I'll help him along for a while."

Rather reluctantly Johnston helped Grant down and put him in Cliff's care while he rode Charity, and they moved slowly off again.

For a while the sleep paid off and Cliff slowly guided Grant across the rough terrain. However, as the heat built up so he felt himself subsiding and the stomach pains returned. He lost hold of Grant and found that Zenda was close to his legs on one side and Charity was on the other, almost as though they were supporting and guiding him.

Josh was distracted. He was trying to keep hold of Trainer and kept peering worriedly at Cliff, and calling to Grant, who was wandering off in the wrong direction. For a while Zenda had appeared to walk by Grant's side, apparently steering him along with the others but now he had abandoned him and seemed to be determined to stick firmly to Cliff. The sad party straggled along the dusty scrub-covered veld. The afternoon sun slowly moved to an angle which threw their shadows across the bushes behind them, and at this point Josh called a halt.

Josh felt exasperated. Why was Cliff being so unhelpful?

He noticed that they had come round well behind a native kraal but even so the dogs had barked and their movements would be noted by many eyes hidden in the bush. Josh looked at the position of the sun and then noticed that Cliff was marching on... and furthermore, he was marching in the wrong direction. He called and then Johnston, coming out of his semi-stupor on Charity's back, called as well. Johnston moved in next to Josh.

"Here, lad, you go fetch him an' I'll 'old onto me old mate Trainer."

Hastily Josh slipped off the horse's back and ran after Cliff. As he caught up with him he noticed that he was walking automatically, like a sleep walker and his colour was high and his eyes glassy.

"Come on," Josh encouraged him back to the group and sat him down on a stone in the shade of a thorn bush. He stared at him perplexed. Cliff stayed bent over trying to relieve the pain in his stomach.

Grant looked up from where he had propped himself against the scrawny stem of another thorn tree.

"Looks sick to me, lad. Seen that colour out East, not good."

"What do I do?" Josh looked hopefully at Johnston.

"Beats me, lad!" Then he seemed to pull himself together and try to think. He waved his empty water bottle at Josh. "Dehydrated, lad, that's what we are, need you to perform a miracle and find some water in this hell hole, then we'll come back to life, I reckon."

Josh looked desperately at the group. He knew he wasn't far from Helpmekaar now but he despaired of getting the group there. He was frightened to find himself the only responsible and fit person of the five. He felt badly shaken by Cliff's sudden collapse.

Johnston looked up again. Grant appeared to have fallen into a heavy sleep.

"You see those hills over there, well that one with the bump on its side, that's just above Helpmekaar. It's not far, lad. It's just that we're all done in, unless you can find some water."

Reluctantly Josh came to the conclusion that he would have to ignore Cliff's concern about not alerting local tribes to their presence.

"I'll take the water bottles and see where the kraal get their water." Collecting the empty cans he moved off into the bush. with Zenda by his side. After a few minutes his quick eyes saw a stirring in the bush. He and Zenda moved rapidly through the grass and found a little girl peering nervously up at him with one hand over her mouth. She was only about six years old and Josh laughed, and spoke to her in his dialect. She looked blankly at him, so he tried sign language and suddenly she seemed to decide that she liked him. She put her hand in his and led him to the entrance to the small kraal. Zenda wisely fell back and lay down in the shadow of a tree to watch Josh's progress from afar. The resident watch dogs could well pack on a strange dog and tear him rapidly to bits. Josh was given a calabash of water but there only seemed to be women in the kraal and they appeared nervous and unfriendly, moving him on as rapidly as possible.

"You're a bloody miracle, boy," Johnston assured him when he returned and shared the water out between them and the animals.

"Now we'll see if we can revive this lot." Carefully Josh dripped water down Grant's throat and he responded by grabbing the bottle and drinking deeply. Cliff drank as though he would never stop and then curled up in pain as the cool liquid hit his stomach. Trainer opened his mouth and gulped gratefully, smearing the drips across his hot face with one hand.

"Wait," Josh said, "I'll soak this bit of shirt material in the last of the water and you can have a bit to cool your faces!"

"Bless you, boy... bless you," Grant seemed to have become aware of their presence once again.

Reluctantly Josh pushed them all to move on. They had to make the camp before sunset.

Grant was back riding on Charity, and Trainer was swaying on Jackalet's back. Josh was walking with Cliff and Johnston and trying to watch all four.

They struggled through the sticky heat for another hour before the army depot finally came into sight on the bleak skyline. The afternoon shadows were lengthening and the sun was not far from the horizon.

Helpmekaar was set in a slight dip in the veld from which the Union Jack protruded like a lone sentinel, the standard hanging limply in the heat above the rows of dusty tents rising like regimented triangular salt pots on a flat brown table. They appeared to be surrounding a couple of rusty sheds. The only relief to the monotony of the scene was a clump of grey-blue pepper trees trailing their fronds round a small dam while a tall windmill waited impatiently for a breeze to encourage its great metal head to turn and pump out more water. Behind the dam were two houses, one stone and one mudbrick, both with thatched roofs.

"At last! Thank goodness!" Josh put into words just what the exhausted men were feeling. Bleak or not, it represented a haven.

A sentry sounded the alarm. There was a flash of light as the lowering sun was reflected off binoculars, and then two horsemen came across the veld on large military horses, to escort them into camp.

"Battle casualties from Isandhlwana?" asked the erect officer, peering curiously at Josh from under his white pith helmet.

"Yes, sah, 24th Regiment, Royal Artillery, Rocket Battery under Major Russell, Private Johnston, sah!" barked Johnston, saluting as best he could and tugging awkwardly at the remains of his shirt.

The officer's face lit up.

"Well done! We heard you were caught by surprise and overrun by the enemy. How many survivors?" he peered hopefully towards the horizon.

"Only three, sah, Major Russell an' the others was run flat into the earth; no chance, sah. The mules took fright an' the battery misfired... it's pure miracle we's here. An' please, sah, what's the news from the camp an' what's 'appened back at Rorke's Drift?"

At this point, as though he had hung on until safety came into sight, Grant began to topple from the saddle. Josh moved rapidly to catch him but his weight was too much for the boy and both of them sank to the ground.

"Sergeant, help me put this man on my horse," the officer dismounted and moved towards Grant and Josh. Immediately Zenda was at Josh's side, hackles up, growling at the approaching officer. The man stopped and peered at Josh.

"And who are you? Too sunburnt for one of our drummers," he remarked, almost conversationally.

Josh was totally thrown by this encounter. He had never seen anything as grand as this tall man in his elegant blue and white livery and he was alarmed to find that the man seemed to talk through his nose and he couldn't understand a word he said. He looked hopefully at Clifford who was leaning against Charity watching the whole scene through feverish eyes as though he was merely an onlooker and not a participant.

"Go on, lad, tell 'im who you are," he drawled unhelpfully.

Josh grabbed Zenda and looked up at the man.

"I'm Josh," he said simply.

"'E bloody saved my life, sir, 'im an' this gentleman, they rescued us from a party of Zulus, back by the mountain," Johnston pointed vaguely back over his shoulder.

The officer's rather stern face broke into a smile.

"Did they indeed, well you all look pretty flattened. And, lad, I'd be obliged if you'd put in a word for me with that hound, tell him I'm not all bad and I'd rather not have his fangs in my person, obliged though I am by his wish to protect men of the British Army!" He put a foot into his stirrup and, still balancing Grant's sagging form, he swung up behind him and looked down at Johnston and Josh.

"I'm afraid its bad news from Isandhlwana... We are waiting for further details but it seems the camp was completely wiped out. You are amongst the few survivors. It's a terrible loss and we can't do anything until Lord Chelmsford arrives. Best get you all to the medic." He paused and moved his horse on slowly, his sergeant leading Charity with Trainer swaying on her back and Cliff sitting in a bemused state on the sergeant's horse, being led by Josh. Johnston brought up the rear limping along leading Jackalet.

"We've a problem here too," the officer went on. "We weren't set up as a proper medical centre. That was at Rorke's Drift. Our doc, Major Spalding, tried to help up at the Drift, but too late."

Josh's first sight of a British Military camp was not impressive. Having been forced back when they tried to go to the assistance of Rorke's Drift, the camp had been barricaded as best they could with the supply wagons, biscuit tins, stones, thorn bushes and sacks of mielie grain.

With bad news surrounding them on all sides they were expecting a Zulu attack at any time and guards were jittery and unsmiling. No one knew the whereabouts of their Commander-in-Chief, Lord Chelmsford, or the exact situation at the other fields of battle. Three officers had brought in the first tidings of the disaster the evening before. Captain Gardener had ridden north with the warning and Captain Stafford and Lieutenant Newnham-Davis had taken the news south to Greytown and Pietermaritzburg. Depressing details were dribbling in with the few survivors, and already the little army surgeon with the bristling moustache was pushed to cope with the soldiers who had reached him, cut off as he was, from the hospital at Rorke's Drift.

Josh stared at the little man suspiciously. So this harassed man with the abundance of whiskers decorating his upper lip, was the white man's medicine man. He smelt strange and the large tent looked white and unfriendly with boxes of shiny tools. He seemed to have two men helping him and was wringing his hands and cursing his limited medical supplies. The sight of four more patients did not hearten him.

Josh hung back as Cliff was lifted onto the couch and the man snorted into his whiskers:

"God, just what we need, seen enough of that in India and Afghanistan! Dysentery man, dysentery!" he nodded to his orderly, "Get him to a tent and do what you can to ease him, man. Next please!"

The orderly, a kindly looking man in a grubby uniform, led Cliff and Josh to a tent.

"There, boy," he said, pointing into the hot interior and indicated two empty camp beds with sheets folded across them. "See what you can do for him while I go to help with the other three."

Cliff tottered to a bed and fell down on it groaning and curling his knees up to try and ease the stomach pain. Josh pulled the sheet out from under him and laid it over him as best he could.

Jackalet and Charity had been led away to be watered and fed with the battalion horses and Zenda came in and stretched out under Cliff's bed with undisguised relief. Josh stared at the other bed space The ground beneath the tent's groundsheet was hard and lumpy but he didn't care, it looked inviting and he could feel exhaustion taking over. The orderly returned with a damp cloth, a bowl of water and a mug.

"Here, boy," he said hurriedly. "Wipe him down and put a damp cloth on his forehead and see if he can take some water."

Despite the stony discomfort of the hard ground, Josh slept soundly and woke in the early hours of dawn, disturbed by an orderly with a lamp who was bent over Cliff, obviously sponging him down with cold water. Zenda was sitting on the man's feet, with his head resting on the bedding, staring fixedly at Cliff.

Josh got up and moved to sit cross-legged next to the orderly on the other side of Zenda.

"He's real bad, eaten up by the fever," the man commented, "an' he 'as been up an' down to the latrines all night, we picked him up several times. The stomach cramps are bad, he's 'ardly conscious at present." The man looked at Josh's frightened face.

"Listen, lad," he said kindly, "out East I seen this a lot an' what 'e needs is reg'lar water. The docs, they don't seem to realise this but I seen many a man saved by 'is bearer just givin' 'im sips of water. At first it will only make him sick again but keep at it and eventually 'is stomach can keep it down and then 'e'll begin to get better." He leant across and put a kindly hand on Josh's shoulder, "Do this for 'im lad an' he might survive. We ain't got the time but 'eres the jug o' water an' a spoon an' a sponge to keep wiping 'im down. It's over to you lad!" The man got up and moved towards the tent flap.

"How's Mr Johnston?" Josh asked.

"He's not too good. Leg's givin' 'im real jip. Infected it is. The other bloke, Private Trainer, surgeon got 'is shoulder back in but it 'urts 'im like 'ell. Whatever you put on 'is wounded leg, once we got the black muck off of it, it looked good, inflammation's down. The other chap, Grant, surgeon's strapped 'im up and lying down is helping 'im. That wound on 'is 'ead's not too deep but there's no doubt he's got a touch of the sunstroke. He's delirious."

The rains came. From being dry and dusty the camp turned into a quagmire. The horses churned the dusty soil into thick red mud and thunderstorms raged to and fro across the gray African sky. At night forked lightning ripped jagged patterns across the black clouds and lit the veld with vivid flashes of spasmodic splendour.

Lord Chelmsford had arrived during the evening of the day that Josh and Cliff arrived. He was now aware of the full impact of the disaster. Six companies of the 24th Regiment had perished along with six full companies of the Warwickshire's and a large contingent from the Royal Artillery, the Natal Mounted Police and the Natal Native Regiments. One thousand five hundred men had perished, not to mention the two thousand Zulu bodies scattered across the hills of Zululand. Rorke's Drift had just held out, at a huge loss of Zulu lives. He was a depressed and worried man with awkward questions lying ahead of him. He hastily convened a court of enquiry at Helpmekaar.

For Josh it was a confusing couple of weeks. All his adult friends were ill and the military organisation, routine and discipline, were quite beyond his comprehension.

"They talk to me but I can't understand them," he confided to Johnston.

"Ay," Johnston nodded knowingly, "it's the different accents'll get you, lad."

Then, seeing Josh's puzzled face, "We're all from the same land, lad, but from different parts, each part speaks the language different... takes a while to catch-on to what they're all saying."

He watched the boy's worried expression, "And you mustn't forget they are all very nervous. We could be attacked any moment and then they've

82

to think of their comrades. Many friends died at Isandhlwana and Rorke's Drift and there's concern for any caught by the Zulu's."

Josh looked at him in surprise. "There'd be none kept by the Zulus," he explained to Johnston. "No, they'd let the spirits out and move on."

It was Johnston's turn to look puzzled.

"Let them out… what's that mean, lad?"

"They'd kill them, sir, rip open their stomachs and remove their hearts…"

Johnston went pale and stared disbelievingly at him.

"It's what they've always done," Josh explained rapidly, "It releases the spirits to return to their ancestors."

"They always do this after a battle?" Johnston queried weakly.

"Yes, it must be done so. How else could they move on to the next world?"

Josh didn't mention it but he knew that they would probably also have killed many of the oxen and the horses in a wild frenzy of blood letting. He recalled his tribal elders talking of this on many occasions as they related the stories of past battles.

"My God!" Johnston exclaimed, "Don't tell anyone else this, lad. They'll only think you heartless. It's not the white man's way."

Josh absorbed this strange difference in silence. He longed to find out more from Johnston but he sensed that the man did not wish to talk any further.

Between storms, Josh was sitting in the sun outside Cliff's tent one day when he overheard two orderlies talking about him.

"He's a strange one, him and that dog what goes everywhere with him," one man remarked.

"You're right there!" the other replied. "Looks like one of us but behaves more like an African… you seen him sitting on his haunches, relaxing?"

"Aye," the other man replied, "and he has no respect for rank. Treats us the same as he treats that lieutenant, young Linden-Brentwood… Seem to get on well they do."

"Well 'spose it takes all sorts to make this world, Jimmy. He'd look odd alongside my wee children but he'd sure outrun any of them. Thank God he's here to help with Johnston, Trainer and Grant and that other man, the one called Clifford."

"Yes, an' him a Yank… did you realise that?"

"Thought he wasn't speaking like anyone I'd heard before, when he was delirious!" the other replied.

The voices faded away as the men moved off to another tent.

Josh sat silently trying to absorb what he had just heard and to make sense of it. He was suddenly aware of someone in blue uniform standing looking down at him. He looked up into the quizzical face of Lieutenant Jocelyn Linden-Brentwood, the officer who had met them outside the camp on their arrival.

"Like to help me with the horses?" he queried.

Josh nodded gratefully.

"Yes, I'd like that."

The two walked away together to examine the Colonel's horse that had gone lame.

"You say nothing about yourself, young Josh," Linden-Brentwood said as they worked together on the leg.

"There's nothing to say," Josh assured him with a laugh. "I'm going down to Port Natal with Cliff. I'll know more then. Perhaps I'll work with him."

"I hope you'll get some education," Linden-Brentwood teased him, adding more seriously, "you've a way with animals and people. I'd like to sponsor you for the army, but first you must get more schooling, lad."

"How'd you know I've not been to school?" Josh asked defensively.

"I talked to Johnston, he told me your story and he thinks the sun shines out of you. You come very highly recommended." He grinned at Josh.

There was silence between them for a few moments.

"Seriously, Josh, I'd like to introduce you to cavalry riding, polish your technique and show you how the British Army works. We need lads like you."

Josh felt quite swamped by this attention. To be accepted by this man who to him seemed like a God. He had no words to express his feelings.

"Just think about it, lad. When you're ready, I'll speak to your guardian, Clifford."

Just then an orderly came over and said that Cliff was asking for Josh.

"He's bad, he's delirious, but your name keeps coming up."

Josh ran on ahead, feeling guilty because he had left Cliff when the orderly came in, and had meant to return in a short time.

Now that Johnston was better and back on his feet, he often relieved Josh at Cliff's bedside. Carefully Josh put his arm behind Cliff's shoulders and levered him forward to give him some sips of water. His eyes were feverish and his face flushed. The orderly came in behind him.

"I think he's reaching the crisis. You'll need to be with him all night to see him through. I'll come in when I can."

With sporadic help from the orderly, Johnston and Josh sponged Cliff down and kept watch, steadily feeding him sips of water all night and Zenda sat for much of the time with his head resting on the pillow, eyes fixed on Cliff's face. The surgeon came in once and shook his head, doubting that his civilian patient would pull through.

"Fortunately," the surgeon commented as he felt Cliff's pulse, "he is a strong, healthy man. He is draining that strength but he has a tough constitution. It may carry him through." Glancing up at the boy's worried face, he added, "Dysentery really knocks the stuffing out of men, but some do survive."

As the first fingers of daylight shone into the tent the orderly came in and said he thought the worst might be over. He told the others to get some sleep. Josh went out to take gulps of cool morning air while Johnston pulled the other camp bed up and fell asleep next to Cliff.

Josh felt very shaken by the suggestion of death. Cliff was all he had. The man, the dog and the horses, had become his whole world. He felt totally bereft at the possibility of losing any of them. He was also very frightened at the thought of being alone in this strange European world where everyone else seemed to know exactly what was expected of them.

While he was outside he met one of the men of the Natal Native Horse, who was acting as a messenger for the field hospital. He asked him what "dysentery" was and the messenger consulted with someone else and returned a few minutes later. Then the two of them went into the veld together and returned just as the sun was putting in an appearance over the far hills. Using some of the embers from the previous night's fire, they pounded up a collection of plants which they then boiled gently, skimming off the scum and keeping the liquid on one side while the rest formed a soft black poultice with a pungent aromatic smell.

As the camp was beginning to come back to life, Josh took the cooled liquid in to Cliff while neither the doctor nor orderly were in the vicinity. He woke Johnston up and together they began to slowly feed it to Cliff, little by little over the next few hours and days. The poultice they smeared over Johnston's leg wound.

Two days later the doctor returned from Rorke's Drift.

"And what is this?" he enquired of the orderly as he examined Johnston's wound.

"That looks terrible, sir," the orderly agreed, "right terrible stuff, sir. But, sir, if you will look at the wound, you will see a great improvement."

The doctor sniffed, "I've enough problems without enquiring too closely into this. It's doing alright, we'll turn a blind eye to the source."

Johnston looked relieved.

"He's certainly feeling much better, sir."

The doctor nodded and hurried off.

Josh noticed that Clifford was at last finding it possible to keep down the herbal liquid. The cramps became less severe and the fever was abating. He still had wild dreams, bordering on delirium. Once he sat up, shouting wide-eyed that an Indian with a tomahawk was upon them. Another time he appeared to fight off an attack from an animal of some sort and once he called for his mother to come back.

"Is he from the Americas?" the surgeon asked Josh curiously.

"Yes sir, he lived with the Indians for a time and rode their horses," the boy explained.

"He has a strong, wiry physique, the sort that comes from living a hard, tough, outdoor existence," the surgeon commented, "it looks as though he will pull through. His pulse is stronger and I think his temperature may be down a fraction." He pointed to Johnston.

"Get yourself off now, Private, you must rest and sleep while that leg heals, the lad will sleep by his side… but I think we are over the worst."

The surgeon rubbed his hand across his eyes.

"Could do with a good night's sleep myself. Not much chance though. All this wet weather has put the Buffalo River into spate and hundreds of bodies have been washed down. I've told them to be careful about the drinking water but I fear it may be too late; we've an epidemic of fever and dysentery upon us. They're dropping like flies." He rose slowly and straightened his back painfully.

Josh sponged Clifford down again and when the orderly returned an hour later he found the boy asleep with his head on his arms next to the patient and the brindle dog stretched out on the man's other side. Cliff was breathing evenly and the high colour had faded.

The orderly told Josh the next morning, "The sight of you there fast asleep next to that man, it made me homesick. I took myself outside to look at that bright foreign moon sailing in the star-spangled southern sky an' for a moment I imagined I was home in Warwickshire with my kid brother an' his spaniel, all together, an' safe, an' waiting for the pigeons to rise over a summer cornfield."

86

Trainer was up and gathering strength. He came in to sit with Johnston and Josh as Cliff began to improve. He was thinner, leaner, but he had regained his dry humour.

"I've not much memory beyond the morning we began that walk towards Helpmekaar. But I do remember the afternoon before and that big Zulu crashing to the ground when a stone from somewhere in the sky suddenly hit him! What a shot, boy, what a shot! There I was thanking the Almighty for his intervention and it turned out to be a small lad, a real live David and Goliath situation, hey lad?"

"Hey," said Johnston, "you're forgetting the lad doesn't know the story of David and Goliath. I'll fill in your missing education, lad!"

Cliff was still very weak but he was improving by the day and Josh was able to raise a watery smile from him as he recounted his experiences round the camp, his formal riding lessons with Lieutenant Linden-Brentwood and the gossip he collected from the grooms and cooks. He would perch on a camp stool, tilting restlessly to and fro as he described the military splendour of Lord Chelmsford and his staff.

"Mind you," Cliff said with some amusement to Johnston, "he has learned more about the horses than the men!"

"Could be he's chosen the better 'arf of this army!" Johnston replied, grinning cheerfully.

They had been at Helpmekaar for three weeks when Trainer came in to say goodbye. His leg was mended and he had been ordered to join his regiment. Johnston had been assigned to take Grant down to Durban and see him onto a ship bound for Cape Town. Grant's ribs were much improved but he remained rather vague and depressed and it seemed likely that after a break at the hospital in Cape Town, he might well be invalided out of the army if he had not improved.

"I'm doing alright on my feet now," Cliff commented to Josh. "It's time we pressed on to the port and found out what's been happening down there."

"Give it two or three days, and meanwhile you can help us with the other men," the surgeon advised. "By then you'll be fit for a long ride, or if you're not you'll know all about it!"

On the third day Cliff awoke feeling almost back to normal.

"Get the horses organised," he instructed Josh, "I'll go talk to the doc, thank him for his kindness, then we'll head on for port Natal."

Arriving back from Port Natal, Johnston came in to see them.

"I've been instructed to stay here a while longer. Lord Chelmsford's got to decide what to do with us men, the remnant of a regiment. I'm going to miss you both, especially you, lad. You feel like my own!"

He looked at Cliff, "Play fair by this one, he's special." He looked again at Josh. You come to old England, lad, an' you need a helping hand, you contact me through the barracks – Royal Artillery, the 24th. You remember this, lad."

Josh nodded, feeling too choked to say much, but he went forward and the two hugged with a huge bear hug and Johnston wiped his sleeve across his eyes.

Zenda sensed the change and was delighted to be on the move. Charity and Jackalet reacted with high sprits and several of the soldiers turned out to wish them well. The tall Lieutenant Lindon-Brentwood waved them off as he had welcomed them. He pressed a coin into Josh's hand.

"Spend it for me one day in Ireland! And remember my offer if you want to join the army. The War Office in London will always find me. He shook hands with Cliff, saluted them smartly, and hurried off.

It was 80 miles to Pietermaritzburg, and early March was proving hot and sticky. The sun was rising as they moved off.

"Come on, Cliff!" Josh shouted as he took off on Jackalet in a mad, joyous gallop across the veld.

Cliff laughed, took off his hat and waved it in the air. How he wished he too could get rid of his emotions as easily. However, the surgeon's words of caution still rang in his ears. He was very aware that his stomach was unlikely to react well to boisterous activity and a long ride in steadily increasing heat. He found himself settling into a sedate canter while watching with amusement and some envy as the boy and pony disappeared into the distance in a whirlwind of dust.

He was going to miss the youngster when he finally left for Ireland. He mused to himself about the possibility of a farm in the rolling hills of Zululand with Josh to help him establish it. Then he brought himself hastily back to reality with the thought of the cash needed for the project. Now that he had actually found the boy and when he had brought him safely to Natal, he must write to the grandmother in Ireland.

Last time he was down in Natal his old friend, John Robinson, editor of the *Natal Mercury*, had found him the family name. It was Barton, Caroline

Barton, and he had promised to try and contact the family in Cliff's absence. However, he was aware that while John had a nose for news he did like proof before he took action and he had been sceptical about stories of the white child.

"This country runs on rumours... half of them aren't true. One cannot raise hopes only to find that some drunken prospector has dreamt it up round a whisky-sodden fireside," he had warned Cliff.

Cliff resigned himself to the probability that John had done nothing. Ah, well, he thought, it will be a letter out on the next mail boat and then perhaps a two-month wait for a reply. I'll have to do a bit of trading or take a job round the port.

At that point Cliff was again aware of the galloping hooves as boy and pony tore back towards him, slowed up, whirled round and pulled to a halt by his side.

"Wow, that was a fantastic gallop!" Josh remarked, his eyes sparkling, his body covered in fine red dust. "What's next, Cliff? Is Pietermaritzburg like Lydenburg? Will we stay there? Will we see Private Johnston? He told me about the sea, I can't wait to see it for myself! Will the army be there? Isn't it good to be back on the road? Look at Zenda, he's glad to be moving again!"

"Alright, alright," drawled Cliff, lifting his hands above his head in a gesture of good-natured defeat. He slowed Charity to a walk and the boy drew in next to him and they rode in contented companionship as Cliff tried to answer the questions.

They camped under the stars that night and reached Pietermaritzburg towards the end of the following day. It was an attractive tree-lined town. The wide streets were edged by long, low, white houses with shady verandas and colourful gardens. It was a severely subdued town, frightened by the unexpected defeat of its protecting army and preparing for a Zulu attack at any time. A town in mourning, having lost many sons and husbands amongst the colonial forces massacred at Isandhlwana.

Nevertheless, Josh was delighted by everything he saw. The neat shiny horse-drawn traps, polished bridles, tidy white houses and the pretty women.

"What are the ox-wagons coming in for?" he asked Cliff as the horses rode up the main street.

Cliff looked round. "Some of them are bringing farm produce for the market and many of them are from the army, looking to buy food for the troops." He pointed across to another building, "That's the school, lad, it's where you ought to be to right now, learning to read and write!"

Josh stared curiously at the building, wondering what it would be like to be inside it.

"Why don't they work outside? Why inside a building?"

"Too distracting for most boys! Look over there, that big white building is the cathedral."

"What's that?"

"It's like the church in Lydenburg, remember? It's a much bigger one for a much bigger town and it governs some of the smaller churches. I'll take you inside."

They hitched their horses to the hitching post outside the church and Cliff led him inside. Josh was awed by the height of the building and by the peace and tranquillity he felt inside it.

"It's beautiful," he whispered, glancing round.

"Sadly," said Cliff, as they left, "there have been many funerals here for men killed at Isandhlwana and Rorke's Drift."

"Yes," said Josh, "from here they will travel safely to their ancestors."

Cliff looked slightly taken aback and then agreed.

The next day they moved on towards the coast, making their way down the mountains towards the gentle hills which led on to the sea. The weather became stickier and the plants more exotic the lower they went. Then Josh saw it. They had just rounded a bend and had a clear view over the tops of lush green trees, when suddenly he became aware of a vast blue sheet which shimmered gently before merging with the matt blue of the horizon. He reined in Jackalet and stared.

"That's the sea!" he exclaimed in tones of wonder. "It's very, very large!"

Cliff turned and looked at his face and laughed.

"It's the Indian Ocean, lad, and it's very deep. There are mountains down in those depths, and fish and monsters unknown to us landlubbers! Great ships sail across its surface with their canvas sails billowing in the wind and now steam ships are doing the same, carrying goods to all parts of the world."

Josh was staring at it, hypnotised.

"Terrible storms blow its waters into massive troughs and towering waves and sometimes the ships do not return to port," Cliff continued, "You must respect the sea and never underestimate its surly moods or the great winds that whip up its surface."

"Come on," Josh urged Jackalet forward, "Let's try to get closer, I want to look at it some more."

They camped that night in the rolling hills at the base of the mountains beneath the scarlet flower-bedecked branches of a flame tree. They watched the sun lower itself like a great luminous orange orb, over the rim of the surrounding hills. The monkeys chattered in the trees and the mosquitoes hummed and droned hopefully over their protective nets.

The next day they rode slowly into bustling port Natal, with its busy harbour and a general air of enterprise and excitement. The presence of the military and the huge back-up needed to keep them supplied and provisioned was forcing the sleepy little port into a frenzy of activity. It was situated on a sea lagoon, sheltered and protected from the waves and winds of the ocean by a long bluff and a hazardous sand spit; it said much for the enterprise of its founders that it already boasted the first railway in Southern Africa, which connected Bluff Point with the town. The new railway line up to Pietermaritzburg was almost complete. By constant dredging the sand spit was kept navigable for small ships. These ships lay bobbing at anchor on the long timber wharf disgorging their cargo and crew into the neat little town.

"You see the large ships," Cliff explained to Josh, pointing into the distance beyond the harbour, "they can't get in because it's too shallow and those little ships going busily to and fro, they move the goods and passengers to the quay."

Josh felt quite overwhelmed. Partly it was the presence of the sea and its steady whispering and crashing as the waves rolled to and fro, and partly it was the sights and smells which seemed to fill all his senses. He was aware that Cliff was watching him with considerable amusement as he sat his horse in lose-legged comfort while his head pivoted from side to side, an expression of bewildered delight on his face.

"Those buildings over there are new," Cliff pointed to the splendid law courts and the adjoining post office in the tree-lined main street. "Suddenly the British authorities are interested in spending money on the town. A war has some advantages for the citizens!"

Cliff had his "home" in a room at the back of "Rosie's Bar" on East Street. This was a long standing arrangement with the plump, motherly owner of the establishment. He paid her a nominal rent while he was away and presents from his trips into the interior whenever he came back. In return she allowed him to keep his few belongings permanently in the room and her girls only used it if business was booming and bed space short. Rosie managed the impossible. She ran a respectable and clean bar with music and pretty girls up front, and for her special customers, the wealthy traders and ship's captains, she could supply a pretty extra in her back bedrooms. It was all clean and as respectable as a small seaport could manage, dominated by the presence of the blousy Rosie, with her voluptuous bosom, creaking corset and the gaudy billowing folds of her lavender-scented dress. Her second-in-command was an equally large but somewhat squatter Zulu woman of uncertain years, who dressed with the same wild abandon as her mistress (usually in her cast-offs) and was known to all and sundry as "Bertha the Bubbler". The name had arisen way back in time when she had been found by Rosie as a small child, abandoned on the banks of the Umbilo (the bubbler) river where it ran down into the lagoon. Rosie had adopted her and the two worked as a cheerful, noisy team of extroverts, remembered fondly by many a homesick young sailor, as Aunty Rosie and Bertha Bubbler.

To Josh's startled consternation he was immediately engulfed in the folds of Rosie's ample bosom. He came up for air through the lavender-scented waves and found himself immediately the most celebrated of Rosie's customers.

"A gift for me?" she declared mischievously, "Always Cliff brings me some little thing! Wait until the girls meet you, ducks! This'll be a story for the town. Bertha, see what we have here?"

Bertha bustled in, threw her hands in the air, slapped her ample thighs and declared herself delighted to meet the young gentleman... "To whom does he belong?"

"To me, Bertha, to me!" cried the exuberant Rosie, while Josh squirmed uncomfortably and wished himself safely back in the army camp.

"Cliff's gift, girl... an orphan, found in a kraal in the Zoutpansberg."

Bertha stared closely at him. Suddenly the smile had gone. Her eyes narrowed in the folds of the plump brown cheeks.

"You not have him!" she declared emphatically, glaring at Rosie.

The sudden change to open hostility took everyone by surprise.

"Bertha!" Rosie exclaimed in surprise, for once at a loss for words.

"*Bertha* is Rosie's orphan," Bertha declared defensively, indicating herself with her thumb. "Nobody else... You take him back to the kraal, Mister Cliff... right now you take him back!" She stamped her foot to emphasize her ill-feeling.

"Okay, girls, okay, let's start again!" Cliff leapt in hurriedly. "He won't be staying long. He has to return to his people in Ireland. Don't worry, Bertha, he belongs to me and to Zenda."

"Bertha, you jealous old bag!" Rosie had finally recovered from her dumbfounded surprise and found her voice.

"I'm joking, girl, J O K I N G, making fun, teasing you. What has happened to you, tickle up those funny ribs, girl – he doesn't *really* belong to me!"

The compassion for which Rosie was famous suddenly came to the fore. She put a plump arm round Bertha's defensively hunched shoulders,

"Of course you're mine... even if I do have to share you with that old rogue, Petrus, now and again... I couldn't manage without you, Bertha. Here, have my hankie, instead of your sleeve. Now, don't make the poor boy feel so silly. Go and get some drinks for us all and we'll have them on the stoop" (veranda) "while we hear about Cliff's trip."

Josh had hastily manoeuvred himself out of Rosie's grasp and taken cover behind Cliff. He didn't care for the malevolent glance which Bertha directed at him as she flounced from the room.

Rosie threw up her arms in despair.

"I'm sorry, Cliff, I forgot about her insane jealousy! She's kindness itself unless she feels threatened or she thinks someone threatens me. We've had some ticklish situations once or twice... you remember some of them! Josh, just leave her be, she'll get over it."

After a day or two, life settled down and Josh began to find his way round the busy port and back to Rosie's Bar without getting lost. It was still a wonderland of smells and sights but he was making friends with the girls although Bertha still scowled. He and Zenda avoided her as much as possible.

Cliff seemed to be busy and he left the grooming and exercising of the horses to Josh and told him to help Rosie whenever he could. Rosie found a camp bed for him but took it away when she found Zenda was using it while Josh preferred the floor.

"What a nerve – a dog on my bedding!"

She kept him busy polishing the metal on the harness and the buggy of her smart little trap. He didn't mind because he sat on a mounting block in the courtyard and watched life going by while he polished.

As Cliff had suspected, the dapper little editor with the bristling moustache and bushy eyebrows, John Robinson, had not contacted Josh's grandmother in Ireland. He was amazed and delighted to hear that the rumour had proved accurate and immediately claimed the credit for the *Natal Mercury*.

It was a couple of days later, having read the large headline: "Lost Boy found in Zoutpansberg Kraal", that it dawned on Cliff that some form of remuneration for the reporter/hunter might be in order.

"After all," he said, sitting casually on the corner of the editor's desk, "it was me who took the risks and now I need to pay the boy's keep because you didn't do *your* bit and write to the grandmother!"

John Robinson laughed tolerantly.

"You Yanks only think of money! I'm surprised you're not digging up diamonds by the ton instead of putting your life at risk over a kid! Sure, I'll pay you, it's a good story with the added bonus of a bit from the kid about life on the camp at Helpmekaar! By the way, the letter has gone off to Mrs Caroline Barton in Ireland saying that her grandson has been found at last and a certain Clifford Wilson is looking forward to the reward and further instructions!"

Clifford grinned at him, scooped up the cash and went off happily contemplating which of Rosie's girls he would take to eat on the sea front that evening.

Clifford was inclined to enjoy life as it came. He had never been one for planning and anyway he had no ultimate goals to achieve except for the possibility of that farm. He relied on his wits, an easy charm and an eye for a "good deal" – usually in horses, hunting or trading. The room at the rear of Rosie's Bar was his first "home", a place where he could return to, where he was sure of a welcome and where people cared whether he was alive or dead.

Men liked him because he could drink with the best of them, gamble at cards, shoot accurately, ride efficiently and had a multitude of tales to tell which spanned several continents. Although he was not particularly aware of it, he also had a reputation as an honest dealer and a man who could be relied upon in a crisis, a man who stuck by his friends but who kept his own council.

Years on his own, or in male company, had not made him at ease with women. He usually shied away from close relationships. He was happiest with Rosie and the bar girls, who expected nothing from him and treated him with fond, friendly disrespect. They were perfectly happy to have him roll into bed with them whenever he felt the need and no charge was ever made. They soon found that if anyone tried to get closer, or became possessive, Cliff would move off to someone else or take himself away on a new trip into the interior while things calmed down. Sometimes they chided him about his solitary bachelor habits, but he laughed and shrugged and refused to be drawn into arguments on the matter.

"I love all women," he would drawl, "I'm not partisan now girls, am I?"

Now for the first time he was a man with a responsibility. He felt uncomfortable and slightly irritated by this new role. It tied him down and forced him to take a reluctant look at his way of life.

He found that having Josh sleeping on the floor next to his bed inhibited his usual bachelor life style and meant that even the easy-going Rosie raised an eyebrow from time to time as he forgot himself with one of her girls or rolled back to his room in the early hours of the morning unable to find the door handle.

"Goddamit," he moaned to the youngest girl, Jessica, "I'm not his fucking FATHER! You'd think I was, the way everyone gets prissy when he's nearby!"

As far as Josh was concerned Cliff could do no wrong. Whatever Cliff did was obviously the standard pattern for an European bachelor. He watched intrigued and the girls teased him.

In the kraal all had been ordered and ordained. At certain ages, and stages of the moon, the youngsters of the tribe were taken on one side by elders and initiated into the next stage of their development. There were unwritten rules handed down through the generations which guided sexual behaviour, protected the young to puberty and then initiated them into adulthood by stages. These laws were tailored to the tribe and punishment for breaking them was severe, at best banishment and at worst, death.

However, Josh was very much aware that this strange new world seemed to have no secure barriers, no guidelines, no watching elders. He felt like a minnow darting round in an unknown lake trying hard to discover whether the fish were friendly, without actually getting eaten in the process.

These sweet smelling, prettily dressed girls were a constant source of amazement to him. They could be distant and haughty, or warm and friendly. Jessica was the youngest, she was like a cheerful butterfly, all flounces and frills and brown ringlets tied up with a matching bow. She was sitting with her arm draped across his shoulders on the top step of the veranda, the sweet smell of her perfume mingling with her natural body warmth. He was suddenly very aware of the delicious smooth roundness of her arm where her skin touched his, her mischievous brown eyes flecked with touches of gold and the slightly pouting pink lips round which she ran the damp darting tip of a pink tongue from time to time as she chatted.

He could not quite account for it to himself afterwards. It was like a wave of emotion which seemed to rise up from his penis to his head and swamp him in a bodily yearning which would brook no argument or commonsense. Almost to his surprise, he found himself wrapping his arms round his pretty companion and bending her back while his mouth searched for that damp wet cavern where her pink tongue was nestling and at the same time his body moved against her breasts in excited yearning.

He was very quickly brought back to reality by a hefty slap across his face and a shove which moved him bodily across the red polished step and put a distance of several feet between them.

"You bad boy, Josh! You are too young to taste the fruit. Is this what they let you do in the kraal? Rosie would have a fit if she saw you behaving like this on the public street." Almost without drawing breath she continued as he picked himself up, "What do you think the people in the road will think, this is a decent house you know!"

Josh could not understand the strange sensation which had overcome him. He often had boyish dreams and laughed and talked salaciously of girls with Napedi and the boys in his iNtanga, but it had all been noise and boasting. This was something different, a reality which was far stronger than he had expected. He felt shaken and ashamed. He had obviously done the wrong thing. For some reason it was acceptable from Cliff but not from him. He got up hastily and walked away, red-faced and embarrassed, heading for the stable to think it all through.

Presently Jessica came to the door and, leaning on the closed half, looked in at him as he pretended not to see her and busied himself with the yard broom.

"Don't worry, luv," she said gently. "I'm not mad really. I won't say nuffing but sometime you an' I better talk."

She wandered off, leaving him to struggle with his own confused emotions.

Clifford sighed when Bertha told him what she had seen from the window.

"You better get him off to where he belongs, Mister Cliff. It ain't right him being with all these girls, it'll only lead to trouble. Rosie, she won't like it neither!"

"She doesn't need to know, Bertha. Come on, be a sport, he can't go until his grandmother sends his ticket and Rosie is only being kind letting him stay with me," he pleaded.

Bertha was staring straight ahead, her face expressionless.

"He hasn't got anywhere to go and the girls can look after themselves *and* him if necessary. Don't you worry about *their* respectability, it's the lad's innocence you should be protecting!"

He put his arm round her shoulders and drew her soft bulk towards him.

"Go on, Bertha, you're so soft on the sailor boys… why be hard on this lad? He's much younger than any of them and he's lost, like you were once."

Bertha laughed suddenly, a harsh little laugh, and pushed him away.

"This is your fault, Mister Cliff, what you want to bring this one here for? He's no good, not for Bertha anyway. He's kraal boy… but not really… why they kept him but no one want Bertha?"

Cliff sighed. He'd not foreseen himself growing fond of the boy. He was meant to be like another load of pelts – a source of cash – perhaps the chance to buy a farm and settle down. Now here he was, protecting him as though he was his own brother.

Bertha, he realised, was jealous and afraid that Rosie might mother Josh instead of her. She hadn't minded Rosie mothering "her girls" and "her sailors", but Josh was a direct threat.

When Bertha was happy she laughed easily but once she got a bee in her bonnet about something she became very stubborn, sullen and rather malevolent. The girls, he knew, loved her because she loved and protected them, but they all agreed that there was a dark side to her nature.

"Perhaps 'er father were an old wizardy man, you know, one of them witchdoctors who cast spells around in the big kraal in the mountains," one of the girls had suggested to Cliff.

"She does funny things sometimes. Gets a sort of wild look in her eyes and mutters a lot, no one can understand, an' she makes potions an' disappears off on her own. Rosie gets mad but she won't say nuffing to 'er. Says she's 'er baby an' there's lots of good in 'er. If you ask me," she had continued, "there's lots of bad too, but she ain't done me no 'arm an' I certainly wouldn't cross 'er!"

"Yes, yes," another of the girls interrupted, "A big black man turned up at kitchen door once, tried to kill her. No one ever knew why, but Rosie said it was her guess someone had tried to drown her as a baby and Rosie had disturbed them and now they had heard the story of Bertha Umbilo."

There was a giggle from another girl, leaning back in a nearby chair.

"Do you remember, Rosie hit him over the head with a bottle. He ran away and he ain't come back! He's a wise man, she keeps a knobkerrie behind the kitchen door now!"

Cliff scratched his cheek thoughtfully.

Just then Bertha bustled in, carrying a tray.

"Bertha," Cliff remarked, "you've half the British Merchant Navy in your pocket, you and Rosie, the girls all love you, don't worry about the past. You'd be dead if Rosie hadn't found you and she couldn't run this place without you. The boy will be gone soon. Leave him be, Bertha, he's no danger to you," he reasoned persuasively.

But commonsense was not what Bertha wanted to hear. She pushed impatiently past Cliff and headed for the kitchen. He watched her kick the door open and disappear purposefully towards the old black range, her shoulders hunched and tense.

Oh, oh, trouble, thought Cliff. She'll be up to her potions before long. So much for that stage coach job I saw advertised! I'd better give thoughts to something round the town so that I can keep an eye on Josh, or my cash and farm will disappear like a whiff of witchdoctor's smoke! He kicked the veranda post in acute frustration.

A couple of days later, just as he was, in desperation, about to consider joining the town militia, a friend with a couple of small "lighters" which plied between the jetty and the big ships beyond the sandbank, asked him if he would like to take charge of them while he went inland for a few months. With the job, went a couple of rooms on the seafront and he and Josh were soon established there with the girls dropping in from time to time to check on their well-being.

Josh was thrilled. He was enlisted as a junior deckhand and once the first pangs of sea sickness passed, he began to enjoy the noisy, colourful life of the lighter, plying to and fro, watching the tides and carrying people and cargo across the dangerous shallows of the sandbar.

He blossomed under the ready teasing of the harbour hands. His language rapidly expanded to include all the most colourful words of the English language, and over the months he was aware of growing physically. He was beginning to fill out and gaining confidence and self-assurance. It didn't go unnoticed that Jessica was frequently down at the jetty to meet him when they finished for the day.

Jessica too had grown and matured. It was a day when Cliff was kept late unloading a gunship of the Royal Navy, that the two found themselves alone in the rooms. Josh was suddenly aware of his emotions beginning to swamp him in a wave of desire as he moved close to Jessica. This time she didn't push him off. This time her body responded to his touch and she slid her arms round his neck and nestled her lithe young body against his strong suntanned frame. The feel of matching desire suddenly encompassed them both. Her breasts beneath the lace blouse pushed into his chest and her lips reached up to his mouth. He dragged her closer and found the tenderness of her damp mouth and he groaned with pleasure as his loins began to rub against her frame. He picked her up and laid her on the bed, her hands pushing back his white shirt with the same eagerness that he struggled with her blouse buttons. Suddenly her skirt was on the floor together with his trousers and he found himself running his hands over the silky whiteness her body as she felt down to his penis and arching her back she guided him into the soft dampness of her body. For both of them this was a first step into adulthood and tender yet exciting love with the promise of passion to follow.

Chapter Six

IRELAND – May 1879

EMMIE LIFTED THE last sheet out of the tub and carried it outside to hang on the line and be flapped dry by the wild wind as it blew across the hills and bogs, bending and dragging at everything in its way. She could smell the scent of the hills in its gusts, moss and bracken and sheep, and a tinge of its origins, a slightly salty tang from the sea itself. As she battled to fasten the dripping sheet to the line she felt its damp folds tugging at her arms and flapping round her face, she was also aware of being watched from afar.

In a small village like this news spread fast and there were many who had always disapproved of the way the O'Connell children had been allowed to play with the family up at the big house. For some it was seen as letting down their religion and others were merely jealous of the advantages it gave the family who were already more prosperous than most people in this depressed area. These feelings were kept carefully covered. After all, Padraigh O'Connell was not only the local miller but also a jovial, cheerful man who smiled at everyone and always had time to exchange a few words with his customers. Both he and his wife worked hard and had suffered with the rest of the community when the blight hit or the price of wheat rose. However, Emmie was well aware that this did not stop the gossips from relishing the situation when word spread, as inevitably it did, that the O'Connells' eldest daughter had been caught in the hay with young master Alfred from the big house.

Emmie trapped the last of the reluctant sheets in a tinker's peg and jammed it to the line with a violence that relieved some of her feelings about self-righteous locals, and made the line jump as though a banshee was using it as a tightrope.

Back in the house her mother was lining up the next job.

"An' now I need the vegetables cleaned," she told her daughter as she came through the door.

"That old critcher from up the road is standing by her wall looking over at us," Emmie complained.

"An' it's not only her, my girl. Since your uncle marched ye back it's been most of the village as has been watching this house. I'm told by Beth Molloy, the parlour maid up there," Colleen nodded over her shoulder in the general direction of the big house, "she says that the young master is to be sent to Africa to look for Miss Florence and her family."

Emmie moved towards the vegetables.

"Meanwhile, we got to sort out what to do with you, lass. Your Da, he's heartbroken. He'd set his heart on you marrying young Rory. Then along comes Rory's dad and says as how the whole thing is off, no son of his will marry a girl who'd play in the hay with a Protestant toff!"

"An' what if it had been a local lad – or even Rory himself?" Emmie couldn't hold back her indignation.

Colleen looked at her sideways. "It'd still have been a disgrace for your family but marriage would have sorted that out, it's happened afore. An' Duggie says Rory shouted at his dad, said he'd still have you, but the old man won't hear of it."

"I'm sorry, Ma, I know yous was set on it, but truly I'll find someone else. I just hate the way the man shouted and waved his stick outside our door so the whole neighbourhood was falling over themselves to enjoy the fun."

"My girl, no self-respecting family round here'd let you join them now. There's many apparently saying we always had it coming," Colleen commented tartly as she lifted the great black kettle back onto the hook over the hearth.

"Lot o' silly old biddies, you'd be thinking their daughters was all perfect!" Emmie said, digging viciously into a carrot.

She was aware of her mother biting her lip and looking sideways at her.

"So, I'm a silly old biddie 'cause I don't approve of what you done, girl? An' I'd like you to know, you's right, I don't an' all. An' ye Da taking his strap to you against his will, then him giving up, an' goin' out when you'd not make a sound, ant Duggie, Peggie an' little Sean all yelling like it was them as had been hit! It's not natural, girl, you showin' no shame!"

"Ma, I'm not thinking of you!"

"I know, nor your Da!"

"No, Ma, I'm right sorry about my family. Even Duggie got his nose bloodied at school. Mind you, they'll not try it again in a hurry."

"No, that McFee boy, his nose was broke ant he'll not call you a Jezebel again in front of your brother… but away from him…"

"I know Ma… ant Father Donohue turning up to sort out our sins, as directed by his housekeeper, an' you an' Da saying naught, an' him going away in a right temper, shouting about mixing with them heathen Protestants!"

"Now that's enough, girl! Give me them vegetables and we'll sort the stew."

Emmie woke before dawn and slid silently out of the bed she shared with little Peggie. She could hear steady breathing from the other bed where Duggie and Sean were curled up together. She was standing by the small window watching the first tentacles of dawn pushing through the clouds round the skyline, when she heard voices from the room next door. It was her parents. She moved closer to the door through to their room and listened.

"I blame myself, Padraigh, I let her go up there to play and to help. We've never minded them an' they was always kind when times were hard," she heard her mother saying quietly.

"And I spoilt her," her father replied. "She learnt the reading and writing and also she's so pretty…"

"At least the boy is to leave the country," Colleen said.

"Not that that really helps us, what if she's in the family way…?" The concern in her father's voice was very evident.

"No," Colleen interrupted hastily, "She's come on since then."

"Thanks be to God for that!" he replied.

"There's folks crossing the road to avoid me," she heard her mother say.

"Take no notice, gal, it's a bit of gossip an' not much else to talk about round here."

"What are we going to do, Padraigh?"

There was a long pause and then her father's voice said uncertainly:

"I'm not sure, it's a difficult time… with the harvest so late them… English panicked… all this wheat from America on the new fast steamers an' now there's a glut… prices are poor an' folks is struggling to pay their accounts…" his voice tailed away.

Emmie was aware of a pang of guilt. She realised that she had just added to his problems. After a moment her mother spoke out. This time she sounded more definite. It was the voice her mother used when she had come to a decision and there was to be no argument.

"It's not the lads who'll mind, it's their parents. They'll whinge an' whine if she steps over their thresholds. There is no hope of a marriage round here…"

Her father's voice broke in:

"McTaggert was in last week, he said we'd a filly with a bit of spirit but this would all blow over when the next piece of drama came along."

Her mother was on a track of her own:

"Padraigh, I've the plan. We must send her to my sister, Kathleen, in Longford. There they'll not know her and she can help Kathy with the little ones, look after the house ant teach them what she learnt at the school."

Emmie felt her heart miss a beat. She strained to catch her father's reaction, almost falling against the door in an effort to hear. There was a long pause.

"Maybe you're right. Sure I'll miss her but then perhaps she'll meet some lad over that way, someone who might bring her back here and be able to help in the mill." She could hear the growing enthusiasm in his voice.

"Ant what's this nonsense about singing – no decent girl sings – she needs marriage to settle her down. Yes, I've thought about it now, it's the only thing to do. Write to your sister an' we'll send her down by train or horse-car."

Duggie turned restlessly in the bed and Emmie drew back from the door and climbed back with the peacefully sleeping Peggie. Her mind was working frantically. The idea which had been circling round in her head was one of escape from Killarga, but not just to Longford. She intended to put pressure on Alfred-Otho to take her with him to Africa. The idea was vague but it seemed like the only way of making an escape to a more exciting future. Hadn't Alfred said to his father that he wanted to marry her? That must mean he liked her. She couldn't marry a protestant but she could travel with him. She hadn't the slightest intention of settling down here. She knew there was a world just waiting to be explored. Many local families had gone to America and some to Canada. She'd always envied those who had gone and been fascinated by their letters home to their relatives. Now she intended to go to Africa. She knew she could sing and surely with this and her youth, she would find work. One day she'd come back and build a fine house for Ma and Da, and the village would be sorry they'd turned their backs on her. They'd want to know her and be able to say that they had gone to school with her.

Africa sounded a long way away, but so was America. Father Donohue had spoken of missionaries and savages, but there must also be cities like Dublin. All she needed to know, she reasoned to herself, was when Alfred-Otho would be going. Then she intended to catch the same train but several stops down the line so that no one could see her and drag her off. How she would manage this she wasn't sure but she had a few pence put by in the small purse her grandmother had given her. One penny she had found down where the road crossed the stream. She had stood on it in her bare toes as she walked through the shimmering water. Another had come from Da as a special present for helping in the mill one busy week. Gran had given her one for her sixteenth birthday. She felt rich.

She wondered when Alfred would be leaving. Somehow the move to her aunt would need to be delayed. She wondered how she was going to keep it all to herself. Outwardly she must appear repentant but sorrowful, while inside she was filled with excitement and a froth of nervousness.

It was Duggie who eventually met Alfred. He was taking some milk up to the crossroads for the O'Byrne cart to collect when he was hailed by a rider cantering in from the Manorhamilton direction.

Alfred swung out of the saddle and strolled over to Duggie, leading his horse by the reigns.

"Duggie," he said, "would you please give your sister a message from me?"

Duggie nodded, hoping desperately that no one from the village was around and listening. He admired Alfred and was flattered by his friendliness, but after the rows at home...

"Tell her I'm off to Africa on the 20th. I'm going to take the train from Dromahair to Dublin the day before. We've had news of Florence's son and I'm to find him and bring him home. Mind you," he grinned broadly at Duggie, "not too fast if I can help it. I'd like to pick me up a few diamonds first. They say they're around for the gathering!"

Duggie was aware of the mixed emotions of envy and admiration. What a chance for adventure. How he wished he could go too.

"Sure, I'll tell her." To Duggie's annoyance his voice came out in an awed whisper.

"Tell her she's a great girl and I'm sorry about the fuss. I'll tell you all about Africa when I get back."

He ruffled Duggie's red hair and swung his stocky figure back onto the horse, adjusting his tailored tan riding jacket with care. He grinned down at Duggie, his eyes sparkling with excitement, waved his riding crop and shouted, "Africa next," as the horse moved to a brisk trot.

Duggie watched him ride off with feelings of frustration mixed with admiration. He was so obviously delighted with his lot and had no comprehension of the chaos he had caused in the O'Connell household.

"I should have told him that Emmie was being sent to live in Longford, all because of him!" Duggie muttered to himself. He kicked a stone against the can and as the clanging noise subsided he heard the rumble of the approaching milk cart.

On his way home, coming round the side of Patsy O'Brien's shop, Duggie was startled to bump into a school friend, Paddy, who handed him a note.

"It's from Rory, for Emmie" Paddy whispered.

"Is it now," Duggie replied, trying hard to sound casual.

"Read it!" Paddy nudged him. "I have!"

That was all the encouragement Duggie needed. He smoothed out the note with Paddy leaning over his shoulder.

Dear Emmie, Don't be worrying yourself. It'll all blow over. Just give the olders time to calm themselves. Rory.

"Shame there's no soppy stuff!" Paddy giggled.

"Don't think it's going to blow over," Duggie added. He turned conspiratorially to Paddy, "It's to Longford they're sending herself!"

Almost as soon as he had said it he regretted doing so. Too late, he thought to himself. Now it'll be all round the village. "Keep quiet 'bout that," he said over his shoulder to Paddy, but Paddy was already off down the alley-way between the houses.

He found Emmie in the house cleaning round the cooking fire. He handed her the note from Rory, raised his eyebrows and shrugged as she read it, pulled a face, and without comment rolled it up and flung it into the fire. Then he told her about Alfred, passed on the messages and waited for the tears and upset. Later he had to admit to himself that, despite his ten years of wisdom, he didn't understand females. To his consternation his messages had met with a grateful smile and an excited hug. He rolled his eyes to heaven and supposed the blessed Lady up there understood, but he was only a mortal man and he despaired.

Emmie's aunt wasted no time in responding to her sister and sent back a note to say that she would be happy to have Emmie to help her and that she would share a bed with the two youngest children. Plans were soon in progress and by deft manoeuvring Emmie managed to set the departure date set for the 19th. After some debate and hesitation it was decided that she might go by train.

"Ay, 'tis more money than the horse-drawn car but sure 'tis quicker, an' fewer changes for the lass," her father commented.

Aware that catching sight of Alfred boarding the train at Dromahair would rapidly change her parents' minds, she took Duggie into her confidence, letting him think she wanted Alfred's company to Longford.

"How am I to get them to take me to Ballintogher station instead?" she posed the problem to him.

Proud to be asked to help, Duggie came up with a solution. "Sure, Em, do you be remembering that Da has a sister, Mary, in Ballintogher. Say you'd like to say goodbye to her before you go off to Longford." He was rewarded with a kiss which he hastily wiped off.

"Ugh!"

Back in the house she broached the subject.

"It's a time since I saw Mary ant her wee ones, can we be going up to catch the train from Ballintogher?"

She saw her parents look at one another in some puzzlement. Relying on their feelings of guilt about the whole move to Longford, she smiled brightly and added, "After all, it'll be a time before I'm back to visit her."

Her mother shrugged, "We can go there, although it'll mean taking the cart an' donkey across the hill by the bog, but then, sure, your Aunty Mary, she'll be pleased to see us all."

Her father nodded silently, the puzzled expression still on his face.

Emmie leapt up and kissed them both, sealing the decision before they could change their minds. Her plans were falling into place.

The 19th was one of those traditional grey Irish days. A hazy drizzle dampened the soul and the hills and vales seemed swathed in misty sorrow. Emmie had the grace to shed a genuine tear as she said goodbye to the wee ones and Duggie and Gran, who were to mind the house while her parents took her in the donkey cart to Ballintogher. They left the little white and grey village in the early morning light just as the first early risers were lighting their lamps, making glowing squares of golden light stand out against the gloom. From there the road wound between low lichen-covered rocky walls marking off small farms, their mearing ditches absorbing the trickles of water which the misty, persistent rain was spreading across the fields. As they moved up onto higher ground the walls fell to fences and then to nothing. The road was rutted and sheep wandered across it peering short-sightedly for sustenance between the gorse and heather. As they came up on the hill above Killamummery a few weak rays of sunshine fought through the drifting cloud. Below they could see the village with its small stone church. Down in the dip they had to ford a stream. The donkeys picked their way hesitantly across the frothing water while Padraigh cracked his whip in encouragement. Another hour found them winding down the last bit of road to Ballintogher station with a soft glow of sunlight shafting through the hazy clouds.

Emmie and her parents were made welcome and children were moved round to make room for them at the large table in front of the kitchen fire.

"Ah, now, an' this is a pleasant shock," remarked Mary as she replenished the large brown tea pot. "An' it's to Longford you'll be travelling, girl, an' all on your own? I'm wishing it was here, to help me, that you were coming!"

Emmie was aware that she was being assessed. Mary's wondering why we came this way and whether I'm in the family way, she thought.

"I've always wanted to see beyond our village, an' this is my chance!" she said brightly.

Mary smiled. "Aren't you the adventurous one! You've come this long way so it's to the station we'll all come, and wave you off."

She went over to a barrel and lifted out some apples.

"I'm putting these in a basket for you to take to your aunt in Longford."

Emmie felt a twinge of guilt which she covered with a hug and a promise:

"I'll be along to see yous when I'm back again!"

Emmie's heart was beating with excitement as they all walked up to the station. She was praying that Alfred would not look out of the window. She need not have worried. The hissing and clanking of the steam engine and the noise of the farewells and the shouts of the children as they ran up and down the platform, meant that her parents were too bemused to do anything other than cling to her tearfully before they pushed her through the carriage door. She leant out of the window wiping the tears off her cheeks with her sleeve:

"I'll be fine, an' you'll be proud of me yet, Da. Look after Ma and the kids." Then the train was pulling away and they were becoming a haze of dots on the platform as she peered through her tears.

Reality took a moment or two to arrive. Then the magnitude of what she was planning began to dawn on her. She sat like a frozen statue, clutching her bag on her lap and staring woodenly at the seat opposite as she began to appreciate that if her plans came off it might be many months or years before she saw them all again. The bubble of excitement and ambition that had carried her along seemed to have burst. What had she done? A feeling of almost painful loneliness swept over her. If she went to Africa, she would be entirely dependent on herself, no loving family support. She felt very alone, very vulnerable and very frightened.

Emmie was aware that if the train had stopped at that moment, she would have leapt off and run back to Ballintogher as fast as her feet would carry her. Slowly the panic subsided. There was one solution. She could go to Longford, get off the train without seeing Alfred, and go to her aunt, exactly as expected. This realisation seemed to ease the load. Yes, she decided, this is what she would do. She chastised herself: Who was she to traipse off to Africa with no money and no prospects?

With this decision made, the trance-like state began to fade and she put her bag on the floor with the basket of apples and loosened her cloak. She shook her unruly red hair out of the hood where it had been captured for most of the trip and at the same time became acutely aware of the pensive stare of her only travelling companion in that part of the jolting, creaking compartment. Peering through her lashes she did not much like what she saw.

He was a broad built lad with a rather flat face and pale blue wandering eyes. His matted brown hair appeared to be plastered flat with grease and the skin over his ruddy cheeks seemed to have been pulled too tight. His mouth was a straight, inhospitable slit, but it was his eyes which frightened her... constantly moving. At first she could not think why this worried her so much. Then she realised, he did not appear to blink. The small eyes flashed across her, then away round the carriage and then back to her. She felt a prickle of fear run up her spine and she tried to see whether there was anyone further down the compartment. It was impossible to see over the seat backs and she felt unable to move, hypnotised with fear.

He's mad, she thought, just like poor Jake down by Tawnylea. But Jake was gentle and harmless and simple. This lad had an air of malevolence, a sinister brooding quality, like a bird of prey. Suddenly the eyes came to rest on her face. The thin lips opened slightly and a pale tongue dampened them:

"Give us 'n apple then, lass!" he leant forward as he spoke and one large, bloated red hand came out and grabbed an apple out of her basket. She cringed slightly and nodded.

As he jammed the apple into his mouth, the eyes never left her body. It was as though he had won the first round and was preparing for the next. Through the crunch of apple he spluttered out:

"Pretty, ain't ye! Who'd let a pretty gal like you travel alone?" He leant towards the window and spat out the apple core. Then wiped a large ham-like hand across his mouth to remove the residue of apple pulp.

"So, where you goin' then, Miss green eyes? Lost your tongue?"

Annoyance was beginning to submerge fear in Emmie.

"My friend is on the train," she said, trying to sound confident. "He'll be along in a minute."

He eyed her with his great head on one side and then laughed unpleasantly.

"A likely tale!" He leant towards her across the narrow aisle.

"You're all mine, lass, there ain't no one else in this compartment... An' I fancy a bit ov a roll!" His breath smelt of alcohol and the eyes glittered.

Emmie realised she would have to act fast. She jumped up and waved to-wards the back of the compartment. As he turned to see who she was greeting, she dodged passed him and sped down the aisle towards the connecting door to the next compartment. With surprising speed he leapt after her and yanked her back by the cloak, almost choking her in the process. One large arm was round her neck and the other was fumbling with the fastenings on her cloak. She yelled and kicked violently backwards. Fortunately, she caught his ankle with her small boot and he let slip his grasp as he yelled in pain. She ran as fast as she could and had her hand on the door handle as he caught up with her. He forced her against the door and was trying to turn her round as the train began to slow down for the level crossing at Balleygawley. The change in motion and the squeaking of the train as the driver applied his brakes, seemed to startle him and he relaxed his grip, enabling Emmie to get the door open enough to slide through onto the connecting platform between the coaches. She was just reaching for the next door when he burst out behind her and grabbed her cloak again. Fortunately for Emmie, precariously balanced on the rocking metal platform, the ticket collector chose that moment to open the door. He stared at her terrified face and let out a yell of consternation, pulling her towards him. The lad let go and turned back into the coach, jamming his weight against the door to stop the ticket collector from following him.

Emmie was engulfed in fear and determined to put as much distance between herself and the "mad one" as possible. She fled down the corridor and straight on to the next coach which was clearly marked FOR FIRST CLASS PASSENGERS ONLY. Suddenly, she saw Alfred in a small private compartment, sitting casually reading a paper. Feeling a wave of relief sweep over her she burst in and almost fell on him.

"Alfred, oh God! Oh God! Save me from the mad one."

Alfred was pleased with himself. He was feeling very much a man of the world. His father had taken him to his tailor and equipped him with a new hacking jacket, and a couple of pairs of new breeches. In his polished leather valise he had new shoes and boots and his mother had added several luxuries for the sea journey. As a concession to his medical studies he had thrown in a text book on tropical diseases. One thing he did not have in vast amounts was money. His passage to Cape Town had been booked by his father's office in Dublin. The preacher who had written to the family lived in Cape Town. It was hoped that through him, he, Alfred, would be able to get in touch with the soldier who had met the boy and the hunter. He was to pick up cash for the journey from his father's bank in Dublin.

Already he was putting Belhavel and his father's lectures behind him and looking forward to the adventure of a long sea trip with boundless possibilities for fortune hunting at the other end. Far from his mind was any thought of the nephew he was to find or his sister and her husband, and even further, any thought of that attractive but unsuitable young lady, Emmie O'Connell. Alfred, at twenty-one years of age, was casually aware that he found it very easy to be entirely selfish and self-centred. The passion of one moment could rapidly become the bore of the next.

The sudden arrival of Emmie, white-faced and shaking, completely smashed his personal image of himself as a debonair and unruffled young man of the world.

Staring at her disbelievingly he felt an unreasonable surge of anger at the way his privacy had been intruded upon and his vision of himself shattered. Overlooking her plea for help he found himself jumping up and moving back from her.

"What the hell are *you* doing here?" he barked unsympathetically.

The girl stopped and stared disbelievingly at him.

"Isn't it you, Alfred?" she asked in a puzzled tone.

"Of course it's me! I'm on my way to Dublin. But what on earth are you doing here, on this train? What's this about some mad person?" he asked, getting a better grip of himself but still feeling put out.

"Ah, sure Alfred, I'm sorry to fall in on you like this but I'm on this train to go to my Auntie in Longford, ant..." at this point she peered fearfully over her shoulder at the corridor, "this lad, he was sitting opposite me in an empty compartment ant suddenly..." She was beginning to shake again, "suddenly he was reaching for me… ant saying he wanted me… ant when I ran he came after me and grabbed me ant then," and now the tears were beginning to fall, "ant then I was between them compartments, on that shaking bit outside the door – ant sure I was that he would push me out onto the line, when this man in a flat hat, he grabbed me from the other side ant… ant here I am." She mopped her eyes with a corner of her cloak, but the tears kept coming.

"Oh Alfred, I wish I was home, I wish we'd never gone to the hay loft… ant me sent away to Longford, ant the terrible fuss in the village ant…" and here she let out a whimper and fell onto the seat beside him, "ant you not interested and not even knowing me!"

Putting her hands over her eyes, she began to sob, wild uncontrolled sobs which shook her shoulders and sent tears dripping through her fingers.

Alfred felt the last shreds of his self-satisfaction fading away. He wasn't used to female tears. This was beyond his experience. He had known his sisters to cry, but they were only his sisters and they did silly things. He had never known Emmie to cry. All the years she had been in and out of the house and running in the fields and paddling in the streams and fishing on the lake, she had never shed a tear. He had seen her in a terrible temper. Her eyes sparking and her hair flying out in every direction. He had seen her boisterously playing leapfrog and riding Beattie's pony full tilt across the cobbled stable yard. But this was something beyond his comprehension. And… what was this fuss in the village? No doubt she had been told off by the family, like he had, but now it was all over… and why, "sent away to Longford", what did the girl mean?

She certainly looked upset and at the same time appealingly beautiful. Alfred sat down and looked rather helplessly at Emmie. The light scattering of freckles gave a softly dappled effect to her creamy skin and her red hair, released from the hood, appeared to be tumbling across her shoulders in wild disorder. Tears were squeezing between her fingers and making glittery patterns on the rough wool of the cloak. Alfred felt himself drawn back reluctantly to memories of the sweet smell of hay and the soft caress of skin on skin. Any intentions he had of getting rid of her quickly, seemed to fade.

"Who tried to frighten you, Emmie?" he enquired, putting his arm round her shoulders and drawing her gently towards him on the seat. "Tell me again and I'll go and see the man. I'll give him a piece of my mind, frightening a girl this way!"

Emmie leant gratefully against him. Haltingly she repeated the story and then remembered her basket and carpet bag.

"Oh, Alfred! He'll surely have stolen my possessions! What am I to do?"

The train appeared to be slowing down again and Alfred peered quickly out of the window.

"I'd best get down to your compartment now or he'll be off at Collooney as quick as a wink!"

Leaving Emmie huddled on the seat he moved rapidly out of the door and down towards the end of the train.

The nearer he got to the last compartment, where Emmie had said she had been sitting, the more congested the corridor became. Something was going on lower down. The time, he decided, had come to exert some command over the situation.

"Excuse me please, I'm on my way down, excuse me please ladies and gentlemen, railway business, excuse me…"

It was working. Reluctantly people were squeezing sideways to let him through. The steady beat of the engine was changing to a slower note as he reached the last door against which three men were leaning their full weight as they tried to force it open. Just as Alfred was about to yell encouragement the door plunged open and like three tipsy skittles the men fell in on top of one another. It was a confusion of arms and legs and yelling and, way ahead, loping towards the back door of the train and the rear platform, was an ungainly figure clutching a small carpet bag.

Regardless of squirming bodies, Alfred used an emerging shoulder as a stepping stone and leapt across to the far side to give chase. The man had a good lead and only halted for a second at the last door, then he was out onto the platform. At this point he must have forced the carpet bag open and rummaged inside it, because, by the time Alfred reached the open door there was no one on the platform but the carpet bag was lying open. There were garments flung across the jolting metal platform and a man's back could be seen rapidly disappearing into a small plantation of pine woods on the outskirts of the village of Collooney. Alfred swore loudly. There was little point in giving chase. The man had too good a start. He was gathering up clothes and stuffing them back into the carpet bag as the conductor and his helpers joined him on the platform.

"Ah, got 'im," said the conductor, pouncing on Alfred and pinning him to the rail at the side of the wobbling platform.

Alfred was stunned. He pointed towards the woods.

"Listen, wait a minute, your thief got away, he jumped over the side as the train slowed down."

"Not likely, an' us on your heels ant closing in on ye!"

"My good man," Alfred suddenly found his dignity, "I leapt across you when you fell over as the door opened. I was the one who chased after him. He opened this bag and then as he heard me arriving he jumped over the side, onto the embankment, crawled up and ran into the woods."

The conductor knew authority when it spoke. He looked uncertainly at Alfred, then enquiringly round at the men behind him.

"He's right, James, he's not the robbing type," one man nodded agreement.

"So you just a passenger, then?" the conductor asked in an affronted way.

"He attacked my fiancée," Alfred thought this the most likely tale to be accepted. "She was coming up the train to join me and he grabbed her bag and tried to attack her but someone, perhaps you, saved her by coming into the compartment at that moment," he nodded in a more friendly way to the conductor as he felt the balance of the meeting beginning to change.

The conductor was pleased to see himself acknowledged as the hero of this piece of drama on his train and immediately began to describe to everyone who was crowding the platform and piling up in the corridor behind, how he had single-handedly saved the young lady. Holding the carpet bag in front of him, Alfred began to push his way back through the crowd and finally arrived with a worried Emmie just as the train was clattering into Collooney station.

Alfred tried the casual approach but it was not a success. Emmie was delighted to see him back and his attempt to pass off his visit down the train with a shrug and a wave, did not work.

"Sure now, Alfred, aren't you the clever one!" she said, clutching her carpet bag gratefully. "Did you catch him too?"

He laughed at her delighted reaction.

"Beaten to a pulp and he deserves it! Only it didn't work out quite like that, gal, much as I'd have liked it to!"

Emmie raised her eyebrows questioningly and Alfred was about to launch into an account of the chase when the door of the carriage opened and the conductor and train driver touched their caps to Alfred and came in, as the driver explained:

"Hope you'll not be minding, sir, we need to put in a report on this nasty happening and talk to the young lady herself."

Emmie went through the story again and there was much indignant comment from the two officials.

"Well bless my soul, ant is that right! He just grabbed ye like that!"

"An' how can anyone be safe with such as him around?" the engine driver speculated.

Alfred watched them in some amusement. They were obviously taken aback to find that his "fiancée" was not a grand lady. Alfred noticed that the conductor was looking sideways at his polished valise and no doubt wondering why Emmie only had a carpet bag and, while very attractive, was only dressed like a cottager. After a few more questions they both left but Alfred saw the conductor wink at the engine driver. They think we're running away together, he thought. He turned away from watching them leave to find Emmie, her bag open, frantically scrabbling inside it and dragging out the jumbled clothes as if her life depended on it.

"What's wrong, Em?"

"He has stolen it!"

"Stolen what?"

"Oh, Alfred, he's stolen my purse," as Alfred continued to look undisturbed by this news, "My purse wit all my money!"

"Was there much, then?"

"No, but it was all I had… what am I going to do?" She looked close to tears again and Alfred felt moved to protect her. He put an arm round her and kissed the chestnut waves. He loved the smell of her, the sensual feel of her body close to his.

"We'll sort this out, Em, but first tell me where you were going on this train?"

"Ah, Al, you'd not know the trouble our time in the hay caused in the village. In the first place it's not done to mix with those grander than ourselves and there were many who were pleased by the comedown. Me Da he had to take the strap to me, an' thanks be to God, my engagement wit that silly sheep, Rory, was ended. Nobody in the village would talk to such a gal an' the Ma had to find me a place looking after her sister's children in Longford."

"Good God!" Alfred commented in amazement. "I never knew you were in that much trouble!" He held her at arm's length and stared at her. "How can I help?"

Emmie dried her eyes on her cloak and looked across at Alfred.

Now, she realised, was the chance to talk to him about Africa. But did she want to go? Her world had been turned on its head and now, here was

Alfred actually offering help. His hands felt warm and strong on her shoulders, his eyes shone with genuine concern. Suddenly the worries about leaving her family behind became hazy and thoughts of Longford, children, and cleaning and ironing, were replaced with an awareness of Alfred and the escape from drudgery he represented. She knew if she went to Longford she would eventually marry some man from a local town and lose the advantages which childhood and youth had given her. Adult expectations would mean that she could no longer mix with Alfred and his family and friends, who would simply become her "betters".

"Al, it's a long time we've known each other ant it's you as taught me to ride an' fish and use your gun."

Alfred nodded. He moved back and sat down, a perplexed expression on his face which made Emmie wonder whether he was regretting his offer of help.

She drew in her breath and wondered how best to continue.

"I'm not cut out for children – or not yet. You know my dream of singing? Well…" She hesitated, looking closely at him. "Well, I'd like to go with you to Africa."

Seeing a look of horror spread across his face she added hastily, "No, Al, not to *marry* you, no, *never* that! I just want to see more of the world ant get a chance to sing!"

"By jove, Em, you had me getting ready to run then! What of your family and your aunt, and what will the village say?"

"I'd come back one day wit the money to build my parents a new house ant perhaps to let Duggie train for building trains, like he's always wanted. They'll all settle down once I write that I'm safe in Africa ant on my way up in the singing world."

"You're the optimist you are!" Alfred teased her. "And how am I to get you to Africa with me?"

"I'm not knowing, especially now I've lost my money."

Alfred couldn't avoid laughing. "Such as that was! You're a great gal, Em, but this will really ruin your reputation. Are you sure you want to risk that?"

Emmie nodded. "No other way, Al, no respectable girls sing, or so my Da tells me, but those 'respectable' girls are also so very dull and know nothing of the world beyond the village. I want some adventure in my life." She smiled hopefully at him.

Alfred turned away and looked out of the window for a moment. Then he turned back and took her small freckled hands in his.

"Em, my family will be very annoyed about this but I'd love a companion on the trip to Africa. I think I could raise the extra money, but things will be tight. You'll have to learn to behave like I tell you and there is no chance of marriage. We may not even come back together. You understand?"

Emmie nodded and bit her lip to stop it shaking. "You're a wonderful friend, Al, I'll not burden you, I promise. I'll find work and make my own way."

"Then that's sorted!" Alfred cried and he leapt up and spun her around and set her back on the seat.

Emmie was speechless. It was as though she had taken the step across the great divide and landed safely on the other side of the chasm. Dear Alfred, she thought, he hasn't a practical hair in his head.

Emmie laughed at him, stood up and removed her cloak and put her hands on his arm.

"Al, I've no booking on that ship, no decent clothes ant my aunt ant my parents, they'll need to know I'm not dead. Your parents may try to stop us too."

"Em, you're the one!" Alfred let out a loud guffaw of laughter. "Don't worry, Uncle Al will think of something!"

He threw his head back and stared at the wooden compartment ceiling

"Money I can get from my father's bank. Old Daventry'll give me a little extra if I cajole him. In Dublin we'll buy you what you need for the trip and a couple of new dresses. As for your aunt, she'll think you missed the train when you don't get off at Longford." He paused to think again.

"I know! I've got the answer for your parents!" he looked triumphantly at her. "You write to them and tell them that you met a family on the train who were going to Africa and that they asked you to join them as a nanny for their small child. Tell them you hope to return with them to Ireland eventually. Tell them you were so busy making plans that you forgot to look out for Longford station and you missed your aunt."

His blue eyes were flashing with delight at his own inventiveness.

"Make no mention of me and I'll send my parents a note saying that I had a pleasant journey and am about to embark for South Africa."

Alfred smiled happily at Emmie and dusted his hands as though to do away with all talk of problems.

Emmie felt impressed, if slightly doubtful.

"When my Ma ant Da hear the name 'Africa', I'm thinking they'll guess whom I'm with, especially when the news gets out that you left on the same day for Dublin!"

116

"Right," said Alfred, obviously in no mood to have his splendid plans rejected, "tell them the family are going to Australia and then you can write from Cape Town and say the wife was too ill to continue the journey so you all disembarked there instead. Then they will not be sure and when you return, happy and successful, they will not like to doubt your word!"

Emmie looked sideways at Alfred. It was difficult not to join in his delight. He so obviously felt that he had everything under control. The practical streak in her wondered whether it would be quite that easy. However, his infectious enthusiasm won her over and she decided to forget about any problems and start enjoying herself. It was, after all, part of the adventure into a new life to be travelling in the company of a gentleman, she reasoned.

A pleasant couple of hours passed as they talked of their childhood and watched the countryside of Leitrim, Roscommon and Longford roll past their window.

At Longford station Alfred turned his back towards the window so that she was hidden from view should anyone be looking in at the window, and Emmie found herself giggling at the thought of her aunt hunting down the platform for her. It was a giggle with a hint of panic and she was glad when the train pulled out and they were able to relax.

Alfred grinned at her. "You've done it now, Em. How'd you feel?"

"Pretty scared, Al, but also very excited."

Alfred nodded towards the fields as the train wound its way through the countryside. "Sad to see so many abandoned homes, the thatch falling in, the land going to weeds."

The change from casual chatter to serious talk took her by surprise.

"Yes, it's like round us. There are still many who will move away given the chance; the famine's a bitter memory."

"Poor Ireland," Alfred commented. "It's becoming a barren land, these empty houses are like memorials to famine and poverty."

Emmie looked at him in surprise. "There are stirrings of change, Al."

He nodded thoughtfully. "Things are bad again with the poor harvests and the Fenians stirring the hearts of the people with talk of rebellion," Alfred tapped the paper which was lying on the seat next to him.

"See... 'The Nation' is full of demands for home rule."

Emmie leant across to look at the headlines. She was aware of Alfred watching her.

"You're a clever girl, Em. The schoolteacher told my mother you learnt to read and write before anyone else when the school started."

Emmie grinned up at him. "Surprised, are you! Surprised the bog-Irish can be as good as the rich folks?" The smile had faded and the question was a challenge.

Alfred gave her an appraising look.

"When my father started the school Father Donoghue was not happy. I believe he said it should only be for boys but my mother said that was absurd and so did your mother."

"I know, me Da often reminds her!"

Alfred laughed, but it was a gentle laugh. "Maybe he's right, Em. If you couldn't read and write you might not have learnt so much about the world around you and you would not have wanted to travel to Africa with me!"

"Yes, I'd probably be marrying Rory and settling to the years of washing ant ironing ant cooking. Me Da will no doubt remind me Ma once again of the damage done by education!"

The noise and hustle of Dublin was something Emmie had not been prepared for. Her dreams had simply envisaged a mixture between Sligo and Dromahair and she found herself dazed by the crowds of people and terrified by the coaches, cabs, and chaise which seemed to flood down the streets. From time to time, as she tried to follow Alfred, she would grab his arm nervously, but he seemed not to have noticed her fear and would shake her off. He was in a great hurry to hail a cab and bundle her into it.

With the cab moving off she turned to him:

"An' yous not very polite to a lady. You bundled me in like a bag of dirty laundry, an' me never in a city before, an all!"

Alfred seemed to have changed as they reached Dublin. Suddenly he was very much the young man and aware of his dignity.

From the safety of the cab he admitted, "I don't want any of my friends to see us together. They'll wonder who the hell you are."

Emmie felt offended.

"An' what's so bad about me, then?"

"Nothing, nothing, well, nothing a visit to a dress shop won't sort. But don't say too much. I'll do the talking."

Emmie would have liked to have argued further but she was filled with excitement at the thought of the dress shop.

She found herself swept into an impressive carpeted shop just off a square near the river. While she was still trying to absorb her surroundings and before she could make any comment, Alfred had instructed the elegant lady who glided up to him from between the velvet curtains as they arrived, to find her two smart dresses for travelling and one dress for evening wear. Emmie's eyes grew round as she heard him asking the startled lady to see to underwear, shifts and shoes at the same time. Alfred retired to sit on a gold and scarlet chaise lounge and was soon deep in conversation with another assistant.

"Will modom please come this way…" the woman indicated an empty room adorned with a mirror and two spindly-legged gold chairs just beyond the velvet curtains.

As the woman was looking directly at her, Emmie assumed, after a quick glance over her shoulder to see whether anyone else had come into the shop, that she was the 'modom' referred to. The woman disappeared and Emmie took a look at herself in the mirror. Thinking of the people she had seen in the street, Emmie was not surprised that Alfred was in such a rush to buy her new clothes. Her best blue skirt and the blouse which her mother had given her, looked battered and care-worn after a day of travelling. Her unruly copper hair had escaped the clutches of her hair pins and was floating in wisps round her face and forming small ringlets across her ears. The black cloak, which previously had looked so smart and grown-up, was drooping from her shoulders in heavy shapeless folds. She felt a slight draft behind her and the woman was back carrying an armful of dresses and a tape measure. She stood back and eyed Emmie critically.

"You've a good figure, mam. We'll have no problem fitting you."

Emmie thought it was just the most exciting thing that had ever happened to her. Her delight was so obvious that the assistant soon eased her critical attitude and began to take pleasure in advising Emmie and helping her to choose. She produced a comb and soon tamed the hair into a neat pleat at the back of Emmie's head. Then there was the excitement of choosing the dresses. Each one was put on and paraded in front of Alfred. Emmie was a little disappointed that he went for the plainer dresses when she would have loved something wildly frilled and lacey. However, the assistant, as she laced Emmie into the dresses, whispered that he was a man of taste and his choice was always the latest fashion.

"Mam, we are into the plain and elegant with the cut and drape being most important," she briefed Emmie. Emmie looked at her from under her lashes, she could see that the assistant was longing to ask her where she was from. She thinks I'm his fancy woman, she thought to herself with some amusement. Then a second thought struck her. Well, I suppose I am, oh what a thought! Then her eyes alighted on the dresses being carefully parcelled up for her to take away and she abandoned the guilt in favour of excitement. She heard Alfred asking for the clothes to be put on his mother's account and she wondered what the reaction would be when the account was presented. But never mind, she'd be back one of these days with the money to pay them back.

A cab was hired for all the boxes and Emmie emerged in a sleek lavender silk dress, buttoned demurely to the neck, her hair in the pleat and a pert deep purple hat with a curving feather adding to the effect of an elegant young lady out on a shopping spree. At the last minute she remembered her clothes from home. She grinned disarmingly at the assistant:

"An' there's me ready to forget the past already! Please put those in a bag for me to take away." She watched the assistant's face as she packed the old clothes into a bag. "Sure ant they're clean an' paid for, not for Dublin perhaps," she quipped. The assistant passed the extra parcel to Alfred with a smile of sympathy. Emmie noticed a look of embarrassment cross his face but he took the looped handle and rather hastily bustled Emmie out of the door.

Their next call was to the shipping office and he came out waving a ticket at her.

"Put this in your purse, gal! Cost me a pretty penny it did but you're in a three-berth cabin in First Class." Seeing Emmie's look of questioning surprise he explained.

"You're in with two ladies. We'll pretend to meet on board for the first time. Tongues will chatter but at least they'll not think we came together. Say you're going to be a lady's maid to someone in Cape Town. No – maybe it better be a governess or they'll think you should be in steerage."

Emmie absorbed this in silence for a minute. "An' Alfred, who'd employ me as a governess?"

Alfred laughed.

"Come on, Em, use your imagination, invent something. Some mad Irish woman perhaps who's homesick for the old country and isn't worried by your terrible grammar and broad accent," he chortled rather unkindly.

Emmie pulled a face at him and made herself a firm promise that she would quickly learn the ways of the grand ladies and mimic their voices.

Alfred was staying at the family home at 27 Fitzwilliam Square and he found Emmie lodgings in a small, discreet hotel nearby. Emmie had the distinct impression that the hotel knew him and were not at all surprised by her arrival. The hall porter winked at her as he struggled up the stairs to the room.

"I suppose I'll get me tip later, from the gentleman," he said cheekily as he deposited the last package in the bedroom.

"Indeed, you'll be lucky!" she told him. "You've the cheek of the devil, you have!"

Emmie knew that she would not see Alfred until they left for the docks the next day. He had explained that he was off to see old Daventry, his father's banker, to see whether he could discreetly wheedle some extra cash to cover her expenses. He also had a meeting that evening with his medical student chums at a gentleman's club for a game or two of cards and revelry to celebrate his release from study. It seemed that women were not invited into these sanctuaries. Emmie did not feel any great surprise. Her Da went up to the local drinking house for a game of cards from time to time. She'd never heard her Ma complaining. She'd heard that the men sometimes drank too much but Da had always come back cheerful and full of the local chat about harvests and politics.

The only person Emmie missed through the evening was her mother and a couple of her school friends. Je-sus! She thought to herself, wouldn't they be surprised to see me now! She tried on her new clothes, played with her hair and hats and twirled in front of the mirror between packing and unpacking her possessions in the new valise. Me Ma, she thought, maybe she'd not be too happy wit me, but she'd love the clothes. Down at the bottom of the bag she packed her old clothes. It's the thrift in me... an' also they're a reminder of home, she thought as she tucked them in.

The other wonder was the bed. It was large, soft, with clean white linen sheets which smelt of summer flowers. There was also a small table with paper and envelopes. It took her a while to work up the courage, but eventually she wrote a letter home along the lines suggested by Alfred. She also asked them to say how sorry she was to her aunt. Then, feeling tired but pleased with herself, she fell onto the bed and slept until the morning light crept through the open curtains and the noises in the street woke her with a start.

She hung out of the window for a while watching the early morning activity in the street below. Then it was time to get ready for Alfred to collect her. Alfred had explained that she would be expected to eat downstairs but she was far too nervous to do that. How would she know what to do in the dining room of a hotel? What would they eat? At home it would just be a bowl of oatmeal and a mug of tea.

Tense with excitement, she forced herself to dress slowly in the discreet checked suit with its full skirt and tight-waisted jacket, set off at the neck and cuffs by a frilly white blouse. She piled her red hair as tidily as possible in coils on top of her head, firmly held in place by an army of hairpins. On top of this, skewered down with hat pins, she fastened the small stylish black and white hat which Alfred and the shop assistant had chosen for her. The effect left her wondering whether her own parents would have recognised her. Gone was the pretty country girl in the shabby cloak and worn skirt who had left Killarga. Instead, she was looking at a sophisticated young lady of Dublin society.

Emmie sat down to await Alfred's arrival. He had said that he would come along with a cab at ten o'clock in the morning. They would travel in two cabs so that people at the docks and on board the ship would not realise that they knew one another. They had to report on board by 11 a.m. and the ship was due to lift anchor with the tide at midday.

By a quarter past ten she was pacing the room restlessly. What had become of Alfred? Was he ill? Had he been hurt in a brawl? Had he forgotten her? Perhaps he had never intended to take her? The insecurities came flooding in but she was also certain that he would not have bought her all these clothes and suggested the letter to her parents, if he was not intending to take her. By half past ten there was still no sign of him. She could not bear the waiting any longer and carried her valise down to the hotel lobby, where an ancient porter looked at her in horror.

"Mam, you had only to ring and I would have brought that down for your ladyship!" he exclaimed. Realising she had made a mistake she felt the colour rise in her cheeks. At the desk she gave them her letter to post but they had no message for her. The receptionist told her the room was paid for by the gentleman the previous night. He offered to call a cab for her. She came to a sudden decision. She would have to go ahead to the docks and see whether he was there. At least, she had her ticket which she could show to the cab driver.

Pulling herself together and smiling at the Receptionist: "I am awaiting a gentleman who was to accompany me to the docks. Should he arrive, could you please tell him that I have gone ahead."

Obviously impressed by her confidence the young man got her a cab and she found herself being taken at a brisk trot through the streets of Dublin and on to the docks.

She joined the queue going up the gangplank at five minutes to eleven, peering hopefully in every direction for the dark, familiar head of curls. There was no sign of him. She was shown to her cabin where two elderly ladies already appeared to be in residence. They stared at her in hostile surprise and tried to insist that she had come to the wrong end of the ship. The steward, hiding a smile, showed them the cabin booking and they reluctantly accepted Emmie.

"And where are you going, all on your own?" the one called Dolly asked her brusquely. Emmie thought quickly of Alfred's story.

"I'm going to Cape Town to act as governess to a family," she lied successfully. The woman looked at her in some surprise.

"You've a country accent!" she said accusingly.

"That I have, indeed, ant the lady likes the sound. Sure it reminds her of home."

The other lady entered the attack. "An' what lady would this be?"

"Probably no one you'd be knowing. Where are you ladies from, may I ask?"

"We live in Dublin," Dolly replied.

"Ah now, you'd not know the Fraser-Haw family from Manorhamilton, I'm supposing?" said Emmie, taking a stab in the dark and hoping Manorhamilton would be beyond their normal circle of acquaintances.

"Did you say she was Lady Fraser-Haw?" asked Dolly.

"No, to be sure, she's just plain Mrs!"

"Ah," said Dolly, rapidly losing interest.

The other sister, Winnie, had one last stab. "Who are your family?"

"I'm from the O'Connells of Killarga," replied Emmie, hoping that the truth sounded acceptable.

"A large estate?"

"No, mam, a small one, but well set-up." Emmie was not quite sure what she meant herself and just hoped that she sounded sufficiently confident for it to pass.

Dolly wasn't going to let her away with it entirely. She sniffed.

"So, why send you First Class?"

Emmie's nerves were feeling shredded. She was out of her depth and felt like a dog trying to paddle against a turning tide. Three quarters of her mind was trying to work out what to do if Alfred didn't turn up.

"Sure, now an' let me tell you, I've been sent First Class because I have the manners not to ask endless rude questions of strangers. Just tell me your names ant I'll be asking to be moved in with nicer people!"

Emmie had the pleasure of seeing Dolly step backwards and Winnie catch her breath, as she hurried off to find the steward. She actually had no intention of looking for the steward, but it was a good excuse to rush up to the deck and hang over the railings peering into the milling crowd below. Knowing not a soul in Cape Town and without a penny to her name she was going to have to get off this ship hastily before it sailed.

It was at this moment of decision that she noticed a disturbance in one corner of the crowd. Then, pushing through the friends and relatives who had come to see people off, she saw him at last. He was shouting and pushing and a boy behind him was carrying a cabin trunk and valise for him. He appeared to have a confrontation with the crew at the bottom of the gangplank and then he was leaping up the steps two at a time. She began to push her way through the passengers and was just in time to see him tip the boy, who turned and leapt hastily down the gangplank as the crew set about loosening the ropes and preparing to weigh anchor.

Completely forgetting herself in her relief at seeing him, she rushed up and flung her arms round his neck.

"Ah, Al, where have you been, I've been right out of my mind about you!" At the same time she was suddenly aware of the shocked faces of her two elderly cabin companions, who had been standing by the rails to watch the departure preparations.

"Whew! That was close," he commented, catching his breath and gently pushing Emmie back. "Girl, you look marvellous, what excellent taste I have! But listen, Em, have I got the mother and father of all headaches!" He tucked his arm through hers and led her up the deck.

"Drank too much last night and passed out! Woke today at eleven o'clock and thanked God I had left everything ready. I grabbed a cabbie and rushed home for the trunk etc. and then straight here!"

Emmie looked at him incredulously, "Didn't you stop at the hotel for me?"

"No, I hadn't time, you saw how late I arrived, any more stopping and I'd still not be here. Knew you were a sensible gal. She'll have gone on ahead, I told myself." He stopped and turned her round so that he could see her properly. "By God, I'm glad to see you though, gal. Would have made for a dull trip all on my own." He smiled cheerfully at Emmie.

She looked at him in exasperated amazement.

"Honest, Al, you are a hopeless case, what am I going to do with you?"

Chapter Seven

AFRICA – June 1879

Emmie clung to the deck rail exhilarated by her first glimpse of Table Bay and the great flat-topped mountain which dominated the foreshore. She was vaguely aware that her meticulously arranged hair was fast escaping its hair pins and, egged on by the brisk south-easterly wind, was blowing triumphantly past her face in russet corkscrew tendrils which flicked her cheeks and brushed across her eyes.

Her thoughts moved to the Misses Caper and Pringle with whom she had shared a cabin for the voyage and she pictured their faces if they could see her present dishevelled appearance. It would certainly have led to pursed lips and yet another sniff of disgust at her behaviour. She chuckled to herself as she suddenly pictured them safely in their cabin below decks, no doubt right now clamping their straw hats firmly onto their grey buns with massive hatpins, determined to defeat the wind at all cost and remain devastatingly "respectable".

She slipped her arm through Alfred's as the canvas flapped and the timbers creaked to the tune of the fluctuating wind.

"Al, what will they do without us to gossip about?" she giggled.

Alfred glanced down at her and raised an eyebrow as he tried to follow her train of thought.

"You, know, the misses Caper and Pringle!"

He laughed into the wind, "We gave them a good run for their money, Em! They never really recovered from the shock of having to share a cabin with a governess with a wild Irish accent! Remember their faces when they caught us playing cards together with the Martins, and as for dancing together on the deck in the moonlight… I think we seared their souls with that one!"

"It's simply not done, young lady!" Emmie mimicked their attack on her. "An' then," she added, still recalling the scene with relish, "they complained to the Captain!"

Alfred squeezed her arm and laughed, "Yes, and the poor man felt he had to remonstrate with me in a clipped little speech filled with innuendoes, which I then misinterpreted! Do you remember how red in the face he went?"

Emmie patted Alfred's hand.

"Mind you, Al, I'm right glad to be seeing the land an' I'll be even more glad to walk on it, God be praised," without thinking she had slipped into her mother's expression. "Remember them storms! The grumpy old sows. I tried to look to them with bowls and cloths and sympathy, an' they were glad enough at the time but once the sea settled they were back to their sniffs and whispers."

Alfred looked down at her.

"Remember," he said, "Jeremy heard them say to Mrs Cogan, 'A mere poor class governess, my dear, and presuming not only to travel First Class, but *also* to have an open and obviously scandalous affair with her employees son!'"

Emmie giggled and looked round.

"Where are Jeremy and the other young men now?"

"They are organising their men down in the Second Class." Alfred smiled tolerantly at her. "You liked the young officers, didn't you, and I must say that young Lieutenant, Jeremy da Souza, quite fell for you, didn't he? Was it undying love and all that?"

Emmie looked coquettishly at him, "He did indeed, an' I told him he'd have to wait in line!"

"You cheeky lass! And by then you had given up the unequal struggle to try and mimic the Englishwomen around you and were back into the strong Irish brogue! I thought that would frighten them away but no, they acted like moths round a candle and young Jeremy declared your voice to be 'like a down duster wrapped round a lilting Irish stream,' or some such total rubbish!"

Emmie looked up at him and raised an eyebrow.

"An' there was no complaint from you! Sure weren't they all waitin' for some sort of jealousy – your girl an' all that!"

Alfred tapped her on the shoulder.

"You're a fine one to talk! There I was waiting for you to simper and say you belonged to me, but no, not a word, just fluttered your eyelashes at them and smiled sweetly and sang your Irish songs to captivate their hearts still further!"

"The singing I couldn't help," she said a little defensively, "sure, the passengers asked me to sing and then that kind lady taught me some English

126

songs, the ones they called 'fashionable', an' people chose to sing with me. Didn't they then?"

"They did indeed, and I must admit you went down well. It was a pity you discovered the steerage and decided to liven life up for them as well!"

"Ah, Al, you should have seen them poor folks. They'd none of the care an' attention we 'ad. There was some poor Irish folk there, pining for 'ome, an' you should'a heard them singing."

"I did, *we* did," he said with feeling. "Mind you, when that little child died in steerage an' you sang at the burial, you had most of the ship in tears. I must say for you, gal, you can sing with a passion and your voice sounds like a summer blackbird."

Emmie looked at him in surprise.

"Well, Al, I do believe that just may be a compliment!" she said, mimicking an English voice.

He laughed and ruffled her hair and they both leant forward over the rail to watch a small boat bobbing up alongside and the pilot being hauled on board to guide the ship to a safe mooring.

Only one small shadow of worry clouded a corner of Emmie's mind. However, she had to acknowledge to herself that it must have been her imagination. It was too great a co-incidence. Once she had peered down into the crew's area and suddenly suffered a flashback to the train in Ireland. She had caught a fleeting glimpse, down in the oily darkness, of a moon face with narrow, mean eyes, leering briefly up at her. Had she imagined the flash of recognition in those pink-rimmed, lashless eyes? She shivered slightly and concentrated on the small boat which was bobbing back towards the docks.

"Look, Em," Alfred nudged her, "we're joining that line of merchant shipping sitting at anchor in the deep water just beyond the harbour. Doesn't it look grand?"

She pushed herself a little further over the rail as the ship manoeuvred round in the wind.

"Oh, Al, de ye see all them little boats, like walnut shells on the water?"

"They are coming out to collect us and our baggage, Em."

"Truly?"

"As soon as we drop anchor they will start to unload the cargo and the passengers."

"An how in the name of God, will they stay upright with all the trunks and passengers?"

"They've done it before, Em, don't worry, they'll manage and without giving you a ducking either!"

Emmie wasn't listening to him.

"Look, look, Al," she shouted above the gusting wind, leaning dangerously over the rail, "it's a *black* man, yes it *is*. I'm telling you it is! He's rowing like the best of them... An' there's another man who's very brown... *Jesus*, I've never seen the like of them! Are they burnt dark by the sun or made that way by God?"

Between guffaws of laughter Alfred reached over and pulled her back to the deck in case she fell over the rail.

"You'll see lots more black men, girl, this continent is full of them. The brown one doesn't look to me as though he's burnt, I'd say he's Portuguese or something."

She was vaguely aware of his arm round her shoulder. It was all so exciting but at the same time it was frightening to be in a strange place so far from home and the arm was comforting and like an anchor with the past.

"Look, Al, the clouds on that old mountain, they look like a frothy mop cap! An' its sort of lavender colour with the town at the bottom spreading about the harbour like a white shawl dropped at the water's edge."

Alfred looked at her in surprise.

"Why, Em, you've suddenly gone all poetic on me!"

Emmie gave him an indignant kick on the ankle but he had seen something which interested him and he hardly noticed.

"Look, Em, do you see how dexterously they bring the boats alongside the ships, and the small boys who are helping with the ropes and ladders?"

"Al, it's beautiful. Can you smell the scent on the wind, it's sure like that camphor your mother kept, that an' a mixture of Cook's herbs and spices... It doesn't smell like Ireland... I wish Ma and Pa could be here to see it all.

"Good God, girl," he withdrew his arm from round her shoulders, "don't wish that on us, we've only just arrived and already you're wishing us back in the misty bogs of Ireland! You're daft! Remember, you're going to sing and we are going to have a good time... look at it, Em, it's all ours! No parents to make the rules!"

Emmie looked sideways at him. "Ah, go on, Al, you'd think we owned the place. No one knows us an' no one cares."

"That's so," he agreed, "but I'm saying that's good. If no one knows us we don't have to live up to standards and if no one cares, then we can do exactly what we like. We couldn't do that in Ireland, gal!"

128

"You're right an' all! It'll be great to have no one to tell us off and to be able to direct our own dreams… sure you're right, Al." She rested a hand on his jacket sleeve.

Really, she thought, she had no regrets. The voyage had been tremendous fun and she had managed quite commendably to mimic the respectable females of the First Class. Her accent had let her down from time to time but she was working on that and certainly she could toss a haughty look with the best of them. Not that she often wanted to, it was all too much fun and Killarga seemed a lifetime away… mostly. There was still that sneaking doubt. She turned to watch the crew, busy with their disembarkation routine. There was no sign of that face, she had definitely imagined it.

A black hansom cab delivered them to a small hotel in the quiet, oak tree-lined back streets of Cape Town. Their trunks were carried in by a Malay servant. Emmie stared round the lofty bedroom in amazement and then her eyes settled on the large, soft bed and she drew in her breath nervously. Alfred had described her as "My lady wife", at the reception desk and she had just managed to bite back a hasty denial as she caught his warning glance.

The bright winter sunshine was flooding through the leafless branches of the oak tree outside their bedroom window mottling the highly polished floorboards with a shimmering dappled pattern of sunshine and shadow. Alfred lowered himself with casual loose-limbed ease onto the velvet cushion of the window seat and stared in amusement at Emmie as she felt the material of the bedspread and peered into the vast stinkwood cupboard in the corner of the room.

"Al, is this room really just for us?" she asked, quite overcome by the size of everything. "Sure, it's big enough to be a village hall… an' all just for the two of us?" She looked at him under her lashes, "I'd not like to have to polish *this* floor! Look on it, just them few rugs lying a-top it!"

"There are servants here, Emmie, no floors to polish. How do you fancy that, then?" he teased her.

"It makes me feel uncomfortable!"

"What else," he continued with a wicked grin, "is worrying your ladyship? You look awkward, you haven't even taken your gloves off!"

She looked sideways at him. "You know Al, you know!" She patted the bed as she perched on the edge of it. "I'm not used to the idea of this bed… an' where are *you* going to sleep?"

Alfred laughed outright. "I thought that was the problem! Come on, girl, you played the game all the way out on the ship, don't let it slip now! You wanted to come! I can't afford two rooms so you'll have to play-act a little longer. We can drop it once we are away from the town, but while we are here it's with me you'll have to sleep!"

Emmie plucked nervously at the bedcover material. "It's true in Ireland I didn't mind, but that was just for fun... here we are among so many grand folk... for sure I feel a fraud! I can't help imagining my Ma's face, she'd take the belt to me for the hussy I am!"

Alfred groaned, "Aw, Emmie, you're a continent away... *they* can't see us... come on, girl, it's an adventure! Let's make the most of it! Unpack your bags and we'll take a look at the town until dinner."

Slowly Emmie smiled at him. "Oh well, Al, you're a cheeky one and I suppose you're right, might as well make the most of this foreign travel." She giggled, "After all, you're Mrs Jameson, an' I'm here as governess to your children... or so my Ma thinks! Not, mind, that you look much of a lady," she swept to her feet and circled round Alfred, "I may have to teach you about ladies' clothes... It's not done to wear breeches all the time, modom. As for climbing into bed with your new governess! It's a strange family for sure... an' me carrying on an' flirting with your son on the boat... right now you'd be having me whipped for my own good. In fact, the Missis Caper and Pringle will be hoping to meet you so that they can tell you the all of it! They'd like some money back on their First Class berths... The suffering those ladies went through, having to share with a poor little governess!"

Alfred laughed, relieved to see her cheering up and joining in his excitement.

Heads turned to watch them as they left their hired carriage and sauntered through the public gardens.

Emmie was commenting on everything she saw like an excited child at a circus. Alfred, although he was nodding, was deep in his own thoughts.

This was a huge adventure for him but he must try to look nonchalant and worldy wise, not only to impress Emmie, but also to impress the people they might meet. He just wished she was not quite so forward about talking to people. They always looked sideways at him as the strong Irish accent tumbled out as she bubbled with enthusiasm and curiosity. However, he had to admire the way she had absorbed the manners and behaviour of those around her. She moved like a lady, she looked like a lady, and a damn attractive one at that, and only her exuberance and unquenchable curiosity let her down... and that accent!

Still, he mused, there were compensations. She was his for the moment. He was very fond of her and he felt excited by the memory of that ill-fated visit to the hay loft. However, there was no family to interfere this time! At last he could teach her some of the tricks the ladies in Dublin had taught him!

She was a sport, always had been, even as a little girl playing with the older children at Belhavel. She would try anything and she didn't howl and blame others when she was hurt.

He had to admit to himself that he was enjoying showing her off on his arm. Particularly, he enjoyed the admiring appraisal in the eyes of other men. He'd make her acceptable in polite society, but marriage... no, that would not be possible, but over here, well away from Dublin society, he could do as he liked, without fear of censure. He was his own man. He drew himself up as tall as he could and felt much older than his twenty-one years, a man of the world, concubine and all!

They walked through the gardens as far as the large slave bell in its white arch. The wind was fresh, with a hint of rain and white clouds were clambering lower down the mountain. For the locals it was winter and they stared in amazement at the attractive girl in an elegant blue and white striped summer dress while they all drew their cloaks around them and cursed the wiley old south-easter which seemed to sing round the corners and whistle under doors, heralding the rain it usually brought in its wake.

"Sure, Al, an' it's not as hot as I thought it would be! An' another thing, Al, where is the jungle? The lions and tigers? Look at that great building with the statue in front... who is it, Al? An' another thing—"

"Steady on gal!" Alfred protested, attempting to stop the stream of questions and speculation.

"Look at them little brown chillen, are they not lovely? An' that man there, he's very dark an' his clothes are near as bad as Sad Sam in Killarga! Oh, it's all that exciting!" She clasped him excitedly by the arm, quite forgetting her sophisticated lady role. Alfred disentangled himself and steered her determinedly back towards their hotel.

"Emmie, you must remember your manners when we are out... a lady does *not* grasp a gentleman by the sleeve and crush his jacket! You talk quietly and indicate what you mean with a nod, no pointing and squealing in delight! A true lady has seen it all before!"

Emmie halted and looked carefully at him.

"Has she now, my fine sir?" she remarked, with a frown and a tinge of sarcasm. "Well, this lady's new in town an' she has-na seen it, an' don't try to tell me your lordship has seen it all before, for I know you haven't, an' I'm thinking you're just as excited as me... So I'd thank you to not give me that nonsense!"

Alfred felt put out. He had just adjusted to what he felt was his tough dominant self with a frivolous and pretty mistress, when he found the tables rapidly turning and the flower on his arm suddenly displaying a side he had not bargained for.

They walked for a while in silence. Emmie managing to indicate displeasure in the swing of her shoulders, while Alfred wondered rebelliously how he had come to get entangled with her in the first place.

Emmie found it impossible to remain offended for long and by the time they reached the hotel she was bubbling with enthusiasm once again and he was forced to come out of his sulk.

Emmie found herself slightly alarmed as she led the way into the dining room. She had learnt to cope on the ship, but would this be the same? Eating seemed to be a highly complicated game in the outside world. At home they had pulled up the wooden bench or the old bentwood chairs and set out to allay the hunger pangs without much thought to anything other than a word of thanks to God for seeing that they had food on the table of some sort. Here there were so many tools and rituals and if they were missing people seemed to stare at you askance. Once again she watched closely the cutlery Alfred used and, confused by the variety of food offered, she followed his lead. The dark-skinned hotel waiter watched her with considerable thinly-veiled amusement and she had the feeling he could see through her act.

"Al," she whispered in some indignation, "that man who brings the food, I think he's laughing at me."

Alfred looked embarrassed, "It's pretty transparent that you don't know what to order or how to behave," he muttered under his breath.

"Ow!" he exclaimed, frowning at her and mopping up the soup he had splashed onto the tablecloth as she kicked his ankle. The next course arrived. "Behave yourself, gal!" he admonished, staring in fascinated horror as she balanced three peas on her knife and steered them towards her mouth.

His expression made her hand shake and the peas fell off, careering across the tablecloth in various directions and tumbling onto the polished floor. Emmie put her hand over her mouth to cover her giggles and suddenly Alfred's shoulders began to shake and they both spluttered as they tried not to laugh outright and break the quiet hush of the dining room with its four tables of sedately chatting guests.

Sharing a bed with Alfred turned out to be far easier than she had imagined. She now understood why he had insisted that they share a bottle of wine. Unaccustomed to alcohol it had gone straight to her head. By the time she had reached the bedroom she would cheerfully have jumped through hoops for him and thought it all part of the fun. She had been struggling into her battered old nightgown, the only one she had ever owned, when Alfred appeared and declared:

"Em, that's the most hideous garment I've ever seen! Tomorrow I'll buy you a negligee!"

"Je-sus," she remarked cheerily, "an' what might that be?"

While she was still trying to sort out why the previously level floor appeared to have a tilt to it, Alfred seized the old shift and, lifting it off her, dropped it to the ground. She was still trying to find her voice to protest when she was pushed into the soft folds of the bed, with his naked skin rubbing sensuously against her body, and she realised with a dreamy thrill of shock that he was as naked as she was. Modesty, she decided rapidly, could wait for another time. Buried in the feathery depths of the bed with the soft lamplight playing shadow games across Alfred's face, highlighting the curves of his muscles, turning his eyes into intense blue pools beneath the glossy, slightly damp curls, he became someone strange and new and extremely attractive.

"By God, Em, you're quite a lass!" he remarked the next day.

She was aware that this was a huge compliment coming from a young man with his worldly experience, who normally kept his compliments for horses and sports. Fleetingly it crossed her mind that she might fit into the last category in some way.

Over the next few nights he set out to teach her some of the pleasurable tricks he had learnt in Dublin and she responded with enthusiasm, tempered, she realised, by the occasional flitting shadows of guilt as she struggled against memories of her mother's lectures and Father Donohue's predictions of mortal sin. She managed to ease her conscience with false reassurance to her inner-self that she was in another world and what folk couldn't see they could not possibly know about. So neither she nor they need waste time on worry!

Alfred took on a new dimension. She felt herself softening to him. He had been an entertaining companion before and a means of escape, suddenly he was more important. She found herself wanting to please him, wanting his approval, and wanting to feel his touch. Worse still, she was aware of a twinge of jealousy when she saw him watching other women.

While Alfred was making enquiries round the town about the whereabouts of the preacher, Karl van de Ryn, the man who had written to Caroline Barton about her grandson, Emmie began to find her way round the colourful port. She was fascinated by the harbour with its perpetual bustle of activity as the lighters plied to and fro with passengers, cargo and crew. There was never a dull moment and she found the variety of people a constant source of amazement.

It took three days for Alfred to discover that Preacher van de Ryn had packed up and moved to the diamond fields three months ago. Instead of being disappointed he came back bursting with excitement.

"Em, he's gone to the diamond fields. There is nothing for it but to follow him up there. I tell you, this is our chance to chase a fortune!"

"What about the missing boy?" she asked.

"Oh, yes, we'll make enquiries, but, think of it, we can do that at the same time as filling our pockets with diamonds! You can have everything you dreamed of, Em!" he grabbed her by the waist and she found herself being whirled round the room, caught up in his wild enthusiasm.

"I was just getting used to Cape Town. I'm sorry we have to move on," she said with genuine regret.

"You'll not be once you're rich," he assured her, his voice filled with excitement.

Emmie pictured herself in satins and silks climbing into a carriage-and-pair of her own. Just as she was beginning to find the picture delightfully attractive, mundane commonsense overtook her.

"Tell me, Al, if there's a fortune for the picking in Kimberley why is Cape Town not empty of people?"

But Alfred was obviously not going to listen to boring reality. She watched him with sceptical amusement. His stocky frame was vibrant with enthusiasm, the clear blue eyes sparkling excitedly beneath the shock of dark curly hair, as he envisaged the wealth to come. She was aware of feeling suddenly older than him, older and more responsible. Yet there were times when his wild enthusiasm was such fun and she did not care if it was irresponsible or impractical. After all, he was a gentleman and he knew how to treat her and how to make her feel as though she was a lady. Little Emmie O'Connell from Killarga, a lady. She pinched herself and did a quick twirl in front of the mirror to enjoy the swish of skirt and petticoats and the flutter of the lace ruffle on her bodice. Alfred didn't notice, he was standing in front of the window, hands clasped behind his back, still fantasizing about their future wealth.

Once he had decided to make the move, Alfred wasted no time. The new rail line to Matjesfontein had just opened. This would take them through the Cape and over the jagged mountains of the Hex River Pass to the fringe of the Great Karroo. From there they would link with the Gibson Brothers' Coach for the last part of their trip to the diamond fields of Kimberley.

They climbed onto the train at Cape Town station and suddenly Emmie was alarmed to find memories of her encounter with the stranger on the train in Ireland, flooding back to her. She tightened her grip on Alfred's arm and he gave her a questioning look.

"It's just that I suddenly remembered that man on the train in Ireland, the one you chased," she explained.

Thinking of Ireland brought back thoughts of home and her parents and young Duggie. She sat in silence for a while, indulging in memories and waiting for the lump in her throat to disperse. Once the train was underway she was slowly dragged back to Africa and pushed her nose against the window to watch the changing scenery.

First the train huffed and puffed past the houses and shops of the suburbs and then it was out onto the sandy dunes of the Cape Flats and heading for the ridge of blue mountains which seemed to encircle and guard the coastal plain leading to the Cape and its Peninsula. Now and then they pulled into small stations and watched local farmers collecting their mail or loading on produce with much banter and shouting in Dutch. Alfred, she noticed with amusement, was at first very aware of himself and their position as a respectable couple journeying into the interior. Gradually the façade fell away and his natural boyish excitement began to take hold. He joined Emmie at the carriage window, quite ignoring the fact that up to this he had been doing his best to pull her back.

They passed rows of lime-washed thatched farm-workers' cottages, which reminded Emmie of home. The difference was that these were lived in by coloured people, a beautiful golden brown people. She had discovered from talking to people at the hotel, that these mixed races originated from the early European settlers and sailors and the Hottentots, Bushmen and Bantu who had gradually mixed to form a group of their own – the Cape Coloureds.

By now many of them had, according to a local lady she had spoken to in Cape Town, even taken on national characteristics. They made excellent fishermen and some were fine craftsmen who were much in demand. However, they were also the peasants of the land, looked down upon by all the pure race tribes... "The sins of the Fathers," she had commented knowingly to a mystified Emmie. Apparently, like so many depressed peoples, they had fallen foul of alcohol. From Friday night to half-way through Monday it was difficult to find a sober worker amongst the Cape Coloured population. As a result many of the more responsible jobs were held by former slaves and by Bantu tribesmen who had drifted down to the Colony from farther north.

Emmie was delighted by the way the women and children waved to the train as it clattered by. In the wine growing area, where the men were trimming and tidying the vines and weeding the soil between them, many looked up and shouted greetings.

The blue mountains gradually turned to purple and then took on the three-dimensional shading of valleys and craggy peaks as the train began to make its way up the escarpment into their midst. The villages grew smaller and the gracious gable-end farm houses were farther apart and the organised fields of fruit trees and vegetable plots and tilled soil, disappeared. Instead the vegetation grew sparser, the soil rockier and the small sidings were barren. The train pulled in several times to fill up with water as the steep climb demanded more steam from the engine and more fuel to keep the fire stoked for the climb to the summit. There followed the strain of the steep descent via valley rims and more peaks, down to the last small settlements before the barren waste of the Great Karroo took over for hundreds of miles of hard-baked scrubland.

"I've never seen anything as bleak as this," Alfred mused out loud, "even the moors up by the turf bog seem friendlier... A man in Cape Town told me they think it might be an old ocean bed but he didn't warn me about the tall hills they call kopjes. Just look at them, Em," he indicated with a sweep of the hand the flat landscape dotted with high, rocky, conical shaped hills, "it looks as though some joker dotted a host of molehills round the plain for fun!"

Emmie laughed. "I think I prefer the bog moor myself, it's got a softer light."

It was sunset before the train finally battled its weary way into Matjesfontein.

"Now, isn't that a wonder!" Alfred remarked excitedly to Emmie, "This puffing iron horse is a marvellous invention. It would have taken us a couple of days by coach or cart to make this journey and here we are in one day!" Emmie was standing up to reach down her hat and he put his arms round her waist and twirled her round in the narrow space between the leather clad seats. She lost her balance and they both fell onto the nearest seat and lay there laughing until they heard the ticket conductor coming down the corridor shouting:

"End of line, ladies and gentlemen... bags and baggage off please. There's a boy with a trolley who'll take your bags down to the 'otel for you. It's back to the ol' coaching service tomorrow, I fear! One day we'll take you all the way to Kimberley – but not yet, ladies and gents!"

They joined the other passengers hurrying off towards the corrugated iron roofed hotel where they would spend the night.

Emmie was grateful for a bowl of clean luke-warm water in their cell-like hotel room.

"Al, that train may be fast but look how that soot blew in through the window and left small grey smuts all over my dress! Dirty bugger," she muttered as she struggled to dust off the specks and wipe the spots with a damp cloth.

"Remember, Em, you're supposed to be a lady!" Alfred admonished her, but his eyes were laughing.

"This room is depressing," he said, looking round at the white walls, red polished floor and white covered truckle bed. "I'm off to have a drink at the bar – to wash the smell of the train smoke out of my throat." He put his hat on the bed, ran a comb through his hair and sauntered out of the door.

How, Emmie wondered to herself in some exasperation, how does he manage to continue looking neat and tidy after a day in a dirty train?

The small, hot dining room produced a stew of unidentifiable origin and then they joined the other passengers on the long wooden veranda to watch the stars come out over the great empty expanse of the Karroo, which disappeared into the distance as they looked northwards, the monolithic kopjes catching the moonlight like foreign planets rising out of a stubble-strewn desert.

As the stars faded into the soft underbelly of the dawn, the passengers found themselves being hustled towards the two coaches for the long journey across the arid plains of the Karroo. Some of the men rode on the roof of the coach with the luggage.

By midday it was a hot, disgruntled and dusty party which drew up in the forlorn little town of De Aar. The hotel in the centre of the town was the only building of any size and everyone headed for the saloon bar to re-vitalise their parched throats from the choking grip of the fine Karroo dust. Beyond the veranda a row of drooping sage-green pepper trees trailed their fronds on the hot earth and gave reluctant shade to three coloured families with a meagre display of produce to sell to anyone interested. The own-ers of the one trading store emerged to collect goods from the coach and then joined the travellers in the saloon bar to see what the latest gossip from the Colony had to say. A tall metal windmill stood on the edge of the town beyond the few houses and now and again it squeaked into languid action as a breath of wind forced the metal head to turn and reluctantly release a dribble of water into the mud-walled dam below.

Emmie licked a finger and wiped it round her eyes in the hope of clear-ing some of the fine dust out of her vision. She had given up worrying about her appearance. Survival in the heat was her main aim. Never had she come across anything quite like the intensity with which the sun beat down on this featureless plain. Nor could she believe the distance which they seemed to have travelled without sign of human habitation. The vast loneliness had reached her even in the depths of the crowded, creaking and jolting coach. She yearned for greenness and the soft misty rain of Ireland. She wished desperately that they were still in Cape Town – in fact, anywhere other than this bleak hell hole of scorching sun and endless scrubland.

Was this the land of diamonds about which Alfred had dreamed?

Emmie turned to the lady next to her. "Mrs Foxton, do you know whether Kimberley is like this?" she asked, indicating the view through the saloon door.

"My dear, I've no idea, but I hope it's a little more hospitable!" the lit-tle woman replied and then asked someone else the same question. It soon became apparent that only one traveller had been to Kimberley before. He proved very reticent.

"It's better than this, an' then it ain't!"

Pressed for more detail, he simply buried his nose in his drink and turned away.

"Well," Mrs Foxton remarked in tones of disgust, "from that we must draw our own depressing conclusions!"

Emmie looked across at Alfred, busy dusting himself down. At least he seemed to have abandoned the attempt to maintain a gentlemanly appearance now that he and the other men on the journey were swopping places on the hot, dusty coach roof. His jacket, and waistcoat had long since been consigned to his leather travelling bag and, in a perverse sort of way, he seemed to be thoroughly enjoying himself, despite the thick layer of reddish dust which coated his clothes from heat to toe. He caught Emmie's eye and gave her a lopsided grin and she could see the bubble of excitement in his eyes... he was probably dreaming of diamonds and riches to come.

He took her arm and excitedly introduced her to a languid, blond Englishman with a white silk open-necked shirt and elegantly trousered legs. The young man threw back the sheaf of blond hair from his eyes with a flick of his head and viewed her with a slow pensive glance which seemed to undress her while it also summed up her parentage and found her wanting.

"Emmie, meet Charles Beauchamp, he's also over to do some diamond prospecting and he knows several people already in Kimberley."

Emmie nodded, too disconcerted by the stare to say anything.

"We may team up," Alfred continued excitedly, "stake a claim together. Apparently that is the way to do it, then you share the workload and the costs."

He grinned happily at Charles. "It's a bit of luck meeting you like this!"

"How do you do, madam," Charles drawled, putting a second too much emphasis on the 'madam', "delighted to meet you!"

Emmie found herself staring him straight in the eye. With her best imitation of one of the First Class passengers on the boat, she said:

"By Jove! What luck! Delighted to meet you Charles!"

She had the pleasure of seeing a look of amazement cross Charles Beauchamp's bored face at this familiar and unladylike greeting. She gave him a winning smile and turned away with as much of a swish of her dusty skirts as she could muster.

Out of the corner of her eye she saw, to her annoyance, a look of amusement replace the smile and he winked at Alfred and raised an eyebrow. She would happily have slapped him but instead she moved with as much dignity as possible, over to where Mrs Foxton was examining a cup of tea which had been pushed across the bar to her. But even so she heard his remark:

"Great gal there, Alfred, a bit of spirit as well. Where'd you collect her?"

"An' where in God's name did such a wet cod turn up from?" Emmie muttered in a whisper. Mrs Foxton put the cup down and stared over her shoulder where Alfred and Charles were now laughing cheerfully.

"Well, Miss O'Connell, you seem to be keeping fine company. I understand from talk in the coach that you've just met the youngest son of an English earl!"

Emmie raised her eyebrows, "Well, his father may be grand but he's not taught his son manners. If me Da caught me brother looking at any lass like that, he'd a hit him straight on the nose an' told him to show more respect!"

Mrs Foxton, put a hand over her mouth to muffle her laugh.

"Quite right too! But one of the other passengers, the man coming to help start a newspaper on the diamond fields, said he'd heard the old Earl bought him a one-way ticket, with instructions to make his own fortune in Africa, after he cheated at cards in his father's club in London," she whispered to Emmie.

Emmie looked across at Charles Beauchamp, patting Alfred on the back and buying him another drink.

"What's he want from Alfred?" she queried.

"Money, I should think," Mrs Foxton replied promptly.

"But don't Earls have lots of money?"

"Not for gambling younger sons! He's probably spent all his money in Cape Town and now he needs a sponsor or he'll have to do some horrible physical work in Kimberley!" she enlightened Emmie with a knowing look.

"Is that so, now?" Emmie looked across at Charles, "I'm not sure Alfred's much better off, so he may be disappointed." She reached for her tea. "Not a friendly or kind face, that one. Looks down his nose like we're all just muck." She found his eyes disturbing. Her Ma had always said, "Look at the eyes, lass. They tell you a lot about the man behind them."

Charles Beauchamp had steel-grey eyes that remained impassive when his mouth twisted into a cynical smile. They reminded her of the slate-grey stones which glowed in the icy depths of the tarn near Killarga in the winter.

He was tall, he held himself with an unconscious arrogance and self-conscious ease, which commanded attention and drew a glance from every woman in his vicinity. How, she wondered, had he got into those trousers; they hugged his figure with a careless ease and the shirt flopped in loose, cool-looking folds, billowing a little in the sleeves, gathered into long white cuffs at the wrist and hanging baggily round the waist without actually

140

coming out of the waistband. Whatever he was saying, it was obviously impressing Alfred who was staring up at him from beneath his neatly trimmed mop of dark brown curly hair, his face alight with enthusiasm.

While fresh horses were being harnessed, the passengers ate a tasteless meal before continuing on towards Kimberly. Emmie shared a table with Alfred and Charles but they hardly spoke to her. They were deeply immersed in their plans for a partnership in Kimberley. Alfred spoke as though his pocket was a bottomless pit. Still, she mentally shrugged, gentlemen seemed to have money whenever they needed it, unlike her father and their neighbours in the village, who struggled to scrape up the landlord's rent on some occasions.

By the time they stopped that evening everyone in the coach, even the most reticent, knew one another extremely well. Sitting out on the veranda under the stars had proved a noisy exciting affair with much talk of their prospecting plans. The experienced prospector was a little less jubilant.

"Aw, lass," he leant towards her, "there's a few young sprigs in for a shock come tomorrow."

Alfred smiled up at her, his eyes alight with excitement. "Em, in the lamplight you look like an angel and here am I, quite the happiest man, with you and now a partner in an exciting enterprise."

Emmie was surprised and pleased. Alfred seldom directed compliments at her.

The following morning the Karroo was left behind and the country, while still flat, was more of an undulating savannah of grassland and hills with clumps of thorn trees and the promise of mountains on the horizon. Now and again kudu and springbok would leap across the road and Emmie heard stories of leopard and baboon in the mountains ahead and wondered what they would look like. The coach followed the well-worn tracks of the main route to Kimberley, turning northwest at Fauresmith, and by lunch time they were in sight of the diamond city.

As a hazy blur in the distance it had charm, the charm of dreams. The nearer it came the more the dream disintegrated. The old-timers knew what to expect – just another dusty, sprawling, untidy heap of corrugated iron and mud houses. The twisting roads fanning out like a crazy spider's web. The town had grown and progressed without any plan as more and more people from the four corners of the earth heard of the sparkling stones to be found in the gravel, and travelled by coach and wagon to join the prospectors.

The old prospector who had been to Kimberley before suddenly rubbed his ear nervously as they watched the town get closer and became more communicative.

"It may sound like quick and easy money, but that's a mirage! Least I suppose it's better than it was at first. There was no law and order, no sanitation and very little water. A stinking hell-hole in the summer."

"So now you tell us!" Emmie said, irritated by the gloom he was casting over his fellow travellers.

"Mind you, I hear it's better now," the man added hastily, "now the law's moved in an' there's better water…" his voice trailed away, "an' sanitation and some decent hotels and bars…"

The coach rumbled slowly down what appeared to be the wide, dusty, main street which was crowded with horse-drawn carts and busy pedestrians. On either side Emmie noticed a hotchpotch of buildings in brick or corrugated iron. Many of the brick buildings had shady verandas and here and there someone had made an effort with a few pots of flowers or a rather tired and dust-laden tree. The shops looked cool and dark and many had hoardings fastened outside announcing what they sold. The town certainly had a feeling of life and action and everywhere men could be seen hurrying about purposefully, many carrying digging equipment and buckets. Here and there she caught sight of women darting through the crowd moving to and fro with bundles and baskets, their bright clothes a relief against the drab brown of everything else. There were many black men as well, some of them appeared to be in charge of carts or sitting on the steps of buildings talking to one another. People turned to look enquiringly at the coach as it passed and many called out greetings to the coachman or asked for news from the passengers. Just before the main square where the coach would turn round and offload its final passengers, it stopped at what someone declared was the "best hotel in town" – The Grand.

Alfred, with Charles close behind him, opened the coach door and invited Emmie to climb down while the coachman unloaded their bags.

"We've arrived, Em, come on," he said excitedly, "Let's see what the town has to offer!"

Charles was standing behind him looking round for someone to carry his bag.

"Is he staying here too?" Emmie whispered to Alfred.

"Of course, where else? Apparently this is the best this town has to offer," he muttered back.

Emmie looked round as the coachman unloaded their bags at the bottom of the front steps to the hotel. The three red polished steps extended from the dusty road up to a highly polished veranda edged with white balustrades and pots of pinky-purple bougainvillea. Inside all was highly-polished wood with stiff horsehair sofas and a few potted palms. The thin, white-faced man behind the desk, who booked them in, wore a stiff collar, starched shirt and black tie. Emmie felt overawed. She noticed that Alfred seemed to take it all in his stride and Charles strolled in as though he owned the place, and was, to Alfred's chagrin, immediately given the best room.

Over lunch the two men began planning their finances.

"I've got some of my money coming over from Ireland shortly," she heard Alfred remark to Charles. "There should be enough from Cape Town to get us started for now." Emmie lowered her eyes but watched Alfred through her eyelashes. When he'd last discussed their finances with her the story had not been so optimistic. He'd said they were running short of cash and he was writing home for more. He very much hoped that the dress shop in Dublin had not sent its invoices to his father as yet. Now, here he was claiming that he had enough to share in a claim with Charles. Perhaps he had not wanted her to know that he had more? she pondered.

"Good lad," Charles said rather condescendingly to Alfred, "tomorrow we'll go out and stake our claim and buy the necessary equipment."

At this point Charles mopped his lips with his linen napkin and, pushing his chair back, declared:

"Got some contacts to make, old chap, must dash." Seeing Alfred's crestfallen look, he added, "Father's friends... you know..." and winked knowingly at Alfred. He bowed towards Emmie. "My apologies for dashing off, see you both later." When he'd left the dining room Emmie looked questioningly at Alfred.

"I expect he has to arrange his money. His old man has probably sent it out to a friend," he explained, brightening up at the thought.

"Well, I'm by way of hoping he's got some!" she declared.

Alfred looked put out. "His father's a wealthy lord, he'd give his son anything he wanted," he said reprovingly.

"Not quite what I heard," declared Emmie, "his Da threw him out of England for cheating at cards. You watch him, Al. He's not got a good face!"

Alfred groaned and looked reprovingly at her. "What the hell do you know, Em, you've never been outside Killarga – give a chap a chance!"

His mood changed rapidly.

"Come on then, lass, let's go and explore the town," he declared enthusiastically.

Washed and changed Emmie felt better and they wandered off together down the main street keeping to the edges to avoid the dust churned up by the cape-carts. Emmie was trying desperately not to look too crestfallen about the town and its inhabitants. It wasn't quite the glamorous hub of activity which she had imagined. There were plenty of people and they all seemed to be scurrying to and fro about their business. Many were greeting one another and shouting news as they passed. Some of the men looked quite prosperous and now and again a pony and trap would trot by, threading its way between the donkey carts, horses, barrows and darting children.

"Sure an' it's not quite the place where one would imagine getting rich, is it Al?" she commented.

Alfred looked round, his high spirits slightly dampened. "The people who strike it rich, they move on and take their money to better spots, the people round here haven't made it yet," he answered her.

"Most of them don't look like they ever will. Al, I'm not sure I like it. It's all so strange."

Alfred hesitated, as though he too felt unsure and was wondering whether he had stepped out of his depth. Then he cheered up and smiled at her.

"Don't worry yourself, Em. Now I'm in business with Charles we'll soon make money and I've told my father that I have traced the preacher to Kimberley and need more money to live while I search for him. He'll be glad and it won't be long before he sends some more, and then, imagine his face if I send him a diamond!"

Their fashionable clothes drew glances from passers-by and one little boy came up to Emmie begging for money.

"Me mam's sick an' me dad went off last week to peg a claim an' ees not come back. We're real hungry, miss."

She gave him a penny and was touched by his obvious delight as he scampered off.

"Don't do that again, Emmie," Alfred remonstrated, "You'll have every beggar in the place fleecing you if you are not careful."

"But it could be true," Emmie insisted, "and who am I to let them starve?"

"It's *my* money you are handing out so liberally," he pointed out, "and what's more, we need every penny now to get started."

"I thought you told Charles you were expecting more shortly?"

"I hope so. This hotel is damned expensive... anyway, I'll see the bank manager tomorrow and get a loan if the money from Cape Town has not arrived yet."

Beyond the hotels, saloon bars and shops were the various specialist merchants and then a jumble of small houses, more like shacks, some with attempts at gardens but most just walling in a tangled wilderness round a small square house with a corrugated iron roof. Each had its galvanised iron tank against a wall waiting hopefully for rainwater, and the inevitable small outside lavatory lurking round a corner like a deserted sentry box. Beyond the houses came the "squatters". This was the area of tents, wagons and carts where the riff-raff of the world appeared to have congregated. It sprawled down a slight incline like a tangled piece of abandoned knitting and disappeared into the distance towards the open veld where native servants and herdsmen appeared to have established their own area along with the donkeys, horses, goats and sheep. It was a depressing sight. Each small group, Emmie noticed, had staked out its bit of territory and some of them were quite clean and neat with their boundaries carefully marked out and tin baths and pails tidily stacked alongside lines of washing and small pens of chickens. Others were an ill-assorted collection of rubble which would have made a tinkers' encampment look like a parkland.

As they turned to start walking back a man standing at a small home-made gate called out to them.

"You new here? Where you from? You haven't believed this diamond thing have you? Ah, sure, there are some sparklers in this earth but they're damn hard to find. You look at your peril, it can get like a sickness. Just one more day, you never know! Meanwhile, your family are starving."

"How long have you been here?" Emmie asked kindly.

"Two years," he said. "An' not all bad. There's a municipality now and they sunk boreholes for water, but still, out here we have to pay for someone to deliver it to us."

Children and dogs seemed to be wandering about everywhere. The infants, happily barefoot and grubby, reminded her of home. Emmie thought that some of the women looked just as careworn and weary, as they peered out from under their large sunbonnets, as some of the Irish women in her village. Her mind reeled at the thought of trying to cook and wash and care for children from a tent or a wagon. They too had come all this way to find the diamonds which would make them rich... and where were they now?

"Where are the diamond diggings, Al?" She shaded her eyes and looked beyond the smoke and dust of the encampments, out to the open veld.

"The Big Hole is on the other side of the town, they tell me. And Emmie, that hat is too small; you need more brim for the sun here." Alfred had noticed her red face.

"Come, we better get you back to the hotel before you become a human lobster!" he observed with amused concern.

"Your lordship's beginning to look a bit dusty round the edges yourself," she replied tartly.

The sun and dust and disappointment had given her a headache and she was glad to wander back into the town and the shelter of their room in The Grand. She lay down on the bed and fell asleep while Alfred went to the bar to refresh himself and listen to the local chat.

The following morning Alfred emptied his wallet onto the crumpled bedcover and counted out his money.

"I'll have to go round to the bank and see whether they can help me with a loan," he informed Emmie, glancing across at her graceful figure determinedly brushing her auburn hair as though she was beating it into submission.

"Will he give it to you just like that?" she asked in surprise, "I thought you had nothing left in the Cape, least that's what you told me!"

"I've only these," he pointed to the coins on the bed, "but the bank in Cape Town said they'd write to Kimberley to give me a reference and then there's my father's letter of introduction… and I wrote to him for more, so they can loan some against that, a gentleman's word is his honour, after all." He hoped desperately that Emmie had not caught the note of uncertainty in his voice.

He finished dressing with a little extra care to the details, remembering that he had to pass himself off as a young man of means. He left Emmie sipping coffee on the hotel veranda and strolled round to the bank with as much casual confidence as he could muster, aware that his stomach felt strangely unsteady. Borrowing from your father's bank account as a student was one thing, but presenting himself well away from an area of family influence, was quite another.

He found himself sitting stiffly in front of a dapper little man with well-oiled black hair and a vast moustache who appeared to be singularly unimpressed by his name or his father's letter. In fact, as the man rather tartly pointed out, "You're nobody here, young man, until you've made a name for yourself in Kimberley. Let your father send the money and we'll be delighted to open the account. No letter has arrived from Cape Town, but even then we need a decent deposit of cash from you."

Seeing Alfred's crestfallen face, he added kindly as he rose to escort him to the door, "Look, sir, we get many hard luck stories and many very competent fraudsters. Once you have money, we can help you, but meanwhile, you're an able-bodied man, get yourself a job, and who knows, you might even find a diamond or two!"

It was the first time in Alfred's life that he had not been able to lean on his family background and the first time he had been treated with such casual disrespect. It was a slap in the face to his ego and he felt both anger and fear battling within him. The idea that he should actually take a job had never crossed his mind. He had wanted the excitement of staking a claim but had not stopped to think of who would dig and sift for the diamonds. With money he could hire labour, without he was left dependent on his own limited resources. He looked down at his hands. They were broad capable hands, good with horses, but also white and soft from the sheltered life of a medical student. He felt he had nothing to offer. For the first time he faced the fact that he had always relied on his father to ease him in and out of situations.

Emmie was sitting on the hotel veranda, sparkling with excitement about the sights and sounds and smells which she had witnessed in his absence.

He threw himself moodily into a basket chair next to her and stared unseeingly across the dusty square.

"Why, Al, you look like someone just stole your toy!" she teased him.

"Bloody bank manager, who the hell does he think he is? Wouldn't loan me any money. Wants money in the account first! Would you believe that?" he stared indignantly at Emmie.

The teasing air faded and Emmie struggled to comprehend what he was saying.

"So he wouldn't accept your father's letter?"

"Pointed out this wasn't Dublin and he didn't know the old man! Some nerve!"

"When will the money from Cape Town come up here?"

"Not until my father sends it to them! Don't ask me when that will be."

"We'll just have to be patient then."

"You don't understand. We're almost out and it could be months before the old man sends some more."

"I thought you were so rich... You told Charles you'd peg a claim with him and you were to buy the licence tomorrow, and the equipment!"

"I know, I know! What the hell can I do about it? You cost me more than I realised. Those dresses and our hotels and coaches. I didn't know two people cost so much. There's nothing for it, Charles will have to pay and I'll pay him back once the money arrives."

"He won't be pleased, Al. I wonder if he has any money? He came past here earlier looking like a storm cloud. I called out to him and he came over but he was almost too cross to talk. Seems some old diamond merchant threw him out. Said he had no room for the inexperienced and something about English titled people being opinionated, idle layabouts." She giggled and then put her hand over her mouth. "Sure, I'm sorry, Al, but he's so full of himself an' all, an' he was so cross!"

Alfred was vaguely aware of what she was saying but his mind was centred on his own problems.

"Don't be ridiculous, Emmie, of course he has money. I'm just ashamed to look a fool with all his smart friends. We'll have to leave the hotel, look for somewhere cheaper."

"Oh, Al, I'm sure sorry I caused you all this problem." She looked close to tears.

"Oh! bloody hell, don't for God's sake start crying! I'm stuck with you, I should never have agreed to bring you, but it's too late to cry now, gal!"

"Please, Al," tears were running down her cheeks, "Please don't be cross. I'll not cost you much now... I'll find some way of earning money... perhaps I could sing..."

"For God's sake, Emmie, stop snivelling and shut up, I'm trying to think!"

"I'm *not* snivelling, you silly boy you! I'll not shut up. I'll scream if I want to... right here on this veranda! I can cope with myself. You needn't think you have to support me, I've got hands and feet. If I can't get a singing job, I'll find something else!"

Alfred looked at her in alarm and was obviously relieved that there was no one else on the veranda.

"I'm not having you working, certainly not the kind of jobs they'd offer you round here. You're *my* mistress, *I'll* say what you do!"

"I'm your WHAT?" Emmie shouted at him. "What the ble'din' hell makes you think I *belong* to you? I'm Emmie... an' sure I don't belong to nobody!" She stood up, her cheeks scarlet and her eyes flashing. "Thank

148

you for your fine clothes, you can keep them. I'm off an' I'll be a burden on you no more, my fine feathered gentleman!"

"Emmie, don't be silly. Stop. I'm just upset but I didn't mean it. I like to have you with me."

Emmie swept down to their room and locked the door so that no one could see the tears brought on by feelings of annoyance and frustration, which were trickling down her cheeks. She gathered together her possessions and carefully left her Dublin dresses hanging in the cupboard. She hesitated over the pretty underwear and the negligee, then, packed them hastily into her bag.

His mistress, indeed! Alfred hammered on the door and she ignored him. She sat down on the bed and tried to pull herself together, wiping her eyes on her sleeve. She'd never thought of herself as "a mistress" and now it was slowly dawning on her that perhaps that was how others saw her. She felt humiliated. She struggled to justify her position in some other way but found she couldn't. So then, perhaps she had been his mistress… but certainly not any longer. Now it was time to make her own way. A wave of loneliness swept over her and she felt frightened by the finality of her decision. She had to think… where might she get a job? Obviously, here in Kimberley, it had to be a hotel or bar.

Alfred was waiting for her when she came out of the room.

"Come on, Em, I'm sorry I was rude. I've paid for our room here and we can go and look for somewhere cheaper. Then we'll talk."

Emmie felt herself weakening. It was such a temptation, what with knowing no one in the town and all… but then she remembered that she was his "mistress", which apparently meant she "belonged" to him… and the determination came back.

"Don't you soft-soap me, Master Alfred! I'm not waiting round for you. I'll go and find something for myself!"

"But how, with no money?"

"I'll ask."

"But *where* will you ask?"

"Maybe I'll let you know, or maybe I won't!"

She moved off down the passage with her bag, walking determinedly. Alfred took a few steps after her and then shrugged.

"Be a proud idiot then. I'll go down to the Bellvue and take a room there. You can join me later."

Emmie heard him but there was no way she was going to look back over her shoulder or say anything. She swallowed the lump in her throat and kept walking, staring straight ahead. Out on the street she walked blindly for a while, trying to fight down her fear.

It was an hour later and she had stopped at five hotels of varying degrees of drabness. No one wanted a maid or a cook and lack of experience apparently counted against her being taken on in the bar. She was becoming steadily more dispirited when she came to "Rafferty's Bar and Dining Club". The place looked clean and cheerful, with bright green and white trimmings and a highly-polished veranda. Several people were sitting on cane chairs chatting and drinking. They hardly spared her a glance as she straightened her shoulders and pushed her way through the glass-panelled door. She moved over to the door marked "Manager" in gold letters, and, putting her bag to one side, knocked cautiously. She pushed the door in answer to the peremptory "Come in", which sounded from the far side, and found herself in a moderate sized room, rather cluttered with highly-polished furniture and a large leather-topped desk strewn with pencils, pens and papers, softly lit by an elegant green-shaded oil lamp. To one side, and masked slightly by a potted palm, she could see the black trousered legs and polished boots of a man who was obviously observing her through the leaves of the palm. There was a tang of alcohol and tobacco smoke on the air. A moment of silence followed, as she stood on the soft rug and wondered whether to try and move round the desk to see him better. She twisted her hands together nervously and was about to speak when the voice said:

"Well?"

"Er, sir, I'm an experienced cook and housemaid ant I, would surely be looking for a post with a good hotel or club... like this one, sir..."

The palm leaves rustled slightly.

"Come round into the light. Let me look at you, girl," the voice ordered.

Emmie moved round and found herself opposite a lean, angular man sitting well back in a leather chair with a glass in one hand and the other fiddling with a riding crop on the arm of the chair. In the dim light his skin had an unhealthy yellow colour and his cold, pale blue eyes, looking at her appraisingly, appeared to be shot with green flecks. She'd seen those flecked eyes before, they were known as "tinker's eyes" back home.

"You Irish?" the man asked.

Emmie nodded. As he moved slightly to get a better view of her, she saw that across his cheek ran a thin scar line which extended to the remains of a mutilated ear. His black hair was straight and greasy and his mouth a thin and bitter line in the bony face. She felt uncomfortable under his unsmiling gaze and began to back towards the door, just restraining herself from turning and rushing out of the room in panic.

The man spoke, but it seemed it was more to himself than to her.

"You've the Irish looks… might cause a flutter in the hen coop… who cares?"

Then, more loudly,

"You're hired."

She thought she caught the strains of an Irish accent but it wasn't familiar to her.

"Be here at 6 a.m. tomorrow, you can work in the kitchen."

"Thank you, sir," she found herself saying and to her annoyance she gave him a bobbing curtsy as she turned to escape hurriedly through the door. At least it was a job and she was unlikely to see much of him from the kitchen, she reasoned to herself.

Out in the street with her bag, she plucked up the courage to ask a woman about rooms and was directed to a house which was really little more than a shed. She did not look up and see the man standing at his office window watching her.

To Emmie's dismay the front door was opened by another pair of hostile eyes. The woman had once been good looking, but life had etched firm lines down her pale face and her wispy blonde hair pulled back into a wayward bun was struggling out of the grip of a collection of hairpins and hanging down despondently towards her shoulders. Almost reluctantly the woman offered her a boxed-off space the size of a small cupboard and wanted money in advance.

"I'm starting a job tomorrow down at Rafferty's bar an' I'll pay you soon as I'm paid," Emmie reassured her, hoping desperately that she wouldn't be thrown out. She felt too tired to go much further.

"You not paid me by the end of the week you're out on your ear, girl," she said threateningly. "S'pose you can use the old range for your cooking. An' another thing, I'm doing you this favour only while my man's away. When he gets back you gotta go. I'm not havin' no other bloody woman round 'ere sharing my man!"

Emmie looked round the mean and grubby little house and wondered whether she should just walk out. But walk out where? It was well known that because of the influx of foreign fortune hunters, there were few rooms to let. So she just nodded and carried her bag into the small space allotted to her and closed the thin door and spread her cloak over the grubby bed. Tomorrow she'd work and then she'd do something about this room.

Chapter Eight

AFRICA – July/August 1879

ALFRED WASN'T USED to feeling lost. He was caught in an emotional bubble, almost unable to think about anything new or to plan his next action. His mind kept circling round Emmie. He couldn't believe that it was now three days since she had gone off on her own and he had not heard from her at all. He had been quite sure that she would appear back, repentant and loving. The first night he had stayed up to the early hours of the morning, expecting her to appear at the Bellvue at any moment.

The next day his anger had taken over and he had hired a horse and gone riding round the various diggings, ostensibly to see what claims were still available. He had been quite sure that she would be back and he had forced himself to stay out until sunset in order to appear nonchalant. However, there was no sign of her and no one at the Grand or the Bellvue had seen her.

Then he had a sleepless night wondering whether she was safe and dealing with that rather nasty, nagging little doubt… could she have found someone else to team up with? The next day he prowled the streets, peering into hotels and, finally, walking through the tented encampment on the outskirts of the town.

He couldn't understand himself. Why, he wondered, did he feel so upset? After all, the girl had left of her own accord. He was in no way bound to her and he could in fact live a lot cheaper on his own. The bars had plenty of girls… he'd soon get over her. By the morning he had forced himself to face the sneaking feeling that he missed her because she was a link with home, and also, dammit, he was responsible for the girl, and, it was painful to admit it, but he had become dependent on her cheerful organisation, and, worst of all, he was actually fond of her.

Crossing the dusty main square, trying to avoid being run over by horse-drawn carriages and carts and lean brown oxen pulling wagons, he suddenly saw a familiar face. It was Charles, hurrying between the traffic and followed closely by two porters from the Grand carrying his bags and several pieces of furniture. Glad to see a familiar face Alfred bounded over to him.

"Charles, old boy! How are you and where are you moving to?" he shouted above the noise.

Charles looked a little taken aback and then grinned and held out a hand.

"Good to see you, been wondering where you two had got to?"

"We've moved somewhere less pretentious," Alfred said, not wanting to admit the real reason just yet.

"Wait a minute," Charles said quickly, "got some news for you. Let's go and eat. I'll just send these two on to my new lodgings with my bags and furniture." He turned and spoke to the two hotel porters waiting patiently behind him.

"Get this stuff over to The Park Lane and the porter there will give you each a tip." He waved in the direction of a smart white building with a corrugated iron roof painted blue and a couple of palm trees in pots at its doors. Across the roof in large white letters, tinted with dust from the square, was painted, THE PARK LANE CLUB.

He turned to Alfred with a grin.

"Come on then, Alfred, let's go to Rafferty's and I'll treat you to lunch. He led the way at a steady pace up a side street and round to the veranda of Rafferty's Club.

Alfred followed him close behind. He was relieved to have met Charles, it stopped his aimless wandering and Charles might have some ideas about where to look for Emmie. He was also feeling shifty about admitting to Charles that he had no money for their claim… well, not at present, anyway… but it had to happen sometime and he'd just have to take the blow to his pride and hope that Charles could subsidise the project for the time being.

Charles, he observed wryly, was bubbling with confident excitement. He led the way at a brisk pace, springing up the steps at Rafferty's and pushing impatiently through the crowd of men on the veranda and commandeering a quiet table towards the back of the busy dining room.

They were just sinking into their seats when he bubbled over with his news.

"I've been offered a partnership in 'The Park Lane Gentlemen's Club'," he declared enthusiastically.

Alfred felt as though someone had thrown a wet towel in his face. However, some response was called for.

"Good heavens… how did you manage that?"

"Know the owner," came the quick reply, "a Londoner, I once did him a good turn and he's returning it now!"

There was something about the over-confident way he spoke that suddenly struck a cord with Alfred. He'd stretched the truth a few times himself back in Dublin and he could recognise the symptoms.

He laughed. "Come on, Charles, who owed whom, I wonder?" and with an intuitive flash, "I bet you aren't in partnership!"

Charles looked thoroughly put out. There was a pause while he decided how to take the challenge, then went for the laugh-off routine.

"Alright! Alright! So I'm a manager for now, but things are going to change pretty quick, my lad!" He smiled disarmingly and changed the subject. "What about your gal? There's a lively one indeed! Not the sort to marry but definitely the sort to bed!"

Alfred felt put out. He'd just begun to fathom the slippery charm of his companion and the tables were turned on him. He'd rather have brought up the subject himself in his own good time.

"Well, the damn woman has up and gone all independent on me! Objected to being called my mistress, would you believe?"

Charles looked startled and raised his eyebrows incredulously.

"Well, I'll be damned! The cheeky Irish hussy! Where's she now?"

"That's the big question! Gone off in a huff to make her own way in the world! Been gone three days and that's the damn peculiar thing… can't find her anywhere in this godforsaken, ramshackled town! Do you have any bright ideas?"

Charles put his head back and laughed heartily.

"Well, I'll be darned! What a nerve! Not really a town to be on the loose in either. Must have found another man to support her – you enquired round some of the bars?"

Alfred groaned inwardly. This was just what he feared and he'd had the ridiculous idea that Charles might come up with something more useful.

"Of course I've tried the bars!" he replied crossly. "Haven't you any brighter suggestions?"

"Tch! A bit touchy are we! Best let her be, man, she'll soon come running back when no one's buying her smart dresses!"

Before Alfred could come up from his misery and make further comment, their lunch arrived and Charles continued as he dabbed his chin with his napkin.

"Forget her, Alfred, no gal's worth it, apart from which there are plenty behind the bars and serving meals!"

Alfred nodded miserably.

"Anyway," Charles continued as he broke the bread on his side plate, "you don't want a tie if you are working a claim… it's man's work."

"I thought we were going into this together?"

"Look," Charles smiled disarmingly at him, "I'm going to be busy with the gaming tables in the club. I'm right behind you though and I'll give you every assistance, partner, but you'll have to sift and sort on your own… get some help with the digging."

Alfred stared at him crossly. "You had a look down that blessed 'big hole'? It's the largest thing I've ever seen and how anyone knows where their claim is or which of the myriad wires, buckets and wheels are theirs, beats me!"

Charles nodded. "Been talking to Wesley at the Club and he tells me that rumour has it that some sharp chaps are buying up all the small claims and trying to amalgamate. Apparently the big names round here are J.B. Robinson, Cecil Rhodes, Alfred Beit, Barnato and a chap called Rudd."

"So what do small fry like us do?" Alfred looked puzzled.

"Not small fry for long, Alfred! Keep that in mind! The advice I got was to move away from Kimberley, down by the dry river beds and along the river banks. Wesley tells me there is still room for more down there and lots of chance of sifting up a good big one… keep us both in comfort that would!"

"So I go out into the blazing sun and do all the work while you flip cards in a plushy club?" Alfred enquired sarcastically.

Charles smiled sardonically. "Right first time, old boy, nothing's simple here! I'll give you cash when I can and we'll share the profits in proportion." He made an expansive gesture, "I'll even go down to the alluvial diggings on the river with you and we'll stake a claim and register. 'Fraid you'll have to fork up the cash for the moment."

There was a short silence as they both finished off their main course.

Alfred laid down his fork and shrugged in embarrassment. "Truth is I'm having problems with my bank manager. I've no letter of introduction from Cape Town and no money has arrived yet. I'm skint, Charles. I cannot put in a penny for the moment." He looked into Charles's startled gaze. "Would you believe it, the damn man had the nerve to suggest that I should get a job! He won't even sub me until the money arrives!"

Charles gaze had turned hostile. "I might have known it!"

Alfred felt a surge of annoyance. The man was not taking it like a gentleman.

He leapt into the attack. "And, pray, where is all this money *you* were going to invest? What's the meaning of this 'I'll give you the cash when I can' – that was *not* our plan when we last talked."

"I'm tied up in business now. I can't spare it!"

"Big talk!" Alfred challenged him. "Don't tell me this chap was just waiting for you to come along! What happened about this job in the diamond industry which was going to fall into your lap? I'll bet," he said with a sudden flash of insight, "I'll bet *you* haven't any cash either!"

Charles looked put out for a moment and pursed his lips thoughtfully, avoiding Alfred's eye.

"So this came up and it's more lucrative, and…" with a disarming smile at Alfred, "maybe you are right about the cash but this way I can get it quickly. What's *your* story?"

"I'm dependent on a sub from home. Keeping Emmie has used up my funds. I'm here to find a nephew but I'm too skint to move until the money arrives."

"If you've relatives over here why not let them bail you out?"

Alfred shrugged, "They're dead and the nephew is only a child."

Charles raised his eyebrows sardonically. "Tough luck, Alfred! It looks, old boy, as though you may, indeed, have to work and sub yourself and I may have to resign myself to missing out on those quick bucks from your labours! Not quite the innocent little rich boy I thought you were!"

Alfred scowled at him. He recalled Emmie's story about Charles. "See you don't cheat at cards again. No Daddy to haul you out of trouble over here!"

Charles eyed him thoughtfully. "Ah well," he said, "much can be made on the side by an enterprising croupier! My advice to you would be to get yourself along to the river diggings and see if some old prospector will let you dirty your hands digging and sorting for him," he raised his napkin to his lips and pushed his chair back, "I daresay you can at least manage the bill." He flashed a cold smile at Alfred and stalked out of the busy room.

Alfred was searching in his pocket and desperately hoping that he had the cash to cover the meal, when the door from the kitchens was pushed open and there was Emmie, wrapped in a large white apron, carrying a tray of steaming soup towards a long table in the corner of the room. He drew in his breath and she glanced up to move sideways round his table, their eyes met. For a moment the soup swayed dangerously but she managed to pull herself together with a cluck of annoyance and a defiant swing of her red hair as she headed back on course for the long table. There she was greeted with several ribald comments and a couple of whistles. Whatever she replied left the men laughing and one slapped her good naturedly on the bottom as she passed him.

Alfred was seething with indignation and it was all he could do to stop himself leaping up from the table and challenging the man to a fight outside. Emmie came back via his table and began to clear it.

"An' kitchen staff's not allowed to talk to clients but I see from your expression yous thinking your property's being meddled with! Forget it, Alfred, I'm earning now ant I have a room for the moment!"

"Don't be an idiot, Emmie… this is no town for a girl on her own!"

Emmie lifted the tray and began to walk away. Looking over her shoulder briefly, she smiled at him.

"Aw, Alfred, if things get too hard, come round here an' I'll be getting you some food!"

Alfred realised just how right she was as he struggled to find the money for the meal. To hell with Emmie, for the moment, he'd have to get down to those dry diggings and find some work.

As he paid and walked out into the street he realised that he must first find that elusive preacher.

Enquiries round the tented encampment outside the town brought some success. He found himself talking to the Reverend Karl van de Ryn, a short wiry man with a black beard and kindly eyes wearing a shabby, dusty old black suit and peering out from under a black felt hat. They sat down together on a couple of wooden boxes by the side of a battered brown tent with a cross painted above the flap entrance.

He was amazed to hear that Alfred had come all the way from Ireland in answer to his letter.

"*Ja,*" he said in answer to Alfred's enquiries, "*Ja,* I remember, this man, he was a soldier… a nice red uniform… He was speaking of this child who helped to save him and his friends. He said the child was brought up by the Kaffirs and this made me think of the lady whose letter was in the Cape papers, asking for news of her son and grandson." He paused to light his pipe. "He said the child and the hunter were going to Natal. No man, you can't reach him, he was sick and they were sending him back to England."

158

There was another pause as he thought and puffed. "'Invalided out' was what I think they called it. No, no surname was mentioned for the child but the soldier said the hunter called him 'Josh'. He didn't know the hunter's surname… let me see… I think he called him Cluff, or was it Cliff?"

It seemed to Alfred as he wound his way back to his hotel, that the wild goose chase was never ending. Africa was a large continent to search. However, at present his most pressing problem was money, having given the Reverend van de Ryn his last five pounds for his information.

It was three weeks before Alfred returned from the river diggings. He felt as though he was several years older and wiser. Certainly he was dirtier and his buckskin breeches and dusty old jumper now fitted in with the clothes of the average digger. He had found a couple of jobs helping with sorting and learnt how to manipulate the mixture of gravel and sand through the 'cradle', watering it down to grade the gravel for the sorting table. With a rug or piece of canvas strung up between bushes to give shade over the old trestle table, a fly whisk of wildebeest's tail and a metal scraper, two men would be bent over the rough surface for hours sifting and sorting hopefully through the gravel from the cradle.

The camp was a rugged, dusty place on the dry river bank, with little privacy, amongst hundreds of other similar encampments. The work was hot and boring, although the company, especially round the campfire at night, had been congenial enough with a rich confusion of accents and enough stories of adventure to fill a young man with wild dreams. The pay was a pittance unless a diamond was found, in which case there was a small bonus all round.

He had managed to put his share into the communal food kitty and to buy a motley collection of second-hand clothes from a chap who was giving up the dream of quick riches to return to his farm in the Cape. Certainly, he had to admit to himself, he had learnt the hard way that very few people made a sudden fortune. He had begun to appreciate that by owning your own claim and working through the daylight hours at digging and sifting, you just might be lucky, or you might only make enough to buy your next meal. It was the infrequent good luck stories of quick riches which kept everyone going, hour after hour, day after day. Any minute one just *might* turn up that priceless gem.

The need for a bath, some female company, a comfortable bed and a decent bar, finally brought him back into Kimberley.

Alfred had swallowed his pride and persuaded Charles to let him leave his baggage stowed in his room at The Park Lane when he went off to the diggings. He arrived back hot and sticky and covered in a fine film of red dust.

"Good God, man, what on earth is this?" Charles commented with a grin, "It's not my smart friend from the Grand Hotel, is it?"

Alfred found himself hastily shepherded round to the back entrance.

"Well, how did you get on? No flags have been run up, so I presume you haven't found the biggest stone on the dry diggings as yet?"

Alfred shrugged. "Even if I had it wouldn't be mine. It's hard work for a pittance for the bloody claim holders."

"Tough life out there!" Charles teased him.

"We found a few small ones, enough to keep us all in food, but I'm telling you, Charles, it's a mug's game unless you own the claim and even then it all rests on luck."

"Couldn't you slide a few in your pocket? It's done regularly you know, by black labour and white!"

"Want me lynched? No, do that and someone would be bound to split. The claim owners are pretty hard on that sort of thing… Several chaps have just mysteriously disappeared. Probably at the bottom of some disused claim!"

Charles gave a mirthless laugh. "Your trouble is you're too honest. No one makes money out of honesty!"

"Least of all you, I suppose?" Alfred said, raising an eyebrow enquiringly.

"We are into Lady Luck here, but we also watch like hawks. The most respectable gentlemen are not above a fast buck! Had to blackball a chap only last week, he and his fearfully respectable friend had worked themselves out a crafty code system!"

"Any partnership coming out of all this?" Alfred asked as innocently as he could.

Charles totally ignored the question. "Listen, I'll wangle you a hot tub to scrub down in, an' old Rafferty's Hotel might be able to put you up!" He winked knowingly at Alfred. "I gather you bumped into her before you left!"

"To hell with you!" Alfred growled, "I hope you haven't been trying to make off with her while I've been away?"

"Wouldn't dare! Anyway, she's a bit of a firebrand and I'm apparently not her favourite person!"

160

"Ah, so you did try!"

"Well… only a first approach as you two were apparently not talking! No harm done, my friend! Oh, by the way, met up with the manager of the Grand Hotel in the Club a few nights ago, said he has a letter for you. Came via the hotel."

Alfred felt cheered. It was amazing how alone a man could feel in this vast continent. Emmie's sudden burst of independence had left him feeling decidedly insecure, he realised with some annoyance. Ah well, maybe it was a letter from home sorting out his finances. Charles, he noticed, was looking very smart and not saying much.

"Well then, if it didn't work with Emmie, who is the lucky lady? You're like a cat with cream on his whiskers!" he enquired as he sat in the tin tub soaping himself down.

"Gal I knew from Cape Town. Dancing with the troupe advertised out front – the 'Parisian Parasols' – rather taking the town by storm, they are."

Alfred's mood lifted still further. A bit of life in the town! Perhaps he wouldn't tell Emmie he was back after all!

"So, and how do I get to meet these valuable gems?"

Charles eyed him without enthusiasm. "You're looking pretty brown and fit, even picked up a bit of muscle, I see. Working on the diggings did you no harm, damned if I'm allowing you near them!"

Alfred stepped out onto the white mat with rivulets of water running down his torso as he languidly wrapped a towel round his waist.

"Anyway," Charles continued, backing away from the drips, "these gals only go out with money. Alas, they also have a prize fighter and an old harridan constantly on guard. You can't get past the stage door! Well, that is, unless, of course, you have class and polish… and know one already!"

"Cough it up then, which one have you collared… And save me the 'closely guarded' bit. I met a lot of show girls in Dublin and there were no hedges of thorns round any of them! You're an old humbug who wants all the fun to himself, Charles!"

A slow smile of satisfaction spread across Charles's face. "A red-headed firebrand called Josy… She's the lead dancer and she's a class gambler as well!"

"Fine, fine, now for the introductions… when do I meet this dream?"

"No way, Alfred, I'm not a charitable institution, you can work that out your way and good luck to you! Just remember what I told you about their minder, old Waldheim, his footwork is fast!"

Alfred walked round to the Grand Hotel and collected his letter.

There was no money in it. In fact, worse than that, there was an indignant line from his father pointing out that the money he had taken and the extra he had loosened from the Dublin Bank, should be more than enough to keep one young man in comfort for several months. The finely scrawled pages went on to tell him that the family had received a letter from a hunter who was staying in Natal, to say that he had found a young, white boy living with a tribe in the Zoutpansberg Mountains and was quite sure that the boy was their missing grandson. The letter instructed Alfred to go down to Natal to meet the boy, ascertain whether he was indeed his missing nephew, and if so, to bring him home to Ireland.

Apparently the hunter was expecting quite a sizeable sum for his services and the family would be sending this money through from the bank in Dublin to the bank in Kimberley. This transaction was expected to take some time but the money would arrive in due course.

Alfred decided to drown his sorrows at the lack of cash at the bar at Rafferty's Hotel, and while there he would talk to Emmie and perhaps get a room for a couple of nights. He needed to think about his Father's instructions and it would be good to talk it over with Emmie.

Emmie had not taken long to be promoted. She worked hard and Jules Rafferty had decided to promote her from the kitchen and instructed the barman to teach her about mixing and pouring drinks. She felt well able to take the customer's banter and to give back cheerful lip without being rude or prudish. She got on well with all the other girls, except for Jules' girlfriend, Maria. It was obvious that Maria was jealous. She was in charge of the staff and most of them jumped to do what she wanted and she made it plain that she would not be usurped by this saucy Irish newcomer.

Jules employed three other girls to serve the drinks and meals. In the evenings they doubled as entertainment with simple dance routines, or led the singing round the old piano. He wasn't fussy about their private lives as long as they brought in the customers and kept them happy. The girls shared a room at the back of the hotel, where they made their own costumes.

Emmie, ambitious to get on now that she was earning her own money, set her heart on joining the troupe. She knew she could sing better than any of them. Commonsense made her cautious. She realised that she would have to gain their confidence before she did any singing or their jealousy would make them unite against her. It was difficult not to show her excitement, she could see her dreams of a singing career creeping closer.

She worked hard and obligingly in the kitchen and made a close friend of the raw-boned Scottish girl, Morag, who was the cook and the two local maids who washed up the dishes.

"Now, you be careful of that Maria," Morag whispered as Maria swept out of the kitchen. "She's right bitter an' twisted just now."

"What's up with her?"

"It's all them girls from the cabaret – och now, you ken them!"

"Ah now, I know, you mean the 'Parisian Parasols'?"

"Sure, them, an every mon in this damn town is after trying to take them out!"

"So what's it to her?"

"Jules… this little party of his we're clearing up after… He gave it for a couple of them and she's eaten up with jealousy, you see she was not invited to attend even!"

"No wonder she's upset… quite a nerve to entertain them under her nose! Mind you, he's a creepy kind. I don't like the way he watches me. Don't know how she lives with him." Emmie dried the last of the plates and seated herself at the table to polish the silver.

Morag nodded. "Do our jobs we do, he pays well, but now, it's not for the love of him." She washed out the drying-up cloth, hung it up and sat down opposite Emmie to drink a cup of coffee.

"Morag, where did he get this silver? He is always so insistent each time he entertains, that it goes straight back upstairs, all dry and polished."

"Don't know, lass. Doesn't look the sort to have family silver!"

"No." Emmie turned the spoon round and stared at the crest emblazoned on the handle. "My God, Morag!" she put down the spoon and grabbed a fork and then a silver-handled knife, "Well, I just don't believe this!"

"What's up, lass?" Morag lowered her coffee cup and stared curiously at her.

Emmie had reached for the teaspoons and unrolled them from the lint in which they were stored. She was staring at the array of cutlery which she had laid out on the well-scrubbed kitchen table.

"It can't be…" She peered closer at the spoon she was holding, "but it certainly is, I'd know it anywhere after all those hours!" She looked across the table at Morag. "This is the same crest as was on the silver of a family I knew in Ireland!" she declared incredulously.

Morag raised an eyebrow. "An' what were you doing eating from crested silver, lassie?" she queried sceptically.

"No, I polished it... I often helped in the kitchens and my favourite job was polishing the silver. Sure now, ant I'll never forget this crest. See, there was a story to it ant Mrs Lyons-Montgomery, she told me what it meant one day when she came into the maids' parlour an' I was polishing a silver dish. Morag, how in heaven's name did this get to be here in Kimberley?"

Morag walked round the table and looked over her shoulder. "I've no idea but there is more of it and I've heard people say," and she lowered her voice to a whisper and nodded her head knowingly, "he's none too straight. He's from Ireland, perhaps he bought it or came by it through some other means..."

"No one ever mentioned a robbery at the Great House and you say he has had this some time?"

Morag nodded as she went back to her coffee.

Thoughtfully Emmie began to roll the spoons back up in the lint and place them in the black box which was kept for the silver. She was thinking back to Ireland and remembering that elder sister in the family, Florence, who had married and moved to Africa. She could recall the preparations for her wedding and the chat in the kitchens at Belhavel. Florence had been given some of the family silver as a wedding present. Emmie had been too young to absorb much of the talk but she remembered hearing that the young couple had disappeared and she knew that it was their son whom Alfred had told her he was looking for. She rolled up the last of the knives and added them to the box which would be left on the table for Jules to collect before he shut the hotel for the night. Morag was closing the windows and waiting, ready to turn the lamps off before they left.

"Morag," she whispered, "don't say anything about this... perhaps I am wrong."

"Morag looked slightly surprised. "No, lassie, there's not much could be done anyway. He's a slippery one that Rafferty and I've no wish to lose my job. It's best forgotten."

Mentally Emmie agreed with Morag's assessment of Jules Rafferty. His cold, snakes' eyes appeared emotionless and unblinking... He shared jokes with his customers, but the smile that twisted his thin lips seldom reached his eyes. He had done her no harm but she sometimes caught him staring thoughtfully at her, she would shudder slightly and wonder at the fine purple line of that old scar on his face.

164

To his surprise Alfred found Emmie serving drinks behind the bar. He glared his disapproval but she just smiled cheerfully and put a hand across the bar to rest briefly on his arm.

"My God, Alfred, and aren't you the handsome one! The brown colouring suits you ant so do the clothes! I've missed you, lad! Were you digging up your fortune then? I'm looking for the money bags?"

Alfred groaned in mock frustration. "And to think of all the time and money I have wasted trying to turn you into a lady and just look at you now, Em! Your accent as thick as ever and you behind a bar! It's not a job for a lady. But... am I glad to see you!"

"Aw, Alfred, you know I'm no lady, but I do enjoy to play at one and I loved the beautiful clothes!" She leant towards him excitely, "I'm hoping I may get to sing with the girls here!" Then, seeing the disapproval on his face, she added, "Come, Alfred, it's a start and I can go on to greater things ant better places, but how else do I start?"

Alfred shook his head in despair and then grinned at her. "Never mind, it's good to see you and I've not come back with a diamond for you but I've enough money for a good meal. Can you join me after you've finished here?"

The barman moved over disapprovingly. "Keep you friends for later, Emmie."

She hastily picked up a glass and began to polish it. "I'll be off at six, meet me here, in the bar," she whispered to Alfred and then moved off to serve another customer.

Alfred booked himself a room at the reception desk and went down the road to Market Square to see what notices were posted on the board next to the coach office.

He was in a thoughtful mood when he and Emmie met that evening. They went round to the new Kimberley Hotel to eat. He told her about the dry diggings and she listened sympathetically and told him about her lodgings.

"She's an odd one, Al, is Maggie, she sits on her own in the house and drinks. Ant she has no friends. I've cleaned the place up for her ant sometimes I cook for the both of us. The furniture is pretty rough ant this husband, he's supposed to come back from prospecting but there's no sign, an' I think he'll never return. I t'ink it's my rent keeping her going at present. She eats like a poor, wee sparrow. I'm glad to get out to work, ant I take no time off 'cause it's better at Rafferty's."

"Em, I wish I could offer you help but my father is not sending any money. He thinks I've had enough!"

"Ah now, Alfred, sure I'm not wanting that. I manage, ant next week I'll see what the girls say to me singing with them. I've done plenty for them ant we get on real well. Now, tell me the news from home. I had a few lines from Ma, ant she is none too pleased with me for taking this job as a lady's maid! I have to make up what it's like ant I'm not sure she believes me! An…" She eyed Alfred with a raised eyebrow. "I'm thinking the word's reached her that yous in the same bit of Africa! My Da's no doubt warming his belt up!"

Alfred grinned at her, "And Father Donohue will be saying his prayers for fallen women again!"

Alfred explained the contents of his letter.

"So, what now, Alfred? There's you a penniless gravel scraper an' me a bar girl! Ant, somewhere in this wild country, there's a boy looking for a home." She summed it up neatly.

Before Alfred could reply she suddenly recalled the crest on the silver. "Ah, ant another thing, Alfred, I found out something odd. This Mr Rafferty here, he's got silver like yours back in Belhavel!"

Alfred raised his eyebrows in disbelief.

She nodded agreement. "Sure, an' I could not believe it either. But I'd swear it's the same lion's head ant the dagger, sword or whatever, next to it, is broken in the same way."

"You're dreaming, Emmie. Old Rafferty would not have silver… Let alone with a crest… out here, in a mining town in the back of beyond! The sun's got to you girl. It's not possible."

Emmie looked offended. "I polished it enough times back home!" She reached down for her neatly rolled-up apron which was on the floor beside her and delved into the pocket. "I put a teaspoon into my apron pocket to show you. The old snake, he counts it all to check we're not stealing it, but he forgot the teaspoons! You'll see," she handed it triumphantly to him.

Alfred stared in incredulous disbelief. Certainly it was the same rather over large teaspoon with the shell design at the top and the double edging line round the sides of the handle. He picked it up and stared closely at the crest etched near the top of the handle. He felt a cold wave of disbelief go through his body. There was no doubt about it. There was the broken javelin on the left and the lion's head on its plinth on the right. He turned it over to confirm the Dublin silver mark on the back. There could be no doubt.

"Well, I'll be buggered!" He stared at Emmie's triumphant face in amazement. "You're absolutely right, girl! But what the hell is going on?" His brow puckered in confusion, as he stared at the spoon again. "How much of this stuff has he got?"

"A whole set. Enough for ten people at least. He's pretty secretive. It only comes out when he has someone to impress and he plays at being a wealthy man. Morag says he had it ever since she came here. She has to wash it and count it for him before it goes back upstairs." She reached over for the teaspoon. "I'll have to get it back next time I take a meal up to his rooms. If he's not in, I'll slide it back into the drawer."

Alfred was drumming his fingers on the table and looking into the distance. "We've no Rafferty in the family and no burglaries that I know of. Em, it could only be one thing... it has to be Florence's silver. It was a wedding present from my parents. Flo would never have sold it. How the hell did this man come by it?"

Emmie leant towards him across the table and whispered, "Alfred, all I know is it won't have been fairly come by. The man's got a mean face, an' all. For God's sake don't go ant ask him. I'd be skinned alive or just disappear! The girls, they say that one lady, a housekeeper, asked a few questions about him once and she never returned to work again an' her landlady said she never cleared her room neither." She shuddered quietly. "Honest, I'd not work here but it's a way to start with the singing!"

"I'll make it known while I'm staying that you are my girl, that way he'll not dare touch you. I'll see what I can find out about your Mr Rafferty. Maybe I'll have a few drinks with his friends."

"I'm scared, Al, when are you going back to the dry diggings?"

"I'm not. A Mr Rudd's advertising for someone to take a load of machinery down to Natal and the money's good. I also have to take a look at this so-called 'nephew' of mine. I'm not sure how I'll tell whether he's genuine." He paused. "You'd better come with me, Emmie."

Emmie looked worried. "Alfred, the moneys good 'cause there's a war on down there. This transport driving. It's dangerous, you know, an' you know nothing about wagons ant oxen... anyway, I can't come, I'm hoping to start singing soon."

"For God's sake, woman!" Alfred muttered in exasperation. "Singing can't be *that* important and how can I protect you if I'm away? There'll be no one to turn to... As to the war, they say the British Army is back in control again and the passes are open. In fact, according to the papers, Lord Chelmsford, the Commander, is about to sail back to England after beating the might of the Zulu army at Ulundi. Anyway, I'll have a couple of tribesmen with me who will know about the country. Come on, come with me, lass, we'll manage together!" he cajoled hopefully.

"No, Alfred," it was Emmie's turn for exasperation, "this is my only chance to get a start in what I've always wanted to do. Besides, I'm not fancying the idea of weeks in a wagon in wild mountain country. I've heard the men talking in the bar. They say they earn their money in danger, an' old Bill Norris, the coach driver, he says the country's still crawling with tribesmen who don't know the war's over. Some chap, Wool... something... he's arrived to take command and clean up, an' Bill, he says there is trouble aplenty ahead! I think the dry diggings would be a lot safer... and nearer."

"Em, be reasonable! Ladies don't sing in bars or on the stage and this is the only way I can hope to earn the money to buy a claim. Working for others is just a mug's game... it makes enough money to feed for a few weeks, that's all."

"What's this about bein' a lady? Who's the lady? Are you planning to marry me then and keep me by your side? I'm Emmie O'Connell, the miller's daughter... remember? You said I was your ... now suddenly I'm a lady, just 'cause it suits you to have company and a bed companion." She looked challengingly at Alfred. "Which is it, Al – am I to return to Leitrim to eat off crested silver or to polish it?"

Her voice had risen in indignation and Alfred looked round in embarrassment, aware that several tables had turned to look at them in some amusement.

"Shush, girl! Alright, you stay behind, but don't expect my damn sympathy when things get difficult. It's not a woman's world, and those bar singers are a tough lot!"

Emmie felt close to tears. She was frightened but she was determined. Over the last few weeks it had dawned on her that Alfred was really only a good friend. His lack of response to her query about marriage had confirmed that, and, in a way, lifted a burden of guilt from her shoulders.

While he had been on the dry diggings she had taken stock of her situation and commonsense had prevailed. One day, she was aware, Alfred would return to Belhavel and she would not be welcomed by the village or the Great House. She had to admit to herself that, fond though she was of him, he had only been a means of escape from Ireland and deep down she had never intended to marry him.

"Lass, you made your decision when you left home," Morag told her firmly when she confided in her as they polished the glasses for the bar.

Emmie nodded. "I know really, and I'm still not sorry, but, sure now, he's like part of home."

"'Course he is," Morag agreed, "you'd know if he was someone special, seems he's not, but he's been a sanctuary and a financial support..."

"Ant also a friend," Emmie threw in.

"Aye, that and all, but now you can make your own way and like as not you'll sing your way to success and perhaps meet the man of your dreams – who knows!" she winked at Emmie.

Emmie lifted the tray and turned to the door, looking back over her shoulder she added, "an' then the family'll know I can succeed outside Killarga and then maybe I could return to the village."

Morag smiled at her. "Go on then, lass, it's dreams we all need... and some do come true."

She cried silently into her pillow that night for the innocent girl who had left Ireland... and for the look of frustrated annoyance on Alfred's face when she would not go back to his hotel room with him... and for her own loneliness without him.

"It's no good, Al, you're my very best friend now, but you're not my lover no longer. Sure, I'll help you in any way I can, but I'll not live with you again," she spoke out loud, setting it straight in her own mind. Brave words, she thought as she lay in bed in her dingy little room and wished she was back home sharing her duck-down bed with Peggie.

Alfred felt disgruntled. Life was full of uncertainties. He'd been hired for the trip to Natal and he'd lied about previous experience. He'd taken on a large Zulu called Umfolozi, who claimed to know the route, and Umfolozi had brought a young child who appeared to be about eight years old and had a name which sounded to Alfred like 'Acorn', who was to be their 'Voorloper' – the one who led the oxen. Between them they would take care of the trek oxen. Rudd had fitted him out with a wagon, gun and ammunition and a letter of introduction to the trader down in Natal. The customer was just outside Pietermaritzburg but Alfred had permission to ride down to Port Natal to see to his own business before returning to the diamond fields.

Back at Rafferty's Bar he found himself on a stool next to a wizened old prospector whose wrinkled face bore testimony to many years of African sun and rough living. The man seemed to know Jules Rafferty.

"Off and on, I known him for many years. Mind you, he's made good and built himself this place... a little diamond field of his own! He used to hunt an' trade. Not always very legitimate, mind!"

Alfred's attention was caught and he tried to sound light-hearted as he probed further.

"What do you mean by that, none of us do things strictly 'legitimately', do we?"

The old man eyed him through a haze of pipe smoke. Then he pushed his glass across to the barman for a refill. As the bartender came up to return the glass he spoke to him.

"Jackson, you've worked for Rafferty for many years, you know what I mean when I say his business isn't always legitimate?"

Jackson, who was normally a rather dour man, laughed harshly, looked round quickly and then nodded at the old prospector. "Joe, you 'n I know a thing or two, but it's best not talked about. If it hadn't been for that fancy wagon I don't reckon he'd have started here. As it is, he's the boss an' I ain't say'n too much."

He winked at Joe and moved off to serve another customer.

"See what I mean?" Joe peered at Alfred.

Keeping his voice as even as possible Alfred asked casually, "What's this about a wagon...? There are hundreds of wagons hereabouts and no one's going to make a mint out of any of them unless they are loaded with diamonds."

"Oh, the diamonds, them's natural hereabouts... a bit of illicit diamond buying had been done by most of the rich boys. Mind, the police they're tightening up these days." He paused to take a swig of whiskey and a puff of his pipe.

Alfred waited politely. He leant confidentially towards Alfred. "Found an abandoned wagon they say. A mighty fine one, all painted fancy like. Sold it to that old Griqua Chief, Adam Kok... I'm hearing the old boy used it to cross the mountains when he set up Griqualand East. Fancied himself in a painted wagon, the old bastard did!" He looked into the middle distance. "Some say there was more in that wagon than anyone knew about." He cast a sly look up at Alfred. "His partners that trip, one had a very strange accident over by the big hole an' the other moved down Grahamstown way... suddenly, he owns a big farm an' his hunting days are over!" He shook his head thoughtfully, "Rum do, rum do, lad... but ask no questions. People round him's mighty tight with information."

"What do you mean, 'an abandoned wagon'? Who'd leave a wagon if it had valuables in it?" Alfred signalled the barman over and ordered two whiskies.

The old boy reached greedily for the glass. "Seems the family who owned it were killed. The kaffirs up there's always given trouble. No one knows no details an' it's old news now, laddie. No trace was ever found." He threw back the last of the whiskey.

"What makes you think he got more than that wagon, Joe?" Alfred leant confidentially towards him.

"Well, such a fine wagon an' all... they do say it was a gentleman from England who was seeking to get himself a farm up north. They'd have had all their possessions, but the police, they could find no trace. The tribes, they would have used what they could and left a lot behind what they didn't understand. No, right peculiar... you know..." he ruminated. "They say he found the trek oxen and sold them in Pretoria. Now, what tribesmen would leave the oxen? That's the main thing they want! If you ask me it weren't no tribesmen, it were brigands or... hunters after a quick dollar!"

"What about the people though? Why would they disappear?" Alfred asked quickly.

The old man peered hard into his face. "You mighty nosey 'bout something what's such old news? Listen to me, lad, those people they just disappeared an' that's the way it'll stay. An' don't say old Joe was talking 'bout it with you, see?"

Alfred realised that he had said too much and shown too much interest. The old man was staring suspiciously at him. "I was only interested," he lowered his voice. "It's a nice place he's got here and I wondered how he'd come by it. I suspect it's illicit diamonds." He winked knowingly at the lined face behind the smoke. "I'm going up to the Mac-Mac Mine to see what's happening there... heard rumours of gold... didn't it happen up that way?"

The old man was showing signs of nervousness. Alfred watched him as he swung away. Then he peered back over his shoulder. "They say it was up near Potgietersrust... you not a dick are you? Police ain't popular in this bar!" He grabbed his empty glass and moved further down the bar.

Alfred shook his head and then sat over his drink, deep in thought. Could that wagon, he mused to himself, be anything to do with Florence and Folly Barton? Certainly they were moving north when they disappeared. Could the silver have been stolen from them, or perhaps pawned and not reclaimed? How could two adults and a child disappear quite so completely? It made him feel vaguely uneasy. He actually had no plans to go north but acknowledged to himself that he would not mind a look at the spot where that wagon had been found. He felt his first stirrings of curiosity about the boy. What would he look like? Would he have any memories which might help to identify him?

Jackson, the barman, interrupted his reveries. "Old Joe's been telling me you's getting nosey. Look, mate, I know you's not police, you's Emmie's boyfriend. But take a piece of sound advice an' keep clear of this bar in future. We're not so fond of nosey toffs; and the boss, he's not keen on anyone who meddles in his business." He added, almost as an afterthought, "You'll make it difficult for Emmie if you come back."

Alfred was tempted to be rude but some instinct made him look over his shoulder. Jules Rafferty was leaning languidly against the bar door looking round the room. His lean bony face gave him the appearance of a hungry wolf, his eyes were dark, narrow gipsy eyes, possibly from an Irish tinker family, Alfred thought, staring at him. He had to admit that the man had a certain grace. He looked as though his lean frame would move with speed if necessary and he might even pack a good punch. Alfred decided on discretion.

"You look after Emmie and treat her correctly or I'll be round to see you," he muttered threateningly to the barman as he moved off.

Walking across the hall he met Emmie. They moved out onto the veranda while he told her in a low voice about his meeting with old Joe and also about the barman's threat.

"I'm really worried about you while I'm away, Em. Change your mind and come with me?"

Emmie shook her head determinedly. "I'm not one for travelling through great mountains on an old wagon. Al, you make your money ant take care of yourself, good luck to you!"

Alfred shrugged resignedly. "I'll be away about a month or a bit more. Please check with the bank about that draft I'm expecting. The hunter will have to come up here to get his money," he looked thoughtfully at her. "Look, if you have any problems, you let Charles know, he'll handle it."

"Oh God! Al, not that gambling toff? Now he'll think he owns me and try to take liberties!"

"He wouldn't dare, Emmie."

"Ah sure, don't be foolin' yourself, the man's no gentleman beneath the fine clothes and the airs and graces!"

"No, I realise that… I mean he's fully occupied! His girlfriend is that tigress from the Parisian Parasols, Miss Josy. She'd chop him into little pieces if he so much as looked sideways at another woman! He's so besotted he's mounting debts like a termite nest trying to keep her in the way she intends to get used to!"

Emmie giggled. "Serves him bloody well right!"

Chapter Nine

AFRICA – May to Sept 1879

JOSH WOKE WITH a start and looked round. He was sprawled on the deck of a fishing boat surrounded by a web of nets draped over casks, baskets and floats. In his dreams he had been back in the kraal, the great marula branches spread protectively above his head. He lay back as the last remnants of the disquieting dream faded and the knot of tension in his throat subsided.

The sun was warm for a winter's morning and he was sheltered from the wind by the net locker. In the cloudless sky above him the gulls were wheeling and screeching and a strong aroma of salt and fish mingled with the spicy land breeze to remind him that he was hungry.

Sundays were the one day when the harbour seemed to quieten down and accommodate itself to church bells and strolling couples. For the remainder of the week it was a cheerful and exciting bedlam of water traffic moving to and fro, to the accompaniment of ship's horns, bells, whistles and shouts, as passengers, cargo and livestock were moved across the harbour between the coasters, clippers, schooners and whale boats.

He sat up and squinted towards the sky. The sun looked as though it might be about midday. It was time to collect Cliff and walk up together to Rosie's bar for a good Sunday dinner. He put the net mending gear back into the basket and smiled at the thought of the lecture he would get from old Ned. He had been learning about mending nets and sea gear from the old fisherman but he had done little this morning. It was so seldom that he had a chance to lie idly in the sun and sleep had swept over him uninvited. Reaching for the coarse brown fisherman's jersey which Ned had passed on to him, he slipped his tanned arms into the sleeves and hauled the rest over his head with increasing speed as he recalled that Jessica had promised to come down and meet him so that she could walk back up to the bar with them… well… with him in particular.

He leapt off the fishing boat onto the pier just in time to be greeted by Jessica running down from the customs shed, her brown hair blowing in a silky stream behind her, blue eyes sparkling with mischief.

"Josh, you lazy lump! I bet you were asleep," she challenged him cheerfully.

"What gave you that idea? Ned's nets were a mass of holes!"

"I bet they still are! Some of them larger than others!"

They linked arms and walked cheerfully up towards the houses on Harbour Road.

"Did you stop in at our rooms?" he queried, looking sideways at her.

"I did indeed." She squeezed his hand and looked up at him with an impish smile. "Unfortunately Cliff had beaten you to it and was scrubbing his hands – I'd hoped for a few secret minutes alone with you. There is no doubt that the girls know something is happening between us and it is really difficult to get away on my own. There always seems to be one of them wanting to come everywhere with me, or finding me work when I don't need it!"

Josh loosened hold of her hand and put his arm round her shoulders, very aware of the soft warmth of her body against his. He smiled down at her.

"We'll find a way to avoid them, perhaps we can get away after we've eaten. "Jes…" he looked seriously at her, "my whole body just aches for you." She lifted her face and gave him a quick fleeting kiss on the lips. Then her mood changed and she asked in a puzzled voice: "What's wrong with Cliff, he's been more moody than usual this week?"

"Mm… it's my relatives, I think. He's found a farm he likes up Port Edward way but he needs money. His money from the work on the cargo lighters is good but it won't buy the place… and he's restless," he added.

"What have your relatives got to do with it?"

"Well… I think he wants to get me off his hands and he hasn't had a letter back yet," he muttered, his good mood suddenly drifting away. "I half hope he never hears… I could help him on a farm… but when I suggest it he just gets cross and walks away."

Jessica considered this for a moment or two in silence.

Josh's arm slid away from her shoulders and they walked in step with one another. He was slowly adjusting to the ways of the white tribe and Jessica had a way of explaining away some of the strangeness, she made things seem quite normal. She was probably about his own age he estimated. He knew from hearing the other girls talk, that her parents had come out as settlers to Natal and their ship had foundered in a storm as it rounded the mouth of the bay. The little girl had been one of the few survivors picked up by the rescue boats. She had lived with an elderly teacher for a couple of years and when the teacher died Rosie had taken her in. She was only allowed to work in the bar but mixing with the other girls made her wise beyond her years.

"What are you thinking?" he asked curiously as he watched several expressions flit across her freckled face.

"I'm thinking he's feeling guilty."

"Why should he feel guilty?"

"Well... He's not much of an example!"

"I don't need 'an example'," he said with dignity.

She looked thoughtfully into his face as though choosing her next words carefully. "I mean... well, I wonder... are they paying him a reward for you?"

"A reward?"

"Well... I heard Bertha saying he didn't do much for nothing an' she'd never known him stay still in one place for so long... and I just fell to wondering..."

"That Bertha! You know she doesn't like me, she'd say anything. She's a jealous old bitch!"

Jessica nodded and changed the subject, but Josh was silent as he turned this idea over in his mind. He had to admit to himself that it might well be possible, although it hurt. Cliff meant so much to him, could it be that he was only a means of gaining cash to Cliff? His mind ran round like a rat in a cage as they walked, more slowly now, towards the house.

Cliff greeted them with a nod. He was bent over a basin cleaning pitch off his fingers. On Sundays he had to see to the repair of the lighters and make sure they were in reasonable condition for work the next week. It was a busy time in the harbour. Over the last year there had been a constant stream of military shipping embarking and disembarking in the small port. Guns, horses, stores, everything had come up by sea from Cape Town. The Zulu war had hit the headlines in Britain and Isandhlwana had wiped the complacency off the faces of the British.

Never had Natal known so much activity and to add to the depressing war news there had been the tragedy of young Louis Napoleon's death when he was in the care of the British Army. This had been followed by the ceremony and military honours of the return of his body to Durban and its sad departure on the voyage back to his mother, the Empress Eugenie.

At last Lord Chelmsford, the military commander, had managed to reverse the tragedies of the last few months with a decisive win over the

Zulu king at Ulundi. Cetchwayo had escaped but the might of his army was smashed. This success had come just in time to save Chelmsford's military career. His replacement, Sir Garnet Wolseley was already in the country but prevented by weather and communications from reaching him before the battle, so the glory was his alone.

That canny old Zulu chief, Cetchwayo, was hiding in the hills and valleys of Zululand and no doubt it would be a while before this new commander would be able to winkle him out. However, Wolseley was only on a 'mopping up' operation and each day ships were arriving to take detachments of soldiers back to Cape Town and then home to England.

To Josh's delight, amid much ceremony and firing of salutes, the harbour had been the scene of Lord Chelmsford's departure two days earlier. The military band had left him speechless with excitement and the scarlet and white uniforms had reminded him of the hospital camp back at Helpmekaar.

Cliff, was less impressed. "So, I'm grateful for their help when I was ill but what else could they do? Don't really feel I owe the British much, and certainly not our horses."

Josh looked up with quick concern. "What about our horses?"

"There's some talk of martial law and commandeering the remaining horses and wagons for military use."

"They couldn't take Charity and Jackalet!"

"Oh yes they could. Apparently, until Cetchwayo is caught we are still a war zone."

"What can we do?" Josh felt lost, he still found some of the rules by which the white men lived, very hard to understand.

Cliff seemed to catch the note of concern. He ruffled Josh's hair. "I'll take them up to a friend in the Valley of a Thousand Hills. It's a remote farm, they'll never find them there."

The walk up to Rosie's tavern was subdued. Cliff was busy with his own thoughts. Jessica and Josh walked behind him talking quietly. Jessica was telling him the little she could recall about England and her parents and he was searching his memory for traces of his own parents.

"My grandparents, on both sides of the family, had died, and both my parents had no brothers or sisters, so my dad said there was nothing to stay in England for. We sold off the farm in Suffolk and he planned to use the money to buy a new one here…" her voice trailed off.

Josh put an arm round her shoulders and gave her a quick hug of sympathy. "At least you remember where you came from. I can only recall that we always seemed to be moving and I can just remember a lovely wagon with pictures painted on its sides and I have a hazy memory of my mother as a lady with a gentle face, beautiful blue eyes and long blonde hair. My father was a tall man with a brown moustache who always seemed to be laughing and throwing me in the air. That's all I remember."

Jessica gave his hand a squeeze. "We orphans need to stand together," she whispered to him as they began to climb the red polished steps to Rosie's tavern.

After dinner Rosie was complaining bitterly about her lot in life. "Would you believe it, after all I've done for their boys, this gentleman in uniform came along and forced me to sell my pony and trap!"

"Yes," Bertha muttered, "we've to carry all our food from the shops and the market. Not good for respectable ladies." Cliff laughed and put an arm round her shoulders. "Don't worry, Bertha, give us a list and Josh will get the stuff and bring it up to you." Josh noticed that Bertha's pained expression did not alter, she just sniffed.

"Mind," Rosie interjected, "we was always a respectable establishment, but with all them soldiers about it's not been so easy these days!"

Cliff snorted, "Come off it, Rosie, you're 'high class' that's all, but 'all them soldiers' have actually made you and the girls a lot of money!"

"I know, I know," Rosie smiled fondly across at him, "but there's a cost. Two of the girls have fallen in love, there 'ave been grand promises of eternal love and money to be sent for their fares to England! How'm I to cope? Recruiting's not that easy."

Cliff didn't waste any sympathy on Rosie. "You and I know how likely that is to happen! An ocean gets in the way and so do families the other end!"

Rosie nodded. "You could well be right," then she looked up as if she had suddenly remembered something. "Ah, Cliff, that reminds me, there's a letter for you from Ireland." Josh caught her flashing a look in his direction as she reached into her ample bosom and pulled out an envelope which she hastily flattened on the table before passing it across to Cliff.

Josh felt himself tense up with expectation. He watched as Cliff tore it open and then spent some agonising minutes struggling to read the spindly copperplate writing.

"Well, I'll be damned!" he finally exclaimed, obviously in some annoyance.

He frowned and looked up at Josh. "They've sent an uncle over to find you and he's up at the Kimberley diamond fields right now!"

Josh felt the colour drain from his face as he stared disbelievingly at Cliff. Half of him had known that something had to happen eventually, but the other half had believed that his family might never actually claim him and he could continue to live with Cliff. But here it was, not just a letter but also an uncle, and worse still, one who was already in Africa.

Cliff went back to reading the letter. "Seems one of your army friends had passed the word round and somehow they got to hear! Who'd have believed it! Seems they have asked this uncle to come down and meet you!" he looked up at Josh, "No word of when though." He read on thoughtfully and then folded the letter and put it into his jacket pocket. "Thanks, Rosie, it looks like we might be needing those horses sooner than I thought."

Josh sat stunned.

"It's happened!" he remarked pointlessly... "I didn't believe it would!" He stared straight ahead, unseeingly. "I don't know these people. They'll be different again... I don't want to go away with them, I'm tired of being different." He swivelled his head to stare at Cliff. "You won't let me go... will you? I feel as if I belong here now... at last."

Cliff looked at him with considerable surprise. "I can't keep you with me always, Josh, you know these people are your relatives and they have been looking for you."

"Not much looking!"

"Well they're here now and we'll have to see what they say!" Cliff remarked almost defensively. "Anyway, give them a chance... you might really like this uncle..." he added lamely.

Josh swung away from him, "You don't bloody care!" he shouted, trying not to show how close he was to tears.

He looked across the table and was aware of Jessica's tear-stained face staring at him and saw that Rosie had her arms round the girl's shoulders and was whispering to her, the words floating like gentle feathers on the air.

"Never you mind, lass, he'll be back. Your home is here where we all love you."

For a split second his mind wandered and he was aware of the emotional turmoil of finding himself in the company of white women with their strange allure and the myriad rules which seemed to govern their rights and expectations. Jessica he knew would be hurting for him. They both understood loss and feared it.

He managed to give her a slightly twisted smile and knew that she was probably aware of the tears the smile masked and the way he ached inside.

"I do care, lad, but I can't take you from your family, I'm not even a married man." Cliff spoke slowly, as though trying to sort out his own emotions as he talked to Josh.

There was whispering round the table as the girls began to speculate about the news and the "uncle" from the diamond fields. Josh wanted to get up and throw his chair over and shout that he had thought they were all his family and he had no need of another. However, he was battling with something called "polite behaviour" which he was constantly stumbling over. Everyone in the world seemed to understand it except him. When he had asked Cliff for an explanation his request had met with a sniff and a sardonic laugh and some equally mystifying drawled comment on "the bloody British…" He'd tried asking Jessica and she'd looked thoughtful for a while and then remarked that Cliff was from a place called America and they did not always like the other tribe of white men called the "British". He recalled that Cliff had ferried the British horses and men and guns to and fro with little comment apart from an occasional aside in Zulu to a native helper. One British lieutenant had tried to make Cliff work for the Army as a Zulu interpreter. When he had refused the man had accused him of "a lack of patriotism" and reported him to the Harbourmaster. Cliff had just laughed and told Josh that the harbourmaster knew he was "a Yank" and they would hear no further on the matter.

Cliff, he noticed, was staring at him expectantly, obviously awaiting a reply to his statement.

"What's marriage got to do with it, we've travelled together and worked together these last few months?" he demanded.

"Yes, but my life's a wandering one, no home, nothing settled. You need a family, boy!"

He could hear the tone of impatience coming into Cliff's voice.

"Tell you what," Cliff sounded suddenly more cheerful, "why don't we sort this out by going up to the diamond fields ourselves. We'll not wait for him to wander down. We'll go as soon as Mac gets back, he's due next week so our job on the lighters will be coming to an end anyway…" He looked expectantly at Josh who looked down at the tablecloth and did not reply.

"It's another adventure, lad… back through the old Dragon Mountains, but this time we'll be able to take van Reenen's pass, a well-worn route." He speculated encouragingly, watching Josh's face.

Josh could not believe what he was hearing. Here was this man, whom he had looked on as almost a brother, trying to get rid of him as quickly as possible. Did he really dislike him this much? Suddenly, he recalled Jessica's comment about reward money and his bitterness boiled over.

"How much are they paying you for me?"

Cliff stared at him, startled by the venom in the remark, and then went red.

"Who the hell gave you that idea?"

There was a sudden expectant hush on the veranda as everyone looked at Cliff.

"You're in a damn great hurry to get rid of me," Josh parried, white faced.

"That does not mean anyone's paying me… It just means I've got a life to live and I can't take hunting and trading jobs until you are off my hands."

"I could help you… And anyway you haven't answered my question? Are my relatives paying you for finding me?"

"Look, kid, you need some sort of education. You need a home, I'm not about to supply that. I couldn't, and anyway you've got a family waiting for you. I went to school when I lived with my uncle's family – they taught me enough to get by, and I already knew about a family and what it meant. I only lost *my* parents when I was nine years old. You need to learn about white people and their ways. Your family are much grander than mine. They can afford to have you back and to educate you. Mine could not. I had to make my own way… you're far more fortunate… but you need to find out about them."

Josh stared closely at him. "So what, I could get by! I could be a fisherman or a hunter or work on a farm. I *don't* need a family I don't know!" Cliff, he noticed, looked angry and strained, and something else, yes, embarrassed. "And *did* you ask them for money?" Josh added challengingly.

Everyone went still, silently watching Cliff.

Cliff scraped his chair back awkwardly and glowered round the table. "What the hell! I didn't have to *ask* them for it… they advertised for you in the papers and *offered* a reward for information. Yes, yes, so I'm getting paid, that doesn't make any difference to me."

"That's not true!" Josh felt himself going red with annoyance. "You know you want a farm and the reward will help you!"

"That's true, but believe me I'd keep you if I could." Cliff drew a deep breath. "Look, you'd be just the sort of son I'd want if I had a chance.

Unfortunately you need a family who can teach you things… you need to do what other kids do, go to school, play games, mix with your sort of people. Josh," he leant earnestly towards the boy, "you *must* do it for your parents. You know that this is what they would have wanted," he sighed, "after all, they would probably have sent you back to Ireland to be educated anyway."

The mention of parents caught Josh off balance. For so many years the parameters of his world had been governed by tribal laws and taboos and his survival had depended on merging, as far as possible, with the children of the tribe. Suddenly he was being made aware that he had never learned to think in terms of these European expectations, in fact, he had no idea what they might be.

"How do you know what my parents would have wanted me to do?" he queried in genuine surprise tinged with indignation.

"You've seen the children going to school. I showed you the school. Even the little children can read and write and tell you about other countries and they can also add and subtract and multiply!"

"I am learning to write and read. The girls are teaching me!"

"When the girls have time they can teach you but you need to be wise in so many ways, your parents would have sent you to school to learn. To be accepted by everyone you must be able to do what other people your age can do."

"In the tribe we were all accepted although we could not do these things."

"I know, Josh, I know, but you are with a different tribe now…"

"Why can't *you* teach me?"

Cliff sighed and looked helplessly at Rosie.

"Josh," she began kindly, "we can all do these things. Even Jessica went to the school here. I taught Bertha. Cliff could teach you but he has to work and you need to be taught for many hours each day. Cliff cannot do this. He is not a school teacher. Anyway…" she threw a mischievous sideways glance at Cliff, "I'm not sure he knows enough to teach you anything!"

Cliff tried to look indignant but Josh saw him throw a grateful look towards Rosie.

"Actually," he grinned at Josh, "Rosie's not far wrong… I didn't have much of an education and now I wish that I had paid more attention and learnt a little more!"

Josh looked down at his hands. He wasn't sure about this argument.

"Lad, your grandparents in Ireland, they'll see you learn, they'll probably get you a private tutor and you'll soon catch up. Then, one day, there is nothing to stop you coming back to Africa and being a rich man here with a farm and many horses!"

Josh lifted his head cautiously and looked round the circle of faces. Bertha had gone to the kitchen and everyone was smiling at him. Jessica's tears had dried to shadows on her cheeks. He felt comforted.

He said slowly, almost hesitantly, "It would be nice to have relatives and to belong somewhere. Even in the kraal I did not really belong." There was a long pause and nobody spoke. His voice sank very low… "it would be nice to read and write properly…" He turned his head towards Jessica, "I'll learn and I'll soon be as good as you, Jess!" He smiled at her and she suddenly giggled.

"'Course you will, Josh! And will you come back to farm in Natal?"

He was aware of the weight behind the question. He smiled across at her.

"Try and stop me!" Her face lit up with pleasure.

Suddenly, all round the table everyone began to speak at once. Rosie came round and clasped him into the folds of her ample bosom in a great bear hug, and the girls, like a wave of colourful cockatoos, were rushing round to kiss him and submerge him in the delicious feminine perfume they each exuded. Cliff started to laugh.

"Dammit, how about me?" he bellowed in the din.

Mac was only a day late returning to Natal. Josh and Clifford were waiting impatiently for him so that they could begin their journey to Kimberly.

The horses were soon loaded with their possessions. The farewells were more difficult. When it came to saying goodbye to Jessica, Josh was aware of a constriction like a rope around his chest.

"I'll be back…" he tried to reassure her unhappy face.

"Yes, Josh, you learn to write quickly so that I can hear from you, and I'll send letters with the coach… and remember that we're two of a kind…" Josh put a protective arm round her shoulders and kissed the damp cheek. "I can write quite a bit now, I'll soon be doing it as well as you, and I'll let you know about my uncle…" he said reassuringly. Hastily he turned away before she could see the aching need in his eyes. It seemed impossible that it was only a matter of months since he had ridden so exuberantly down these same roads from Pietermaritzburg. He felt years older and wiser.

The bulging saddlebags, guns and water canteens obviously spelt a long trip to the two horses and they were in high spirits. The rains had churned the roads into corrugated quagmires and Cliff and Josh found themselves hampered by constant stops to try and help wagons and carts back onto the road, or to dig sinking axels out of the reddish mud.

It took them a day longer than they had expected to reach Pietermaritzburg. Everywhere they came across remnants of the British Army ponderously moving equipment and supplies towards the depots at the coast. Cetchwayo was still avoiding arrest and they were warned to take care. Apart from the army, they met a few tribesmen crossing the road, but most of them appeared to be intent on their own business and one man told Cliff that he had fought and been wounded and had hidden up in the hills until he was fit and was now returning to his kraal to help with the crops. Cliff gave him some food and wished him well. The occasional transport drivers stopped to share a cup of coffee but mostly they had the appalling roads to themselves. During the months of the campaign the army had moved some thirty-two thousand draft animals up these roads and somewhere in the region of two-thousand wagons and carts had wound their way across their rugged surfaces to keep the army provisioned. What had never been more than well-worn tracks in the first place, were now so pitted and pocked with holes that they were nothing short of a wagoner's nightmare.

On the 8th of August, as they began the ascent through the foothills, they were caught in a storm of incredible ferocity. All afternoon the horses were jittery and hard to control and Josh and Cliff watched the gathering barrage of storm clouds build up across the mountains ahead of them. They had crossed the Tugela River at Colenso the day before and its rushing waters had warned them of heavy rains ahead. From the top of a hill Cliff peered through the gathering gloom in the hope of finding a homestead or a roadside trading store but the countryside rolled out ahead of them lush and broodingly gloomy against the deep purple sky.

"Over there," Josh pointed across the shallow valley to the next hillside. "See, there's an outcrop of rocks and bushes. We may find shelter under an overhang or in a cave. We'd better hurry." Cliff nodded.

They spurred their horses down the track trying to avoid the rocks and churned-up cart tracks. The wind died away and in its wake the first fat drops of rain from the glowering clouds began to hit the galloping riders as they raced for the rocks. Veering off the track and setting themselves low in their saddles they guided their horses across the open veld. Suddenly, a flash of lightning like jagged quicksilver lit up the scene, making both horses jink in their headlong flight. Josh just saved himself from flying headlong over

Jackalet's head and saw Cliff straighten himself for a second to check behind that he was still there. Then, with an ominous crash of rolling thunder the storm was upon them and the rain began to fall in a heavy curtain of drenching water.

Both horses slowed down as they lost their clear vision and began to stumble against slippery rocks. Ahead of him, Josh could just make out Cliff reining Charity to a stop and springing down from his saddle to lead her up the path between the rocks. Josh heaved himself over the little mare's steaming, shaking flanks and began to lead her ahead, staring into the gloom and hoping desperately that he had been right about the overhang. By now the lightning was rending the gloom into almost perpetual glaring phosphorescent light which lit the rocky area up with an ethereal glow, giving it a frighteningly unreal quality. The thunder continued to roll and roar overhead like an infuriated God reducing mountains to rubble. The wind had risen into a howling banshee rage and was wiping sheets of rain viciously against every intervening object.

In the next silvery flash they suddenly saw a quiet corner of darkness where a veranda-like projection of rock seemed to link up with another great boulder to form a haven from the rain and a recess into which they could scramble together with the horses. Between them, tugging and pushing, they managed to manoeuvre Charity and Jackalet up the slippery incline, through the barrage of water which was already pouring over the lip of the rock and into the dark dry recess of the shallow cave.

Both horses stood shivering and breathing heavily, the whites of their eyes flashing in the darkness as they snorted and blew from their exertions. Cliff and Josh, panting and soaked, sank slowly and almost in unison, down the rough wall of rock onto their haunches and then into an exhausted sitting position. There was no point in trying to talk against the wild noise of the storm and they were content to have found a sheltering roof and a ringside view of an electric storm in all its glorious fury.

Across the towering, craggy peaks of the Drakensberg Mountains, and some way down the other side, a canvas-covered wagon was drawn into the face of a rocky ravine, and another overhang was sheltering Alfred, Umfolozi and the Voorloper, Acorn. The storm had taken two hours to sweep by and they were sleeping off the after effects of a long struggle over inhospitable mountain tracks with a wagon which seemed set on sliding over every precipice. To add to their problems they appeared to have a span of pig-headed oxen that had never heard of team work, hated storms and were either naturally obstinate or exceedingly stupid.

Alfred had not found any natural talent within himself for the job of Transport Driver. Umfolozi knew the way but little else, and Acorn, whose job as Voorloper, was to guide the lead oxen down the tracks, added little to the trio as he turned out to be partially deaf. It was not until Alfred was about to set upon him in considerable frustration with the wagon whip for his casual insubordination, that his uncle, Umfolozi, had managed to convey to him that the boy was not ignoring him but simply could not hear the instructions. By then they had put a good two days' deadly slow travel between them and Kimberley and it was too late to send them away. Alfred suspected that this had been carefully orchestrated by Umfolozi.

Alfred woke first and it slowly dawned on him that the storm had passed and a watery sun was sending hopeful shafts of sunlight through racing clouds. He stretched, shook out his damp shirt and put it back on and clamped his old buckskin hat on his head. He spared a thought for the family back in Ireland. How they would reel with amusement if they could see their debonair son now, black hair like springy turf and trousers creased and crumpled from sleeping in them yet again.

"Get moving, you lazy louts," he shouted over at the recumbent forms of Umfolozi and Acorn as he headed out to dry off in the intermittent sunshine and breeze. They had managed to outspan the oxen before the storm had hit them in full force and had kraaled them against the cliff face encircled in branches of dry thorn bush.

He now observed that, unfortunately, in their hurry, they had not packed the bush thickly enough at one end and some determined or storm maddened ox, had broken through, leaving a gap which had then been used by two more. Alfred counted thirteen oxen and shouted for Umfolozi.

"Three of these lazy bastards have gone on a walking tour. Now what do we do, Umfolozi?" Umfolozi scratched his ear and peered round the rocky mountain side. He was joined by a sleepy looking Acorn and they both stared at the tracks.

"We follow boss, Swartkop, Rooibos *en ou* Riempie, they won't go far." Alfred viewed them sceptically.

"I'll go the other way and see whether I can find anything for the pot while I'm looking," he growled.

It was two hours before Alfred returned with two guinea fowl for their evening meal and by then the light was fading rapidly. There was no sign of Umfolozi and Acorn so he checked on the remaining oxen, lit the fire and busied himself with the various camp duties. Eventually he resigned himself to the fact that he was on his own for the night. He settled down in the wagon with his gun by his side and slept fitfully, waking at the least sound. Gradually the dawn arrived, heralded by all the usual early morning bush noises, and in some relief he struggled up and looked hopefully about the mountain slopes. The oxen needed to graze and he was just resigning himself to keeping an eye on them and the wagon at the same time, when he was hailed from the ridge where the track wound out of sight.

"Inkos! Bayete! We come baas, with the sun, we come!"

To Alfred's relief, he saw the silhouetted figure of Umfolozi followed by the piccanin, Acorn, bringing up the rear behind three oxen.

"It was Rooibos who give the trouble, boss."

"Uh-huh," Alfred acknowledged their arrival at the camp and waved towards the coffee and remains of the previous night's guinea fowl. It was their casual disinterest in the food which first alerted him to something not being right.

"Where have you two been?" he asked suspiciously. Umfolozi appeared to make his eyes as round and as innocent looking as he could manage, in a face well-tramped upon by time.

"We find the oxen, baas, but they go long way. Right down the valley. First we find Riempie, and then Swartkop. Rooibos, he was in pound by Jabie's kraal. Jabie, he want money. I say, 'Good baas will pay.' He will find us by Van Reenen's Pass."

"I see," said Alfred thoughtfully. He noticed that Acorn's deafness had suddenly become acute and he had wandered off to organise the grazing.

"So, you slept on the mountainside with the cattle?"

"We take good care of the oxen," replied Umfolozi, avoiding the issue neatly.

"What you mean is that you had a good indaba with this Jabie chap and his family and after the party you slept off the beer while I had a sleepless night trying to protect the cattle and the wagon? ...And *now* this Jabie wants payment for your indulgence?"

Umfolozi looked puzzled and rather hurt. "I no understand baas, no harm is done to the oxen. Rooibos, he is always bad, he makes the other bad. Rooibos he should be eaten!"

Alfred watched the old Zulu hedging and steering the subject away. He laughed dryly, "Alright Umfolozi, I'm just glad you're back. What's this man going to want for his hospitality…? I'm not a complete idiot, you know!"

Keeping the carefully cultivated look of puzzlement on his face, Umfolozi said, "Twenty shillings, baas."

"What! Who the hell does he think I am? Bloody get cleared up here and we'll move off."

They battled on yard by yard, shouting encouragement to the reluctant oxen that were double-spanned to move the weight of the wagon over the rugged rutted track and round the bends leading to the pass.

"Let them blow!" Alfred shouted at intervals as the oxen heaved and pulled, "let them blow or we'll kill them!" To avoid the wagon sliding back-wards Acorn was helping Alfred with the brake and then rushing back to chock the wheels. Umfolozi's giraffe-hide whip whisked to and fro, a touch here and there, steering the animals in the right direction to put the great-est pulling strength on the skeys, yokes and reins. Sometimes the wagon wheels became wedged between rocky outcrops and at others they sank into soft sand or mud.

"Chocks away!" Alfred found himself shouting, his voice edged with tension as he watched the load shift slightly. Too much of a shift and they might lose the lot down the mountainside. They were repeatedly digging the wheels out and wedging them up with stones so that the oxen could move the reluctant axels back into action. It was another three days before they reached sight of the pass. By that time Alfred's nerves were frayed almost to breaking point.

The final part of the climb to the summit and the pass was fraught with problems. On one area of rock face, which extended round a narrow bend, they were trying to keep the wheels in the grooves of previous wagons to give them greater grip and the reluctant oxen were straining at the chain and their yokes while Acorn tried to guide them wide of the corner to avoid cutting it and bringing the wagon up against a clump of boulders. Suddenly there was a shout, followed almost immediately by a shot which echoed off the rocks and shattered the comparative peace of the high peaks. Rooibos, ever temperamental, reared back and began to jink to and fro and his part-ner, Witneus, confused and frightened by the noise and his nervous compan-ion, tried to move off hastily in the direction of the track edge. Alfred and Umfolozi watched helplessly as this set in motion a train of havoc down all fourteen remaining oxen. No one had time to enquire as to who had fired the shot. All three were too busy trying to calm the frightened beasts and save what they could of the rapidly tangling span. The wagon was dragged towards the track edge and it was obvious that any moment now one of the maddened oxen would begin to slide down the steep incline and drag the others and the wagon with it. From there the whole team would have a steep drop which would shatter the wagon and kill the oxen.

Above the bellowing and noise Alfred shouted to Umfolozi, "Unhook the bloody centre chain! I'll do the reins." Alfred leapt onto the side of the wagon and ran forward to hang down from the front and cut the reins with his knife to separate the cattle from the wagon. As they felt some of the weight lifted from their backs, the oxen began to charge forward, only to find themselves entangled in the broken straps and reins. Yokes began to shatter and the chain ran free licking round the entangled hooves and legs of the hysterical animals. The wagon halted shuddering on the brink of the track and then, just as he had jumped free, Alfred noticed to his horror that some of the load had begun to slide sideways and the weight was tipping the wagon relentlessly over the edge. With a great creaking groan the whole wagon disappeared over the side, scattering machinery parts in every direction. As the dust cloud settled the three men peered over the side to find that the wagon and most of its contents had only slid a short way before becoming entangled in a small clump of thorn bushes which were clinging to the rock a short way down the slope and well clear of the main drop. The bushes were low but dense and showed no sign of being dislodged by the wagon.

"Let it be, let's try and sort out the oxen," Alfred called to Umfolozi.

It was difficult to get near the oxen who, in their confusion, had become wildly dangerous. Suddenly Alfred was aware that he had two new helpers. As if by magic a young white boy and a tall, brown-bearded man were moving in front of the chaotic scene trying to calm the frightened animals. Cut off on both sides, the oxen began slowly to calm down and within ten minutes they were all standing, glistening with sweat and shaking, their eyes still rolling, but no longer threatening to tear one another apart in the remains of the harnesses.

Alfred pushed his hat to the back of his head and scowled at the newcomers.

"What the hell were you shooting at right by the pass?" he shouted accusingly. "The echo threw this lot into chaos and the wagon over the side!"

The man with the brown beard rubbed his face thoughtfully before shouting back, "We didn't do it. Seems you were being ambushed. Round the corner there we have the one responsible."

Umfolozi and Acorn were gingerly approaching the lead oxen to begin the process of cutting them loose from the remains of the harness. Alfred picked his way round the debris to join the newcomers, still somewhat suspicious that they were in some way connected with the devastation which faced him.

The brown-bearded man swung down from his dappled mare and offered his hand to Alfred. "I'm Clifford Wilson and we were just coming out of the pass at this side when we saw this beauty lying against a boulder on the roadside with his gun trained down the road towards you and your wagon." He indicated behind him and looking round the bend Alfred saw a wizened old black man propped against a rock with his hands and feet firmly bound. An ancient gun lay against the rock next to him and an alert-looking dappled hound was lying a yard away, obviously on guard duty.

"It seems," said Clifford, "that he was intent on a bit of highway robbery… have you ever seen him before?" Alfred shook his head and then recalled Umfolozi's talk of the African who would meet them at the pass in the hope of getting money for having kept Rooibos in his pound.

"Umfolozi, bring yourself over here!" Alfred shouted. Indicating the old man, he asked, "Is this your friend Jabie?" He noticed a look of some confusion crossing Umfolozi's face. He appeared to be struggling between the wish to protect his friend and considerable indignation that they were in this mess because of him.

Finally, he reached a decision. "Yes, baas. Maybe he jus want to stop us? He wan his money perhaps?"

"Well," said Alfred with feeling, "this was not the way to get it!"

It took them two hours with Clifford and his young companion helping them, to sort out the oxen. Then they all viewed the upturned wagon.

"I wonder whether we could get that back on the road?" Alfred speculated out loud. "As far as I can see the wheels still seem to be intact."

"Yes," Clifford looked at it thoughtfully, "most of it just slid over and it looks as though the contents are strewn across the shelf." He walked round to look from another angle. "Looks as though the salvage bag is there, so we can get at the ropes, chains and tools." He nodded at Alfred. "Should be alright, just tedious dismantling it bit by bit and reassembling up here."

"Thank God you came round that corner," said Alfred with feeling, "I wouldn't have any idea where the hell to start!" He ran a hand through his hair and grinned at Clifford.

By early evening they had most of the pieces up and decided to leave the collecting of the machinery until the following morning when they would be able to grapple it out of the thick thorn bush which edged the brink of the plateau.

The last piece of the wagon was hauled up the incline just as the shadows were lengthening on the track.

"What on earth do we do about him?" Alfred asked Cliff, nodding towards the silent figure of Jabie, still sitting against the rock like a trussed-up chicken.

Clifford took the old man a drink and talked to him in Zulu. "It seems," he called back to Alfred, "that his family did not have good crops this year and the young boys were all called away to fight for Cetchwayo. He's not committing himself, says his gun went off by mistake, but I think he heard from your man, Umfolozi, that you were coming this way and thought he might make himself something extra as times were hard... he is actually thoroughly frightened and thinks you may kill him."

Alfred walked over to join Cliff. "He deserves a damn good fright after causing this mess." Alfred shrugged and looked at Clifford, "What would *you* do? You obviously know more about travelling in this country."

Clifford looked thoughtful for a moment. "We all have to travel this road through his tribal lands... I think perhaps it would be wise to pretend to accept his explanation, give him some food but refuse him the cash he is due for impounding your ox. I'll tell him you lost money through this delay and cannot afford to pay him. He'll understand that and be grateful to get away with his life."

Alfred looked down at the wrinkled old face, the dark eyes peering nervously at him and felt sorry for the old man. "We can give him a bag of maize and some biltong."

Clifford nodded at him, "Sounds like a good idea, the food will keep the family from trying it again too soon and hopefully their own crops are almost ripe so they will be over the worst in a few weeks."

Alfred noticed with some amusement, that Umfolozi was not happy to be sharing out a proportion of their food and kept up a steady mutter as he filled the sack. Jabie set off into the gathering darkness looking relieved despite having had to leave his ancient gun in Clifford's care. "I told him it was dangerous... and so it damn well is. It's so old it could blow up in his face at any time and it's as well to avoid the risk of having our brains blown out in the night... Just a precaution..." he explained to Alfred, with a laugh.

After they had eaten that night they sat peacefully round the camp fire. Umfolozi and Acorn curled up to sleep under their blankets while Alfred, Clifford and Josh sat and talked.

"So, you're going down to Natal, then?" Clifford asked Alfred.

"That's it. I've to get this machinery delivered to Pietermaritzburg and then I have some people to meet in Durban. What is the road like down the mountain? I don't fancy any more accidents."

"You not done this before then?" Clifford asked.

"No, I haven't driven transport before and I think that once I get this wagon back to Kimberley, I'll not undertake it again!"

Cliff laughed, "Didn't think you looked like a regular transporter! You on the diamond fields then?"

"For my sins!" Alfred looked ruefully across at the partly assembled wagon on the edge of the flickering firelight. His eyes rested on the young boy who had worked like a man as they hauled the heavy wagon parts up the incline. "You riding home someplace?"

"We're going up to Kimberley to meet an uncle of mine," Josh replied.

"Yes," Alfred remarked, "I'm actually going down to Port Natal to meet someone…" He looked speculatively at Josh, "Must be about your age too… You meet a lad called Josh Barton in Durban town, at all?"

There was a stunned silence as Josh and Clifford digested the question. At the same time Alfred saw their expressions and the answer dawned on him.

"Well I'll be damned… don't tell me! *You're* Josh Barton and *you* must be the hunter chappie… yes, Clifford Wilson! Would you believe it! Up here in the Drakensburg, round a campfire! Good God, lad! I've been hunting for you across the country!"

Alfred noticed that the boy had a frozen expression like a fawn faced by a cobra. The flickering flames played across his stunned face throwing his eyes in and out of shadow.

Cliff broke in on the moment of electric silence. "I'll be damned! What a bloody coincidence! So *you're* the uncle we were going to the diamond fields to find! I'll be jiggered! Thank God we didn't just pass on the road without comment! I never expected to find you driving transport! In a coach with a topper perhaps, but not picking up bits of wagon on a mountain top!" Cliff stared at Alfred in wide-eyed amazement.

Alfred tried to collect together the tangle of emotions he was feeling. Here was the boy in whom he had never quite believed. With an effort, he pulled himself back to what Clifford was saying and searched for a response, "When I heard from your family that you were in Natal, I decided to try this transport business… thought it might be a bit of fun and earn at the same time… and get me down to you."

Clifford was still staring at him as though he was a ghost and Alfred added, with a laugh and a shrug, "Not exactly that topper I fear. Just might have looked a bit out of place up here!" he turned towards the boy again, trying to make his voice gentler. "Here, lad, come round next to me, let me see what you look like."

The youngster stirred uncomfortably, stood up slowly and walked reluctantly round to him. The firelight sent new patterns of dancing shadows across the boy's face, turning his blue eyes into deep unfathomable pools beneath the thatch of fair hair which alternatively flickered burnished gold and platinum silver as the flames gyrated across his face. He sank down on his haunches next to Alfred, his hands hanging loosely over his knees. Their eyes met.

Alfred thought out loud. "You're taller than I thought... I forgot about fair hair... yes, Flo had fair hair... Folly's, I seem to recall, was brown. What colour are your eyes?"

The boy whispered so that he could hardly hear, "Blue."

Alfred nodded, still peering at the shadowy face with its guarded expression. "You been living in a tribe, I understand. You any idea what became of your parents... my sister and her husband?" The boy said nothing. "You must have been a very small, child... perhaps too small to remember?"

The boy turned his gaze towards the leaping flames. For a while the crackling of the fire and the restless movement of the tethered horses were the only sounds to disturb the deep indigo of the surrounding night.

Then the boy spoke, almost as if the words were dragged out of him, "Majinga said they were killed by white hunters. They had the mosquito illness... these men killed them for their wagon, their oxen and possessions..." His voice tailed off into a hesitant silence and his face continued to stare expressionlessly into the fire.

"White hunters?" Alfred queried in amazement. "Surely not, what would white men want with those possessions... surely it must have been black tribesmen, trouble makers, the sort who have been making this war?"

There was an almost imperceptible pause while Cliff and Josh stared intently at Alfred.

"Majinga said they were bad *white* men," Josh insisted.

"Who was this Majinga, how did she know?" queried Alfred.

"She was my tribal mother, she was there. She saved me and brought me to manhood with her people."

On the other side of the fire Cliff cleared his throat and joined in. "You have been lucky not to have come across these bands of brigands. I have met them and they are a dangerous lot, the scum of the earth."

Alfred looked puzzled. "Who are they and where do they come from?"

"They are men who have escaped from convict ships, discontented and unsuccessful diamond prospectors, sailors who could not take the discipline of the sea and jumped ship, murderers and thieves. Every country has them but here they tend to join up in groups and live by hunting and pillage. Farmers here don't keep their guns solely for wild animals and marauding tribesmen. They also keep them by the door for these brigands."

This was a new concept to Alfred and he thought about it for a few minutes while Cliff packed tobacco into his pipe.

"Do you remember anything of your parents?" he queried again, wondering how on earth he was going to decide whether this strange boy, who sat swaying next to him, in the same hunched position that Umfolozi often adopted, was really his nephew.

The boy had dropped his eyes. Now he raised them again, "My mother had beautiful long, fair hair, she had soft skin, freckles on her nose... I think she had blue eyes... she told me stories. This is all I remember... my father had a brown beard, he laughed a lot... he rode a horse. That is all."

"Do you recall any names?" queried Alfred hopefully.

"No. Majinga never mentioned names. Maybe she did not know them... But..." he hesitated, "...we had fat, brown oxen and a long wagon. This wagon was painted with pictures. I have seen no other wagon like it. I *think* my mother painted them, and they told stories from my mother's land... But I'm not sure now... I can only just remember this... and Majinga told me once that my mother was very clever with making pictures and our wagon was the most beautiful anywhere in Africa."

Alfred digested this information thoughtfully. He could recall his mother reading out extracts from Florence's letters to them all as they sat round the huge dining table. However, like all young boys, his mind had been on other things and his attention was only caught when there was mention of wild animals and guns and black men. Vaguely, almost through a haze, he was sure he could recall his parents laughing over the description of the wagon. His father had said, "Good old Flo, her artistic talent would come out. No paper and she'd paint on the wagon instead... fancy a wagon crawling up Africa covered in figures from Irish legends! That'll mystify the locals!" Alfred's expression softened as he looked at the boy. "How old are you, lad?"

194

Josh shrugged. "I came to my manhood one moon before Cliff came for me," he said, by way of an explanation.

Cliff puffed thoughtfully at his pipe, then removed it from his mouth and cleared his throat. "I'd estimate him to be about fourteen now. How'd that fit with your sister's child?"

"About right," Alfred nodded.

"So, what do you think?" Cliff could not keep the expectation out of his voice.

The silence seemed to stretch on for ever. Finally, Alfred scratched his boot on the rough soil and looked up at the expectant eyes. His mind was drifting back to his talk in the bar back at Rafferty's... but, if it had indeed been white brigands... In his mind's eye he saw Jules Rafferty leaning against the door at the back of the bar, the shifty dark eyes which darted snake-like round the room, the scarred bony face, thin tight lips...What, he wondered, became of brigands? He recalled old Joe's comments about the partners... the strange accident which had befallen one, the large farm and respectability. Could there be a link, he mused, was there any reason for the woman to tell the boy a lie? No. If it had been tribesmen they could simply have killed the child as well. White brigands might well have overlooked the child or assumed he would die in the bush. But, was *this* Florence's son? Africa was full of strange tales... other families had simply disappeared. The child remembered so little. But he did recall the wagon and there was no doubt that apart from some of the traders, few people decorated their wagons beyond a name and a few trimmings. Still... He'd like to see that wagon, like to look closely at the paintings. He had seen some of Flo's paintings, they were distinctive. Nothing soppily feminine about them. She had been a lady of considerable character and determination, with an abiding interest in Irish folk tales and legends. He made up his mind.

"Look, Josh," he said to the boy now sitting cross-legged facing him at the side of the sinking fire, "you have the right name, are about the right age and my sister was certainly an artist, so that gives you a head start. However, I really need to see that wagon to be sure."

"What the hell do you mean?" Cliff could not believe his ears. "How are we bloody well going to find that? It will have been sold on and possibly broken up, many years ago. Wagons don't last that long you know, look at yours, pretty bashed up already."

"Whoa!" Alfred raised a hand in the dark. "I'm not finished...!"

Cliff snorted, but said nothing. The boy simply continued to stare into the flames as though carved out of mountain rock.

"I've done a little enquiring from my end and I've heard a strange story of a family who disappeared and a beautifully painted wagon which was sold to a native chief, Adam something…"

"Adam Kok," Clifford completed for him, "He trekked to Natal with his half-caste tribe. It's called Griqualand East now."

Alfred nodded and continued. "My informant said the old chief travelled in this wagon, and, also…" Alfred paused and threw a twig onto the lowering flames. "Also, I have found some of my sister's silver in Kimberley… In the possession of a strange Irishman who hides it and keeps his life a guarded secret." He was aware that he now had the full attention of Clifford and the boy and they were both staring at him expectantly.

"How do you know it belonged to your sister, and anyway, when families get hard up they sell such things," Cliff remarked quickly.

"It had the family crest on it. I know people sell things but this man hides this silver and also he became suddenly a rich man and no one knows how. He allows no curiosity about his affairs."

"You *sure* about this 'crest'?" Clifford queried.

"Oh, yes, no doubt, and my sister would only have sold her silver in extremis. This was never mentioned in her letters home or she would have been offered help. No, that silver was not gained by fair means… it's too closely guarded. Rafferty only uses it when he wishes to impress."

"Rafferty?" Clifford whistled, "Jules Rafferty? That old rascal, a rich man you say! Then I agree. I've met him about the country and he'd certainly not pay for anything unless the money was dragged out of him bodily. He had two friends, they always moved together, like a pack, and a threatened one at that."

"Certainly sounds as though you know him," Alfred commented incredulously.

"A nasty trio," Clifford continued, "and quick with their guns. Rumour had it they'd met up in the interior, in the wild outlaw country where men disappear without a trace and I'd bet they put a few of them away at that!"

Alfred nodded in the dark at Cliff. "A large piece of mining machinery slipped onto one of them, killed him instantly. The other man has a wine farm in the Cape. Rafferty has this hotel in Kimberley. He is a respectable citizen but folks keep their distance and leave him to his own devices."

196

"Well, by God, that's the last thing I expected to hear! How'd you get a line on the silver? A friendly little dinner for two?"

Alfred laughed dryly at the sarcasm. "Like hell," he paused, wondering whether to come clean about Emmie, then, realising he had no alternative, he gave them a thumbnail sketch of his life-to-date in Africa and Emmie's discovery of the silver in the kitchen of Rafferty's hotel.

They went over all the possibilities as the fire died down. Finally, it was decided that once the wagon was mended Cliff and Josh would turn round and ride with Alfred as far as Pietermaritzburg. There Josh and Alfred would take the coach road towards Kaffraria, which would lead them to Kokstad in Griqualand East, where they could enquire about the wagon. Meanwhile, Cliff would deliver the machinery and collect the return load and head back for Kimberley. In Kimberley he would make contact with Emmie and they would await the return of the other two. By then, Alfred prayed hopefully, the money to pay Cliff would have arrived in the bank.

Finally they rolled themselves into their blankets and slept the remaining few hours to dawn.

Josh woke once and heard the distant rumble of drums. He rested his head on his elbow and listened intently, then sank back into sleep as the first slither of a silky pink dawn touched the purple of the horizon. The drums beat out the news that the great Zulu chief, Cetchwayo, had at last been captured in the Valley of a Thousand Hills. An Empire had toppled and a new epoch in African history was beginning. It would be some time before the Zulu nation rose again to prominence.

Chapter Ten

AFRICA – September 1879

JOSH WAS INDULGING himself in a daydream as he trotted along the rutted track between Kokstad and Pietermaritzburg. His mind was way back in the misty realms of childhood, trying to unravel any forgotten memory traces of his parents, or the stories his mother had told him.

The familiar but elusive feeling of warmth which usually accompanied memories of his parents was rapidly giving way to emotional waves of confusion. The memories were there but they were misted over by time and distance and hard to distinguish from the African legends which were more immediate and recent. The visit to Kokstad had brought his losses back to him in a tumbled mixture of happiness and sorrow.

He was jolted back into reality when a large eland buck sprang with easy grace, across the road in front of him. Jackalet's steady trot faltered momentarily as she too was startled out of her usual even pace. Rider and horse both watched for signs of pursuit but there were none. It was a chance encounter on a calm, clear day. Josh looked back over his shoulder to see whether Alfred was still in sight. He suffered a pang of conscience when he saw how far ahead he had ridden. Alfred was a dot and a small puff of dust about a mile back. He slowed up and stopped in the deep shade of an Umbrella Thorn. Alfred was still weak from a bout of fever which had delayed them in Kokstad for an extra week.

Josh's relationship with Alfred had built slowly and warily. To start with, the meeting in the mountains had been shattering. Somewhere in the back of his mind he had treasured the view that this unknown family of his would never materialise. He acknowledged to himself that he had wanted to stay with Clifford Wilson, to join him in his roving life. Over the months they had been together Cliff had become the centre of his insecure world. Then, suddenly, with the arrival of that floundering wagon on the mountain pass, he had been thrown into reality by the presence of a living uncle. The shock had sent him reeling into a painful silence for several days. Clifford had been too busy to notice and Josh had helped with the salvage operations and kept his confused emotions to himself. Decisions seemed to be made with the assumption that he agreed with them and, while he was still trying to come to terms with events, he found himself being turned back to Natal with Clifford and Alfred.

He was not sure what he had expected to happen. The haze of shock had stayed in place until they reached Pietermaritzburg and Clifford had nonchalantly turned to him,

"Josh, it's over to *you* now, lad! I'll move on with the wagon and get this machinery delivered. You two take the southern road and head for Kokstad."

Josh realised now that he must have looked shocked and dazed. Clifford had stared at him impatiently.

"No need to look like a fish out of water! You and Alfred have a mission to complete."

His voice rasped a little. "You have to see whether the Kok family still have that wagon with the pictures you described… make life a darned sight easier for Alfred if you find it… no doubt then as to who you are!"

His patience finally seemed to have worn out:

"Dammit, kid!" he had drawled, "Got to find you a family *some* time!" He had roughed up Josh's hair with one hand in a familiar gesture. "Get on with you and keep an eye on that young uncle of yours. Get him back to Kimberley where I'll be waiting!" Nobody had said it but Josh had only just resisted completing Cliff's sentence with "for my money". Josh recalled the feeling of loneliness which had flooded over him; he had turned away without a farewell and gone to rest his head on Jackalet's saddle, hanging his arms dejectedly across her rump. He'd been aware of a groan from Cliff and heard him mutter, "Moody little bugger!" as he led his horse out of the yard.

It had taken a couple of days for the two of them to reach Kokstad. At first he had said little and Alfred had tried to break through the wall of resentful silence. When none of his enquiries or stories met with any response he eventually commented out loud and to no one in particular:

"Keeping people in my family quiet is normally more of a problem than making them talk! I wonder, have I perhaps not found the right boy yet?"

This remark fell like a pebble in a pool. The ripples seemed to break a reflection and catapult Josh into the present and the realisation that in his loneliness and resentment he had been blaming this man. Alfred had not been annoyed with him, in fact he had done his best using vivid descriptions, to try and introduce himself and his family in Ireland and had met with no response. Josh was sitting on a rock while the young man who was his uncle, was making coffee over the fire. He dragged one foot in the sand, watching the grains fall steadily back to earth. He looked out from under the brim of his hat at the man with the merry eyes, thick wavy hair and soft sunburnt skin, concentrating awkwardly on manoeuvring the pot over the flames.

"I'm sorry!" he blurted out with a flash of youthful insight, "*You* don't know about Africa and *I* didn't want a family."

Alfred had lifted the pot onto the ground and sat back on his heels and stared at him.

"Why?" was all he said.

"I had Clifford... he saved my life... I'd like to hunt and farm with him."

Curiously, and unexpectedly, this uncle had seemed to understand. "Quite a character," he agreed. "Couldn't help liking him myself, seems so in control of his life. My God, doesn't he know how to handle oxen and wagons!"

Josh nodded, feeling bad about his long sulk.

"I know about Africa, I don't know about Ireland... is it very different?"

"It is, it is, lad! There's a lot of rain and not much heat... but compared to Africa it's soft and safe. People are not always as friendly... except that is, for your own family." Josh felt the blue eyes looking quizzically at him. "You'd not find it easy. Life is full of rules you are not subject to here, but all the same there are advantages... few biting insects, no wild animals and everyone speaks your language!"

Josh could not imagine this world. It sounded very boring. He smiled. He had decided to like this uncle.

Sitting in the shade waiting for Alfred to catch up with him, he thought of the frustrations and fears and heart-rending emotions which, for him, would always surround the name of that small town, Kokstad, in the hills of Kaffraria.

Kokstad was a sprawling village serving a close-knit farming community most of whom were members of the mixed-race Griqua tribe. They had emigrated from Griqualand West some years ago in an epic two-year trip which involved a group of two thousand people hauling their wagons and twenty thousand head of cattle over, first the Maluti mountains of Basutoland and then the formidable Drakensberg range, in search of a piece of land aptly named "Nomansland". Adam Kok III, their leader, had led the exodus. He had travelled in a wagon which had remained a memorial to the tribe ever since. Every available space was painted in figures and scenes. No one knew its origin.

By the time Alfred and Josh hitched up outside the Royal Hotel in Kokstad with its red corrugated iron roof and long red-polished veranda, Alfred was obviously beginning to weary of the constant barrage of questions he was having to answer.

"I'd like an honourable promise from you of ten minutes' silence while we wash the dust down our throats with a well-deserved drink and consider our next move!" he pleaded.

Josh grinned. "I thought your family *all* talked too much!"

Alfred had groaned as he swung painfully down from his saddle. Josh had looked up to see a large black man in full European dress, with a felt bowler tipped to the back of his head, leaning against the bar door watching them arrive. He had wondered about him, trying to fit him into his experience. The man had come forward as they came up the steps and had held out a hand to Alfred.

"I'm Yankee Woods, the proprietor of this li'l ol' joint, an' you're right welcome."

Josh had been fascinated by the man. He had spoken English with a pronounced drawl, not unlike Cliff's. He looked completely at home in his smart waistcoat, shirt and trousers. When curiosity finally overcame politeness, Josh had asked him in direct fashion,

"Are you a Zulu, sir?"

Yankee had given him a long hard look.

"Where you bin, kid? I ain't no kraal kaffir me, no, for sure, I'm a Yankee from Ah-merica, aiming to see the world an' pick up riches while I's about it!"

At this point he laughed and clapped a hand like a ham joint down on Josh's shoulder.

"An' look where it's got me, kid! From diamond diggin' to proprietor of this select joint in this one-horse town," he had laughed cheerfully and shaken Josh's shoulder as though it were a feather pillow.

Josh had removed himself hastily from the hand and stared up at the man. It was a new concept for him. Cliff had not told him about black Americans, only about American Red Indians. Finally, he felt forced to ask:

"Are you a Red Indian, sir?"

Yankee roared with laughter.

"No siree, I'm black right through, kid, good ol' slave stock from the Southern States." He had laughed like a roll of thunder.

"God-dammit, first time I been taken for a red injin, bless you kid, you'd best call me 'Black Feather', huh? Wait till I see a Red Injin again, I'm gonna see what he says when I claim him as a blood brother!" He had gone off to get their drinks, still shaking with rumbling chuckles.

Over the drinks Alfred had explained that they needed to see the Griqua chief with a special request.

Yankee had scratched his head thoughtfully, then explained:

"The old boy died 'bout four years back. The elders look after things now. The sheriff, ah now that's a slip…" he rolled his eyes to the roof, "this here, Chief Magistrate, Mister Charles Brownlee, he sees to affairs round here."

Josh could hold back no longer.

"Have they got a painted wagon?" he had demanded.

Yankee looked puzzled, "Lots of wagons round here, which one'd you be talkin' 'bout?"

Alfred had interrupted.

"The old boy who died, he came over the mountains in a special wagon – we want to see this wagon."

"Don't know 'bout that," Yankee had replied slowly, then brightening visibly, had added, "but old Ma Kok, she's still around. Gone to visit some relatives but should be back soon – she would know 'bout that wagon. Yous looking to buy a wagon, then?"

"No," Josh had interjected, "We want to look at it – it belonged to my parents."

A cautious look had crossed Yankee's face.

"You folks here to claim this wagon, to make trouble for the Griquas?"

Alfred had hastily spoken: "No, it's interest only. The boy's parents are dead and he remembers the wagon. He just wants to see it once again because his Ma painted the pictures on it."

Yankee looked relieved.

"Aw, that's good. Could do without more trouble round here."

He had marched them off to their rooms at the back of the hotel.

202

With an introduction from Yankee, they had gone round the following day to call on one of the Griqua Elders, Abraham Jantjes. Jantjes confirmed that there was an old wagon which had survived the trek and which was brought out on celebration days, but was a bit vague about its whereabouts. He had walked them slowly up to "the palace", a long, low tin-roofed house with the traditional veranda. At the back they had been attacked by three excitable terriers. The old man had flapped his arms at them and shouted, *"Braks, loop weg."*

To Josh's amazement the dogs had promptly slunk away and kept up grumbling growls in the background.

"What are they called?" he had asked the old man.

"They's Brak one, two and three," the old boy said with a gummy smile. In answer to Alfred's raised eyebrows Josh explained, "Mongrel one, two and three!"

One of the sheds at the rear of the house was an old whitewashed mud-walled building with no windows and a pair of solidly built black-painted wooden doors. It was firmly locked and bolted. Jantjes examined the doors.

"This must be where it's kept, the old Ma has the keys. Never mind, she'll be back before long. She goes to Pietermaritzburg once a year, for a week. She'll be back," he thought a bit, "probably next Monday."

Yankee was delighted to have their company for the next five days. The only other residents were two old prospectors who came back at night. The District Commissioner sent up a couple of inspectors on general duties and they added to the number of evening guests, together with the local Griquas who called in to drink their "sundowners" and talk about the good or bad "old days" and the "troubles" in February of the previous year when, during an uprising led by outlaws, the powder magazine had exploded killing eight local people.

It had only taken Yankee twenty-four hours to wheedle out the reason they were there. He had then passed the news on to each visitor. There had been much discussion between the Griquas about the wagon, and stories of the trials of the two-year trek through the mountains were brought out and embellished. So were the grievances left over from the short administrative rule of Captain Matthew Blyth.

In the evenings, sitting out on the red polished veranda watching the setting sun, with the background accompaniment of a trilling chorus of crickets, the stories of treasure and secret caches of diamonds and gold and great hunting exploits, had been exchanged by locals and visitors. Josh and Alfred had sat enthralled.

They had been invited out to a couple of local Griqua farms where they tried the home-made brews which were now allowed in what had once been a tea-total area under the old chief. Much later they would stagger back to the hotel to sleep off the effects. Another day was spent eland hunting with Yankee, to the benefit of the hotel menu.

Josh recalled how he had found himself constantly walking up the hill to Ma Kok's house and staring at the shed. Would it be the correct wagon, he had wondered. Would there be that golden giant with the flowing locks blowing behind him? Would there be that strange musical instrument, with the graceful shape? Would the faces of the fairy folk be peeping round the wooden edges? Or had it all been long since painted over… or perhaps he had only dreamt it. If so, would Clifford let him live with him if there was no money forthcoming…? If not, what would become of him? All the locals could tell him was that it was "special" but no one could recall exactly what was painted on it. "Just bright, with many colours," had been the usual reply. Some thought it was, "Just squiggles of colour – like the medicine man has on his wagon."

Alfred had also seemed restless and uneasy. He had questioned Josh closely on what he could recall of the wagon. I suppose he was wondering what to do with me too, Josh speculated to himself. The five days had stretched into ten and Alfred had pointed out that his money was running out. Yankee, reluctant to part with his unusual visitors, had said that they could have some days "on me" because more locals came to drink while they were there. On the fifteenth day, just as Alfred had been declaring: "The old bat must be dead en route," there was a clatter of a horse and cart coming up the rise and someone shouted that she was back.

As by now the whole village was involved in the saga, it had not taken long for an invitation to arrive at the hotel for them to attend "at the palace", in two hours' time after the old lady had had a quick nap. Josh was convinced that those were the longest two hours of his life. Alfred had paced to and fro muttering about heat and complaining of a headache which he declared was all Ma Kok's fault for delaying her return so long. Josh remembered noticing that he was white-faced with beads of sweat running down his forehead.

The old chief's wife turned out to be a wizened little old lady who closely resembled a dried-up walnut kernel wrapped in a pink checked dress. Two beady black eyes shone knowingly out of the wrinkles and she made them both sit down in her front parlour and "take a cup of tea" so that she could hear the story in more details than the excited gossip which had come her way. Looking kindly at Josh, she asked "*Ag ja*, tell me, little man, what were your parents' names?"

"Folliott and Florence Barton," Alfred had answered for him before he could reply. Ma Kok nodded and her wizened face broke into a smile.

The "niceties" seen to, she plucked a big black key from inside a flowery teapot on her dresser, picked up a candle and matches, and led the way in small uneven steps to the shed with the large black door. As she went she recalled the wagon's past.

"I didn't like the stranger who sold it us. A mean-eyed man with a scar down the side of his face... no name given. I loved this wagon and it was strong and beautiful. Not many survived those terrible mountains. I often prayed for its safety as it was roped up to be pulled over cliffs. It never lost its colours to the sun, either. Always strong and beautiful. A magic wagon I used to feel."

Josh's heart was in his mouth, and slowly choking him, as he helped her push against the stiffly resistant and creaking doors, gradually swinging them open. The lack of windows made the inside of the shed a black hole against the bright exterior light. The old lady had moved in to the edge of a wagon and balanced her candle on the back step while she lit it. Then, triumphantly, she had led the little party into the gloom. Out of her pocket she had taken an old duster with which she had begun to rub the sides of the wagon to move the dust and spiders' webs which had accumulated over the paintwork. Holding the candle high to throw its light more generally over the scene, she had beckoned to Josh and Alfred to come and look. There, all along the sides of the old wooden wagon, were a dancing stream of very distinctive characters, painted in bright blues and yellows, reds and greens. In between there were castles on hills and spinning wheels and there, right at the end, a tall giant with golden hair blowing out behind him and he held a harp aloft as though he was protecting it. Alfred had pointed to him.

"Look, Josh, it's the giant you told me about and that thing he is holding is called a harp. It's an ancient Irish musical instrument and that must surely be 'The Harp that once on Tara stood'." He hummed a line of the song and Josh recalled trying not to burst into tears as a wave of emotion swept over him conjured up by the notes of the familiar tune his mother used to sing.

"That's it," he managed to say in a choked whisper, "That's what she used to sing to me… there should be some little faces in other places too."

They followed the soft candlelight round to the front of the wagon and climbed up the creaking steps. Looking at the back of the box seat and down the inside of the low wooden sides, a host of little faces peered back from every corner. The flickering candlelight made them seem alive. The old lady laughed in delight.

"Ag, man, I remember them now. They used to amuse us when we were sleeping and sitting in here. We often wondered who had been so clever with the paint and had invented such a collection of different faces… now I see that she must have painted them to amuse her baby." She moved the candle and Josh became aware that the soft glow was highlighting his face. He had pulled back but not before the old lady had seen his tears. She had hastily put her candle down and put a small bony arm round him.

"It's all still here, boy… she loved you so much and she did it all for you… I always had a feeling that this wagon was special. See, it was one of the few to hold together over two years of travel through terrible mountains, and once we even had to build our own pass – Ongeluks Pass – in order to get through. I think your little people have been waiting for you to return to them. I think they will stay with you now." Thinking back Josh could still feel the sense of comfort which had seemed to surround him. It had been as though he had suddenly felt more confident and no longer alone.

The old lady knelt painfully by the back of the box seat and motioned Josh down next to her.

"Look," she whispered, and carved into the back of the box and inlaid in metal, were the initials F & F.B. & J.B. Josh ran his fingers over them again and again. It was like coming home and knowing you are loved. She lifted the lid of the box. "No bible in the bible box, boy or I'd a given it you."

The next ten days had been something of a blur. As soon as they got back to the hotel Alfred had collapsed in a heap, instead of being pale he was now burning up with heat despite the fact that it was a cool evening.

Yankee had looked at him and declared him: "Eaten up by dat darn fever. You better sponge him down an' I'll go see if the doc's in town."

With the help of one of the prospectors, Josh had got him into bed. While the man sponged him down, Josh went off to see what herbs were down by the stream on the edge of town. He made up a poultice, wrapped it in a cold cloth and put it on Alfred's head. Then he brewed some liquid and began to drip-feed the delirious man with a teaspoon.

The fever had run its course in forty-eight hours. He and Yankee had stayed together at Alfred's bedside to see him through the worst. Old Ma Kok and many other locals called regularly as he was recovering and brought him eggs, fruit and broth to encourage back his strength.

Despite the old felt hat which Yankee had insisted that Alfred should wear to protect his neck as well as his face, Josh thought he looked worn out by the time his horse brought him into the shade of the thorn tree. He spread out the bedroll and Alfred gratefully collapsed onto it beneath the protective branches of the tree while Josh busied himself plucking a guinea fowl he had shot earlier in the day.

Chapter Eleven

AFRICA – September / October 1879

EMMIE WAS FEELING restless. Whenever she broached the subject of singing with them the girls looked embarrassed and said it was up to Maria. Although Jules Rafferty seemed to approve the idea, Maria wasted no time in pointing out that three could cope very well and four would be too many.

When she approached Jules his snake-like eyes slid away over her shoulder and he shrugged.

"Sure, she probably knows what's best," was all he would comment as he moved on to speak to someone else.

"It's only the chance I need," she groaned to Morag as she helped her clear the kitchen. "I know I could hold them diggers as well as anyone. I'd have them all joining in with me in no time."

Morag nodded sympathetically. "Had you thought of getting one of the men who drink at the bar to call out your name and suggest you sing an Irish song for the many Irish diggers who are far from home? I'm sure Maria couldn't do anything about a personal request like that and there'd be plenty of men shouting approval, an' ay, if they like'd ye they'd soon make the requests themselves an' she'd have to allow it, like it or not!"

"Ah! Now sure, that's a splendid idea, Morag!" Emmie gave Morag a quick hug of excitement.

"Mind you," Morag commented, "you could do with a new blouse. The skirt'll not matter but a crisp white blouse would make a big difference... an' I'll make it for you, if that'd help. Bring me the material an' I'll do the rest."

The evening went on till late and it was nearly two in the morning before Emmie finally kicked off her shoes and fell on her bed in a state of total exhaustion. She noticed as she tiptoed by that Maggie's bed was empty but she was too tired to wonder what had become of her.

In the morning she filled an enamel basin with water to wash and then put the kettle on for tea. There was still no sign of Maggie, but just as she was filling the teapot she heard the noise of someone being sick outside the front door. There was a thump against the door and when she opened it Maggie fell in, white as a sheet and wreathed in pungent alcohol fumes. "Whiskey!" Emmie identified them for herself as she pulled the woman through the door and onto the tattered remains of an old rag rug which was on the floor next to Maggie's bed. She looked down at her thoughtfully. "Ant how did you manage to afford that, my girl… has that man of yours hit it lucky with a nugget or a diamond, at last?" she enquired of the comatose Maggie. "Not bloody likely in my view…" she muttered to herself, "…more likely yous found a man to drown your sorrows with." She lifted Maggie's head onto a pillow, put a bowl next to her, covered her with an ancient bedcover and went back to making the tea.

Emmie was drinking the tea and trying to ignore the whiskey fumes in the air, when she recalled Morag's offer to make the blouse. Checking first that Maggie was still unconscious, she went behind her screen, knelt down, and using a teaspoon handle, levered up the floorboards under which she kept her savings from the long days at Rafferty's bar. She felt around in the earth below but there was no cold metal biscuit tin to greet her fingers. She scrabbled frantically in every direction beneath the floor, then found a match and peered through the gap. The space was empty. Her savings had gone. She rocked back on her heels and tried to stop the rising tide of panic which was sweeping over her.

"Think girl, think," she remonstrated with herself. Gradually she became aware that her heart had stopped beating so frantically and that she was beginning to focus on her position and the practicalities.

"Who might have known about the money?" she asked herself. The answer was no one. She had brought it back in her apron pocket on pay day and deposited it beneath this board when Maggie was out of the room. "Wait a minute," there had been times when she had needed to rush the process because she could hear Maggie coming in? Could there have been a time when Maggie might have seen her when she had not been aware that she was back? Yes, there was a space between the bottom of the screen which divided off her corner of the room from Maggie's, and the floor… Maggie could have bent down and seen her putting the board back… Or perhaps even heard something which gave her the clue to what her lodger was doing. Of course! The whiskey, that was probably what she had done with the money! Slowly logical reasoning was returning. But what to do now?

She went over to Maggie and searched through her pockets. Nothing. She had either gone out without a purse or it had been lifted off her long ago… or all spent in one of the local bars. Emmie's natural instinct was to hit her and demand that she give an explanation. Once again, reason came to her rescue. She sat down on the floor with her head in her hands and tried to think. For certain it was gone. There was no hope of getting a penny back. I'll have to leave these lodgings… But where will I go? I'll take my things and see whether Morag can help me. Her decision made, she opened her eyes and looked straight into a pair of apprehensive grey ones, watching her from the grubby rag rug on the floor.

"I'm sorry," Maggie whispered, "so very sorry… I had this letter from him. He was getting a ship in Cape Town… Doesn't want me no more. Returning to Holland and doesn't want to see me ever again. No money, no love, nuffing… an' all the time I've waited for him!" Tears of self-pity made rivulets down her puffy face.

Emmie just sat staring at her and trying to drag up pity from somewhere, with no success.

"So, what did you decide to do?" she found herself enquiring with an almost impersonal interest.

Maggie put her hand to her brow and groaned.

"I wish I'd just die."

"You are not going to, so tell me what happened."

Seeing that there was no sympathy forthcoming, Maggie pulled herself gingerly onto an elbow.

"I'd 'eard you move that board and I knew you must be keeping money underneath. I knew I had nothing left so I thought I might get the coach to Cape Town an' see if I could kill him 'fore he left…"

"Ant…?" Emmie looked coldly at her.

"An' then I reached the square, I heard the coach was delayed so I went in the hotel. I felt pretty frightened. I thought I'd have a drink to give me strength for the journey… somehow it turned into quite a few an' I must-a missed the damn coach. I woke up propped up on the streetside all on my own… reckon they must 'ave thrown me out… rotters! Any money I might 'ave 'ad left was gone, so was my coach ticket." She looked up pleadingly at Emmie, "Sorry again, not much I can do now." She slid back down with a groan.

Emmie stood up.

"So much for me, then! All my savings gone down your throat wit' only a 'sorry' to show for them." She looked down at the crumpled body on the floor. "Fend for yourself from now on, gal."

Emmie grabbed her carpet bag from under her bed and bundled her few possessions into it. All this delay had cost her time and she would be late at Rafferty's. She could only hope Morag would cover for her. She threw her key on the table, slammed the door and walked gratefully out of Maggie's life. Outside she came down to reality.

Although spring was on its way, the African morning still had a cold bite in the air and the temperature dropped sharply at night. Where, she wondered, was she going to find a new roof to protect her? She hurried across the dusty main square, dodging the carts and wagons as they jostled for position to sell their produce to the local early risers. She had bumped into Charles before she saw him.

"Hullo, Emmie! What a pleasant surprise, I should get up early more often!"

"Charles! Have you news of Alfred yet?"

"Not a murmur... you look a bit distracted, is there any help I might give?"

Caught in her immediate problems and pleased to see a familiar face, Emmie confided more than she would normally have passed on to Charles.

Charles appeared to be taken aback to find himself suddenly a confidant. From the distracted look in his eyes it was obvious that he had other things to think about.

"Ah... it's a problem just at the moment, Em, I'd like to help you but I'm owed a bit from gambling debts... bugger's not paid up... and..." he looked round nervously, "mustn't be seen talking to you or someone might tell Josy and then there'd be hell to pay!"

As he was turning hastily away he suddenly halted. "Hang on, Em, can't help you myself but Alfred left his baggage at the Club and one of the bags was yours... heard you were too proud to take it, but I bet it has a few things you could sell, if pushed to it... and after all, gal, they *are* yours!"

Emmie's eyes lit up.

"Come round after four o'clock this afternoon and there'll be no one about. I'll leave the bag with our club porter. He'll pass it on to you."

"Thanks, Charles, that might be a help." He gave her a hasty pat on the shoulder and moved off quickly.

Maybe things aren't going to be so bad after all. I could get something for that negligee – certainly enough to get a room again, she pondered as she raced up the street towards the backdoor of Rafferty's Bar.

She met Morag at the door carrying in a bag of fresh vegetables and she handed some to Emmie to carry without any comment. Maria was standing in the kitchen, hands on hips, scowling at the back door, but when she saw them come in with the produce she shrugged and went out again.

"Phew! Thanks, that was all I needed, my job gone and I *would* be destitute!" Morag listened sympathetically to Emmie's tale of woe as they scrubbed the vegetables together.

"I do have a friend who might be able to help. She's got a tiny wee house down towards the west end o' the town and her man's not well, so she could do wi' the money right now. She's from Scotland, like me. I'll give you a note for her."

"Morag, you're so kind an' I don't know where I'd be without you."

Morag laughed and wiped her hands on her apron.

"In life you usually get a chance to return a favour, mark my words, lass, one of these days I'll be asking one of you!"

At a quarter past four Emmie walked in at the door of the Park Lane Club and looked round at the velvet draperies in some awe. Johnson appeared from behind a potted palm and before she could say anything he said:

"And you must be the young lady come to collect the portmanteau?"

Emmie nodded.

"Come along this way, miss. Mr Charles is in after all and he'll pass it on to you himself."

Emmie felt a twinge of regret. She would have preferred to escape without having to parry any of Charles's comments. She followed Johnson through to the rooms at the back of the building.

Charles was sitting writing. He pushed away the papers as he thanked Johnson.

"Come in, Emmie, care for a drink?" He indicated a bottle of scotch on the table.

"No thanks, Charles, I'm obliged to you for this idea about the portmanteau. I'll take it and go."

"Not so fast, my fine young lady – or do you still call yourself a lady these days?"

"What are you talking about?" Emmie asked in shocked surprise.

"Well, since you stopped sharing Alfred's bed things haven't been so easy have they, sweetheart?"

"You call yourself a gentleman, and this is how you speak to a lady?" she enquired indignantly.

"Come on," he put an arm round her shoulders, "come, let us see what sort of a 'lady' you are, darling," he said, pulling her roughly towards him. "You scream and I'll let every man in Rafferty's know you're easy meat," he laughed menacingly as she tried to push him off.

"You lay a finger on me, you make-believe gentleman, ant I'll see that your tigress, Josy of the Parisian Parasols, hears all about how you spend your afternoons while she is rehearsing… sure she'll make certain you 'ave nothing to play around *with* no more!" Charles hands fell away from her bodice.

She swung round rapidly, picked up her bag and moved to the door with as much dignity as she could muster. As she stepped into the passage he kicked the door closed behind her with a resounding bang which echoed round the whole club and left the door vibrating in its frame.

It was the third week of October and temperatures were rising towards their summer heights. The few trees which had survived in the town were beginning to collect their summer coating of dust and the bougainvillea and golden shower creepers were a vivid splash of colour on the veranda posts. Emmie was a well-established lodger with Kirsty McDonald and delighted to be part of a family once again.

Walking to Rafferty's one morning, Emmie met one of the Irish diggers, a man called Tom Maguire, from County Fermanagh. They were exchanging news from Ireland when Emmie remembered Morag's suggestion about the singing.

"Are you coming into the bar this night?" she asked him.

"Sure," he said, "an' bringing several friends."

"Would you do me a favour?" she smiled shyly at him.

"Sure, lass, what would it be?"

"When Maria asks what you'd like her ant the girls to sing, could you ever say you'd like to hear the Irish barmaid sing a true Irish song?"

"It'd be a pleasure," he winked at her. "You can rely on Tom for that!"

The bar was so busy that night that Emmie completely forgot about Tom's promise. She was reminded when Tom and four of his Irish friends came in and he winked at her across the bar and then turned with his drink in his hand to watch Maria and the girls singing "Cockles and Mussels". As it finished he clapped with the rest of the customers and then shouted above the heads.

"I'd like to hear this wee Irish lass, up here at the bar, sing a song for us Irishmen, so far from home!"

Immediately, his friends and several other Irishmen in the bar, began to clap and add their voices to the demand.

Maria looked taken aback. She looked as though she was going to refuse but Tom was having none of that.

"Come on, love, it's time the Irish had a turn," he swung round on the rest of the room. "Let's have a new voice for this once lads, one of our own." Immediately there were nods of agreement and other voices backed him. Maria gave her characteristic shrug and a little mock bow towards Emmie.

Now that her chance had come Emmie felt quite overcome with a sudden wave of shyness. However, it did not stop her smiling and moving through the crowd to the piano on the small stage.

"An' now what would you be wanting?" she asked the crowd, her voice a little tight with emotion.

"Aw, give us that old tear jerker – 'The Rising of the Moon' – go on, lass, show them how the Irish do it," a voice called from the back of the room. There were several shouts of agreement. The pianist played the opening bars and Emmie floated her voice into the haunting, well-remembered refrain. As she finished, there was a pause while everyone seemed to come back to earth, then the clapping burst out across the room. The Irishmen stamped their feet, demanding more. Maria tried to intercede and send her back to the bar but was shouted down. Emmie sang three more songs before discretion told her she had already tried Maria's patience beyond the limit. She waved to everyone and slipped back through the crowd to the bar, followed by a string of friendly comments and much teasing banter.

When they finally closed at one in the morning and she was preparing to walk home to Kirsty, Maria appeared in front of her, hands on hips, eyes flashing.

"So, I suppose you think you're God's gift to the singing world? Well, you ain't round 'ere, your Irish bog-boys may think so, but we want some decent songs... and *decently* sung. Don't try that one again too soon or you're out on your ear... do ye 'ear me?"

Emmie nodded silently. She was just winding her way through the last customers as they were leaving the saloon bar of the hotel, when Jules pounced on her.

"Here, you," he tapped her on the head, "I've been hearing that you tried to 'go-it-alone' tonight. Don't do that again. Maria don't like it. An' jus' remember your place, you're the bar girl round here…" his voice dropped to a menacing note, "An' I don't like my staff to get above themselves."

Suddenly, they were both aware of a tall, lean, bearded and suntanned man leaning casually against the doorpost, listening to what Jules had to say and observing them both closely.

"We're closed, an' that means right out the door for you too, no loiterers unless you're a paying guest. This is a high-class establishment," Jules said abruptly to the man.

The young man stayed where he was and laughed shortly.

"Come on, Jules, don't give me this 'high class' bit. You mean your saloon is like every other bloody mining saloon only the food is better and sometimes the singing is exceptional," he said pointedly, smiling at Emmie. The bright blue eyes turned back to Jules. Emmie was aware of the drawl. Not English or Irish or Scots, she ticked them off mentally to herself.

"You're going to have to give way somewhere, man, the boys liked her and they'll be wanting more. The word'll get about and it will boost business."

"Well, if it isn't Wild West Wilson himself," Jules said, recognition dawning. "Pardon me, I didn't recognise you without your gun or your hat and that infernal dog… you still got him?"

"That nip healed then?" the man asked affably. "Never nips those he likes, creeping up on my tent must have frightened him. Anyway…" the young man pushed himself casually off the doorpost, "I'll escort this lady off the premises if you're finished your lecture. See you around, Jules." He put a proprietorial hand behind Emmie's shoulder and moved her off towards the entrance.

Emmie was vastly impressed. She had never heard Jules silenced quite like that before. She heard the door slam behind them and wondered whether Maria would get the bitter edge of his tongue.

They were standing out in the street and she became aware that they had stopped and he was looking down at her in some amusement. Before she could say anything he asked:

"Well, lady, are you by any chance Emmie O'Connell, the guardian of Alfred Lyons-Montgomery's funds?"

Emmie looked thoroughly startled. Somehow her thoughts of Alfred had faded in all the recent excitement and she was taken aback to be reminded that she had some sort of responsibility towards him.

"How did you realise it was me?" she asked curiously.

"Aw, well now, Emmie is not exactly a common name and I heard the Irishmen shouting for you! There again, I also have a guilty conscience. I should have contacted you a few days ago when I first came into town. Afraid I've been catching up on diamond news and who's defrauding whom in this tin-pot town." He was leaning back against the veranda steps of Rafferty's, eyeing her quizzically. "I assume I guessed right then?"

Emmie could not stop herself from smiling broadly at him. "Are you the hunter who was travelling with Alfred's nephew?"

"I am indeed... Clifford Wilson at your service, madam!" He gave a mock bow.

Emmie stared at him, wondering whether he would disappear as suddenly as he had arrived. What, she wondered to herself, had she been expecting? Some old wizened hunter whom she hadn't been looking forward to having to placate while waiting for Alfred's wagon to get back? Instead, here was a young man who could not be more than twenty-five, with a friendly drawl, laughing eyes and an air of confidence which quite swamped her.

Emmie was suddenly self-consciously aware of her fixed smile on her face as she stared at him in amazement. She mentally shook herself and tried to return to the practicalities.

"You must have news for me from Alfred... what does he think of his nephew? ...why not walk me back to where I am boarding and you can tell me what has happened?"

Clifford laughed. "I think you've stolen my lines. I'm supposed to be the gentleman and ask to walk *you*! But of course," he added quickly seeing her embarrassment, "I would be delighted to do so!"

As they walked through the dark streets of the town, Clifford told her about the ox-wagon incident and Alfred's decision to take Josh down to Griqualand to identify the wagon.

"So, I went along as far as Pietermaritzburg to try and keep that wagon together. Josh and Alfred took the road to Griqualand East – and good luck to them with that quest. I just hope that wagon still exists. As for myself, well I got the wagon to Durban port in one piece and had to buy a new one for the return journey and the new cargo."

"Sure now, you speak of it all so calmly, as though bringing that wagon back was no effort!" Emmie was staring at him in the dark in frank admiration. Clifford shrugged and laughed again, "I've been trading and hunting and travelling with wagons for several years now. I know every bit that can come off and how to improvise another. I know about the cussedness

216

of oxen. I know about their strength and their varying temperaments and I'm not bad on mules and horses either! I'll tell you more another time!" He lifted the lamp he was carrying and looked round. "We seem to have reached your lodgings and we can't stand by your gatepost all night, so I'll be off now and see you soon."

Emmie laughed at his long speech, although she felt sad to see him go.

"Ah now, an' you've a lot of adventure behind you, ant no doubt more to come. I'll be making enquiries at the bank about Alfred's money, although sure we'll have to wait till he arrives to pass it to you."

"I'll be round by Rafferty's to hear some more singing!" he called over his shoulder as he strode away.

Emmie realised that she had no idea where he was staying, or whether he was married, or in fact, almost anything about him! All she knew was that the stars seemed brighter.

To Emmie's alarm Clifford did not appear at Rafferty's for several nights. Meanwhile the Irish contingent managed to persuade Jules to let her sing more Irish songs on one of the nights.

He shrugged off Maria's complaints, "It's all good for business and you girls have the floor most of the time."

"Yes," Maria wailed, "but her reputation is going round the town as the 'Irish Nightingale'."

"So then, you'll just have to watch *your* reputation, won't you," was all the comment he would make.

Emmie was surprised and annoyed with herself. She was constantly scanning the bar and watching the doors. Whenever a tall young brown-haired man with a neat beard came in, she was aware that her heart missed a beat. Jackson found her preoccupied and chased her several times to get things done, where normally she needed no reminders. Kirsty, her landlady, watched her closely as she put things away in the wrong places.

"Tell me, Emmie, someone's not running away with your heart as well as your sense, are they?" she asked with a giggle as she rescued a cup from the top of the plate rack.

Emmie sighed and brought herself back to reality.

"I'm sorry, Kirsten, I've not found myself like this before... it's a real trial I am to me too!"

The next night the world turned the right way round again. Clifford wandered into the bar at lunch time. He seemed genuinely glad to see her, although quite casual.

"I'll have a beer to quench the thirst and you can tell me some good news!" he declared.

"And what makes you think I could do more than the beer?" she asked him with a smile which she hoped covered her true delight at seeing him.

"Oh, I just wanted to see those Irish eyes smiling at me!"

"Well, it just so happens you're in luck anyway. I called in at the bank and they have your money ready and waiting for Alfred to come and claim it from them!"

"Well, there, see, I was right, you do have good news for me. Now all we need is some news of that same person and young Josh, and confirmation that all went well in Griqualand."

Johnson was polishing glasses behind Emmie and casually listening to the conversation. He interrupted briefly.

"You looking for news from Natal, mister? The coach should come in today and someone may be able to help you. The driver always stays overnight here."

"Thanks," Clifford nodded. "I'll come up this evening myself."

Jackson moved off to serve another customer.

Emmie was so delighted to hear that Clifford would be back in the bar that evening that she put a hand on his sleeve and smiled at him.

"Don't get too excited, girl, he may not make it back on this coach," he said, returning the smile.

Emmie looked puzzled. "You mean Alfred may not be back tonight?"

"Yes," he nodded, "isn't that who you're excited to see?"

"No, ah, now, I'm not saying I won't be glad to see him safe an' sound! But he's only a friend, you know?" she replied hastily.

Cliff looked astounded.

"But I thought you two were engaged and all that?"

"What gave you that idea?"

"Well, I suppose it was Alfred. He said 'my girl Emmie, back in Kimberley'."

"Aw, him. Him ant me's only friends." She looked shyly at him under her lashes. "Sure, we came over from Ireland together, but we parted up here and I make my own way. Alfred knows that. Don't get me wrong. Sure we used to be close, but now it's only friendship. I'll not return to Ireland with him."

Cliff let out a low whistle and seemed visibly to relax.

"And here was I being careful not to get too close to this beautiful gal in case Alfred whipped out a gun and shot me 'pon his return!"

He leant forward and put his hand on her sleeve.

"I can only say it's poor Alfred's loss!"

Emmie went scarlet and looked nervously over her shoulder.

"Sure now Cliff, I'd better get back to the customers. You'll be back?"

"You bet. Try and stop me!" he drawled, laughing at her consternation.

The coach was late arriving that evening and Cliff ate in Rafferty's and then came to sit in the saloon bar. Emmie noticed with interest that he seemed to know so many people. Men greeted him politely and several women waved to him, somewhat to her annoyance. Tom Maguire was sitting at the bar joking with some friends and he noticed her watching Cliff.

"De ye know the Yank, lass?"

"No, but he brought me a message from a friend. Why does everyone seem to know him?"

"Ah, now surely, he's a well-known fella. He has an open, friendly way with him, but mind, he can be secretive. There's no one could say they really know him. Keeps to himself, he does. They do say he jumped ship in Cape Town and has made a life for himself in Africa. He's a dab hand with the gun and can ride with the best of them. He traded for some years with Henry Hartley. Got a fair introduction to the country that way and learnt a bit about wagons and oxen. He's a well-known hunter, earned a lot of respect and made himself a bit-a cash too. Always willing to help a chap out, although they do say he doesn't keep the cash long!"

Tom's companion chipped in:

"One of the old boys from Natal told me once he's very well-known there. Lives in a bordello down Durban way, but doesn't seem to make any steady attachments amongst the ladies. Helps them out and then he's away again, him and that dog and the horse. Sometimes he does a bit-a work in the harbour but mostly it's inland. Reckon he knows the tracks of Africa better than most." He pondered for a moment… "Funny for a Yank to be so familiar with Africa. Would have thought he'd go for the diamonds or the gold, but no, seems he's not much interested there. Nice chap, mind."

It was nearly eleven o'clock before the Natal coach driver came in with some of his passengers. There had been some problems coming down the Drakensberg and they had found themselves delayed for repairs.

"Must say, I'm glad to be here, need a damn good whiskey to bolster me up and a large plate o' Morag's beef stew," he informed the various bar customers who greeted him cheerily.

When he had eaten he came back to the bar to have another drink before bed. Cliff moved over and sat down next to him, paying for his drink. They chatted about the hazards of the track for a while and then Cliff asked him whether he had seen or heard anything of Josh and Alfred.

The driver lit his pipe and thought for a moment.

"Yes, now you mention it, I did hear from one of my travellers who picked up the coach in Pietermaritzburg. Said he'd heard a right weird tale down in Kokstad in Griqualand. Something about a painted wagon an' a murder." Jackson was pouring a whiskey for someone and his hand hesitated over the glass and he spilt a drop on the counter. He wiped it up and looked with curiosity at Cliff and the driver. He handed the drink to the customer and then busied himself with a cloth and a water decanter on the far side of them.

"What else did he say?" Cliff prompted the driver.

"Seems there was a man and a boy down in Kokstad and they were waiting for the old lady – you know, Mrs Kok, to come back and show them the wagon that led the trek to Griqualand East."

At this point Jackson put down his cloth and quietly left the bar by the rear door.

"Did they get to see it?" Cliff asked eagerly.

"Don't rightly know," the coachman replied slowly. "Aw, now I recall. This chap, he said he left before the old lady had come back from her trip to Durban. Seemed the story caught his attention because it was one of those tales of a lost family one hears here-a-bouts." He paused for another drink and drained the glass.

Clifford looked for Jackson but he was not around, so he called down to Emmie.

"Emmie, another drink for Hal here. He's had a rough journey and he's some news from Griqualand."

Emmie brought the drink over and stood waiting for the story to continue.

"Has he heard of the others?" she whispered to Cliff. He nodded assent.

Just then Jules came in closely followed by Jackson.

Emmie looked suspiciously at them. Jules very seldom came behind the bar and Jackson looked flushed with exertion. Why, she wondered, was Jules so interested in the bottles on the shelves in front of Cliff? Cliff did not appear to have noticed him coming in.

The coachman seemed to get his second wind and remembered where he had stopped his tale.

"This youngster, seems was brought up by a tribe after his parents was killed by some white brigands… Way back some years ago now. Seems the boy has been brought back to civilisation by the chap he is with an' they are trying to track back to who it might have been who killed his parents… an' where it happened." He drew on his pipe and watched the smoke curl up towards the ceiling. "Seems the kid may be worth something now and the grandparents have put up some reward money, or something. The wagon may have had family valuables on board… or some such story."

Cliff let his breath out in a whistle of simulated surprise.

"And the wagon…?"

"Aw," the Coachman grunted, "Can't rightly remember that. Seems there is something 'bout this ol' wagon the boy needs to see, something he recalls from when it happened… may help to identify him and give the authorities a clue to the killers. Seems old Kok may have bought the wagon off the killers without realising where it came from."

Jules straightened up and swung round to face Cliff and the Coachman.

"An interesting tale, gentlemen, but one as common as dung in Africa. What's this searching gentleman called?" He looked at the coachman.

The driver scratched his head thoughtfully, not happy at having his dramatic tale ruined by Jules.

"The gentleman what told me got off back in Harrismith but it was something long, I gather the man was from Ireland… Mont-something I think."

"Montgomery?" queried Jackson from the background.

"Now that sounds likely," the coachman sounded relieved. "I think that was it."

Jules swung round and stared at Emmie. "What's he doing down there, that toffee-nosed nosy parker? What kid's he paid to lie?" he sneered.

Emmie was thrown off-balance by this sudden onslaught. She looked blankly at Jules and then over his shoulder at the startled face of Clifford.

"I don't know 'bout it, Jules. He went to find his lost nephew… Seems he may have found him…" she tailed off, wondering whether she was saying the right thing. She noticed Jules swing round to stare at Cliff. He must have caught her glance at him, trying to tie them together.

Cliff seemed to sense the atmosphere. He leant back languidly on his stool and yawned.

"It's a fine tale," he told the coachman. "Poor kid, what a thing to happen, and all those years on his own in a tribe. Let's hope the authorities can piece it together and the kid can live in peace." He reached for his drink, "You spin a good yarn, Hal. Tell me if you hear any more."

The coachman looked gratified, gulped the last of his drink, picked up his hat and headed for his room where he would fall onto his bed with his boots still on and be snoring in two minutes.

Emmie moved hastily down the bar away from Jules and began to give out last drinks to the few men left in the bar. Cliff moved off to greet a friend and Jules and Jackson were left talking quietly together. Emmie realised rather nervously that she had not heard the last of this business from Jules. Out of the corner of her eye she could see that Clifford was glancing in her direction occasionally. This gave her a feeling of comfort. She had not been entirely abandoned. Presently Jules came up to her and said abruptly:

"Finish up here and then get upstairs to my office. I want several words with you an' don't think you can jam-spangle your way out of this one with yer pretty face and yer winning ways." He swung out of the bar and passed Cliff without a glance.

Never had the bar been so carefully cleaned or the last customers listened to with so much attention. Jackson was close behind her every move and Cliff had retired to the far side of the room where he had lit his pipe and was chatting to none other than the diamond magnate himself – Judd.

"Enough's enough," declared Jackson at last. "You got to get off to the boss now or 'is temper'll be even worse than it already is. I'll clear this last couple out."

Reluctantly Emmie headed for the door. The stairs seemed suddenly very steep. The big wooden door marked "Manager" loomed ahead of her and was snatched open just before she reached it.

"Ah-ha! So you see fit to grace me with your presence at last, ye ungrateful spalpeen, ye! An' wasn't I by way of taking you off the street and giving you a chance to earn a pretty penny, an' all ye do is bring the English divil wit you to plague me," he spat out at Emmie.

Emmie stared wide-eyed at him.

"Ant I'm not certain what it is you're talking about?"

"That ye do! Ye scheming hussy. It was you as had that grand young man as your special bosom companion?"

"You mean my friend, Alfred Otho? The man I travelled from Ireland with? Sure, *he's* no Englishman, he's from County Leitrim. Ant, another thing, Jules, he's *not* my 'bosom companion'. He's a friend and nutting else, no matter what Jackson may think!"

"Tell me more," Jules sneered disbelievingly.

"He was here for his own purpose, nutting to do with me. He didn't discuss his business with me but he did tell me he was sent by his family to find a missing nephew.

"Ant how, Miss Clever-clogs, was he supposed to do that – and where, pray, did he find this mysterious nephew?"

"He said that someone in Africa was writing to his family in Ireland to say that a boy was found in a tribe far distant, a boy who might be the missing relative. He was here to find the boy."

"And how long ago might this amazing occurrence have been?"

"I don't know Jules, really I don't. We 'ad a disagreement, Alfred and I and he didn't tell me what had happened. I only know he got the news and decided to go and meet the boy himself. Truly I don't know nuffing more." Jules eyes had narrowed and he peered at her like a puff-adder deciding where to strike.

"'Ope you wouldn't consider lying to me, girl. It won't be just your job'll go if I find there is just one grain not accurate in that story." There was a long pause during which he seemed to be reviewing the situation himself. "Not that I got anything to hide, see, but I don't like bastards who pass themselves off as diggers when they're really spies."

"Spying on what?" Emmie asked, genuinely puzzled.

"You shut up now an' listen to me! What's that bloody Yank got to do with you – an' why's he so damn interested in what's going on in Griqualand?"

Emmie felt as though she was stepping into a bog and might well sink without trace if she gave the wrong reply.

"He's a friend of Alfred's. He was concerned that Alfred was not back yet. He has some goods for him, an' he wants to talk to him."

"So bloody well do I," shouted Jules with feeling. Then, as though it was a sudden frightening enlightenment, "Hey, they're not both coppers, are they?"

Emmie had heard about people being so surprised that their mouths fell open, but this was the first time she had been aware of it happening to her.

"What?" she said in genuine amazement, "Coppers! ...Alfred Otho an' Cliff... *now* you got to be joking!"

"Oh, alright then, sure I'll nail their hides to a door if I find they been double dealing me! An, as for you, my lass, if I ever find you knew more than you told me, I'll see that pretty face of your is scarred to make you look like a witch. Now get out o' my sight!"

Outside Emmie found Cliff sitting on the edge of a cart across the road, watching the hotel and waiting for her to come out.

"God, Emmie, am I glad to see you!" he leapt up and strode across to her as she came down the hostelry steps. He put a hand on each shoulder and looked into her face. "I was afraid that bugger might be trying some nonsense. I was going to give you another five minutes and then crash in at his office door."

"Well, I'm glad you didn't, 'cause here I am ant no harm done... 'cept to my nerves and my soul!"

"He's a bad sort," he lowered his voice confidentially, "I heard about the silver from Alfred. Now we know from his reaction that he is definitely involved in some way... and one can guess how too."

"He makes me scared though, Cliff, he threatened to scar my face if I hadn't told him the truth."

"By God, I'd like to kill him by slow degrees. He's a cruel brute, no feelings, no emotion. A straight killer. If he was a rabid dog we'd gun him down and be thanked for the task. Because he's a man we have to be more careful how we do it."

Emmie looked nervously at him. "Don't you start, Cliff. One man mad for violence is enough."

"I know, Emmie, I know. It's just that his sort get away with it so often. Look what they probably did to Josh's parents."

Emmie nodded soberly. "What do you think he'll do now?"

"I'm not sure but I think we'll find out tomorrow."

They had reached Kirsty's gate and Emmie opened it hesitantly, then turned round to say goodnight. Clifford was close to her and as she turned she was suddenly very aware of his warmth and the smell of his leather waistcoat and the sweet aroma of tobacco mixed with soap. She looked up at his face, which was dark against the midnight blue of the African night. His arms wrapped gently round her shoulders and he pulled her towards him. Neither of them said anything for a minute. She enjoyed the sense of safety and security his presence gave her and she had a sudden yearning to lean on him and feel the soft cotton of his shirt and the warmth of his breath on her face. Slowly she moved her face and his came down to greet her. It was to Emmie as though the world had stopped. Their lips found one another and she seemed to drink a wave of emotion which flooded through her body and found expression in her mouth, her hands and the tingling of her toes. It seemed like a multitude of years before she came down to earth, it could only have been precious seconds. "Goodnight, sweetheart," he said gently.

The next day Maria had a black eye and a temper to match. The staff were scuttling around trying to make themselves as invisible as possible and she was pouncing on every move they made and dissecting it with noisy hysteria.

There was no sign of Jules and word had it that he had been seen in an equally black mood, riding down to the squatters' camp.

It was mid-morning when the kitchen door burst open without warning and two large men marched in and threw their canvas bedding roles in the corner. Emmie had her hair up in a business-like bun and was swathed in a large apron as she scrubbed potatoes. She swung round to look at the intruders and then swung hastily back to the sink and held onto the china edge as the shock ran in waves through her body.

One of the men had a large, flat face and mean narrow slanting eyes. They were the unblinking eyes of the man who had robbed her on the train way back in what felt like another life, in County Leitrim. She was sure of this and she wondered whether he had recognised her. She kept her back firmly turned away while Morag poured them each a mug of coffee and handed out hunks of bread.

"The boss says you're to pack us several days' rations for three and put them in these saddlebags," the lean lank-haired man announced, pushing the dusty leather bags onto Morag's clean kitchen table.

Morag swung round on him, hands on hips.

"Get your filthy bags off my table and you can sit on the back steps while I find some mutton an' bread for yon bags. Move your stinking carcasses out o' my kitchen," she unceremoniously opened the door and slammed it on their retreating backs. Then she moved hastily over to Emmie and put an arm round her shoulders.

"What's up, lass? They're great barbarians from the squatters' camp but they'll not harm you here, gal. An' sure they know I'm quick with the meat cleaver!"

Emmie turned her white face to Morag.

"The one with the flat face ant the snake eyes, he's from Ireland, he robbed me on a train once."

"Aw, that's exactly what I'd expect of them lot. Scum of the earth gather in that camp. Don't worry, lass, he'd not recognise you any more, an' he'll not try nuffing round these parts for fear of Jules. Take the polish through to the bar until I've got rid of them."

"Where do you think they are off to, Morag?"

"Seems Jules is to be away a-while, lass. Give us some peace. Mind, I wish he'd take that wild woman, Maria, with him an' gi' us a bit-a quiet!" She patted Emmie sympathetically on the back and bustled off to prepare the bags.

On her way through the lobby Emmie heard Jules' voice shouting at Maria.

"You'll damn well do as I say while I'm in Natal, woman. Any slip-ups an' I'll have your hide an' no man'll ever look at you again."

The upstairs door slammed and she could hear Maria crying.

I almost feel sorry for her, Emmie thought to herself as she rubbed beeswax into the bar tables with unnecessary vigour.

Any feelings of sympathy for Maria faded very quickly once Jules and his unprepossessing team had ridden off. She needed someone to take out her ill feeling on and it was Emmie she chose.

"You're causing me grief," she claimed, leaning on one of the newly polished tables. "An' I don't like that, miss. You an' your menfolk are a menace. I'd like to throw you out but it seems some people might find you useful, so, like it or not, I gotta keep you around. Still, miss high-an'-mighty bog-maiden, I see no reason for you to work in the bar no more. I want you down in that kitchen so quick a fly wouldn't notice you passing… get going…"

As Emmie headed for the door she sent her parting shot behind her, "An' I'm reducing your wages as you won't be up for the customers to see, no more!"

"Sorry about the wages," Morag comforted her, "but I'll enjoy having your services down here, lassie."

"I won't see Cliff," Emmie moaned sadly.

"Rubbish, lass, he's not too proud to lounge on the kitchen steps, now, is he?"

"You're so kind," Emmie laughed, "you always cheer a girl up!"

Clifford was disconcerted not to find Emmie in the bar at lunch time. Jackson was non-committal and told him he did not know where she was. There was something about the way he said it that left Clifford feeling uncomfortable. For the first time in his life he had become aware that he actually cared for someone and that person had somehow found a way under his skin. He found it amazing that this small, flame-haired Irish girl with the clear green eyes, softly freckled skin and enchanting singing voice, could reach him where no one else ever had, and was extracting from him a tenderness he had not known he possessed. I must be getting soft, he had told Zenda as he fondled the dog's ears.

Clifford went round to the kitchen door and tapped on it. Emmie opened it.

"Ah, now, that's a relief, gal! Jackson was of the opinion that you'd faded away without trace," he drawled, a large smile lighting up his face.

"No," Emmie pulled him delightedly into the kitchen, "I'm demoted by Maria. Jules has gone down to Natal and she's in charge, she's got her chance at last to get back on me for my cheek in singing in the bar…"

Cliff stopped her.

"Wait, Em, what's that you said about him going down to Natal?"

"He's set off for Natal with two very rough look'n men," she did not get any further because suddenly she seemed to realise what he was thinking.

She put her hand over her mouth and looked back at him, "My God, Cliff, could it be that he's after Alfred and Josh?"

"What did Maria say to you?" Cliff asked quickly.

"Now I think on it, I heard Jules shouting at Maria that she was to do as he said or she'd be sorry, ant then, Maria, she said I was causing her grief 'with my men' ant she wanted me out of the way in the kitchen with less money."

Cliff looked thoughtful as he perched on the edge of the kitchen table. "I think he is going down to see what he can get from Josh and Alfred. It's my bet he'll kill them if he doesn't like what he finds out. He could be holding on to you as some sort of hostage."

Emmie looked alarmed. "Me? What for?"

"I suspect he thinks a threat to kill you may get what he wants out of Alfred. I wonder if Maria's been told to watch you carefully while he's away?"

"What's best to do? Certainly she checks on me from time to time but I thought that was just to harass me more."

Cliff looked thoughtfully out of the window. Then seemed to make up his mind.

"Alfred and Josh will be out of their depth with guys like this. I think I'll need to find them as soon as possible. But, just in case things go wrong and he has taken action before I get there, I want you safely out of the way."

"What about you, Cliff? He'll not like you interfering in his business."

"I know the type. I've been moving round Africa some years now. I can look after myself."

"There is nothing else for it, gal, it's right out of Kimberley you need to be. I've friends in Pretoria will put you up. I'll write you a letter to give them and I'll fetch you from Pretoria when we have this business about young Josh sorted out."

"I'm not sure I want to move away from Kirsty and Morag. I'll be alright, Cliff, I can look after myself."

"No, Emmie," he shifted himself off the table and put a hand gently on her shoulder, "No, lass, I can't risk anything happening to you. These are desperate men who will take desperate measures if they think it will save their skins. Can you trust Kirsty and Morag?"

Emmie was staring at him with a bemused expression but she managed to nod, "Yes, of course I can."

"Then this is what you must do. I'll write to my friends and give you the letter. I'll book you onto the Pretoria coach for tomorrow afternoon. When you don't turn up for work Morag and Kirsty must say they are worried and rather disappointed as you didn't say anything to them about leaving. Maria will be in a panic and she'll soon find that I have left town and will assume that I took you with me. Meanwhile, you will be safely in Pretoria while I find out the truth about our Mr Rafferty and his undoubted concern about Josh and his parents."

To his relief Emmie seemed to see the sense in his instructions and she reached up on her toes and gently kissed him on the mouth.

"I shouldn't be saying this, Cliff, it's real forward of me, but I'm going to miss you something terrible."

For what felt like the first time in his life, Cliff felt his face growing hot.

"My God, Emmie, you've made me blush," he laughed out loud and took her in his arms and kissed her firmly on the lips. "As soon as I can I'll be back, mark my words. It seems to me we've some years ahead to plan!" He noticed with considerable amusement that it was Emmie's turn to blush, but he was off out of the door before she could think of anything further to say.

Chapter Twelve

AFRICA – September 1879

BY THE TIME they reached the streets of Pietermaritzburg Alfred was beginning to gather strength and had remembered to look in at the Grand Hotel to see whether he had been left any messages. There was a note from Clifford to say that he had delivered the goods and bought a new wagon and was on his way back up to Kimberley.

"By now," Alfred calculated, "he should be kicking his heels in one of the Kimberley hostelries. Damn good thing he had the foresight to leave us some cash with the hotel proprietor!"

He ruffled Josh's hair as they stood on the hotel veranda watching the townsfolk drifting about their business.

"Suppose he'll be wondering where the hell we are! That old girl really delayed us and then my fever didn't help," he commented, a note of frustration surfacing in his voice.

Josh moved away abruptly. He could not understand this European wish to pat people smaller than themselves on the head or ruffle their hair. It was an intensely irritating habit and he was not sure why they did it. He was aware of Alfred looking sharply at him and then tapping his fingers on the veranda rail as he looked thoughtfully into the street. They both turned to watch a coach come bowling up the road and Alfred leaned his arms on the rail, then removed his hat and scratched his head thoughtfully.

"Josh, I've been thinking... I believe ships call in at Durban on their way round to Cape Town and then to England and Ireland..."

Josh dragged his eyes off the activities on the street and turned to give Alfred his partial attention.

"It's just that the family back home will be hoping to meet their grandson as soon as possible... would you like to be put on a ship down in Durban before I go up to Kimberley?"

Josh's fingers gripped the wooden veranda rail until his knuckles went white.

"So, you want to get rid of me too then?" he asked in an icy voice.

Alfred looked startled and stared at him, replacing his hat rather hastily on his head.

"No, never. I want your company, lad, but I wondered whether you'd like to get on with your new life?"

Slightly appeased, Josh shook his head.

"I've… things to put straight here… Alfred," he spoke slowly because he was formulating emotions into thoughts and finding words to express them.

"See… I'm not going anywhere until we know who killed my parents… It would be like abandoning them… seeing that wagon and remembering Majinga's words about the Cave of the Ancestors. I want to know who would do such a thing. You have found the silver with the special markings…" he tailed off into thought.

Alfred nodded and said what had been circulating in his thoughts since hearing the description of the man who sold Adam Kok the wagon.

"At one time, Josh, I thought I'd go back home once I found you, but Africa has trapped me with her beauty, I think I'll stay on. I too feel I owe it to Florence and Folly and our family to find out what happened." He put a hand gently on Josh's shoulder and with uncharacteristic awareness of the boy's feelings, added, "I think, perhaps we can help each other to sort this out, then we can go back to Ireland together! How does that sound?"

Josh had noticed the two words "our family" and they had meant a world to him. For those two words he felt he would go anywhere with Alfred.

Alfred extended his hand, "Shall we shake on it then? 'Blood Brothers' as Yankee would have said!"

"Sure," Josh smiled and clasped his hand, "You're a blood uncle anyway!"

They set off at sunrise the next day, heading up the road towards Colenso and the Drakensberg range, the same route that Josh had travelled with Clifford. They reached the small cluster of buildings called "Weston" well before sunset and decided to rest their horses and themselves in a shack known grandly as the "Wayside Hotel", and cross on the pontoon over the Mooi River the next day. They handed their tired horses to a small African child who led them off behind the old corrugated iron building to a makeshift stable. They carried their saddlebags inside and piled them just through the door. They were the only travellers staying in the place and the owner, a large fat lady with untidy strands of hair sticking out from under a headscarf, looked as though she resented their arrival because it meant work. Their drinks were slid unceremoniously in front of them and two plates of indifferent food appeared after a long delay. Alfred was just thinking that they would have done better to have camped out, when they both heard the sound of several horses arriving and being hitched to the post outside the building.

"This'll be a nasty shock for her, more work coming in!" Alfred commented dryly. Alfred was sitting back in his chair with his boots resting on the seat opposite, tipping the last of his beer down his throat when the saloon door swung open. He glanced casually through the amber liquid and saw a man look in. The man then kicked the door and came into full view and even through his distorted vision of glass and beer, Alfred recognised the lean, predatory shape of Jules Rafferty.

It was too late to explain the situation to Josh – who was bent awkwardly over a piece of paper trying to use his slowly advancing knowledge of the written word to send a message to Jessica down in Durban.

Alfred stiffened and lowered his glass. Jules was looking full at him with an expression that could only be triumph.

Ah, now, well, if it isn't my friend from Kimberley, Mr Alfred!" He advanced across the wooden floor with an extended hand and a disarmingly pleased smile.

Alfred put his feet firmly onto the floor and leant forward to shake hands, feeling as though he had stepped into a tiger's den.

"Ah, Mr Rafferty," was all that he could manage.

Josh, he noticed, had stopped writing and was looking up with interest.

"Well, Mr Alfred, and a *pleasure* it is to meet a familiar fellow traveller on these lonely roads... and who have we here?" he nodded towards Josh.

Alfred thought fast, if this man had anything to do with the murder of Florence and Folliott Barton then he must not know who the boy is, he reasoned to himself. He moved his glass round as casually as possible and said slowly:

"This is Josh Maynard, son of an old friend, a Natal farmer."

Aware that Rafferty was watching them closely, he could only look steadily at Josh and hope he would not look too taken aback.

Josh looked from one to the other and kept silent. He put down his pencil as though sensing something in the atmosphere which required his full attention.

At that moment the door was kicked open again and two ugly looking men swaggered in. They strolled over towards Rafferty who, half turning, introduced them in a meaningful way to Alfred.

"Ah now, here we have my travelling companions, Big Ox," he indicated a six-foot hulk of a man with a bald head, a down-turned mouth and no eyebrows over red-rimmed ice blue eyes, "an' Killer Quinn from Ireland."

Not much to choose between them, Alfred thought as he nodded and eyed the round expressionless face and tiny pig-like eyes of Killer Quinn.

"You keep safe company, then," was all he could find to say.

Rafferty nodded and waved the two over to a table on the far side of the room.

"An' so my friend, Mr Alfred, let me buy yous a drink now an' you can fill me in on your life history then." Rafferty moved over towards the woman behind the bar and returned with the beers.

Although Quinn and Ox were sitting back with their beers, feet on the table, surveying the room, Alfred managed to whisper across to Josh as Rafferty paid for the drinks:

"Rafferty of the silver!"

For a moment Josh looked blank and then comprehension slowly dawned across his face and the casual interest was replaced with an alert watchfulness.

Alfred was busy wondering what to tell Jules. Does he already know my surname? Above all, why is he here... or is it, indeed, just a chance encounter? He weighed the likelihood but the memory of the look of triumph on Rafferty's face as he saw them in the room, made chance seem unlikely. However, it was only Cliff who knew their whereabouts... What had happened in Kimberley? Whatever the answer might be, Rafferty, he speculated, was not travelling in his present company for a happy picnic or by chance. All his senses were on the alert as he looked at the three men.

Rafferty sat down, pushing Alfred's beer towards him.

"And where are you going then Mr Rafferty, is it business?" Alfred thought he should get in first with the questions.

Rafferty raised an eyebrow. "Aye, business it is!" he answered, giving away nothing.

"Now, mister, you'd have another name, what is it?"

Alfred eyed his speculatively. "It's Lyons-Montgomery."

"Ah, indeed!" Rafferty looked thoughtfully into his beer. "From Ireland, is it then?"

Alfred nodded.

"An' now you'll tell me why you're touring Africa if it's not the gold you're after?"

Alfred felt like refusing but decided a casual approach would be better. He supped his beer thoughtfully. "I'm sent to find out about a missing family."

"Someone you know then?" Rafferty enquired equally casually but with a razor edge to his voice.

"Yes."

"Perhaps I know them?"

"Doubt it, it was some time back." Alfred felt as though he was mentally walking on quicksand.

"You in an official capacity for family or police?"

"No, just family."

"Where did you hear of them last?"

"Transvaal way."

"Why you in Natal then?"

"Collect the boy. His dad's a friend. The youngster speaks several native dialects."

Rafferty shifted his gaze to the boy.

"You speak Zulu, then?"

Josh glanced at Alfred, then shook his head.

"What you speak then, boy?"

Josh shrugged and looked away. Rafferty looked at Alfred.

"What's wrong wit' him? An idiot or something?"

"No," Alfred replied, "just resents your questions as much as I do. What's it got to do with you?"

"Maybe something, maybe nothing. In Africa, mister, we like to know one another. Big spaces can be lonely…" he added ominously, "people disappear in big spaces."

"So, tell me *your* business, then?" Alfred pushed.

Rafferty's small eyes darted between Alfred and Josh.

"I'm looking at some long-term insurance. Want to expand my business without questions."

Alfred absorbed that in silence for a minute. Then he nodded towards Ox and Quinn.

"Thought you travelled *with* your insurance?"

"Useful company for a lonely road," Rafferty confirmed.

"Now, mister, let's try again on where *you* been?"

Josh pushed his chair away from the table and got up. He put the note he was writing in his saddlebag on the floor. He stretched casually and walked to the door. Rafferty turned to watch him, as did the other men. He pushed open the door and put a chair against it to hold it open, then leant against the doorframe looking out at the gathering darkness.

"Not thinkin' of leaving us, is he?" enquired Rafferty sarcastically.

Alfred ignored the sarcasm.

"Just getting some air."

"So you're here to look for a missing family – why you looking in Natal if they were in the Transvaal?"

Alfred sighed, "Mr Rafferty, why are you so curious? I came to collect Josh because he speaks some of the Transvaal dialects – he can help me."

"I know a lot of people all over southern Africa. Give me the details ant I can guarantee I'll soon find out what you need to know," Rafferty volunteered.

Yes, Alfred thought to himself, I bet you will, some cock-and-bull story to put me off looking any further.

"Not much point in trying the authorities, they keep no census of families, particularly if they are trekking," Rafferty continued.

"What makes you think they may have been trekking?" Alfred queried suspiciously.

"Only guessing, that's the way most families move around until they find a spot to settle. I heard from the Durban coachman that you were down in Kokstad. An' why, I wonder, would you be visiting the Griquas then? Some story of an old wagon, I understand." Rafferty narrowed his eyes slyly.

So, Alfred thought to himself, Yankee's chatter to his customers had travelled fast. "That's so," he said, "we found what we wanted."

Rafferty looked a little discomforted. "So you found what you wanted. Was it the wagon of the folk who disappeared?"

"It was," Alfred confirmed, watching Rafferty closely for a reaction.

"How'd you know that?" Rafferty demanded.

"We had a description," Alfred parried. "The family, they'd a description from their daughter." Alfred felt he had avoided implicating Josh. He recalled Ma Kok's description of the man who sold the wagon to her husband, and enquired, "What interest is it to you?"

"I was interested because," Rafferty stopped to clear his throat, "perhaps the Kok family told you, I gave that wagon to the old chief in return for some help with hunting in Basutoland?" Rafferty stated, struggling to look off-hand.

Alfred tried not to look as taken aback as he felt at this open admission.

"Indeed, and where did *you* get the wagon?" was the only reply his whirling brain could muster. What was Rafferty trying to gain with this piece of information, he wondered.

"It was a sad story," Rafferty continued, "while I was hunting in the far north of the Transvaal, I came upon this small farmhouse burnt out and empty except for the dead bodies of a man and his wife. The poor souls, God rest them, must have been attacked by a local tribe. I buried the bodies and looked for papers or possessions with names; unfortunately they must have been burnt in the fire. The wagon was on its side next to the house, but untouched, so I took it with me rather than leave it to rot in the bush."

"Did you have oxen to inspan it with?" Alfred enquired.

"But of course," Rafferty filled this gap quickly, "I had a wagon and a span of oxen for my hides and tusks. I inspanned two of my oxen to pull the wagon."

Alfred was silent while he considered this.

Rafferty continued, "I had an agreement with a man down in the Free State, at Wepener, to buy all my skins and tusks. I went down to see him and on into Basutoland to do some hunting. While I was there I met up with some of the trekking Griquas. The old boy, old Adam Kok, he helped me out with some gunpowder when I found mine was running low. In return I gave him the second wagon. He liked the pictures painted all over it."

"You mean you took it with you all that way?" Alfred queried. "It must have slowed up your progress, why didn't you sell it in Pretoria or Kroonstad?"

It was useful to have two wagons while I was trading," Rafferty shrugged his shoulders. "Would it be that wagon that yous was looking at? It was handsome alright but I'm surely surprised to hear that it made it through those mountains and out the other side. I told the old boy he was mad but he wanted to avoid grazing and watering fees an' you couldn't blame him. He had thousands of cattle."

Out of the corner of his eye Alfred noticed that Josh had joined them again. He was sitting on his haunches with his hands out in front of him, arms resting on his knees, eyes on Rafferty's face.

"Sounds like the same wagon, Mr Rafferty. So it could be the same people. Strange that you should hear about our visit and then suddenly arrive here to tell us you gave Adam Kok the wagon. You got some other interest in the matter?" Alfred asked, struggling to keep his voice on an even keel and suitably casual while his eyes watched Rafferty's face closely.

Rafferty's face stayed blank. "The boys and I, we was just coming down on business, like I told yous. If those were your folks, God bless them, they was well and truly with their Maker when I found them, and not an item remained to say who they were... all burnt by the savages or such like."

Josh spoke at last, "Where was this place?"

Rafferty looked closely at him. "It was somewhere in the Waterberg Mountains. A lonely spot. I'd not find it again. Came upon it quite by chance. Shame I was too late to help."

"Did you have partners on that hunt?" Alfred asked, remembering Old Joe the prospector, in Rafferty's bar in Kimberley and his story of the partners and the cattle and sudden wealth.

"Ah, sure now, no. I'm one for doing my hunting on my own. More profits and less complications," Rafferty assured him quickly.

"So you'd say these people who owned that wagon were the ones you found dead in the burnt-out farmhouse?" Alfred queried.

Rafferty nodded, "Seems likely. That was certainly where the wagon came from and there'd not be another wagon painted quite like that, I'd say."

"What else did you find with the wagon?" Alfred queried.

"I've told you now, there was nothing. Whoever attacked them had burnt or cleared out everything. Not a sinner left an' no animals neither."

Alfred tried again. "What of tin trunks or silver money or jewellery – things that robbers might not have valued if they were tribesmen?"

Rafferty shrugged. "They could always have sold them. Could be a band of cattle thieves from Khama's country, just across the mountains. It's foolish for one family to try and farm so far from other folk."

Alfred nodded. He hesitated, but then he could not resist asking, "Not even family silver?"

Rafferty had been turning his glass round slowly as he talked, the picture of a sorrowing man. Suddenly his head came up and a startled look crossed his face, rapidly replaced by a hard stare.

"I've told you, haven't I, there was *nothing!* An' what makes you t'ink they'd be having such things on a small farm in the Waterberg?" he challenged Alfred.

Suddenly, out of the corner of his eye, Alfred became aware that Josh was swaying strangely, and then, before he could fully comprehend what was happening, the boy had leapt from his squatting position with a screech like a cornered baboon. He had his hands round Rafferty's throat and was shaking him wildly and shouting between bursts of tribal babble:

"You lie, you lie, that wagon came from Makkapan."

Rafferty's chair tipped backwards as he struggled and the boy fell on top of him, hands still round his throat. As Alfred leapt to pull him off, the two men from the far side of the room arrived. Big Ox lifted the boy by his braces, slammed his hand away from Rafferty's throat and dangled him, thrashing helplessly, in the air.

Rafferty scrambled to his feet, rubbing his throat and gathered his composure as he dusted down his clothes. By this time Quinn was lifting a chair ready to slam it across Josh's dangling body. Alfred whipped the chair away from Quinn and threw it to the floor, the legs shattering into spinning splinters.

"Lay off the kid," he yelled above the noise.

By now the woman behind the bar had come to life and was screaming for her husband and littering the air with noisy obscenities about the family background of her customers. Just as Quinn was reaching for Alfred, Rafferty raised a restraining hand:

"Ah, now, boys, boys, please let us get to the bottom of this attack."

He turned to Ox. "Please lower the cub and let us look at him more closely."

Ox let go and Josh fell to the floor where he lay for a second, totally winded. Then, just as the men closed round, he bounced up as if to go for Rafferty once again. Quinn aimed a blow at him which sent him reeling into the nearest table. Hastily Alfred stepped in front of Josh and Quinn's next punch caught him full on the nose. When he came round it was to find Ox pinning a furiously squirming Josh to the floor with one foot while Quinn, his eyes narrowed to fine slits, kicked Josh repeatedly on the side of his body with his boot.

Rafferty appeared to be in no hurry to stop his companions, so Alfred rallied himself for another attack, knocking Quinn back into Rafferty. Quinn regained his balance and swung round on Alfred, who hastily shoved a table between them.

Ox advanced on him from one direction, Quinn from the other and a blood-bespattered Josh clambered back onto his feet just as Rafferty drew a pistol from a holster under his jacket and waved it at them all.

"Let it be, boys, yous can have them later," he shouted above the din.

Ox stopped his advance and signed to Quinn to stop as well. Glancing across his shoulder, Alfred caught sight of the fat woman and a nervous looking man peering in round the door. They obviously had no intention of moving any closer or trying to intervene. Quinn raised a warning fist at Alfred with a jerk of his shoulders, but made no move. Ox took a vice-like grip of Josh's shoulder and twisted him to face Rafferty.

"An' now, ye young welp, let's hear what you have to say 'bout attackin' a man for no good reason?" Rafferty fixed Josh with an angry stare.

"He's not in a state to talk to you," Alfred interjected. There was a large bruise developing across one side of Josh's face and one eye was already showing signs of closing. His nose was bleeding, there was a slash across one cheek and blood was running down to join a soggy purple bleeding lip.

"He'll do," said Rafferty "an' for sure he was asking for worse," he ran his hand round his neck where the red marks left by the boy's fingers were still visible.

"Well?" he demanded.

Josh stayed silent.

Ox shook him as a terrier might shake a rat.

Rafferty looked at Alfred.

"The son of a friend from Natal, is he?" he sneered disbelievingly. "This one's not one of us. This one's a bush baby – brought up by the baboons or some lost tribe," he turned to Ox and Quinn, "You seen how he squats? Sits like a bloody bushman, on his haunches!"

He swung round to Alfred again. "Time you came clean 'bout this kid. Who's he and what's he bloody jabbering about? What's this Makkapan place?"

Alfred was weighing up possibilities. Rafferty had the upper hand with a gun and his two companions. How best to bluff their way out of this one. If he accused Rafferty directly then they would join the colonial "Missing Persons Index". Rafferty could not afford to leave them alive.

"The kid's confused. You come marching in here with two rough looking guys and start on about his parent's wagon and then you're surprised when he goes for you?"

"An' what do you mean, 'his parents' wagon'? I know where I bloody found that wagon and there was no kid there."

Alfred looked sternly at Josh, hoping he would keep quiet.

"The boy was able to identify the wagon. I am satisfied that it is the one he described, but he also knows where his parents were killed and it was not on a farm in the Waterberg."

"Who'd believe a kid like that?" Rafferty interjected, "he'd have been too young to recall anything, even if what he says is true."

"The maid who took him away can remember it all... and where it happened."

"A maid can be paid to say anything. It would not stand up in court. Those people died on that farm."

"If you say so and you found the wagon, then you must be correct," Alfred said placatingly. He threw another warning glance at Josh, aware that the boy was staring at him. "Did you report this to the authorities when you reached Pretoria?" he asked Rafferty.

"Authorities? You mean Paul Kruger and his Raad?" Rafferty sneered, "What do you think they'd have done? Families who go into remote areas, without joining an official trek, take their chances. It was too late to do anything."

Alfred shrugged as nonchalantly as he could manage. "We'll have to accept what you say then. It was most fortunate that you happened this way and were able to advise us of the details..." he wondered whether Rafferty would let it go at that.

Rafferty slid his gun back under his jacket and leant back against one of the tables.

"So, behind your polite words, you threaten me; this boy who has grown up as a kraal kaffir attacks me and my men and accuses me of lying," he turned to Josh, "an' about what is it I lie?" His eyes narrowed. "Sure, that is, if yous feel able to conjure up a reply in a language we can all understand?"

Alfred was aware of Ox and Quinn stirring restlessly.

"If you say so," Josh muttered through his swollen lips, looking down at his feet.

Rafferty shoved his face close to the boy. "Why did you attack me? I want to hear from you. What was it you thought I'd done, exactly?"

Josh wriggled himself free of Ox's iron grip and rubbed his shoulder ruefully. "I know my parents were murdered somewhere below Makapansgat. So you say you didn't do it, but I'll find the men who did."

There was something about the grim determination with which he said this that made all the men give him their full attention.

"So, it's more than one man now is it, an' how'd you expect to do that?" Rafferty barked at him.

Josh shrugged and then winced, "I'll see what I can find," was all he would say.

Rafferty laughed sardonically. "Buried folk don't talk, praise be to God, ant ten years or so of rains and sun soon hide signs of passing wagons. Don't t'ink to waste your time. Anyway, I intend to give you two a chance to start again. Ox here, an' friend Quinn, they fancy a little trip round the fringes of Basutoland and then cross country to the railway line and down to the Cape. There they'll see yous onto a ship for England and you'd be wise to keep away from Africa, the both of yous."

"Why not down to Durban?" Alfred queried.

"And I'm the fool if I'd do that, ant you two jumping off in Cape Town and heading back up here to cause me grief," Rafferty explained with a shrug. He swung round as if on a second thought and looked at Alfred.

"An' don't you be worrying 'bout that lass, Emmie, for I'll be marrying her ant using her talents to run a string o' hotels, an' any argument ant she'll find her pretty face has scars like mine. Make a pair we will!"

Alfred looked at him in consternation. "What makes you think you can kidnap us and force Emmie into marriage?"

"You got friends who're going to stop me?" Rafferty enquired.

Realisation dawned on Alfred that they were very much on their own in this vast country. Here there was no family to call on and even law and order was difficult to reach.

Rafferty turned to Ox and Quinn.

"You got your orders then. I'll arrange for you to share the room with these two tonight. You sleep by turns."

Alfred did not care for the look he saw pass between the two men.

"We'll ford both rivers then head for the high peaks via Gourton – we'll be back in Kimberley for the cash," Ox addressed Rafferty briefly.

Rafferty nodded. "I'll clear off up north then meet you back in Kimberley… for the wedding!" he laughed, and looked at Alfred for a reaction.

Alfred felt sick with frustration.

"You'll not find it that easy. She's a lady who makes up her own mind!" he commented over his shoulder as Ox and Quinn pushed them towards one of the doors at the rear of the building. Rafferty's harsh humourless laugh rang in Alfred's ears through the closed door.

Alfred looked over at Josh, who appeared to have retreated into himself. His bruised and battered face was totally expressionless but Alfred noted that he had picked up his saddlebag from the debris round the tables as they marched through.

He could not be as shocked as he appeared, he thought with some relief. It was bad enough to have landed them both in this mess but it was going to need some fast work to get away from these two alive. He had kept mixed company on the diamond fields for long enough to recognise that neither of these men had the slightest intention of doing the long trip to Cape Town. Alfred acknowledged to himself that it had been naïve to leave his pistol in his saddlebag with his rifle. However, he also wondered whether he would have had a chance to use it, and decided that Rafferty would still have had the upper hand.

Before they marched them to the room where they would all sleep, Quinn had frisked him and laughed sourly when he found no sign of a weapon. Ox had picked up Alfred's saddlebag by the door and extracted his rifle, broken it to check whether it was loaded and then confiscated his gunbelt, the pistol and ammunition and slung the useless rifle back into Alfred's bag. Ox clouted Josh across the ear when he tried to stop him looking in his bag. He rapidly disarmed the boy's rifle.

Josh sat down on the bed clutching his painful head and Alfred checked his face to make sure his jaw was still intact after the pounding he had taken. To his relief the jawbone was just severely bruised.

"Keep you silent for a day or two!" he winked at Josh, trying desperately to lighten the mood.

Ox took the first duty on a chair in front of the door. The boy preferred the floor. Alfred dipped a cloth in the water jug and put it across Josh's forehead and swollen cheek. Quinn lay down on the narrow truckle bed, put his hat over his eyes, his gun by his side, and was snoring in two minutes. Ox put his feet up on another chair and turned the lamp low while he dug at his nails with a splinter of wood and then took to lovingly cleaning his pistol. Alfred lay on his bed feeling very vulnerable, with Ox on one side and Quinn on the other.

He went round and round the meeting in his mind trying to work out whether he could have engineered a different outcome. He knew he should have been carrying a pistol. He probably should not have mentioned the silver cutlery. It had seemed to jerk Rafferty onto another level of awareness and it might have precipitated Josh's attack on him. It was clear that Rafferty had planned what he wanted done with them long before he reached them. He fretted to and fro over the incident getting no further but feeling horribly guilty. He finally fell into a fretful sleep filled with angry frustration, dreaming he was caught up in a web which was under constant attack from an angry bluebottle. Somewhere else in the web he was aware of Emmie also struggling to release herself. Several times he surfaced sufficiently to realise that the bluebottle drone was Quinn's snoring. Then he would lapse back into the same disturbing dream.

Josh woke at the best time of the morning in Africa, very early dawn. He reached to make his customary stretch, almost as an obeisance to the dawn, when suddenly every muscle protested and his head seemed to scream with pain. Hastily he eased his aching frame back into a foetal position and tried to open his right eye. When it wouldn't co-operate he tried the left one and was greeted with the sight of Quinn's filthy old boots resting on a chair. Painfully his mind fought back to the night before. He put a hand up to his puffy face and it passed across a painful ear. The one useful eye wandered up to the rest of Quinn. He was slumped against the door with his hat low over his eyes and a finger idly picking his nose. The eye closed and he struggled again with the other one and realised he had a cloth across it. It must have been cold and damp once but now it was dry and prickly. He moved it away gingerly and tried the eye again. It opened and the world moved back into a better perspective. Gingerly he went over all his other moving parts and found they were working. He felt relieved and fell back into a light sleep. This was interrupted by a creak on the boards and he looked through his lashes to see Quinn rise gingerly and look across at the sleeping Ox.

He needs a pee, he thought to himself, as Quinn very slowly turned the door handle and inched the door open enough to let himself out. Josh looked up at the bed above him and noticed Alfred's foot sticking out. He reached up a hand and gently shook the foot to and fro. Alfred rolled over and looked down at him through bleary eyes. Josh pointed silently to the door and Alfred took a moment to respond. Just as they were both lifting themselves upright they heard voices outside the door and hastily lay down again. Through his lashes Josh saw Rafferty look into the room and then pull back and shove Quinn in through the doorway.

"Have your pee at change-over," they heard him say, "not when you're on duty, ye stupid bugger. I'm off. I'll catch the first pontoon this morning," he added.

Quinn peered suspiciously round the room and then slid sullenly back onto the chair. Half an hour later they were all moving and Ox was shouting for food. Reluctantly the fat woman slopped in with a greasy offering and some bread for the road. She avoided looking at Josh or Alfred and was obviously very glad to be rid of them all. Her attempt to get compensation for broken chairs met with a snarl of contempt from Ox and a hollow laugh from Alfred.

Josh looked at Alfred as they were marched out to their horses. If it was Cliff, he found himself thinking, we'd have these two tied up.

He wished he could talk to Alfred. With Ox and Quinn stuck close to their heels there had been no chance to exchange more than a look.

We should be able to get away on horseback, he reasoned to himself. Or perhaps they could get some help at the pontoon when they crossed the Mooi River. Perhaps that was what Alfred had in mind.

The recent rains had made the ford impassable and a pontoon had been constructed to help travellers. The next river would be the broader reaches of the Bushman River, there a pontoon was the only means of crossing. Surely Alfred would not let them be marched meekly down to this town in the Cape where they would be bundled out of Africa and all that was familiar. Africa still held the tenuous memories of his parents and the reality of Majinga, his tribal mother. The more he thought about it, the more determined he became that he had no intention of leaving Africa because it suited this man, Rafferty. The man was a liar and back in the kraal they'd have "smelt" him out with the witchdoctor. An induna would have been detailed to kill him or Gadunga would have called on the ancestral spirits to designate a form of death suitable for one who murdered for gain. Out here in the white man's world it seemed there was no built-in protection, no laws to live by. In Durban there had been a form of law and order administered by white men who were called policemen. However, it had appeared to be very weak and people seemed able to just move on if they wanted to avoid being locked up. At the fort in Durban they had sometimes hung people but it seemed to Josh that most white folk simply did what they liked. Cliff had called it "the law of the gun" and said that the gun holder held the power.

Josh realised that this was his first experience of that other side of the white man's world. Cliff's friends had been his friends and Cliff's word was respected. He'd heard talk of the people who scrabbled in the ground for riches. Almost all these white people seemed to have tried it and he'd listened to many tales of sudden riches and equally sudden death. Yankee Woods had been one of the lucky ones. He said he'd seen what greed could do for a man and he'd used his diamonds to buy the Royal Hotel. All these thoughts circled round in Josh's head as he loaded his saddlebag, watched closely by Quinn. Ox was standing by Alfred, his hand resting on his pistol holster in readiness for any attempt by Alfred to alter their travelling plans. Jackalet and Alfred's black stallion, Jupiter, seemed ill at ease and restless, as though they had caught some sense of threat from the atmosphere. Quinn and Ox had a pair of brown roans who looked strong and resilient. Josh realised that the men could not be out-ridden. Their horses were well used to travelling fast over rough terrain. He felt a wave of despair as he recognised that with the combination of ammunition and hardy horses, their travelling companions certainly held all the cards at present. As they mounted the two men did the same, one on either side of them, so that they made a close band riding four abreast.

Ox was having no ambiguity about the present situation. "Behave yourselves and we'll have a good trip. Try any funny business and we'll shoot to kill. Don't care about you, kid. You'll be treated same as 'im," he nodded towards Alfred.

Alfred spoke at last. "Where do we leave the main track to head for Basutoland?"

Quinn spat onto the road and commented:

"An' that's none of your bloody business."

Ox ignored him. "We'll use the hunters' track up Gourton way and cross the Little Tugela."

Alfred shrugged. "Be quicker by the main track," he commented casually.

Ox threw him a knowing look. "Sure," he said, "an' give you more chance to meet a convoy coming the other way. Forget it, we'll be off the beaten track as much as possible, and after the Bushman River it'll be up into the peaks where few people travel." He hung onto the word "few" and smiled unpleasantly at Alfred.

Josh noticed that they didn't head for the pontoon but Ox led them off onto a left-hand path which meandered through the rocky terrain and led them down into a steep dip. Below them the river snaked like a frothy pink earthworm, carrying debris and silt from the recent rains. The path led them to where the river narrowed into a waist between two rocky projections. By careful manoeuvre they were able to slide the horses down a narrow defile to what Ox assured them was a slender but firm rock-based ford across the river. Josh noticed that Quinn made sure that Ox was leading. He was behind Alfred and Quinn brought up the rear. At least this meant that the crossing must be an acknowledged one and not a fatal trick to send them into the frothing river to be swept away by the current. Ox's horse balked at the prospect at first, but then, after some cajoling, stepped gingerly into the water, and finding a firm base, began to wade cautiously across.

They followed in a line, each horse firmly behind the other. There was a nervous moment when a large piece of wood swept down on them but Josh

244

eased Jackalet to a stop and the wood passed through the gap between her and Jupiter. When the horses climbed out on the far side they were shivering from tension as well as the cold water. It crossed Josh's mind that perhaps this would be the time to make a dash for freedom while Ox and Quinn seemed preoccupied with calming their horses, but the path ahead was still narrow and not knowing the countryside could prove fatal for horse and rider in this terrain. He decided to wait.

The Bushman River was a far wider and more treacherous reach of water than the Tugela. They spent most of the morning moving up the escarpment, back towards the acknowledged track which would lead them to the pontoon and a safe crossing.

The weather was hot and sticky and voluminous clouds formed great grey banks in the sky, threatening downpours which never arrived. The flies were persistent and seemed to stick in the sweat and perspiration on Josh's face. He wished that the threat of rain would turn into a reality and cool the thundery atmosphere and wash them free of the unwelcome insects.

Round the middle of the day they stopped in the shade of a spreading acacia thorn tree. Ox was restless and ill at ease as they ate their bread. Josh noticed that he frequently looked over his shoulder and scanned the surrounding bush, especially towards the valley where the road lay. He drew Quinn briefly to one side and this gave Josh his first chance to exchange a word with Alfred.

"Shall we make a dash for it when we are back on the track?" he whispered to Alfred.

Alfred shook his head. "Where to? They'll outride you in ten minutes," he murmured. "I'm hoping we might find someone else using the pontoon and be able to make a fuss at that point. I thought we might jump off the pontoon but with the river in spate there is no point."

"What about the boys who man the pontoon?"

"One or maybe two tribesmen? No, they wouldn't help, especially not once these two whip out their pistols. If we meet no one then we may have to move out at night, on foot."

At this point Quinn came back and signalled them to mount once more. He went over to his horse and unhooked a coil of rope. Ox led his horse in front and to the consternation of Josh and Alfred. He began to rope the horses loosely together.

"Just in case yous has any funny ideas down by this pontoon or on the road!" Ox explained briefly. "An' don't forget now, we're armed an' yous are not," Quinn added with a look which almost passed for a smile, as it slid across his thin lips.

They joined the track shortly before the pontoon after Ox had gone ahead to check that there were no other travellers on the road or approaching the crossing. The far side of the river was thickly edged with reeds where the road came down to the crossing, making the track almost invisible in the slanting shadow cast by the afternoon sun. A few birds were wheeling to and fro across the turbulent brown water and a skein of wild ducks stood out against the blue sky as they headed for new pastures. Two grizzled Zulus with broad smiles and smooth muscles, were manning the winch which controlled the pontoon. Their acute hearing had picked up the sound of the small party long before Ox led them onto the track, and they had hauled the pontoon across ready for the travellers. Reluctantly Ox threw them each a coin and the men bowed politely as they caught them. Their smiles faded when they saw the rope and they looked more closely at the faces of Ox and Quinn. Josh guessed they remembered them from their previous crossing, and obviously not with any enthusiasm. They glanced quickly and furtively at Alfred and Josh and then turned away to busy themselves with getting the pontoon close enough for the horses to walk onto it. Josh tried to catch the eye of either man but their gaze slid hastily away and when he turned to talk to one he felt the tip of Quinn's whip across his already bruised ear and winced. A wave of frustration and hopelessness swept over him.

Because the river was running so fast and there was always the danger of debris, the maximum weight the pontoon could manage safely was one man and horse at a time. However, Ox was having none of this and roared at the two men that the pontoon would have to take *two* men and their horses at a time. Eventually, and very reluctantly, they conceded and shrugged and Ox said that he would go over with Alfred first. Quinn removed the rope connecting the horses and re-coiled it.

As they edged the nervous horses towards the insecurely bobbing pontoon, Alfred managed to come up alongside Josh. Under cover of the noise as the two Zulus debated how best to manage the gradual release of the pontoon rope that would keep the heavy platform stable, Alfred muttered to Josh:

"Something's up. One of those old boys used a bit of mirror to flash across the river and I don't think it was just the signal to start hauling."

Josh felt himself tense up, "And they pretended not to remember us from our previous trips," he whispered back. Holding Jackalet's face close to his

246

he rubbed his bruised cheek gently against the velvet texture of her nose, trying to sooth her nerves and his own, while he stared across the choppy water trying to make out anything unusual on the far side.

With the two horses carefully placed in the centre of the pontoon with their riders holding their heads and steadying them, the first crossing was underway. On the far side Josh could just make out the two pontoon winders who were steadily pulling them across while the two on his side equally steadily chanted the rhythmic tune which maintained the steady unwind.

Chapter Thirteen

AFRICA – September, October, November, 1879

By ALFRED'S ESTIMATION the pontoon was almost half-way across the broad reach of the river. The rhythmic refrain of the "unwinders" was fading steadily while the lilting song of the "winders" on the far bank was gathering strength above the rush and swirl of the turbulent water.

He was trying to picture the terrain on the far side of the steep bank. Was it the moment to try and ride for help, he pondered as he stood holding Jupiter's head and watching the bank draw closer.

He glanced across at Ox. Ox had an old felt hat pulled down over his bald head and appeared to be concentrating on the bank. His lack of eyebrows made him look disturbingly alien. The expressionless, almost egg-like smoothness of his face, with the small red-rimmed eyes and crease for a mouth, added to this general impression.

Alfred tried to size up the situation. If he and Jupiter made a dash for it on the far side at least he would only have Ox to contend with, but then, what of Josh. No use to separate himself from him. If Quinn thought he had got away from Ox he would almost certainly use that as an excuse to shoot the boy. There was also the matter of ammunition. Ox had the upper hand with a loaded rifle. Regretfully he returned to his vague plans for an escape under cover of darkness. It looked like their only hope.

Ox moved his horse forward rapidly as the pontoon touched the cause-way edge. Alfred followed him and greeted the two Zulu "winders", paying them for their efforts on this bank as he led Jupiter past them. He noticed in some puzzlement that they, like the winders on the other side, avoided his eyes and failed to return his greeting.

Ox had placed himself in the centre of the road at the top of the sloping bank. He was sitting astride his horse, his rifle across his lap, watching the pontoon begin its return journey. He signalled with a wave of his gun to indicate that Alfred should remain below him.

Both sides of the landing area were enclosed by dense beds of reed which wound up the bank on either side of the track. It was hot and sticky at the water's edge and Alfred moved himself and Jupiter to the side of the track where the reeds offered some protection from the afternoon sun. The two Zulus reached the end of their chant, jammed the chain and rope and sat back to rest. One of them went down to the river edge to splash himself in the swirling waters.

There was a flash from the far side of the river and it was time for the pulling chant to re-start. Presently the watchers on the bank could see the pontoon with its cargo of horses and riders, swaying across the water as the winders stretched their muscles on the winch.

Alfred dismounted and let Jupiter move back to the water's edge for a drink while he sat down on the roadside with his water bottle. As he lifted it to his lips he glanced up at Ox on the rise above him. The bottle stopped half-way to his lips and stayed suspended in the air, dribbling a silver stream past his chin, as he absorbed the sight above him on the rise. Ox was sitting watching the pontoon unaware of a rider behind him with a gun pointed at his head. Simultaneously, and almost as though he had caught the thought waves from Alfred, Ox jerked his head over his shoulder and tried to lift his own rifle at the figure of Clifford behind him. Instantly Clifford's voice rang out ordering him to lower his gun and throw it to the ground. Every inch of Ox's body language screamed reluctance as he rapidly assessed his position and then dropped the rifle with a clatter to the road below him. His horse jinked sideways in fright and sent the rifle spinning to the edge of the reeds.

With Ox's back to him Alfred saw his chance and moved rapidly up the rise towards the spot where the rifle had landed. Just as he put his hand over it Ox must have seen him and directed the roan towards him with a sharp kick. The roan, thoroughly thrown by the quick sequence of events, rolled its eyes and rose on its hindquarters, crashing down close to Alfred. Alfred and the gun rolled into the reeds and the horse tipped forward as its hooves missed the hard track and went into the mud on the reed edge. As it tensed to avoid falling forward it threw its rider into the middle of the reed bed, then teetered sideways, found its balance again, and galloped back down the slope towards the two Zulus, who had stopped winding and singing and were now staring open-mouthed up the slope. They dropped the winch and both leapt for the water edge. The winch wheel began to spin and unravel the cable, gathering speed as it found there was nothing restraining it any longer. The horse galloped a few feet into the river and stopped next to a startled Jupiter. Both horses wheeled round as if deciding that the river was not the best place to escape and stared wildly at the two frightened Zulus and the clattering, whirling winch handle.

Alfred found himself being dragged out of the reed bed by one leg and fought to lift his head free of the sharp leaves. He was suddenly aware that it was Clifford bending over him and urgently trying to pull him onto the hard surface of the track. At the same time there was a roaring curse from the middle of the reed bed where Ox was struggling to get a foothold in the deep mud.

"Quick man, get down to that winch or we'll lose the kid on the pontoon," Cliff hissed, "I'll watch your friend in the reeds."

Alfred rolled hastily over and gathered his legs up for a spring forward. He found himself rushing head first down the track towards the winch while looking frantically towards the centre of the river where the pontoon was acting like a spinning top caught triumphantly by the hungry waters. He reached the winch just as the final yards of cable were unwinding. The handle was going too fast to catch it without knocking himself out or breaking his arm, so he reached for the metal jammer key and dropped it down. There was a deafening grating noise as it slid into the whirling ratchets. Sparks flew in every direction and the whole mechanism tilted dangerously as the rope took the sudden strain once again. Some of the sparks had seared the rope and although it had stopped running it was now in danger of burning through and breaking away. Fortunately, at this moment the two Zulus overcame their fear of the horses and rushed for the rope adding their weight and pulling the mechanism back so that the strain on the damaged rope was eased for the moment.

Alfred looked out into the river and groaned. The pontoon was bobbing about, the empty platform flailing wildly in the river and with a distinct list to one side. By now the operators on the other bank appeared to be trying to wind in their side to drag the pontoon back towards their bank. However, having lost its balancing rope it would be a difficult task until Alfred's side was back in action and the rope disentangled from the pontoon logs and river rocks.

Meanwhile, Alfred had no clear picture of what had become of the horses or Josh and Quinn. Leaving the Zulus to operate the mechanism he ran back up the hill to where Cliff was standing with his gun pointed towards the wavering reeds which marked Ox's unsteady progress, while his head appeared to be looking out across the river for any signs of life in the water. Both horses followed Alfred up the slope and stopped near Cliff.

Alfred heard a shout, and whirling round saw one of the Zulus pointing urgently towards something in the river. It was a blob bobbing like a cork round some rocks. It definitely looked like a head. Then a swirl of current caught it and whirled it nearer to the bank on Alfred's side. At the same time Alfred saw Quinn's large roan swimming for the same bank, his head straining above the water. Meanwhile the Zulu who had shouted now pointed down river and began to run along the bank. Alfred was about to follow him when he heard an urgent shout from Clifford. He turned round just in time to see a mud-covered Ox reaching into his saddlebag for his pistol. Before he could make a move to use it Clifford had fired and the bullet appeared to hit Ox in the arm. For a brief moment he swayed and creased up, then, grabbing the saddle, he levered himself hastily up with his other arm, whirled the startled animal round and began a headlong flight up the track towards the high peaks.

Alfred heard Cliff give a short harsh laugh and saw him pick up Ox's pistol and drop it into his own saddlebag. At the same time he lifted a coil of rope off his saddle and started to run towards Alfred.

"Get down river a bit further, the current could carry them in beyond those rocks."

Alfred turned to look where Cliff was pointing.

"Yes, there's a pool down there which seems to attract debris."

Alfred began to leap down the slope towards the bank. Could the lad swim? He didn't think so. His best chance would be to cling onto the pontoon... but that was possibly a vain hope, he speculated.

The Zulu was waving and pointing and Alfred felt Cliff outpace him in the last two yards. He arrived on the river bank as the two men were looking out across the river, both chattering excitedly in Zulu. Alfred followed the direction in which they were pointing and he too could see a log of wood bouncing across the water, drawn by the current towards the indent in the river bank. It looked as though someone was clinging to it. They ran down the bank as the log swirled in and Cliff dived in and dragged the log and its body to the bank.

Alfred wanted to scream with frustration as he recognised the flat-faced features of Quinn staring up at him. The man was only just alive. Somehow he had managed to cling on to the log as his body was tossed between the rocks. Alfred was aware of Clifford looking up at him, his face a mask of disappointment. With the help of the Zulu they pulled Quinn up onto the bank and then turned to look back at the swirling waters.

"Here comes his horse too," Cliff shouted as the great roan was also carried into the indent by the current and all three of them waded into the water to steer the terrified animal into the bank.

"By God! There is something attached to his far side – could be driftwood," Cliff shouted as he waded round the horse.

Alfred had grabbed the great beast's sodden reins to try and lead him up to the bank and he stepped round and saw a small hand, almost blue with cold, clutching the stirrup leather on the far side.

He dived into the water by the side of the horse and he and Cliff came up at the same moment with Josh clutched between them. The Zulu, who had grabbed the reins from Alfred as he dived into the water, let out a great shout of triumph and the horse reared and tried to gain a foothold on the bank.

Alfred was aware of Cliff pushing the boy into his arms and swinging his rope round the horse.

"Lumba," Cliff shouted to the Zulu, "Pull this rope!"

As the Zulu began to pull so Cliff was breaking away part of the bank and making a path up it for the horse. Slithering and slipping as he went, the horse fought his way up the bank and stood heaving at the top, the whites of his eyes rolling and his legs shaking uncontrollably. Alfred had struggled up the bank with the horse, clutching Josh and keeping him from harm. Now the three men concentrated on prising the boy's icy fingers from the stirrups. Lumba, the Zulu, had come round to hold the boy.

"Massage his arms," Cliff ordered Alfred tersely, as he struggled with the fingers.

Suddenly Josh let go and the men lifted him gently onto the bank.

"Lay him face down," Cliff ordered. He moved the boy's head sideways so that his mouth was free and began steadily to pump his back, forcing great gouts of river water out of his mouth. Gradually Josh's blue lips began to turn to white and presently he opened his eyes and just lay on the grass like an exhausted rag doll.

"Better get him into something warmer," Cliff muttered, struggling to remove the boy's clothes.

Lumba was the only one with a dry shirt and he tore it off and they wrapped the boy in it, making him as comfortable as possible while he struggled to recover. None of them were paying any attention to Quinn. The roan was still standing shaking and steaming on the river bank and Alfred had just turned back to him to check his front legs for any damage. Suddenly he felt his legs kicked away from under him and he fell, bumping against the horse. He heard Quinn shouting, "Bloody toffee-nosed bastard, leave my damn horse alone. Where's that bugger Ox?"

Rolling hastily out of the way, Alfred looked up in time to see him stretching groggily for his soaked saddlebag. Before Alfred could do anything the roan had reared up with fright and leapt back from Quinn with a whinny of terror. Quinn seemed oblivious and came on, hands outstretched, for the saddle. The horse could not retreat further without falling back into the river and came down with both hooves on Quinn's shoulders, knocking him to the ground where he hit his head and lay unconscious, blood pouring from a gash on his head and jagged splinters of bone protruding from one arm where a hoof had lashed into him.

Lumba grabbed the horse's broken reins and hung on, seeming to overcome his own fear of the animal in his sympathy for its terror. Cliff whirled round from Josh and helped him to calm the animal. The horse stopped bucking but its eyes were still rolling. Cliff blew into its nostrils and held its head tightly. Slowly it calmed down and stood shaking gently on the riverbank, with Lumba holding onto its bridle.

Alfred looked in horror at Quinn. "What the hell do we do with him?" he asked no one in particular.

It was then that he surprised himself by recalling some of his medical training in Dublin. While Cliff and Lumba watched him in amazement he tore his rapidly drying shirt into strips and began making a pad to put over the wound in Quinn's head. Then he looked carefully at the fractured arm and shouted to Cliff:

"Bring me some straight pieces of wood from beneath that tree."

Gingerly, he found himself straightening the bones, removing some splinters, and pushing the flesh back as best he could. Taking a couple of the straighter sticks from Cliff he bound them to the sides of the arm and twisted the strips of shirt round the crude splints and then bound the arm to the man's body for support. He sat back on his heels to view his handiwork and, suddenly aware of a strange silence, he turned to find that everyone, including a dazed looking Josh, was staring at him in awed amazement. He suddenly felt incredibly tired. He shrugged and went over to sit under the thorn tree and closed his eyes while the happenings of the last few hours whirled in front of him in nightmare confusion.

Slowly he became aware of Cliff standing in front of him asking him something.

"The sun is low, shall we camp here tonight?"

He nodded. Then he roused himself. "Sorry, a touch of shock. What shall we do with my charming Irish friend? Given half a chance he'll shoot us all – not the grateful type, I fear!"

Cliff nodded agreement.

"I think he's coming round – the head wound has stopped bleeding but he'll have one hell of a headache. That arm will need hospital attention," then he added hastily, "You did a hell of a job patching it together, but in this hot and humid weather poison will soon set in without regular clean dressings."

"It needs a doctor to reset it properly, that is only a temporary job," Alfred got to his feet as he spoke.

Cliff went over and spoke to Lumba. The man seemed reluctant but then he spoke rapidly to Cliff and finally they seemed to reach an agreement and he nodded, handing the horse's reins to Clifford and moving off towards the track. Clifford returned to where Alfred was leaning against the tree trunk.

"We'll camp here for the night and then your charming Irish friend will move over to the shade near the pontoon until the Thursday postal coach arrives. Lumba reckons they'll take him on board and drop him off, probably at the hospital in Pietermaritzburg."

Alfred felt relieved.

"It's Thursday tomorrow, isn't it?" he asked.

"It is, thanks be to God because we can leave him to it and take his horse for the boy!" Cliff grinned at Alfred.

"So now," he continued, "you'd better fill me in. Just tell me first, did you find the wagon and make up your mind about Josh?"

Alfred nodded. "He's the right one alright!"

He walked over to where the boy was propped against a rock and ran his fingers through Josh's damp hair.

"He's kept an eye on me and I can't tell you how grateful I am to have him across that river in one piece."

Josh managed a half-hearted crooked smile.

Josh felt as though every bone in his body was aching and weak with exhaustion. He kept drifting in and out of sleep, jerking himself upright to scream as he relived the slide off the tilting pontoon into the sucking, whirling waters. Jackalet had been swept away from him as they entered the river and he had no idea how he had caught hold of the stirrup or how he had avoided rocks or the horse's hooves as he swam or struggled for a footing.

Finding Cliff bent over him had been no surprise. It had seemed almost natural that he should rescue him once again. Then he had looked round for Jackalet and found that she had not appeared and the general feeling was that she had probably drowned, not being as strong and large as the roan. He had wanted to search the banks but when he tried to get up his legs buckled under him. Cliff had searched the bank before sunset and found no sign. He had seemed to understand the depth of Josh's misery and had wrapped him in his own bedding and made him sleep next to him, close to the fire.

Josh heard Alfred getting up and down all night, keeping an eye on Quinn, giving him water and trying to calm him as he moaned with pain and cursed them all roundly for his condition.

As the sun rose the two Zulu pontoon operators, Lumba and Toti, arrived to take Quinn to sit by the causeway and await the coach. When this was explained to him he flew into a rage which made his wounds bleed again.

"So, yous might as well have shot me, bloody well abandoning me wit these heathens! For sure, they'll like as not kill me when you leave. An' what of my horse...?" he added as Cliff handed his saddlebag to Lumba, having first opened it and removed his pistol and ammunition and taken out some coins for the two carers.

"Don't howl to me," Cliff rounded on him, "your caring for this kid extended to kicking his face so that it is still black and blue. You don't deserve to still be alive and once Rafferty finds you, you won't be. He doesn't care for losers. As for your horse," he added, "you're contributing it to the kid in return for the damage you've done him."

Josh looked at the big roan. His heart ached for his pony but the big horse had saved his life, pulled him through the nightmare of the river.

Toti laughed as he watched Quinn's contorted face and he made a comment to Cliff. Cliff grinned and turned to Alfred and Josh.

"They've named him 'Flat-faced-river-fish'. Apparently he was rude to them when he crossed previously and they are not too worried about his welfare. News travels fast round here and they already knew that he and Ox were on their way back with you and Josh when I reached the pontoon."

"Ah," Alfred nodded in understanding. "That explains why they were so reserved when we crossed over. They knew there would be trouble."

Quinn tried self-pity and then threats thrown over the shoulder at them as he was led away by his escort.

"I'll get you buggers for this. I'll say you left me to die. I'll get even with you..."

The protests floated back across the fresh morning air.

Cliff shrugged. "Rafferty was digging low for that one... Pity the river didn't claim him."

Josh heard Alfred mutter:

"It's only a matter of time before someone gets him."

Josh was feeling better but he still missed Jackalet and sat staring across the river hoping that she would suddenly appear. The two men drew him into their discussion and tried to distract him by asking his opinion about the plans. He listened to Alfred explaining the need to find the graves and to see if they could discover any way of proving that Rafferty had been implicated in the murders.

"It was him alright!" Josh said with feeling, "If I'd had a gun where I could reach it, I'd have shot him last night!"

Alfred nodded sympathetically.

"Mention of the silver got him going alright! That story about the Waterberg didn't ring true. He had it far too neatly explained... I think he'd tried that one before."

Josh felt anger rising like bitter gall in his throat as he recalled the meeting.

He swung round to Cliff, who raised both hands defensively.

"So now, Cliff, we know that he was involved in some way. Why has he gone up north?"

"I suspect his quick departure is probably to check that there are no other ways he could be implicated in this crime."

"But..." Alfred appeared to be thinking out loud, "...he was right, Cliff, after all these years there wouldn't be any proof – and he took the wagon and probably sold its contents... so, why rush back? Perhaps there is someone around who knows more? ...or, perhaps he didn't destroy everything?"

Cliff took up his train of thought:

"Mmm, he'd not want anyone finding anything which might prove who the man and woman were, especially not now that Josh has identified the wagon and Rafferty has agreed that he sold it to Adam Kok. His story of a burnt-out farm house and a dead couple would be totally discredited! In fact, with that and the family silver we'd have a case for a murder trial!" He looked triumphantly at Josh and Alfred.

"Ox and Quinn were, I'm sure, meant to kill us, once off the trail and near some convenient mountain precipice," Alfred added.

"I have no doubt that was what was intended. That's why I came down to warn you," Cliff confirmed.

A feeling of desperation swept over Josh. He put his head in his hands and rocked to and fro.

"I'd like to have Gadanga cast the evil eye on him," he said, struggling to keep control of his voice and emotions.

"He'll have my evil eye to contend with first!" Cliff tried to reassure him.

Alfred suddenly straightened himself up.

"Do you know, that sneering toad told me cheerfully that he was going to force Emmie into marriage and make her run his hotel – or he'd slash her face."

"The bastard!" Clifford swore with feeling.

"We'd better get her away from that hotel before he gets back," Alfred added.

"Luckily I thought she would be next in line for trouble, so I put her on the coach for Pretoria, to stay with friends," Cliff explained quickly. "I'm hoping Maria doesn't track her down too soon but word gets about fast and Maria'll have the fear of the devil upon her because Rafferty left her to keep an eye on Emmie."

Alfred looked at him in some surprise.

"So you got to know Emmie, then?"

Cliff nodded.

"Of course I did, you said to update her and see that she was alright."

Alfred laughed in obvious relief.

"Thank goodness for that. She can be so cussed, I was afraid she'd be so caught up with her singing that she'd not want to listen to you."

Cliff looked speculatively at him.

"You worried about her then?"

Alfred shrugged.

"She's tough, but I brought her to this country so I feel responsible... She's not like most girls, she can fight her own battles, well... generally... but not with someone like Rafferty, he's too slippery, she'd need protection."

Cliff looked at him with a furrowed brow.

"You're a bit casual. She's got a killer on her hands and that's all you can say?"

"That young lady has a mind of her own and she'll go her own way."

Cliff raised an eyebrow.

"You talk from experience, then?"

Alfred nodded ruefully.

"Fantastic gal but no lady, I fear!"

Cliff smiled quizzically, "That mean you're not interested in taking her back to Ireland when you go?"

"No way, she'd not come anyway. She's smelt freedom now," he laughed easily.

Cliff looked relieved. "No duel to the death then if I show an interest?"

Alfred threw back his head and laughed.

"I'd be delighted to be relieved of the responsibility," he put a hand on Cliff's shoulder. "She's got real guts and you'd be a lucky man if you can hold her!"

Cliff smiled confidently. "I'll cope, but for now we'd better plan on getting to her before Maria or Rafferty do!"

Josh had never met this "Emmie" person and he felt resentful that Alfred and Cliff now seemed more concerned about her than about plans to see that some form of justice should be meted out to Rafferty.

"What about *our* plans then? We can't go off after some girl while Rafferty makes sure there's no proof that my parents ever existed…"

Cliff turned round and looked at him.

"We've not forgotten, Josh, We'll try to collect Emmie on our way north as we chase Rafferty's shadow. Don't worry, lad, it's all gonna sort out!"

Josh was aware of a wave of relief as Cliff's words eased the tension he was feeling.

"It has to be a quick route," Cliff added, turning back to Alfred, "Rafferty's got twenty-four hours start on us. He probably went down to Howick and then up the old Transvaal road through Helpmekaar and Rorke's Drift. He may go via Pretoria or he may use hunting tracks to Bronkhors Spruit and then cut up on the old coach road through Potgietersrust."

Cliff sat and thought for a few moments. Then he voiced his thoughts again.

"No one from Kimberley is going to reach him to tell him that Emmie and I have disappeared. He thinks you two are being taken care of by Ox and Quinn. He will want to get up to Makkapan but he won't be pushing himself. Yes… I think if I was in his place, I'd go cross country. Some of it will be fairly tough but he's used to that… In that case it's going to take him roughly six or seven days to reach Makkapan."

Alfred was nodding wisely but only to give encouragement, Josh realised, he could have no idea of the possible routes himself.

258

"We'll need to go via the Biggarsberg to make up any time and then, once into the Transvaal, we'll use the hunting paths to cross the Whitewater reef to Pretoria. This will again shorten the route for us…"

He continued to ponder and the others waited expectantly.

"Unfortunately the detour to Pretoria to collect Emmie will delay us a bit more. We will just have to hope that he is in no hurry and will give his horse plenty of breaks. By moving rapidly ourselves, we may well arrive on his heels." He swung back to Josh with a cheerful grin. "Not much goes on in Africa unobserved, so we'll soon hear what he did when he reached the big cave."

Chapter Fourteen

AFRICA – November, 1879

EMMIE HAD FOUND the move to Pretoria very traumatic. It had all happened so suddenly that there had been no chance to get used to the idea. She had just had time to give a brief outline to Kirsty McDonald and to ask her to tell no one that she was leaving. Cliff had collected her bag and she had gone in to help Morag in the normal way. Then she had slipped out of the kitchen and met Cliff in the dusty square where the mid-day mail coach was disgorging its passengers as the stable boys replaced the horses with a fresh team.

Cliff had wasted no time on pleasantries. One minute he was coming up to her with a smile on his face and an extended hand and the next he was seeing her onto the coach, well wedged in between a perspiring, fat lady and a short, worried looking little man, with a pince-nez balanced precariously on the bridge of his nose.

Cliff had seen the consternation on her face and leant into the coach to say:

"Watch out for pick-pockets when you change in Johannesburg, 'cousin' Anna is expecting you. Here is the address in case she can't get to meet you."

Emmie tucked the piece of paper into her bodice and strained to see through the window, but he was already out of sight. He had warned her that they would need to move fast and draw no attention to her departure.

She was glad to get out of the stuffy, dusty and rancid atmosphere of the coach in Johannesburg. The final leg of the journey proved to be more pleasant and less crowded.

Here, in Pretoria, life seemed to follow a quieter and less frenetic pace than had been the order of the day in Kimberley. The little town had a great white church on a spacious square where the townsfolk paraded in leisurely fashion and farmers with cattle and produce came in to sell their goods. Around the square, flowering trees threw patches of shade onto the sunbaked earth and local tribespeople spread out their goods for sale to the housewives and workers of the small town. Although three people alighted from the coach they all seemed to move off very purposefully, leaving Emmie, bag at her feet, looking round hopefully for her "cousin" Anna. The coach moved off with much shouting and dust to find its way to the hotel yard where the remaining passengers would spend the night. Feeling in her bodice, Emmie pulled out the slip of paper with the address and walked over to a blacksmith. He set her off in the right direction and she walked down a long, wide, dusty road lined on both sides with small houses set well-back behind a deep storm ditch.

Emmie noticed the neat small gardens, well stocked with bushes and flowers and the dainty metalwork, like petticoat lace, on the verandas, and eves of the houses. It all had a far more settled, well-established and contented air than the rough-and-tumble of Kimberley. Turning left, as she had been instructed, she came to a neatly fenced, white-washed house set back behind the fronds of a well-established weeping willow. A young woman with bouncing ringlets opened the front door and immediately threw her arms round Emmie's neck.

"I received the note from Cliff yesterday. Sorry I couldn't get away to meet you. Cliff forgets about babies and small children!"

Anna's home was a happy, chaotic mixture of children, their toys and her sewing. Her husband, John, was a pharmacist who had got to know Cliff when he was peddling goods for Hartley. He seemed quite unperturbed by the chaos in the house, although none of the children were allowed in his "potion parlour" which was a small room tacked onto the side of the house where he dispensed medicines and handed out advice on minor ailments to his customers.

Emmie was quickly absorbed into the family life. Looking after the little ones brought back memories of Ireland and a realisation of how much she missed her family, especially Duggie and little Peggy. However, reality always crept back in and she thanked God that she had escaped to explore the outside world.

No word came from Kimberley and she wondered what had passed between Morag and Maria concerning her disappearance. Maria would not be able to sack Morag because her cooking was one of the reasons for the Hotel's success, she reasoned to herself.

When she was not helping with the children she felt too restless to settle to anything and would walk round the little town looking at the people, their houses and gardens. It was almost as though she expected to find someone she knew. When there was a gathering of people she found herself looking eagerly at their faces and wondering whether they knew Clifford. Once she even asked someone if they knew him but was met with a shake of the head and a blank look. However, Anna and John were always ready to regale her with stories of Cliff and his trading days. When asked about his present life they were very non-committal.

"We know he lives some of his time in Port Natal and now he seems to hunt and trade for himself. His life is something he never discusses but he's not married or we'd have heard," Anna said sympathetically.

To her surprise Emmie felt herself blush. She looked at Anna from under her lashes. "Is it that easy to see that I care about him?"

Anna laughed, "Why else would he be saving a lady in distress? He's never been one for romance. We've always told him it would catch up with him with a large bang one day! Frankly, we're delighted!"

Anna was a dressmaker of considerable talent, a fact soon unearthed by the local ladies of Pretoria. As a result she found her services in constant demand and Emmie, when not busy with the children, helped her with seams and hemming.

There was a hint of the soft warmth of early spring in the air and from her seat on the swing bench on the red-polished veranda, Emmie could look across the budding front garden to the street and watch the trades people, hawkers and neighbours going about their business. She was hemming a dress for Anna. With her toe she set the seat gently swinging and moved the silky material across her lap to stitch a new section. She heard a giggle from the street and glancing up saw a young man and a pretty dark-haired girl walking up the road. As she watched, the couple stopped and the man leant forward and kissed the girl on the cheek. Then, as if drawn by a magnet, they moved closer, into a long intimate embrace. The girl pulled back but she held his eyes and put up a hand to touch his cheek in an intimate gesture of love. Then they both appeared to become aware of where they were and the magic moment was lost as they looked round and began to walk rapidly on, as though embarrassed by their lapse.

For Emmie the intimacy and love expressed by the two cast a shadow of loneliness which left her feeling bereft. They had expressed something in their body language which she suddenly recognised was missing from her life. She thought of Cliff. She recalled the urge to touch him, to run her hands up his arms, to put her body next to his and feel the warmth and strength of him. Her whole body yearned for his presence. She closed her eyes and pictured his tanned face, the determined strength of the chin and mouth, the clear blue eyes with the laughter lines like delicate fans at their outside corners. She recalled the way his mouth went crooked when he felt sceptical and then his laugh, a whole-hearted chuckle of warm amusement which would tumble out as though out of his control. How different he could look when he was concerned or angry, his eyelids would lower and narrow and the laughter lines were smoothed away as the full mouth compressed into a thin line. His body she had noticed, seemed to become lean and active and he moved from easy going charm to brisk action within split seconds She smiled to herself. This was a man she felt she could trust. A man who would keep her interest because life with him would never be boring.

She was suddenly aware of someone standing in front of her and opened her eyes to find Anna standing looking keenly at her.

"You were thinking about him, weren't you?" she queried gently, with a look of quizzical amusement.

Emmie nodded, not wanting to trust herself to talk.

Anna sat down next to her.

"It's been ten days since you arrived and we haven't heard a word. We will hear very soon, Em," she added reassuringly. "Look, why don't you go down to the coach office and see whether the afternoon coach brought in any post for us."

"They're probably tired of me asking!" she laughed and put her needle away, standing up to shake the dress and put it back on a hanger. "Thanks, Anna, I think I'll do that. It'll be like trying to help myself instead of sitting round worrying."

The Booking & Enquiry Office was quite busy when Emmie reached the square. The most recent coach had come in earlier than usual and two men were sorting out the mail mid much discussion and ribaldry as they tried to guess the contents of some of the townsfolk's mail. There were company messenger boys waiting hopefully for letters and people trying to buy tickets for the coach. There were also people complaining about lost and damaged luggage and a man cursing the coach company for inefficiency. Emmie pushed her way into the crowded little office trying to see how close she could get to the mail sorters.

She found herself wedged between a fat farmer in a grubby felt hat with a stinking cob pipe who, in guttural Afrikaans, seemed hell-bent on declaring the sorters to be a murderous collection of thieves, and an old lady with a walking stick who was using this weapon to poke at the people in the front row to improve her jostling position. It was while trying to avoid the stick and the pipe that Emmie caught sight of a head of black ringlets beneath a large flat red hat, bent across the counter. There was no mistaking Maria. Emmie's first instinct was to run in the other direction as fast as possible. However, wedged as she was, there was no easy escape route and just at that moment Maria swung round and Emmie heard her say:

"Keep an eye out for her, I'm offering a reward, you know." The small bespectacled man behind the counter nodded and Emmie could not hear what he was saying but the final part of his parting sentence sounded like: "...not paid as a missing persons' agency, but sure, we'll let you know, mam."

Emmie bent her knees and shrunk as far as she could to try and avoid being seen by Maria as she pushed her way out of the office. Fortunately, she was well hedged in and one man put out a hand to try and help her up.

"You feeling alright there, miss?" he queried in concern.

"Just dropped my hanky," Emmie lied from her crouching position and he leant forward and took her arm and helped her up. She looked nervously between the heads and shoulders behind her and was in time to see Maria disappearing through the door.

Devil take her! she thought to herself, how did she ever manage to trace me to Pretoria?

She pushed her way over to the grubby, barred window of the office and watched Maria in her red and grey dress, sweep across the square towards a small hotel on Breede Street, with a little boy trotting along behind, with her valise.

I'd better get back and talk to Anna and John – in a small place like this it won't be long before someone recalls seeing me and tells her where I'm staying, she thought.

She used the back streets round the square, moving somewhere between a scamper and a run and her heart seemed to cartwheel into her mouth as she heard her name being called as she crossed Plein Street.

"Hey, Em, Emmie, *Emmie*, stop a moment, wait a moment!"

She swung round, instantly on the defensive, with her back against a white wall. Then she could have cried... and shouted, with joy. There, coming up the street on horseback, were three men. Really she only had eyes for the one in front but she was aware of his companions. All dignity forgotten she tore down the street and Clifford had to leap off Charity and grab

Zenda's collar as he had gone into a crouching position ready to spring at this strange being who appeared determined to throw herself at his master. With his other arm he caught her as she reached him and hugged her to him.

"Darling," she heard herself whisper into his collar, "I've missed you so much!" She felt his body stiffen and then relax and the arm round her held her more tightly. Zenda had now had time to recognise her and she felt a wet lick on her arm. The other two had caught up and were sitting astride their horses looking down at them. She looked up at Alfred's howl of laughter and pulled a face at him.

"Well, by God, Emmie," he said, "Now haven't I seen the lot! Imagine you falling for *him*! There's no accounting for a woman's taste! And him only a wild man out of the bush with a Yankee accent! Imagine explaining that to your folks back home! The shock'll knock Father Donohue into kingdom-come!"

She grinned back at Alfred.

"An' sure you're a cheeky lad, young master Alfred, this one's worth ten of your kind!"

Alfred doffed his leather hat in respect, still laughing.

"You're right, lass, you always have known what you wanted!"

She became aware of a solemn pair of blue eyes staring down at her from the back of the roan.

"And this must be Josh? How do you do, Josh." Her quick glance took in the green and blue bruising across his face and she felt a wave of sympathy for the boy. She reached up a hand to him and he shook it awkwardly.

"It's a fine uncle you have there, even if he is a bit forward with a gal. Ant now, let me tell you that you have a fine set of uncles and aunts back in Ireland waiting to see you." Josh's blue eyes registered surprise.

"Emmie lives near your grandparents in County Leitrim in Ireland," Alfred explained quickly.

The blue eyes took on a friendly quality and the boy smiled slowly at her.

Suddenly she recalled Maria and swung round to Cliff.

"By God, Cliff, and who do you think has just come to town this very day? It's that Maria. She's asking folks if they've seen me, and sure she'll soon track me down. I was on my way to ask John and Anna where I could move to next."

Cliff's eyes narrowed and he stared solemnly round the street.

"Best not waste time then. Let's escort you back to John and Anna and we'll need a horse for you." Then, almost as a second thought he asked:

"By the way, can you ride?" Just as Emmie was nodding Alfred interrupted.

"Cliff, she's never ridden these sort of distances astride, but she can ride alright, taught her myself!"

Cliff looked thoughtful. "We could drop her off further north with other friends, or we could put her on a coach to Potgietersrust and meet her there."

Emmie felt indignant.

"I can do as well as you Alfred-O, don't you interfere in my life." Alfred laughed and raised both hands in the air.

"So I give up, I give up! It's over to you Clifford… and good luck!"

Emmie measured Josh with her eyes. "Give me a pair of his trousers an' I'll ride with the best of yous."

It was Josh's turn to look indignant, but he couldn't resist her teasing eyes as she looked at him through lowered lashes.

"She can use my other pair for now," then almost as a second thought, he asked, "Can you read and write?"

"Of course I can!" She looked puzzled.

"That's alright then, you can teach me to do the same!"

Emmie laughed up at him. "It'll be a pleasure – mind, I'm a hard taskmaster!"

Cliff swept her up onto his horse and climbed up behind her. They moved off to navigate the back streets to Anna's home.

Sitting up on the horse with Cliff's arms encircling her as he held the reins, she felt a glow of contentment for the first time since arriving in Pretoria.

Josh had been so involved in the daily realities of the fast ride from Natal and the new experience of listening to two men who were very different, but between them seemed to open up a whole new world for him, that he had quite forgotten their main aim in coming through Pretoria.

He was thoroughly taken aback when, as they trotted through the town, Cliff suddenly called out and a slim red-headed girl in a blue and white dress, spun round and stared in alarm at him. Suddenly she was running towards Cliff and he was swinging down off Charity to calm Zenda and then to clasp her in his arms. When she finally looked up at Josh he was amazed by her clear green eyes and the porcelain delicacy of her complexion behind the soft scattering of freckles. He recalled the conversation down by the Bushman River. So, this was the girl whose face Rafferty was threatening to slash. The wave of jealousy which had swept over him as Cliff hugged her, subsided and was replaced by a feeling of protectiveness towards her. There was also something about her that reminded him of Jessica. A way of moving her head and that mischievous look in her eyes. For the first time he was aware of a need for female company, for someone special who looked at him the way that girl had looked at Cliff as she ran towards him.

They rode round the back streets to Anna's house. Cliff explained that Rafferty's girl friend was in town looking for Emmie and warned John and Anna to keep their doors locked at night and to tell any callers that Emmie had headed back to Kimberley. After they had eaten, Cliff had gone out with John to get a horse for Emmie and Josh and Alfred had been introduced to the three children.

Somewhat reluctantly, Josh gave Emmie his spare trousers and was amazed at how good she looked in them when she came in to show off to Anna. She had put on a blouse with soft, puffed sleeves and long cuffs and the fawn trousers accentuated her slim legs and trim ankles in the short riding boots. Anna and the children laughed and Anna commented:

"It's very unlady-like to go round in breeches, Emmie, but I must say you look better than a lot of men I know!" She got up and put an arm round Emmie's shoulders, "I'm going to miss you. You've been like a sister to me," she said quietly.

"You'll not lose me!" Emmie reassured her hastily. "We'll have to come back this way and I'll be collecting that beautiful dress you're making for me. An' sure, you never know, I might be here to stay again."

"I hope so," Anna kissed her on the cheek.

Once the men came back with the extra horse, Cliff had them all mounted and riding off as rapidly as he could. Josh heard him explaining that they needed to be well away before Maria traced Emmie to the house. It seemed to him a little strange that a woman could be quite so dangerous. He wondered why Cliff, who had rescued them so calmly from Ox and Quinn, should be in such haste to avoid a woman. Cliff must have seen him looking at him speculatively.

"It's not Maria that's the problem, Josh, although I think she could be quick with a knife, but it's really *who* she has brought along in the background. There'll be someone to do her dirty work, you may be sure. I could do without them following us either," he drawled, as he swung into the saddle.

They had to cross the low ridge of the Magaliesberg hills and then move down onto the Springbok Flats, an area of rolling grasslands and acacia thorn trees, renowned for its prowling lions.

"Alfred," Cliff swung round in his saddle as they moved into a steady jog on the road out of the Pretoria, "could you ride behind Em and Josh, and guard our rear. This is lion country from just before sunset. I'd like to reach Joubert's farm on the edge of the hills and stay there for the night."

Josh fell into place behind Emma. Alfred laid his rifle across his pommel and brought up the rear. The horses moved into an easy canter and then found their pace in a steady jog.

Josh noticed that Emma was moving smoothly in the saddle, her shoulders under her short jacket rising and falling evenly with the horse's stride. Her auburn hair caught the rays of the setting sun in waves of soft russet hues as it rippled in the breeze. He could not help wishing that it was Jessica but felt a pang of disloyalty as he wondered whether she could have ridden as well as Emma. To distract himself he looked back over his shoulder at the distant outline of the town, fading into the soft afternoon sunlight behind them, as they moved into the shadow of the Magaliesberg hills.

Cliff was relieved to turn up the track to the Joubert's farm just as the sun was sinking like a scarlet ball into the black skyline of the veld. To his surprise no one came out to meet them as they rode up to the long low mud-brick house with its straw roof extending out over a narrow veranda. The homestead was set on the side of a rock-strewn kopje and there was a square outhouse or barn to one side of it and a cattle kraal behind. There were sounds of cattle moving around in the thorn-bush edged kraal and a sliver of smoke from the kitchen chimney was drifting up into the rapidly darkening sky. A dog moved idly out of the outhouse and began to bark at them, a disturbed chicken squawked in the vicinity. The soft light of an early lamp glowed in a window. Cliff dismounted and, leaving the others watching his progress, he went over and knocked at the main door. One of the old black rockers on the veranda was still swaying slightly, as though it had only recently been vacated.

Presently a male voice called out *"Ja? Wie is dit?"* enquiring as to who they were. Clifford replied and asked to speak to him. Slowly a crack of lamplight appeared as the door was opened an inch, then another inch, and an elderly bearded man stood defensively in the gap, with a shotgun in his hand. He demanded an explanation for their presence in guttural Dutch. Cliff felt somewhat taken aback by the reception as most lonely farms were only too pleased to help strangers as it was their way of getting news from the world beyond their immediate locality. Quickly, one eye on the shotgun, Cliff explained:

"We need a roof for the night as we are travelling north and we have a lady with us."

The old man peered out suspiciously into the twilight.

"*Verdomste Engels*, you steel our republic without even a warning and then you expect our hospitality. Be off with you before I use my gun!"

Cliff was stunned into silence. Then he recalled that two years previously Britain had indeed sent an emissary to Pretoria who had announced in the public square near the church, that the republic was now annexed as a British Colony. The residents of Pretoria and the local Boers had been stunned and had realised that they had been tricked out of their republic by murmurs of gold and an inexperienced President. They had been seething at the injustice ever since and there were murmurings of an uprising to come. Pretoria itself was now garrisoned by the British Army and between the soldiers and the town's inhabitants there was an uneasy truce.

"Wait a bit!" Cliff hastily put the toe of his boot into the rapidly closing crack of the door. "I'm no British subject. I'm a Yankee and we have our own arguments with the British. My friend here, he's Irish, he'll support you too, and for that matter, so is the lady."

The crack widened a little as the old man looked past Cliff and examined the other three. There was a short whispered discussion with someone behind him and then he opened the door a little wider and told them, rather reluctantly, that the barn was the best they could expect. Cliff was about to protest when Alfred remarked:

"Seems that's the best offer he'll be making. Let's get over there and shake out the snakes and the hens and make the most of it. At least the lions will be deprived of our company!"

Cliff led the way over to the barn and they moved some of the carts round, disturbing a rooster and sending a group of hens squawking into the darkness of the far corners. A farm cat stalked out and the dog arrived to inspect them all. They were just settling down, using some of the hay which was making an untidy heap in the centre of the barn, when Mrs Joubert arrived with a lamp and some bread and meat. She was apologetic about their sleeping accommodation, and embarrassed when she saw Emmie. It seemed that her husband was adamant that he would not have them in the house, whatever they claimed to be.

Josh had curled up on the hay under his rug and slept contentedly. He awoke to the dawn fluffing and clucking of the hens and the strong smell and restless movement of the horses. Emmie was silhouetted against the haze of light coming in round the door and for one split second he thought she was naked. Then, just as he was aware of a rush of excited warmth creeping up his body, he realised that her slim, lithe figure was clad in his trousers and shirt and she was stretching upwards, extending all her joints after their night curled up on the floor. He caught Cliff watching him with amusement from a seat on a nearby sack. Cliff winked at him and he felt himself grow hot and hastily looked down at his hands, relieved that the dancing shadows hid his embarrassment. Emmie bent forward to let her hair fall like a gleaming straw-bespattered russet curtain towards the floor. She shook it and began to pick out some of the bits which had settled in over night.

"An' why is it the straw falls off you lot and glues itself to me?" she asked in a pained voice.

Alfred laughed at her. "You should sleep *on* your rug, not under it! I can tell you're used to the soft life, Em! We seasoned travellers sleep with our hats on in case we have to move hurriedly!"

Emmie pulled a face at him and went back to pulling bits of straw off her clothes.

"Master Alfred-O, you're a fine one to talk of the soft life, an' you riding round Dublin in your fine carriages an' all!"

Cliff, Josh noticed, had dragged himself away from the pleasurable task of watching Emmie and was standing up stretching.

"There's a jug of water from Mevrou Joubert over by the door, and bushes and boulders outside if you want privacy... just watch out for snakes," he grinned mischievously, looking meaningfully at Emmie.

She caught the look and flung one of her boots at him, which he caught deftly.

"I'm no lady yet, Clifford, ant I've a better aim than most women!"

He grinned and tossed the boot back to her, adding: "No doubt also taught by Alfred!"

Cliff made them ride steadily northwards until the sun was up and they stopped in the shade of a clump of trees and a mud house which boasted a placard outside that stated rather grandly, "Pienaars River Inn". Josh stuck his head through the door and a friendly man shambled out and introduced himself as Jacob Fay. He produced food and drink and waved them on their way towards the hot springs. Josh wanted to view these natural wonders but Cliff pointed out that they needed to get to the area known as Naboomspruit before sunset, allowing themselves a short ride to Potgietersrus the next morning. In Potgietersrus he knew the Landrost, a man of importance in the area who was responsible for keeping law and order and calling up the local militia in times of trouble.

Naboomspruit was a dusty little patch on a small stream where a couple of traders ran a rest house and shop, encircled by a vast number of fat-leafed euphorbia trees, which flourished on the banks of the river. Their very poisonous sap meant that they were largely left to grow undisturbed and the early settlers had called them nabooms – or nasty trees. There was something almost primeval about these huge, tall succulents, each one reaching up their grey-green branches in supplication to the heavens in a huge single crown. Josh cast an interested eye over them.

"*UmHlonhlo*," he murmured, remembering their tribal name.

Cliff looked at him. "What use are they, Josh, do you know?"

"Spirits live in them," Josh nodded solemnly. "They are sometimes cut down but only if the witchdoctor advises it and then it is first surrounded by fire to move the spirits on. Sometimes the sap is used on…" he hesitated, searching for the word, "…bumps on the hand or foot."

Cliff nodded. "I'd heard that too, things we call 'warts'."

The sky line was darkening as the sun sank like an orange Chinese lantern behind the navy blue hills. The great nabooms stood out like sinister black monoliths against the reddening sun.

The four travellers were eating a meal beneath the uneven thatch-covered veranda of the little mud-brick rest house.

Accommodation in the house was sparse and water was short. The stream was running dry and the locals were searching the skies hopefully for any sign of rain clouds. The stream could turn from a trickle in a dry sandy bed to a roaring torrent of water within a few hours if rain fell in the hills. Josh had slept better on the hay the previous night. He still found it easier to sleep on the floor than a bed but he was sensitive to the fact that Emma was in a room on the other side of the mud wall and might find out that he could not cope with a bed. He was not sure why this worried him. He was also beginning to feel tense about the whereabouts of Rafferty and how much of Majinga's story he could remember when it came to identifying the spot where his parents had been murdered.

He tossed and turned on the lumpy coir mattress and, for the first time in a long while, allowed himself to think of the kraal in the mountains and his dark-skinned "mother". He found himself longing for her comforting presence and the placid commonsense with which she had always treated his questions. He was aware of a great need to be back beneath the protective branches of the giant marula tree. Sleep would not come to give him release from the turmoil of his thoughts. He eventually crept out of the uncomfortable bed and went to sit on the veranda steps in the moonlight. There he found himself joined by the silent presence of Zenda, who sat down against him as though to offer comfort. Alfred found the boy and the dog curled up together, fast asleep, as the first glimmer of dawn washed across the sky.

They left before the sun was fully up. Cliff explained that he was eager to find out whether anyone in Potgietersrus had seen Rafferty.

The man who ran the rest house in Naboomspruit had been sure someone of that description had passed that way in the last two days. He had only stopped for a meal and to rest his large black horse.

They rode to Potgietersrus largely in silence, each wrapped in their own thoughts. Emmie sometimes asked about the countryside and the strange flat-topped mountains which seemed to push their way out of the bush-covered plains. Josh noticed that she was interested in everything and seemed well able to keep up with Clifford on her horse. He and Alfred brought up the rear with Zenda loping, seemingly inexhaustibly, beside their horses.

Josh looked at Alfred. It was strange to think that this good looking, tanned man with the unruly mop of dark curls which bounced out from under his leather hat at every chance, was his uncle. He wondered whether his hazy memories of a small fair-haired mother had been correct.

"What was my mother like?" he asked Alfred as they followed the rutted road across the veld. Alfred looked startled and then smiled as he recalled his sister.

"Well, she was always the daring one, always ready to try something new. The other girls had dark hair but Florence was different. She had fair hair and very bright blue eyes... like yours, Josh. She was full of energy and she was the artist of the family. She played the piano for us all in the evenings and could ride as well as any of us. My father adored her. She was a very warm person and she was going to study art in London. Then she met your father, Folliott and they decided to go out to Africa, so that he could find work as an engineer. She wrote home regularly and we knew all about you when you were born. Then the letters stopped. Round that time the Bartons, your father's parents, also stopped getting letters, so we guessed something had happened."

"Did you try to find us?' Josh asked.

"Of course we did. We wrote to everyone, including the governor in the Cape and we put advertisements in the Natal and Cape papers. That's how Cliff was able to identify you."

"It took you a long time to come out here," Josh said accusingly.

Alfred pushed his hat back on his head in a gesture of embarrassment and unruly curls escaped and fell forward over his forehead. He looked thoughtfully at Josh, a perplexed frown lurking beneath the curls.

"I know, Josh, I know. You see it was some time before we realised that neither family was receiving any letters. Then we tried official sources and had to wait for replies. We kept hoping that you were simply in too remote a spot to get letters to us. Also, with all the older children in our family being girls, there was no one available to travel out to look for you. Hugh, my eldest brother, died in '73. Henry and Lambert were in business. I was the only one they could send and I was at school when they first suspected a problem."

Josh nodded slowly, trying to accept and understand.

At one point the road wound down to a swampy area where a sluggish stream meandered through the bush and the horses had to pick their way across the stony ford to the far bank. The place had an ominous feeling. The far side of the stream had a triangular pile of boulders in the path of the travellers.

Cliff reined in his horse and pointed to the cairn.

"This is Moorddrift where the chief Mapela and his men attacked several wagons, killed the men, women and children and flayed alive a man called Hermanus Potgieter."

Josh noticed Emmie giving an involuntary shudder as she looked round.

"Why did they attack them?" she asked.

Cliff shrugged. "Cattle and land. The usual arguments. The farmers had taken the land and put some of it under cultivation and mostly they were cattle ranching. The local tribes, especially Mapela, resented the influx of strangers and weren't averse to a bit of cattle rustling. Then, once the trouble started, it spread and soon more people were murdered, this time

273

by Chief Makhapane. The local farmers banded together and began to hunt Makhapane's people down. When the tribe realised that the farmers were after them they retired to hide in a very deep cave called Makapans Gat."

Josh felt his heart start. "Cliff," he said quickly, "that's the 'Great Cave of Sorrow'."

Cliff reined in Charity and fell in beside Josh.

"How do you know?"

"Majinga told me that the wagon had struggled up the mountain track because my father wanted to see the great cave where the people of Mapela and Makhapane had died. The cave, she told me, was known for many moons and since the beginning of time by people seeking safety. The white attackers could not get them out so they blocked the entrance. Neither food nor water could go in. For many weeks the people stayed there until most were dead. So, from being called 'The House of the Ancestors', it became 'The Cave of Sorrow'. It was considered a place of restless spirits and few would go there." He paused to think.

Cliff nodded encouragement as he sat his horse alongside Josh.

"Majinga said she tried to stop them from turning up towards the cave but my father said it was all past history and he had heard that the cave was so large that no light could penetrate to its end. He wanted to see this wonder for himself. Majinga said she only went because my mother was not feeling well and needed her care."

There was a long pause and all three sat their horses in silence, waiting for Josh to continue.

"She said my parents had paid heavily for trespassing on the graves of others. She felt that the ancestors had worsened my mother's fever and given it to my father. Then the bad white men came. She picked me up and fled into the bush. She returned only to find they'd taken the wagon and the cattle and killed my parents. They had buried them and once she had found their graves by the cliff-face she knew she must take me to join her tribe on her own."

Josh was aware that he had been over the story so many times in his mind, but now they were probably moving up the same track that his parents had taken ten years ago and he felt very alone and frightened. He was vaguely aware that Cliff stayed silently by his side and Emmie moved up on his other side. It was as though they were offering him what comfort they could by their presence close to him. He was grateful for their silence.

Slowly he felt himself coming out of his emotional trance and back into reality. He was aware of the three of them watching him. He felt awkward and Emmie released him from his embarrassment.

"Well, Josh, back in Leitrim they'll be glad to know at last what happened to Miss Florence. It was not knowing that was wearing down your grandparents."

Alfred nodded agreement.

"I've written back to them. They will be glad to have a grandson."

Josh absorbed this solemnly. His eyes slid over to Cliff. Cliff smiled at him.

"It'll be great to have your own family, won't it lad?" he said encouragingly.

Josh hesitated. Then his feelings swamped him.

"You're my family, Cliff, I don't need another one. I don't mean to be rude, Alfred, but Africa is my country, not Ireland." He looked appealingly at Cliff.

Cliff moved his hands awkwardly on the reins.

"Look, lad, you've a real family back there. It's not fair on them if they never see you. You've your mother's parents to meet and your father's mother and plenty of aunts and uncles. Give them a chance and then you can come back and I'll be here to help you if I can. But take a look at other places first and get a bit of education while you can."

Alfred nodded, "You'll be able to earn more with an education," and then in a flash of inspiration he added, "You might be an engineer like your father, and then you could come back and buy a farm of your own."

Josh turned this over in his mind. "Could I come back to you definitely?" he asked Cliff.

"I'd be pretty upset if you didn't," Cliff reassured him.

Josh looked him in the eye. "I might try it for a while then," he conceded.

"Good lad!" Cliff commented, relieved, and then began to move his horse slowly forward, pointing ahead as he did so.

"See those trees? That's Potgietersrus. It's not a bad little town and I bet we could all do with a meal?"

There were murmurs of agreement all round and the horses moved off briskly as though sensing a water trough and nosebag ahead.

Chapter Fifteen

AFRICA – November, 1879

JOSH GLANCED ROUND the small town with interest. It was the first sign of organized habitation they had found on this vast plain of thorn bushes, aloes, prickly pears, sluggish sandy streams and strange rock formations. Occasionally they had seen the traditional sign of a homestead, a distant roof, a well-worn track or the inevitable windmill; but the track had been theirs alone for most of the way.

Potgietersrus looked promising and the small veranda-fringed hotel had been friendly and their meal very welcome. To judge by the carts and wagons it was market day. A haze of reddish dust drifted over the busy village, stirred up by carts and wagons as people moved about their business and farmers offered their produce for sale in the local market square. Drifting through the dust, and a magnet to the local population, came the aroma of newly baked bread, wafting from a small bakery opposite the hotel.

Cliff excused himself when Emmie went in search of the hotel bathroom to wash away the mask of fine dust which had accumulated over her face and arms. He set off, together with Josh, to find the local magistrate, the Landrost, and anyone else who might represent law and order in the town.

In the twenty years since the town had been established the trees planted down the main street had grown and flourished and now threw a welcome dappled shade along the dusty side path which the two were following towards the small white-washed town hall with its red corrugated iron roof. Fastened to a row of hitching post rails along the fence in front of the building were several smart horse-drawn buggies and a couple of donkey carts. The horses and donkeys were all drooping visibly in the heat as they patiently awaited the return of their owners, tails and ears twitching against the onslaught of the local flies. Across the square Josh could see two farmers arguing over the cost of a load of fodder. In the deep shade of the building several tribesmen appeared to have settled down to sleep off the mid-day heat.

Cliff strode up the two steps to the entrance and Josh looked casually at the sleeping tribesmen as he followed. Then he stopped. He stared again at the sleeping form of the young man nearest to him. He was wearing a baggy pair of trousers and an ancient but clean shirt which had long since lost most of its buttons. Josh leant over and shook him by his shoulder. The eyes opened and stared uncomprehendingly at the white face. Then a veil seemed to lift from his eyes and the young man leapt up in one smooth athletic movement with a cry of *"Ikona!"*

Josh grinned at him.

"Napedi, bayete! It is I, Josh!"

The two boys clasped one another by the shoulders, delight spread across both faces and they began to talk fast in the tribal tongue of Josh's formative years. Cliff swung round in the doorway and stared back in amazement.

"Found a friend, then?" he speculated needlessly as the voices pitched higher and the other tribesmen gathered round to enjoy the excitement.

Josh looked over his shoulder towards Cliff.

"It's Napedi of my iNtanga," he explained excitedly.

Cliff nodded, shrugged and went on into the building.

Josh crouched down on the ground to catch up on the news and the men did likewise. The noise drew a few spectators and some European children gathered round to watch the unusual sight of a white boy involved in a tribal discussion and talking a dialect not generally understood on the Springbok Flats.

"Times are hard up in the mountains," Napedi explained. "We hear of the great hole which is being dug for the glittering stones and the money which can be earned in this way. It was decided that four of us would go down and see whether we can bring riches back to the tribal lands."

He went on to tell of their travels so far and the mixed reception they had had from other tribal areas and from white farmers. Then he looked hard at Josh.

"Tell me, Golden Cub, who has changed to a man and widened in body and in height and cut his hair short like his fellow whites... how have you fared? I would wish to tell Majinga when I return with my wealth and my gifts."

Josh wanted news of Majinga and was disturbed to hear that her grieving for him had made her ill for several moons.

"But now," Napedi hastened to tell him, "she is better and she is with child and she tells everyone that she will have another little cub, this time he will be black, not golden. You will always be her golden child and this is how the tribe will remember you."

"Napedi, should I go back?" Josh asked earnestly, a great longing sweeping over him for the simplicity of the kraal life, the security of Majinga's love and the need to sit beneath the great Marula tree once again.

"No," Napedi said quickly. "You must settle in your life and allow her to find a new contentment, but…" he added, seeing the disappointment in Josh's eyes, "give her time and love her always and life will bring you back in a great curve, such is the way of being. You have touched and will touch again. Time cannot break this bond."

Josh nodded slowly and the boys settled down to a general chat. Josh told him of his life and took some good natured teasing for the way he looked.

"But what are you doing here?" Napedi enquired curiously.

"It's a long story," Josh replied. This was just the sort of invitation Napedi and his companions wanted. A story meant entertainment. They all moved closer to Josh and prepared to listen. Using his hands and face Josh told them the story, backed by Napedi as they recounted Majinga's tale between them.

"You see," Josh finished, "if we can find where my parents were buried and prove who they were, then there can be no doubts as to who I am and I can lift my eyes in the company of my white family and know that I have roots with them as well as with my black family. I also seek vengeance for my parents. They died cruelly and I need to make sure that their murderer takes some punishment in this life."

The three young men said nothing. They just looked at him thoughtfully. Eventually Napedi spoke.

"I understand what you say but you put yourself in danger acting for the Spirits. The ancestors will take their time but they will mete out justice in like kind to him."

"I cannot wait. I want to see it *now*. I want to enjoy my revenge. Why should he get away with it?" Josh insisted.

Napedi shook his head.

"He will not escape but perhaps they have sent you to see to it. Is he in this place?" Napedi indicated the town with a sweep of his head.

"We think he will have gone to the place of his evil, to the Makkapan Caves, the Caves of Sorrow," Josh explained.

Napedi looked startled.

"That place, guarded by the UmHlonhlo trees is not for mortals to trespass upon. Pass by there as quickly as possible, Cub. Most certainly this man is cursed if he has killed by those caves, do not be led into repeating his error."

Josh looked at the real concern in his friend's eyes.

"I'll heed what you have said," he sought to reassure Napedi.

At this point Cliff came out onto the veranda with a short square man in dark trousers and a white shirt. He introduced Josh.

"This is the young man whose family disappeared by the caves. Josh, this is my friend, Johannes du Toit, who is standing in for the Landrost until a new one is appointed."

Mr du Toit looked slightly taken aback when Josh stepped up to him and offered him his hand as the girls in Natal had taught him to do when meeting someone new.

"Ag, now boy, I mean, Josh, it is indeed a terrible loss and you have grown up in the Zoutpansberg, I hear?" He looked curiously at the four tribesmen behind Josh. He had obviously seen Josh rise with an easy grace from his squatting position amongst them.

Josh nodded.

"Few people go near those caves. They have seen too much death and now we hear of yet another tragedy. Rest assured, we are happy to do anything we can to help you and bring me some evidence and also the man who did this, and we will see that justice is done." He turned to Cliff and extended his hand.

"Good day, Cliff, keep an eye on the boy and watch out for that Rafferty. His is a tricky one, never straight in his dealings, a glib talker." He swung round to go back into the building and then looked back over his shoulder, "And... an excellent shot."

The tribesmen had been talking amongst themselves and now one of them spoke to Josh. Josh translated to Cliff.

"They are sure they saw a man on a black horse turn up the road to the caves this morning, very early. They were walking along the road to Potgietersrus and could not see him clearly."

"Thank you!" Cliff acknowledged the news and added, "Yes, Johannes says he spent a night at a house near the hotel which also lets out rooms. People round here remember him from his hunting and trading days but he did not go into any of the bars, it was as though he did not wish to be noticed or recognized... and then left before the sun was up."

"So, we have caught up with him!" Josh exclaimed excitedly.

"Yes, he has not pushed himself too hard, but what, I wonder, does he hope to gain by coming back here?" Cliff pondered aloud.

"Perhaps there is something left at the site," Josh suggested.

"After ten years? No, not very likely. Johannes du Toit says the local tribes have told the authorities that two white people are buried near the caves but they don't seem to know much more. Do your friends here," he pointed to the tribesmen, "know anything about it?"

"They know the story because they can speak some of the local dialect but Napedi also knows more because he used to sit with me when Majinga told us the tale."

Cliff looked at Napedi. He looked about Josh's age but he was more muscular and had a straight proud stare.

"Would your friend come with us? He could go on his way to the diamond fields with us when we return?"

Josh looked excitedly at Napedi and asked him. There was a long silence while Napedi subjected Josh to one of his searching looks. Then he turned and spoke to his companions. After a while they nodded. He spoke rapidly to Josh who translated for Cliff.

"He says he will come but he will not go into the great cave. He will come because he is my friend and he wishes to see that I do not upset the Spirits. He will then travel with us to the Great Hole where he will join his friends again to find the stones which glitter."

Cliff nodded.

"Good, he will join us until then. He will need to ride. Does he mind this?" There was considerable laughter from the other three tribesmen and Napedi rolled his eyes to the heavens but pointed out that if Josh could do it he would also be able to do so. He saluted his friends and they returned the greeting with a loud shout and he and Josh followed Cliff off down the dusty road towards the hotel.

Alfred and Emmie were a little taken aback to find themselves joined by a tribesman, and one who had never ridden before. Cliff purchased the horse on their way past the market and its owner almost withdrew the sale when he discovered it was for Napedi. Josh hoped Napedi could not understand too much of what was said. The man's indignation was fairly clear and he kept reiterating that no black bastard was to ride his horse.

Napedi ignored him and stared into the distance above his head and Cliff called him "A bigoted old bible puncher" and added that he was lucky to get that much for a scrawny horse good only for the knacker's yard!

The saddle and bridle had been part of the bargain and after a quick lesson from Cliff, aided by advice and translation from Josh, Napedi, looking

280

decidedly uncomfortable, was balanced in the saddle. The cavalcade moved slowly off towards the craggy hills north-east of the town.

The dusty road wound up through the acacia thorn bushes and here and there a waft of sweet perfume drifted across the track where the bushes were bursting into fluffy yellow balls of spring blossom and bees were humming hopefully between the threatening thorns. The early afternoon sun was moving across the arc of the sky casting shadows in dappled patterns on the sandy road with its embedded ruts of wagon tracks and hoof imprints. The heat acted like a soft, smothering blanket, making everyone drowsy and Josh wondered whether the heavy stillness heralded a storm. Even the horses seemed reluctant to move into anything more than a lethargic jog.

Napedi swayed dangerously on his horse but was obviously determined to master the jolting without complaint. He reminded Josh of how, as youngsters, they had sometimes ridden the more biddable of the oxen and encouraged them to a brisk trot when possible. The two laughed together at the memory and Josh was grateful for this lightening of the rather oppressive mood which seemed to have descended on him and the rest of the party, as they neared the caves.

Cliff had ridden a little ahead and was waiting for them in the shade of a buffalo thorn tree at the sandy junction where a track turned off towards the steep and rocky mountainside. His wide-brimmed leather hat threw a dark shadow across his face and Josh noticed, as the dust from the trotting hooves settled down, that he, like the rest of them, was coated in a fine red powder of dust outlining every crease in his face. Cliff pointed up the track through the rocky bush-bestrewn hillside from which the tops of euphorbia and marula trees were protruding above the acacia bushes.

"Come, Napedi, tell me, is this the track of only one horse, which we follow?

Napedi climbed down and examined the road closely. He nodded to Cliff.

"Alright, we'll ride ten minutes and then it's a case of getting off and leading the horses. When we come close to the kloof, I'll signal for you to wait and Napedi and I will go on together in the hope of surprising anyone who may be round the cave entrance. Give us a few minutes and then come on yourselves. Ride in single file with Emmie at the rear in case you have to turn back quickly."

The track was turning into a rocky path bounded on either side by sentinel-like aloe plants. Their scarlet and gold blooms resembled flaming torches, held to attention as if to salute or warn newcomers of their approach to a special arena.

The riders stopped to dismount as Cliff, handing his reins to Alfred, moved off on his own into the ring of bush. Napedi slid off his horse and swayed as he tried to adjust and gain control of his reluctant leg muscles.

Josh couldn't resist a comment:

"You look like a spider trying to work out how to get all your legs moving at the same time," he quipped in a whisper to his friend.

Napedi grinned at him and whispered back:

"It would be easier to control eight legs than two which have been turned inside-out!"

He moved off, a silent shadow behind Cliff.

Josh, Alfred and Emmie waited a few minutes and then began to follow. They found that it was virtually impossible to travel quietly over the last few yards as their horses hooves were slipping and sliding on the uneven shale which had slid down the mountainside over the centuries. The sun was hidden behind the berg and the hillside was in deep shadow. Almost without warning they found themselves on a grassy plateau in front of a high kloof almost encircled by giant succulent Euphorbia trees, their branches lifted towards the African sky like priests offering supplication to the gods of past ages.

Josh pushed his hat back and tilted his head to look up the precipitous rock face towards the sky above them. At the base of the great kloof and slightly sheltered by other rocks, was the dark entrance to an underground cavern. The only sign of life was Clifford bending over some disturbed soil some way to the left of the cave entrance. He signalled them over.

"No sign of anyone here but there are tracks going that way," he pointed in a northerly direction where a path wound its way off along the mountainside and was soon lost in the surrounding bush. "Something has happened here recently," he pointed to the loose earth that looked as though it had been freshly dug over.

Josh sat and looked round, white faced and silent.

Napedi glanced at him and then moved over to join Cliff and Alfred at the cliff face. Alfred went off to fetch the spade he kept tied to his saddlebag, but when he returned, intending to dig on the same site, Napedi put a restraining hand on his arm and shook his head. Alfred pulled back impatiently and looked at Cliff.

"Better not," Cliff said hastily, nodding towards Josh, "by the look of the soil it's been well dug over and we'll find nothing more than mortal remains… It's almost bound to be his parents' grave and they should be left to lie in peace."

Cliff said a few words to Napedi, who nodded and then indicated the cave.

"I think he is saying that if we desecrate the grave the ancestors will come after us and some disaster will follow," Cliff explained to Alfred.

Alfred shrugged, "Seems like ridiculous superstition, if you ask me." He replaced the spade and felt for something in his saddlebag.

Josh slowly emerged from the trance state he had entered when he first saw the cave and the whereabouts of the graves. He had the strange feeling that his mind was slowly rejoining his body. Mentally, he realized, he had been back in the kraal listening to Majinga's description of the kloof and the graves and now it was fitting together. The story was taking on an aura of reality. He almost thought he recognized it… but commonsense came to his rescue… and he became aware of Emmie standing at his side.

"Josh," she said gently, putting her hand on his arm, "we know they were very sick, perhaps neither would have survived… I am so thankful for you that the little maid was able to take you to safety."

Josh stared at the churned up ground and nodded.

"Majinga saved me or I too would be in that grave. I have tried to recall something but there is nothing there… I always thought it would come back if I could stand here… but it makes no difference." His voice ran down to be submerged in the silence.

Cliff heard his last remarks and seemed to pull himself back from contemplating their next move, to a sudden recognition of the youngster's dilemma.

"Probably the wagon was outspanned on the plateau below us and you will have been totally unaware of what was happening until Majinga picked you up and fled with you into the bush," he said kindly.

"But how will we ever know that they really were my parents? *How* can I prove that I *am* Alfred's nephew, that I *am* a Barton?" He looked up, appealing to Cliff.

Cliff looked puzzled.

"Why does it matter? *We* all know who you are and you described the wagon, didn't you?" Cliff took his hat off and wiped his brow with it, still looking closely at the boy. "How did you imagine that coming here would prove anything, anyway?" he queried more gently.

Josh sat down on a nearby rock and put his head in his hands. He was aware of the presence of Napedi behind him and heard Emmie snap at Cliff.

"Ah now, an' are you not the uncle to be proud of, then Cliff? Sure, and the lad has lived here in his mind for all those years, struggling to recall the family who loved him. Ant you may be sure he didn't know *what* he'd find but he hoped there'd be something, even a rusty bucket or something." She paused and put a hand on Cliff's arm, looking up into his face. "Can you see that this might be a shock?"

Cliff nodded. Josh felt him touch his head with his hand.

"We believe in you, Josh. Alfred knows you are his nephew, don't you, Alfred?" He looked round for a response but there was no sign of Alfred. Napedi seemed to realize this at exactly the same time. Josh saw the concern flash across his friend's face as he looked round. Napedi shouted something at him and leapt away. It took a brief second for Josh to comprehend what he had said and then he too began to run towards the mouth of the cave. Before he could run into the velvety darkness Napedi backed out and caught him in a vice-like grip, shouting urgently at him. Cliff came up behind and Josh turned round to him.

"Do not try to enter. Napedi says it is sacred to the spirits only."

Cliff nodded.

"Mr du Toit told me that close to a thousand tribes people died of starvation in there and no one knows if there are more bodies in the caverns and passages which lead off the main cave." He turned to look at Napedi. "Do you think he went in there?" Napedi nodded and spoke quickly to Josh.

"Napedi says he thinks he did not believe in the stories of spirits."

Emmie joined them at the entrance to the cave just as they noticed the flicker of a small flame deep in the interior, which grew closer as they watched. A white-faced Alfred came out holding a small stub of gutting candle in front of him, the wax streaked down his hand like a soft cobweb.

"Never have I smelt anything quite like that! By God, the place is sinister. I didn't go far but it is certainly vast and the darkness is like black velvet… putrefying velvet, with a heavy sinister stillness."

Napedi groaned and turned away, muttering something as he went.

Josh found his voice first.

"What the hell did you go in there for? It's not for us that cave. It's a cave with an ancient and terrible past." He nodded solemnly at Alfred. "It's said that all the people who have entered there in the last few years have met a violent death."

Alfred paled and stared at him in surprise.

"That's superstition, Josh. You've been brought up on that rubbish and you'll have to get rid of it before you go back to Ireland, young man!"

There was a sharp intake of breath from Emmie.

"Ant you from Ireland an' you can say such rubbish, Alfred-O, I'm ashamed of you!"

"Oh, Emmie, don't you go for this catholic superstitious nonsense, it's only for uneducated peasants. You and your fairies and bogeymen and leprechauns!"

Emmie had gone red in the face and put her hands on her hips.

"Don't give me that 'uneducated, superstitious, peasant nonsense' or I'll start on your heathen, filthy, liberated Protestantism, young *master* Alfred!"

Alfred shrugged and rolled his eyes heavenwards.

Josh was staring at them in amazement. He turned to Cliff for enlightenment.

Cliff looked equally puzzled.

"Come on, Alfred," Cliff interjected, "what on earth made you go in there? This is Africa, not Ireland. You obey the unwritten laws of the local tribes unless you want to find yourself in serious trouble." He looked quizzically at Alfred.

Alfred eyed the ring of accusing faces. It was obvious that he felt slightly indignant that what had seemed to him like courage had backfired so badly.

"I wanted to see what Folliott went to look at," he said defensively.

Emmie threw her hands in the air, "Ant look what happened to *him*! An' you go on about superstition!"

Alfred shifted awkwardly when everyone just continued to stare at him in silence.

"Well, I don't know what you are all on about… after all no rock fell on my head!" he declared defensively.

He began to walk away and then turned back to look at Cliff.

"What now, no sign of Rafferty, so are we back to Potgietersrus?"

Cliff had an arm protectively round Emmie's shoulders.

He looked up at Alfred.

"No, I think we'll find out what it was that Rafferty found – follow his tracks. He didn't dig in that grave for nothing."

Josh was glad to leave the caves. Whatever he had expected had not happened, he wasn't sure what it might have been, but the place had a strange air of foreboding and a feeling as of time standing still.

They led their horses down the narrow path which showed signs of recently having been used, to the next level area and then along the mountainside to the accompaniment of the chatter of monkeys and, way in the distance, a baboon barking a warning. The afternoon was cooling down as the shadows lengthened and Cliff pushed them to ride harder. Their path had improved but it was still uneven and had a habit of suddenly narrowing just as they were making reasonable headway. Then it would be back into single file and watch for the overhanging thorn bushes. The path stayed on the hillside but ran almost parallel to the coach road they had originally come off. Cliff seemed puzzled by it at first but as they rode round a narrow defile they found themselves amongst a group of mud huts and tin shacks, mostly empty. A movement in the shadows caught Josh's eye and he saw two men leaning against a door with their gold panning equipment piled at their feet. They eyed the riders with interest.

One looked at the other and remarked:

"Well, Ben, with all this traffic around I think I'll just pop along and catch a trolley bus back home in time for my dinner!"

The other man pushed off from the door frame he was leaning against and scratched his neck thoughtfully, as he eyed the five riders.

"And so, gentlemen, ah!" and his eyes lit up as he spotted Emmie, "and that treasured rarity, a *lady*, welcome to our flourishing town. The hotel is right down the road, you can't miss it." He pointed towards a tin shack whose door was down to its final hinge and tapping persistently against the metal wall.

Cliff went straight to the point.

"Have either of you seen a man on a black horse ride this way today?"

The two men exchanged looks.

"With all this traffic and us out of whiskey and panning all day bent double in the stream, how do you expect us to see anything?" the first man asked slyly.

Cliff grinned at him and put his hand into his saddlebag, bringing out a half bottle of amber liquid.

"And wasn't I warned that this was a dry town?" he commented as an eager hand reached up for the bottle, which he lifted higher. "And what of my question?"

"They say there are still torturers around!" commented the man, his eyes never straying from the bottle.

The other one shrugged.

"Well, it's true that while we were sleeping off the heat of the day a man came through. A mean, lean lookin' man of few words, whose appearance could only have meant that he'd sold his soul to the devil."

The other man picked up... "He rode through without comment, although we extended the hospitality of the town to him."

"Thank you!" Cliff said, lowering the bottle into the waiting hand. "And could you make a guess at where he might be going on this highway?"

The taller man loosened the lid of the bottle, his every movement closely watched by his partner.

"He could only be heading for one of the small mines along this route, it ends at Eersteling – you know, Pigg and Button's rocking boulder gold mine."

Cliff nodded. He touched the brim of his hat.

"Thank you, lads, and good luck!"

The two men were already perched back in their doorway arguing about how much constituted a mouthful.

The track wound on along the mountainside past a couple more small deserted encampments and then began to climb steeply towards a ledge which ran unevenly in front of a steep rock face. Balanced on one side of this area was a huge boulder. Rising up to one side of the boulder and towering incongruously against the mountainside, was a huge granite smokestack.

Josh stared at it in amazement.

"What's that?" he enquired, voicing what the others were thinking.

Cliff pushed his hat onto the back of his head and stared at it thoughtfully.

"I've heard about it but it's more impressive than I thought. This gold mine belongs to two characters called Button and Pigg. They crush quartz under that rocking boulder and that chimney is built of granite shipped from Scotland. I'm no expert on gold but I've heard men say that that chimney is a power plant for smelting the gold."

"How the hell did they get that lot up here?" Alfred queried in wonderment. "What made them transport it all that way?" he looked at Cliff for an answer.

Cliff turned his horse back to face the steep twisting track and pulled his hat back over his forehead.

"It's a well-known story now. Button and Pigg were convinced they had found enough gold to make themselves, and the owner of this farm, very rich; only the best tough Scottish granite would do. Their stories and enthusiasm picked up some investment abroad and locally, and they threw everything they had into it."

Josh looked up at the mine clinging to the mountain above them.

"I don't see much happening – is it still open?"

Cliff nodded and swung off his horse to lead it up the steep path ahead.

"I understand," he said over his shoulder, "some of it is still in action, but there are lots of tunnels into the rock face all round here and some of them have been a great disappointment and business has slowed right down."

A sign on the way up the well-worn path declared that they were trespassing on the registered property of Pigg & Button. As they neared the mine several corrugated iron sheds came into view. They had been carefully painted and one appeared to be living accommodation and the other bore the rather grand notice "OFFICE" painted on a white board. It was obvious that Pigg and Button had style and intended to maintain it. The whole scene was dominated by the rocky cliff face which rose behind it. Although no hive of activity, the place still had an air of organization which lifted it above the average mining venture in the area.

Cliff led the five of them and their horses onto the little plateau and towards a metal hitching post on a well-baked square of earth. The afternoon sun was throwing a rich pink light across the mountainside, giving the whole scene an almost surreal effect, as though viewed through a piece of pink glass.

A man came rapidly out of the shed marked "OFFICE". He was a small, nuggety man with deeply tanned skin and an air of authority. He was pointing a shotgun at them and shouting:

"Who the hell do you think you are? This is private property and people come up here by invitation only."

"Reaching you for that invitation might be difficult – is it Mr Pigg or Mr Button?" Cliff asked conversationally, totally ignoring the gun.

"Who wants to know?" the little man asked belligerently, still raking the barrel of his gun across the line of riders and horses. Then he suddenly saw that there was a woman among them. He lowered his gun.

"It's Button. Can't be too careful, you know, but I see you've a lady with you. What's your business then?"

"It's a long story," Clifford began, "and we are in a hurry to meet up with a gentleman who has something of ours he may be planning to dump in one of your old shafts."

Clifford swung off his horse and moved towards Button with an outstretched hand.

"Clifford Wilson at your service, sir."

Button leant his rifle against the office wall and extended a hand in friendly fashion.

"Good gracious, you're the young man who used to trade with Hartley! You've become quite a legend in your own time. Pleased to meet you, son. And the others?"

Clifford waved towards Emmie, who was staring down at the miles of bushveld spread out below them.

"Miss Emmie who travelled over from Ireland with Mr Alfred Lyons-Montgomery," he nodded towards Alfred, "in search of this young man…" he indicated Josh, "who has tribal links in friendship with our tracker, Napedi."

Napedi nodded nonchalantly. Josh realized that he was still struggling to follow Cliff's quick conversation, but he seemed to have gathered he was part of this introduction.

Button looked rather taken aback.

"How can I help you? Our accommodation is sound but not comfortable and we are not equipped for young ladies."

"It's information we are after," Cliff explained. "Have you ever had dealings with a man called Jules Rafferty?"

A wary look crossed Button's face.

"Why him?" he asked.

"So you know him?" Cliff queried cautiously.

Button nodded, giving nothing away.

Cliff and Alfred exchanged glances. Josh watched the faces with interest, lit up as they were by the late afternoon sun.

"Has he passed this way today?" Alfred tried a direct question.

"Not that I know of, no, but then he would take care not to come near me and he knows these mountains and the shafts round here pretty well. In fact, he claimed to have bought the first concession from the local farmer."

Josh wished they would come to the point. Tension pounding through his head like a rattling stone in a metal drum. He burst out before anyone could say anything else:

"The bastard killed my parents and he is hiding something that might prove he did it!"

Button swung round and stared at him. Then he laughed, a hoarse hollow laugh which echoed off the rock face and then seemed to fall away into the valley below.

"Sorry," he said, "it's just that I'm not surprised. The man has the nine lives of a vicious, prowling, vindictive tom cat and I've been waiting for his luck to run out. He's one of the reasons we are armed round here."

He led them over to a fire where a kettle was bubbling on glowing coals and wood smoke drifted slowly up in the afternoon air.

"Coffee. Help yourselves," he indicated the pile of metal mugs in an enamel bowl nearby.

"We need to find him quickly," Cliff explained. "By morning he may well have gone and we need to know what he is trying to hide."

Button ignored him, he swung round to Josh.

"And so, boy, what is your name?"

"Josh Barton," Josh surprised himself at how quickly and confidently he replied, how he used the surname without a second thought.

"Ah," said Button, comprehension dawning on his face as he looked at Josh.

"I recall now. There was talk up at the Mac-Mac Mines about a wagon that was coming that way and never made it. No trace was found, although it had left Potgietersrus... it became another of those bush legends."

Josh was staring at him as though hypnotized.

"As I recall, the relatives made enquiries from the local Landrost but no one had seen them. Word was passed to other areas but with no results." He looked at Josh's startled expression. "Now tell me, how is Rafferty involved?"

Josh swung round to Alfred, "So now I know the family *did* try to find us!"

Alfred grinned at him, "Glad to get that one cleared!" He turned to Button, "We think Rafferty was part of a group who attacked and killed my sister and her husband. We also think that it happened down here, near the big cave, Makkapan's cave, it will have been about eleven years ago."

Button looked thoughtful.

"Yes, that was before we started this mine and Pigg and I were prospecting in the Murchison Range round then. At the time there were many rumours of gold and an old farmer told me that there were roaming bands of white men who were far more dangerous than any of the local tribes, even Mapela, who killed many of the Potgieter trek. I gather most of them had jumped ship somewhere between Cape Town and Durban and then they'd form a gang who'd live outside the law by robbing and looting and trying to throw blame onto the local tribes."

290

"So how did you come across Rafferty?" Cliff interrupted.

"Ah, yes, Rafferty! Well no one ever knew where he'd come from and rumour had it he was off a convict ship bound for Brisbane. The old farmer who owned this land, he told me that a masked man robbed his house once and tied his old lady to the kitchen chair. Years later, the old lady met Rafferty when he tried to get permission to prospect on the farm. She told her husband she would never forget the voice or the eyes and he turned down Rafferty's offer."

"So, how did you get to know him?" Alfred enquired as he drank his coffee. "When Pigg and I came along we were able to come to an agreement to share the rights with the farmer who owned the land. We found old shafts and realized that someone had been removing ore before we came. Then Rafferty and a man called Krane, turned up and demanded to know what we were doing on their land. We showed them our documents and Rafferty made threats and said he could prove he had bought the land from the farmer. However, no documents were ever produced and the farmer warned us to keep clear of him.

"Did he try to come back?" Alfred enquired.

"Yes, we had plenty of trouble. We would find machinery broken and ropes cut and on one occasion our water supply was poisoned."

"What!" Clifford exclaimed, obviously aghast at the thought.

"For a while we had protection arranged by the local Landrost but then we expanded and all over these hills and mountains there were other prospectors trying to find that vital 'rich vein' and Rafferty came in our direction less and less. Then we heard he had made it big down Kimberley way and we all sighed with relief. Now you bring me the bad news that he is back up here! Look, any action to get that man slammed away and I'll back you."

Clifford poured the dregs of his mug of bitter coffee onto the dry soil where it sank instantly away.

"He's somewhere here. Which shafts would he know best? He'll be armed and he's come all this way to cover evidence so we best move fast or we'll be too late," he drawled thoughtfully. "He might be an hour ahead of us but I doubt he knows we are on his heels so perhaps his rush will be only against the failing light."

Alfred looked at the sun.

"We've about three hours at the most."

Button swung round to Emmie.

"Look, mam, you best stay here. The going's hard up to the old shafts and if he sees us first he may shoot at anything that moves."

Emmie looked indignant.

"I've come this far and I'm not staying to cool my heels ant worry 'bout you all!" She nodded at Napedi, "If he can come then I can too!"

Cliff looked at a loss. Alfred pointed out to her that Napedi was going to be tracking but she might slow them up. Emmie was having none of this.

"I'd be more frightened on my own here," she declared.

Cliff glanced at the afternoon shadows and then quickly at Emmie.

"You come, Em, but you stay at the rear all the time. Alfred, you make sure she is close behind us but always at the rear."

Alfred raised his hands in despair but nodded. Emmie frowned at him and tucked her blouse firmly into the trousers Josh had lent her.

Button gathered up his rifle and began to lead the way up one of the tracks which wound its way along the plateau away from the main mine buildings and then narrowed down as it turned up the kloof.

Josh noticed that they were passing several shafts which ran into the mountainside where the rock face joined the plateau. Some of the shafts had numbered boards and several others had planks of wood across their entrances. He was walking just in front of Alfred and turned and pointed enquiringly at one of the blocked entrances. Alfred whispered:

"Closed – worked out or perhaps too dangerous to enter."

They came to a division of paths where four tracks seemed to take slightly different angles, two running down an incline, and one bending round into a ravine and another going almost vertically upwards. Button slowed down and Cliff signalled to Napedi to examine the paths. The exertion of the steady climb with the added stress of trying to do it as silently as possible, was showing on them all, despite the comparative cool of late afternoon. Alfred went back a little way to help Emmie round a rocky cleft in the path where torrents of rain had at some stage worn the path away altogether and left only smooth slippery rock surface.

Napedi examined the paths and then, extending his arm with his palm in a halt gesture, he went on down one path very slowly and silently so that he merged into the gathering dusk beneath the shadow of the overhanging bushes. They all stood as though carved out of the mountain rock. In two, seemingly endless minutes, he was back and whispering to Josh. Josh moved over to Button and passed on the message that Napedi could smell a horse on a lower level of the path but the horse appeared to be tethered and

292

so far had not picked up their scent. Napedi scouted round the confluence of the paths and suddenly chose one. He raised his hand in a beckoning fashion and they began to move slowly behind him, trying hard to copy his silent, almost fluid, co-ordinated hunter's prowl. Presently they passed a small path leading to another opening into the rock face, with a barrier across the entrance. Napedi stopped and stared hard at the dark ground, then moved on upwards. Button put a hand on Napedi's shoulder. He signalled to Cliff to close in. They bent very close together and Josh joined them to translate for Napedi.

"The next shaft is the last up this path. It's been long closed and is one of the shafts begun before we bought the mine – we went down it but the wood shoring up the roof was rotting and we could find no trace of workable veins, so we closed it up," Button whispered.

Alfred was straining to look up the path in an effort to make out what was happening in front of him. He saw the others in a huddle and looked behind him to see what progress Emmie was making. There was no sign of Emmie on the path so he slowly picked his way backwards, watching his steps on the uneven earth. At the bend he thought he could see her trousered legs through the branches of a bush, but, almost as he saw them, he heard a crash just below him and then a muffled cry.

As he covered the last few yards at a run he was aware of breaking branches and a dragging noise. Diving round the next bend he could see no sign of Emmie but he was back near the first path up to the closed shaft. He reached it in two leaps and caught hold of a small tree trunk to arrest his downhill run. Standing back in the dark of the entrance was Emmie, clutched in Rafferty's arms and sagging like a rag doll. As far as Alfred could see she had a red mark across her forehead and appeared to be unconscious.

Alfred was aware of a triumphant smirk on the man's face as he let Emmie slide from his arms and the next thing Alfred knew he was cocking a pistol and it was only his own instinct to let go of the tree and fall to the ground, which saved Alfred from getting the bullet full in his face. As it was, it flew past his right ear and embedded itself in the lichen-encrusted bark of a nearby tree. There were muffled cries from Emmie who was evidently regaining consciousness, followed by a disconcerting silence.

Lifting his head cautiously, Alfred realized that Rafferty and Emmie had disappeared into the dark passage of the shaft. Alfred was just pulling himself upright as Cliff, followed closely by Josh and Napedi with Button in the rear, came tumbling down the path summoned by the gunshot.

Everything had happened so fast that Alfred was in a state of shock. He was still staring incredulously at the entrance to the shaft when Cliff collided with him on the path. He pointed silently and Cliff shook him by the shoulders.

"What happened? Where's Emmie?"

Alfred found his voice and croaked out:

"It's that bastard, that Rafferty. He's got her in there." He pointed helplessly at the shaft entrance.

Cliff shook him again and shouted accusingly:

"You were to look after her, I told you to! Where the hell is she?"

The others arrived around then and were trying to glean what had happened. Josh watched as Cliff turned a despairing look on the shaft entrance.

"He's there!" he said. "The bastard's got Emmie with him and he could kill her or—"

Button's voice came out of the gathering shadows,

"No, he'll try to use her as a hostage to give him a chance to get away. In fact, he had probably heard us coming and was trying to get out down here when he bumped into Emmie. Then Alfred arrived and he was cornered, so he took her back with him."

The others clustered round him uneasily, staring up at the shaft entrance.

"Pigg and I always wondered if these shafts were interlinked but we didn't dare explore too far because of the old timbers and crumbling rock face."

Napedi sat down as though in a state of shock. Josh moved over to him and they spoke for a moment.

"Napedi thinks it's his fault because he could see no sign of a track to that shaft," he said to Button.

Button looked impatient and then seemed to relent.

"Explain to him that he probably went in at the top shaft."

Napedi stood up and turned as though to go up to the top shaft but Cliff prevented him.

"We've a hell of a situation now and rushing in to either shaft could result in us being shot or him killing Emmie. He knows his tunnels and we don't!"

Emmie sat back against the cold rock face and clutched her head. It hurt to try and think but she was attempting to piece together how she had come to find herself gaining consciousness, as someone dragged her up a narrow tunnel with rough stone sides. She was conscious of dripping water and felt almost stifled by the stale, bitter smell of bat's droppings and rock-rabbit pellets and the eerie wisp-like tug of spiders' webs as she was dragged through their long-established homes. She was aware of tripping and moaning and being pushed and dragged on into the pitch dark for what felt like an eternity. The passage appeared to narrow and to go uphill and round bends and she was being bumped from side to side, bruised by the rocky surface and with her boots giving little protection to her battered feet. At last her assailant stopped in what appeared, when he lit a match, to be a huge cavern. He had pushed her against the wall so that she fell in a heap on a rocky outcrop, his saddlebag illuminated for a second on the far side of the outcrop.

"Shut up! You whining little bitch, an' for sure don't even consider getting away from me. This place is a mass of passages, many made by underground rivers and there are deep drops which fall away down hundreds of feet to other caverns and passages. If you lose me you'll end up a heap of bones for a hungry jackal to gnaw on – or drowned in a pitch-black river, thrown up months later in some distant canyon."

Now that she had regained consciousness and caught her breath, Emmie recognized Rafferty's familiar voice. She felt an ice-cold shiver run through her body. How had this happened? She had no recall beyond struggling up the rocky path behind Alfred. She was also well aware that the last thing she needed was to lose Rafferty in this alien environment. Hate him she might, but without him she was lost. He removed a miner's lamp from his saddlebag and was lighting it so that the dim little light threw their surroundings into flickering relief.

"An' so, you thought you'd catch me an' pin those murders on me! Well, you cunning little divil, you, I'm not about to hand that kind of evidence over to a judge an' jury, sure I'm not. How was I to know that kid'd grow up and some bloody tribe would hand him back alive an' kicking? How the hell'd he slip away from Ox an' Quinn? I should've known better than to depend on anyone else. I'll see them dead for this… and him."

Emmie kept quiet as he lifted a bottle of golden liquid to his lips and drank deeply from it. Immediately the air filled with whiskey fumes. His eyes in his heavily shadowed face slid sideways and wandered down her body.

"For a country lass, you've some nerve, I'll say that for you. You're one above the usual colleen from the old country. Your parish priest'd consign you to the devil, but then I don't suppose that'd get you too concerned!"

Still she kept quiet.

He wiped the top of the whiskey bottle with his sleeve. Then carefully replaced the cap and put it into his bag.

"Now," he said, "'fore I show you what I do to girls who step over the mark and try to frame me, I'm going to a spot where I can look down on your friends and find out what they're planning to do. You stay here or you'll be sorry an' I'll be sending your remains over the edge to entertain your friends."

Emmie felt another shudder run down her spine. Reluctantly she heard herself say, "Jules, you'll not be long?"

He laughed harshly and flung himself to his feet, leaving his saddlebag on the stone floor and picking up the lamp by its handle.

"Prepare yourself, my darling, I fancy you… ant Maria will be sick as a cow when I tell her I've sampled what you have to offer! It'll be 'double the cards' if I can finish off that kid *an'* that thieving mine owner, Button."

He picked up his rifle in his other hand and headed off into the dark with a sure-footed walk of someone who knew their way.

Emmie cleared spiders' webs from her face and sat clutching the rock like a shipwrecked sailor in an ocean of darkness. The weak flicker of the oil lamp seemed to move up towards the ceiling of the cavern and then it disappeared altogether like an extinguished firefly.

Gradually her nerves steadied in the velvet blackness and she found her breathing slowing down and her mind beginning to work. Then there was a flutter of air near her face and something swept past her. Terror returned and she flung herself from the rock and onto Rafferty's saddlebag.

Bats! she thought to herself, damn bats!

Gradually she stopped shaking and took reassurance from the reality of the bag beneath her cheek It represented the outside world and the smell of horse perspiration was like perfume against the stale stinking air of the cavern. Her hands ran over the bag and she felt something large and heavy inside it. Her fingers moved into the canvas interior and she found a square parcel wrapped in an oilskin pouch. Curiosity overcoming fear, she felt round the pouch but it was well bound and she could find no way of assessing its contents. It felt like a fairly heavy metal box. Searching through the bag in the darkness she found a metal water container and several rounds of pistol and rifle ammunition in cartons.

She struggled back into a sitting position with the bag on her lap and surrounded by the oppressive black silence, she began to recapture her thought processes. He was bound to have a certain amount of ammunition with him but at least losing the rest would restrict him in the future, she reasoned. She began frantically gathering up the cartridges and bullets and when she had a handful she flung them to the far corners of the cavern and listened to them cracking off the rocks. She became aware that when she flung them directly ahead of her and in the opposite direction to the one Rafferty had taken, she was hearing no thud or landing. This had to mean that there was a deep gulf on that side of the cavern and she aimed closer to see whether she could assess where it started.

Josh felt very helpless. Cliff had sent Button and Napedi up to assess the higher entrance to the shaft and he and Alfred were speculating on the possibility of moving into the lower passage and inching their way along hoping to catch some sound which would tell them where Rafferty was hiding out. The big problem was that shooting into the dark might prove fatal for Emmie. The sun was now almost on the horizon and darkness would give Rafferty the cover under which to escape.

Josh listened to Cliff speculating out loud on possibilities, his voice hoarse with stress.

"Emmie'd be a hindrance if he was trying to creep out silently, especially if his escape involved climbing down the cliff face but then I suppose he might kill her or leave her imprisoned in some underground chamber where we'd never find her... on the other hand, if he was coming straight out, he could use her as a shield knowing that we'd never shoot."

Josh made up his mind that he couldn't stand around any longer, he craved some sort of action. He'd see if he could be of any use to Napedi, higher up. He had just set off at a brisk pace up the twisting path when a shot ricocheted off a nearby rock just ahead of him. He threw himself over the edge of the path into the gloom of the bushes and stared up the rock face above him. High up above the path he picked out the figure of Rafferty on a ledge with an overhanging rock above him. He was laughing wildly and his voice came down to those below him in a hollow echo.

"I can see all the paths from up here and I know all the exits from this mountain with its potholes and caverns. When I choose I can just walk out where I wish, but if you want the girl alive, it'll be in exchange for the boy."

Josh heard Alfred shout:

"That'll be over my dead body," and there was another harsh laugh from above.

"Indeed, it might be, but it's the boy I want and once the dark settles in you've lost – so think quickly or the girl dies. Once I've the boy, yous can forget about all this an' be assured I'll move on… and I've a wish to cross an ocean."

Josh recalled the distraught look on Cliff's face as he tried to decide what to do about Emmie. He remembered Emmie looking small and vulnerable belted into his trousers. She, he was sure, wouldn't hesitate to help him if he was in trouble, she was so fearless. There was no time to talk this over. He had no alternative. He'd throw in his lot with this man and then perhaps he'd kill him.

He shouted up from his hideout in the bushes:

"So I'll come then, Rafferty. You bring out Emmie and I'll join you."

From above him there was a furious shout and he recognized Button's voice.

"You'll do no such thing. Stay where you are. He'll shoot you from above."

Emmie was beginning to get used to the dark and she remembered Cliff laughing at her when she told him how much she hated bats. He had explained that they could see in the dark or certainly had the ability to fly without bumping into anything. She began to feel a little braver. She tried to assess which way Rafferty had gone and realized that it had been the opposite side of her rock from his saddlebag. She reached into the bag for the last carton of bullets and pulled herself up slowly bringing the bag with her. Moving his bag elsewhere would also delay him, she reasoned. She began cautiously to move in the direction Rafferty had gone. After all, he had said he would be able to see her friends. The thought of reaching the outer air made her heart flip with excitement. She found herself on a steep upward slope; the roof seemed to slide upwards as well, allowing her to walk upright. Every few steps she threw a bullet from the carton ahead of her and listened to it bounce off rock. Sometimes they rolled back down to her, but at least there was no ghastly silence as it fell away to unimaginable depths. The rock base reached a rough wall and she felt along it to a narrow tunnel. At this point she wondered whether she was choosing the right way forward but she also recalled the way that small glimmer of light from the lantern had suddenly disappeared quite high in the darkness. The first passage was very short and ended in rough rock face and she had to back cautiously down again. A little further along was another passage and this time it seemed to wind away in an erratic fashion, still going steadily uphill. Just

298

as she was beginning to wonder whether she had missed a third exit from the cavern, she was startled by a gust of fresh air which blew across her face like a cool wave. The quality of darkness suddenly changed from dense black to a dark blue haze. At the same time she was aware of Rafferty's voice shouting somewhere beyond her. She slowed down cautiously, her emotions suspended between relief and fear. She glanced round for somewhere to hide the saddlebag and found herself looking round a bend which ended on a ledge looking out at a sinking sun and miles of hazy bushveld country.

Rafferty was standing on the ledge shouting down to people below. She heard the bargain about exchanging herself for Josh and she heard Alfred's reply and then Josh's offer.

Surely, she thought, Cliff would think of something. At that moment a shot rang out and Rafferty fell hastily backwards. However, the angle of fire from below must have been almost impossible and a few shards of rock from the edge of the ledge flew wildly into the air and plunged into the gathering gloom. Rafferty rolled over, staying close to the edges but keeping well out of sight of those below him. As he rolled over he must have seen Emmie's white face in the passage behind him. He bounded to his feet and before she knew what had hit her he had dragged her onto the ledge with him and was shouting to the frustrated group below:

"So here's your little Irish slut – an' now I'll show you what will happen if you don't do as I say." As he spoke he ripped off her already tattered blouse and the bodice top she wore beneath. She pushed at him and screamed but he threw her onto the floor of the ledge and began to rip off her trousers. She yelled and kicked and tried to bite him but all the time she was desperately aware of the terrible fall down to the bushveld below them.

From the base of the cliff there came a blood-chilling shout like an animal in desperate pain. Rafferty paused, momentarily puzzled, and Emmie, whose panties were being ripped off, managed to stick a thumb as hard as possible into one of his eyes. He reeled back and a naked Emmie leapt to her feet and kicked at him. At the same time she saw out of the corner of her eye, as Rafferty caught her foot and wheeled her close to the edge, a black body leap from amongst the gnarled rock-face undergrowth of the kloof and throw itself through the air at the ledge. By some incredible feat of balance Napedi reached the ledge, swayed slightly and then threw himself forward before the impetus of his body could drag him down to his death on the rocks below.

A look of incredulous horror swept across Rafferty's face and he tried to give Emmie the final push which would have sent her spinning down in the wake of her floating clothes. However, his balance was wrongly co-ordi-nated and Emmie was able to push back towards the rock face. At the same time Rafferty must have recognized that his only hope would be to get back into the mountain. He dived for the tunnel entrance just as Napedi regained his balance. Napedi spent a split second pushing Emmie to safety against the cliff face and in that second Rafferty had tripped over his saddlebag, regained his balance and, aware of Napedi bearing down on him, turned round and flung the bag with all his body force at Napedi. It bowled Napedi over and the impetus of the swing sent it on and over the edge of the ledge and down into the bush below. This manoeuvre gave Rafferty, bending low, time to take off down the tunnel at high speed. His rifle had spun away as he tripped over the bag but he still had his pistol.

Leaning against the rock face, shaking with fright at her narrow escape from both rape and being flung over the edge of the ledge, and the shock of Napedi's sudden, seemingly magical, arrival, she slid down to the rock floor and put her face in her hands.

The rock beneath her felt rough and sharp and she realized that she had no clothes on. She had a vague memory of them being ripped off her body and flung away. They must have floated down to the bushveld below the kloof. She giggled slightly hysterically at the thought and then she recalled Napedi and that dark cavern below and the crevasse which awaited anyone who could not see the danger.

The miner's lamp which Rafferty had brought up with him was still flick-ering at the entrance to the tunnel where he must have put it down when he emerged into the daylight of the rocky shelf. Emmie picked it up and moved off the shelf into the dark passage.

Josh had turned round and found Clifford and Alfred at his side just after Button's warning to him not to move. They had slithered down the path to join him, keeping to the dark shadows at the side.

Alfred put a hand on Josh's shoulder.

"Good lad, but there is no way I'm going to let that bastard kill another member of my family."

"But what of Emmie?" Josh queried. "We can't let her…"

Before he could finish Clifford had aimed at the figure on the ledge with his rifle. There was a crack and then they saw pieces of rock flying in differ-ent directions and Cliff cursed bitterly.

It was at that moment that Emmie's scream came floating down through the clear air. They stood transfixed staring upwards. Then Rafferty was back there shouting at them and obviously ripping her clothes off. As each garment floated down to the rocks and bushes below, Josh heard Cliff groan, saw him cover his eyes.

"No, Cliff, no," he said, reaching out to the man in his obvious pain, "See, it's only her clothes."

As the girl disappeared, flung to the floor, Cliff let out a cry of immense pain and despair. It was at that moment that Alfred suddenly saw a black figure reflected in the rays of the sinking sun, clambering at high speed up the kloof face, swinging from frail tree to rocky crevice and leaping gaps to grab hold of gnarled branches. Alfred was so riveted in fright at what Napedi was doing that his voice broke as he said to the others:

"Look, look, it's Napedi. He's almost up to the ledge."

Frantic screams were coming from the ledge and Josh found himself staring up, a hand tensely gripping Cliff's arm, and echoing Cliff's prayer.

"Dear God, let him get there before she rolls off!"

They all froze as Napedi made the final jump. They saw him sway backwards, totter on the edge of the stone shelf and then throw his body forward with a final frantic transference of body weight. At the same time they saw Rafferty push Emmie towards the edge, her frail body swayed and then bent away from the edge and disappeared with Napedi seemingly between them. The next instant something, which looked at the distance like a small boulder, flew across the shelf and plummeted down to the bush below.

Still transfixed, the watchers suddenly saw Emmie stand up and move back into the rock face, a small pink wraith against the darkening rock.

"Bloody hell!" exploded Cliff. "He's made it back into the passages and shafts and Napedi has gone after him. What chance has Napedi against a gun? And why has Emmie gone back too? At least from here we had a chance of reaching her, just as Napedi did – and, by God, was he brave!"

Alfred nodded, still staring up at the kloof, "That last jump was defying the laws of gravity… It was a superhuman effort."

Josh was shattered to find tears streaming down his face. He wiped them with his arm. The two men looked at him and Alfred was quick to respond. He put a hand on Josh's shoulder:

"Cliff and I will find them," he said with as much conviction as he could muster.

As if Alfred's words had broken his trance, Cliff began to plan the next action.

"I'll go in and I want you two to cover the exits in case Rafferty tries to make a run for it. Alfred, you stay near his horse and Josh you come with me and we'll join Button although I'd like you, Josh to cover the shaft entrance while Button and I go in. Don't say anything, no discussion, just shoot for his legs. No news from any of us by daybreak and you two link up and get help."

Moving rapidly through the gathering gloom, Cliff and Josh reached the higher shaft entrance and found no sign of Button but only one lamp sitting outside the entrance.

"He must have gone inside once he saw Napedi climb to the ledge and disappear," Cliff surmised. "You wait there, lad, keep a close watch," he pointed to a vantage point from which Josh could watch both the cliff face and the entrance to the shaft. "Remember he'll be like a deeper shadow in the dark – any of us would be carrying a lamp." He bent down and lit the lamp and strode into the shaft entrance. Josh sat down cross-legged with his rifle across his knees and his back in against the rock face.

He recalled how in his tribal hunting days Napedi had made him blacken his face and he put his hands round the roots of the cliff climbers and smeared the dirt over his white face.

This time, aided by the lamplight, Emmie found herself quickly at the end of the first tunnel. She stepped gingerly down the sloping rock face which would take her to the cavern, resting the lamp on the tunnel edge. Just as she was about to reach for it, it was blown to pieces by a pistol shot. She leapt back with a scream and tumbled a yard down the steep incline feeling every outcrop and rock making an imprint on her naked body. She felt a dull ache in her back and another on her neck. However, she had the presence of mind to remain lying on the incline and to peer down into the dark cavern and shout to Napedi.

"Napedi! Don't go to the far side of the cavern, it drops away. Then she remembered he might not understand. She searched frantically through her mind for the few words Josh had taught her. "Danger, Napedi. Stay still," was all she could muster. Then, from somewhere down in the depths of the inky blackness she heard a man's voice shout instructions in Venda. Immediately there was another shot and the cave echoed to the bangs and crashes of the bullet and the rocks it loosened. Emmie froze and then her heart leapt. It might be Cliff, he might have found his way into the mountain.

"Cliff!" she shouted, "Cliff, I'm here!"

Almost immediately a bullet hit the rock above her head and brought another shower of debris down onto her body.

The same voice called up, "Are you alright, Emmie?" she managed to scream, "Yes!" as another shot was sent in the direction of the voice, which she now recognized as that of the mine owner, Button.

There was something close to a snigger in the dark. Then Rafferty's voice rang out:

"I'll get you all. It's only a matter of time. Either you'll fall to your deaths or I'll find the target!"

Dead silence settled into the darkness as each person listened for a tell-tale sound. Emmie had crawled back against a cold damp stone wall and was beginning to be aware of the ache of various wounds inflicted by the flying stones shattered by the shots.

It was then that they all heard it. At first it sounded almost like the rushing of water and then it changed to an ominous rumble. She stood up, clutching the wall and tried to peer into the darkness. Then she was aware of the wall beginning to shake and the sound of falling rocks. As the horrible truth dawned on her, she found herself grabbed by a strong black shadow which whispered, "Napedi," in her ear and picked her up like a bag of feathers and began to run down the slope with her. Suddenly the weak flicker of a lamp appeared ahead of them and Button's voice boomed out above the roar of moving rocks:

"Napedi, Emmie, quick, this shaft is still intact."

Napedi ran like a wild buck across the collapsing debris towards the light and fell against Button just as another rockfall crashed behind then. Button had the lamp held up high to guide them to the passage and suddenly Rafferty's voice, behind them, yelled:

"Help me, help me!"

Button lifted his lamp and they all turned just in time to see a large boulder bounce with full force onto Rafferty and carry him screaming helplessly over the crevasse edge. There was a split second of eerie silence and then a terrible thud a long way below the rocky shaft.

"Quick!" Button brought them back to reality, "Get down this shaft before it too collapses!"

Emmie found herself between Napedi and Button, running on all fours, stumbling and trying to avoid the outcrops of rock in the tunnel. There was a final great roar behind them and they all hesitated for a brief second and then ran for their lives as the tunnel became wider and the old wooden stumps which held up the roof could be heard creaking and groaning and puffs of dust were moving ahead of them as stones came loose and fell into the passage. Then they could see a light and Napedi shouted a warning to Cliff.

"Emmie?" Cliff shouted.

"I'm here, Cliff!" she managed to choke out.

Napedi slowed slightly and grabbing her arm, forced her past him and down towards Cliff.

Emmie could remember nothing further. She regained consciousness wearing Cliff's shirt and lying under the stars as dust poured out of the shaft behind them. She was aware of a circle of concerned male faces looking down at her.

Cliff's worried expression broke into a huge smile as her eyes met his.

"Thank God! In future you'll stay right with me, girl!"

She tried to move but every inch of her body cried out in protest.

Alfred sat down next to her.

"Listen, Emmie, that medical training came in useful at last! I've checked you out and it's all bruises and bumps, but nothing broken, you've been incredibly lucky and you've Napedi to thank for your life. In a few days you'll be moving around and then in a week it will be back on a horse! Meanwhile, you have us all at your service and Button & Pigg Mines have been put at your disposal – the quarters are cleared for you. Josh and Napedi have even found most of your clothes that floated down to earth!

Emmie looked at them all gratefully and smiled, and Cliff picked her up gently and she fell gratefully asleep on his shoulder, aches and pains merging into sleep, as he carried her back to the Mine's quarters.

It was three days before Emmie could move around normally. Three days filled with talk and speculation as they all exchanged their experiences.

Josh was subdued. He was annoyed with himself; he had every reason to be delighted with the outcome of the expedition to the north. Rafferty had admitted to the murders. What was more important, Rafferty had met an end which appeared to be just retribution for his murky past. Despite the dangers, everyone else had come through and they were contentedly celebrating life and making plans for the future. Alfred was making plans to take him back to his family in Ireland and had reassured him that as soon as his schooling was finished he could return to Africa if he so wished. Emmie and Cliff were talking about a hotel and farm so that Emmie could still sing and Cliff could farm and go hunting when the mood took him. Napedi was a hero and wanted a while on the mines and then he planned to join Cliff. No, the more he thought about it, the more annoyed he felt with himself – why the feeling of let-down?

Emmie was looking at him thoughtfully. "Josh, you've got all you want, I think? Rafferty is consigned by the good God, to hell. You wanted proof of what became of your parents. You have this now. Sure, we do not know what Rafferty was trying to hide, but we know he was after you." She smiled at him and then she recalled the parcel in the saddlebag. "Josh, Rafferty had a saddlebag, I wish we knew what it had in it but he flung it over the edge with my clothes."

Josh looked at her and suddenly his face lit up.

"It's probably nothing, Emmie, but I did find that bag when I was looking for your clothes. I forgot about it in all the excitement of the mine collapse and your escape. I found a parcel wrapped in waterproof cloth and I dumped it in my own saddlebag to look at it later."

He jumped up and ran over to where their travelling possessions had been piled. He scrabbled round in his bag and ran back with a medium-sized parcel. The others came over to see what had caused the sudden movement. He put it down on the floor and carefully peeled back the oil cloth. Inside was a family bible and he stared at it in puzzled disappointment. Emmie leant forward and opened the cover. There was a list of names and the final entry was:

JOSHUA FOLLIOTT BARTON, born 4.6.1865
Beloved son of Florence and Folliott Barton
of Belhavel, County Leitrim, Ireland and
The Waterfoot, Co. Fermanagh, Ireland.

He turned to Alfred and his eyes shone, I *am* your nephew, Alfred, I *am*, I *am! I know who I am! I have both an Irish and an African family* – he smiled up at Napedi – Napedi grinned back. "Majinga too will celebrate," he said quietly.

Glossary

assegais	slender iron-tipped hardwood spear
BaVenda/Venda	South African tribal language originating from the Soutpansberg mountains
berg	A mountain or hill
biltong	strips of salted and dried lean meat
impi	an armed band of Zulus
indaba	a council or meeting
induna	tribal councillor, or head man
iNtanga/n'itanga	Youngsters of a similar age group
kaffir	contemptuous term for a black African (origin: Arabic for infidel)
kaross	a cape, blanket, or rug made of animal skins
kloof	a wooded ravine or valley
knobkerrie	a weapon – short stick with a knobbed head
kopje	small hill
krantz	a precipitous or overhanging wall of rocks
Mearing ditch	a boundary ditch (Irish)
mfecane	a series of tribal disturbances in the early 19th century
piccanin	a very young tribal child

rimpi	a leather thong
Skeys, riems and strops	Part of the reins, shaft and braking system of an ox wagon. Skey being the wooden bar passing through each end of an ox-yoke, to which the neck-straps are fixed.
veldskoen	strong handmade suede or leather shoe/boot